Award winning author Adriana Kraft

When It's Time to Heat Things Up

PUBLISHED BOOKS

SERIES

RIDERS UP Romantic Suspense novels
Book One *Cassie's Hope*
Book Two *Heat Wave*
Book Three *Detour Ahead*
Book Four *Willow Smoke*

I0659205

SWINGING GAMES Erotic Romance novellas
Book One *Anticipation*
Book Two *Hook-Ups*
Book Three *A Tempting Taste*
Book Four *Complexities*
Book Five *The Adventure Continue*
Book Six *Who's the Coach?*
Book Seven *Dare to Adventure*
Book Eight *Pushing the Limits*
Book Nine *Too Close for Comfort*
Book Ten *Triple Play*
Book Eleven *Summer's End*
Book Twelve *Foursomes and More…*
Book Thirteen *Epicurean Delites*

COLORS OF THE NIGHT Erotic Romance novels
Book One *Colors of the Night*
Book Two *Aria Returns*

PURGATORY POINT Erotic Romance novels
Book One *The Mistress of Purgatory Point*
Book Two *Return to Purgatory Point*

THE DIARY Erotic Romance novels
Book One *The Diary*
Book Two *Writing Skin*

STAND ALONE NOVELS AND NOVELLAS
A Gift for Adam Erotic Romance novella
The Lady Wants More Erotic Romance novella
The Heist Romantic Suspense novel
The Unmasking Romantic Suspense novel
Cherry Tune-Up Erotic Romance novella
The Reunion Erotic Romance novel
Atlantis Woman Found Erotic Romance novella
The Best Man Erotic Romance novel
Santa's Boss Erotic Romance novella
Through the Mirror Erotic Romance novella
Sheila's Prenups Erotic Romance novella
Full Circle Erotic Romance novella

SHORT STORIES IN ANTHOLOGIES
Accidental Contact, in *Sapphic Planet*
A Taste of Ginger in *The Cougar Book*

WHAT THEY'RE SAYING
ABOUT ADRIANA KRAFT

Romantic Suspense

Heat Wave (Riders Up, Book 2) Five stars at Goodreads *Heartfelt with mystery and hope...made me cry. Spot on interplay between the main characters...well written and extremely enjoyable to read.* Donna H.

Cassie's Hope (Riders Up, Book 1) Five Stars at Goodreads *An emotional roller-coaster, with twists and turns you never see coming! ...I feel I know them, I took their journey with them. I felt their pain, their sadness, their struggles, and most of all their love. And that is the mark of a truly good book.* Faith

Erotic Romance

The Reunion, Winner of the 2014 Bisexual Book Award for Erotic Fiction. *This book sizzled as two incredibly sexy women and one gorgeous guy form a super hot triad, eventually. These three are by far and away the best smoldering trio I have read about. Oh, bring on more of this, but read this one first!* JJ, Rainbow Reviews

The Best Man, Top Pick at The Romance Reviews, Five Stars at Amazon *Kitty and Jared are my new favorite characters. I love this book. It kept me on edge because Kitty was so unpredictable, which gave this story its twist and turns.* Cheryl B.

Riders Up
Book Four

Detour Ahead

by

Adriana Kraft

Riders Up: Book Four
Detour Ahead

By
Adriana Kraft

Copyright ©2008 and ©2015 by Adriana Kraft
ISBN 978-0-9907476-7-3

B&B Publishing
1970 N. Leslie St. #560
Pahrump, NV 89060

Cover by
Rebecca Poole
Dreams2Media.com

Riders Up

Book One: Cassie's Hope
Chicago, 1996

Book Two: Heat Wave
Iowa, 2000

Book Three: Willow Smoke
Chicago, 2002

Book Four: Detour Ahead
California, 2004

Dedication

To a pair of very real horses we have known and
loved:

Ransom, a Saddlebred/Arabian
now training in dressage

And

Cory, a Quarter Horse who missed his calling

Prologue

She screamed silently and squeezed her eyes tight, trying to shut down her senses.

It couldn't be happening. But it was. Their bodies clamped her to the ground. Their words seared her brain. Their hands groped. They penetrated her innocence.

What had she done? What had she ever done to deserve this?

California,

2004

Chapter One

Traci Steele peered through the rain-splattered windshield of her rental car trying to focus on the taillights ahead. She'd climbed the foothills east of San Diego for nearly an hour. Abruptly, the traffic slowed to a snail's pace.

Why so slow? The rain was letting up some. Traci loosened her grip on the steering wheel to rub first one forearm and then the other.

She squinted trying to read the orange road sign. Damn. The sign grew clearer with each few feet she advanced: *Detour Ahead.*

A lanky deputy sheriff leaned down to answer her unasked question. "Sorry ma'am, the road is closed. We had an oil tanker jackknife and roll on the slick pavement. This road likely won't be reopened until sometime tomorrow."

"I'm headed for Buteo. To the Live Oak Resort."

"No problem. Just stay on this route we're sending traffic over." The deputy gestured toward the narrow road to Traci's right. "About a mile down that road you'll have an option to come back to the main road you're on now. Don't take it. This detour is actually a short cut to Buteo, and the views can be spectacular. Just don't try going too fast."

"Thanks." Traci nodded, raking fingers through

her hair. "I won't be rushing on these roads."

She took the right hand turn. A small, paint-chipped sign read "Buteo Canyon Road." Another stated "Open Range." What did that mean?

Three miles farther the road climbed sharply. It twisted and wove its way through deep ravines and across a dried up creek bed. A bright yellow sign proclaimed: "Dip Subject to Flooding". Easing closer she looked up and down the ravine as far as she could see and then sped across. Safe, for the moment, anyway.

Brilliant sunshine suddenly broke through the clouds. "Yes," she cried. How quickly things changed here! On a rare straightaway, she scrunched her shoulders forward and rotated her head trying to ease tension and strain in her neck muscles.

She glanced quickly up the hillside and saw countless boulders dotting the landscape, making it look like nature's private graveyard.

Her spirits sagged. It was no use. Even here she was never far from that gaping hole. Her father's gravestone was already up—it had been there beside her mother's, waiting to receive him since before she could remember. That had always bothered her. She remembered the first time she'd been old enough to read the words, her tiny hand held securely in his. She'd looked from his name on the stone, up into his face, and back at the stone again. Had he known, even then, he would never remarry?

A twenty mph curve loomed in front of her. She

slowed, made the turn and sped up again. How far could civilization be?

"Good God!" She screamed, slamming both feet on the brake pedal. Her mouth fell open at the sight of the largest animal she'd ever seen up close sauntering into the left-hand lane. He was huge. And he was obviously and enormously male. The mammoth range bull was followed closely by seven of his harem.

The great beast came to a halt directly in front of her car and turned its head to stare at her. His eyes were enormous. Traci couldn't think. She couldn't react. She just sat numbly and gaped. Shaking his gigantic head, the bull ambled on across the road and the cows followed.

Traci didn't twitch a muscle for a full minute after the road was clear. Breathing shallowly, she shook her head at her white knuckles still gripping the steering wheel as if it was the last anchor to reality. Flexing her fingers, wetting her lips, she eased the car forward, cussing Cassie Travers more heatedly as she cautiously rounded each serpentine curve.

Why had she allowed her best friend to send her on this wild goose chase? She'd been vulnerable, worn out, used up—that was why. And Cassie's offer of two months in her condo high above San Diego had been tempting. "You need to get away and relax," Cassie had said.

This wasn't Traci's idea of relaxing.

With pursed lips, she refused to look over the side of the road again. She'd seen enough to know

7

that some of the drop-offs were sheer. Sheer or not, over the side was certain death.

Keeping her foot on the brake pedal, Traci hugged the steering wheel and proceeded down a ten percent grade. Twice she pulled off to the side of the road to let irate drivers pass. If she ever got to Live Oak, she promised herself she wouldn't budge for her entire California stay. There would be no easy day trips to San Diego—not over this road!

After executing a sharp left turn some ten minutes later, to her surprise, she descended gently down onto a wide valley floor. The vegetation turned several shades of green. Palm trees, cypress, eucalyptus and oak lined the roadway. At a crossroads stop sign, arrows guided her the remaining three smooth miles to Live Oak.

Traci blinked. The glistening adobe buildings with red tile roofs were no mirage. She had finally reached her destination. Pulling into a space near the resort office, she put the car into park, leaned back in her seat, flexed her fingers and massaged her thighs.

She'd made it. Had any traveler ever welcomed a desert oasis more? Where was the Jacuzzi?

She slid out of the car and stretched to her full height. Her long legs cramped. She stumbled and grabbed the car roof for support. Closing her eyes, she rested her head against the car and offered a brief word of thanks to whoever had been guiding her across that horrific curvy road.

She opened her eyes; her heartbeat jumped. There some hundred feet away in the horse stable doorway stood a tall man dressed in a short-sleeved blue work shirt, with a brown Stetson pulled low over his brow. She'd have to be blind not to see that the well muscled man appeared poured into his jeans. The cowboy pulled on his hat brim before turning on his heel to retreat into the shadows of the stable.

Not very friendly. So much for western hospitality. Traci shrugged. She didn't have time to worry about cowboys stuffed into clothing two sizes too small.

In any case, she had no interest in cowboys, horses or range bulls. Who had been more menacing: the range bull, or the wary wrangler?

- o -

"You handled that real well, McCord. Real smooth. The woman must think you're a Neanderthal idiot." Scott McCord berated himself as he broke a bale of hay apart to divide among his horses. No doubt the woman was Traci Steele. She fit Cassie Travers's description. Hair as black as night falling below her shoulders, and tall.

She might only be a few inches shorter than him, and he was six one even. And there weren't a lot of single women in and out of Live Oak. It was a nice enough resort, but it wasn't Club Med.

The Chicagoan was a looker, all right. Very nicely proportioned. Yep, Traci Steele looked as attractive as Cassie had bragged her up to be.

But he wasn't interested in a woman — no matter how attractive or how intriguing. And he definitely was not interested in a lawyer. It could be fatal to trust a woman, and it damn near just about had to be fatal to trust a female lawyer.

Nope, Cassie could do all the arranging she wanted to do. He was a bona fide member of the confirmed bachelor club and damn proud of it. Oh, he had his moments. When he watched his brother, James, with his twin daughters — sometimes there'd be a tug at his heart. But he got over it soon enough.

His assessment of Traci Steele was crystal clear. Class oozed from the woman: high cheek bones, glances peering over her sunglasses — and she strutted. He'd be surprised if she'd even step into the stable — likely too afraid she might get dusty, or, heaven forbid, step into something untoward.

Still, he'd have to do better than he'd just done. There was no way he could ignore Cassie's friend for two whole months. He owed them, Cassie and her husband Clint. But he wasn't about to play nursemaid to some damn uppity city slicker.

"Here you go, Jet," he said, placing two leaves of hay in a rope net for a chestnut quarter horse. "At least they had the good sense to geld you so you don't have to get all hot and bothered about women planning to change your life."

What infuriated him most was that Cassie had gone over his head. The resort had a non-fraternization policy between its employees and guests. Yet the condescending resort manager had taken him aside and said, "Mrs. Travers called yesterday. Seems like she has a close friend arriving day after tomorrow to be with us for two months.

"Mrs. Travers tells me the woman needs the kind of rest we provide here, but that she knows no one in the area. The Travers are very good owners. Mrs. Travers and I agreed that it would be okay, even desirable, that you free yourself up to see that her friend has a good time with us."

Scott remembered trying not to go berserk. "I thought we had rules about that?"

The manager had scowled in return: "Mrs. Travers helped me understand that rules are made to be broken, sometimes."

Scott walked back to the doorway, crossed his arms over his broad chest and stared at the woman's red Grand Am. She sure had looked drained when she'd gotten out of that vehicle. The furtive once-over she'd given him hardly mattered much. She looked as high strung as some of his classy thoroughbreds. Was she a head case, or just exhausted? Maybe she should spend her entire two months in bed. Alone.

Tomorrow, maybe the next day, he'd go say hello and welcome Traci Steele to Live Oak to satisfy Cassie Travers.

- o -

Resting her head against the Jacuzzi ledge, Traci delighted in the cascading water. This was an epicurean paradise. Layers of stress melted from her tight muscles. Tomorrow she'd go out and stock up on groceries. The one bedroom luxury condo came with coffee, a bottle of Chardonnay, and fresh fruit. That was more than adequate for now.

Into her second glass of wine and her second half hour of letting the water jets strum her body, Traci let her eyes close from weariness. Her long legs bobbed up like two corks. She laughed, without any effort, seeking equilibrium.

With one hand, Traci lifted mounds of soap suds to cover her breasts that were now shivering against the cooler air. Smiling languidly, she welcomed the tightening of her nipples. With the toes of one foot, she repositioned the furthest jet. Water crashed against her loins.

Gradually, she sensed a tightening, a coiling deep within. Soon her flesh tingled with sensual anticipation. Shuddering, she jerked away from the coursing water and crossed her legs. She held herself rigid, not giving in to the lure of the screaming desire of her body.

Moments later, pulling her knees to her chest, Traci sobbed. Why did she even try to tease herself anymore? It was a frustrating waste of time.

The next morning, Traci startled awake in an unfamiliar queen sized bed. Rubbing her eyes vigorously, it took her a few moments to realize

12

where she was.

Bounding out of bed, she reached for the terry cloth robe and then padded into the living room area. A sofa and two easy chairs were arranged in front of a fireplace furnished with one of those compressed logs that burned for hours. Traci passed a tasteful glass dining table, turned into the tiny kitchen nook, and pushed the button to start the coffee.

Grabbing a banana, she walked over to the patio door, pulled it open and smiled broadly. Sunshine! It felt so warm. She smiled at the sounds of crows greeting her. She was puzzled by birdcalls she didn't recognize. That would give her something to do later; she'd find a bird book.

After filling a cup with coffee and grabbing a novel, Traci stepped out onto the balcony and sat down at a round metal table. Why hadn't she come to southern California before during the middle of a Chicago winter? "This is so delicious," she moaned, stretching her long legs under the table.

Traci swallowed her coffee, savoring its heated bite. It was an unfamiliar specialty brand, and it tasted great. Coffee was her usual breakfast. The banana was an add-on.

From her position, she had a good view of the tennis courts. Later, she might walk over and see if anyone wanted to play, or she could just hit some balls.

Cocking her head to the left, Traci was puzzled by sounds coming from up the street. It was a steady bop, bop, bop. Curious, she stared as the noise came closer and closer.

"Oh, damn," she muttered. Below her balcony, not fifty feet away, came the wrangler she'd seen the afternoon before, only now he was astride a black horse followed by three other horses and riders. The sound of horse hooves rhythmically hitting the pavement was steady and loud.

Quickly, before he could notice her staring at him, Traci ducked her chin and focused on her book while watching him out of the corner of her eye. Up close, he was more than she'd imagined. Many women would think he was a heartthrob for sure. His body displayed that natural toned and muscled look, a product of hard work rather than the often exaggerated look acquired in a gym. She swore his full brown mustache twitched when he passed by. He moved with the horse as if they were of the same body.

Damn, damn, damn. She pulled her robe tighter around her shoulders and her nipples turned pebble hard against the soft terry cloth. That had to be Scott McCord, the man Cassie wanted her to talk to about suspicions that someone was sabotaging racehorses. McCord had contacted his friends for assistance because Clint Travers had a partnership in a detective agency.

Traci winced. Did Scott McCord know *she* was the assistance? She'd agreed finally that she did need rest after successfully prosecuting the Marlin rape case. Actually, she'd had a series of high profile grueling cases, and her boss had asked her—no, told her—to take time off. One reason she'd accepted Cassie's offer of the condo was the chance to help one of Cassie's friends.

Why couldn't Cassie's friend be a nice ugly guy? She didn't know about nice, but she certainly knew Scott McCord wasn't going to win any ugly contest.

After he'd ridden by, Traci turned to assess him more closely. Just as she did he stood in his stirrups and looked back at the riders following him, and then back up to the balcony where she sat staring dumbly.

Traci grimaced. He'd caught her gawking. Again, he pulled on the brim of his hat. Was that some sort of cowboy greeting, or was it an attempt to hide? Before looking away she thought she saw the hint of a smile on his lips, but it was hard to tell because of the mustache. Was that mustache coarse or soft?

Shaking her head in disgust, Traci pushed back her chair and retreated to the safety of her living room. She'd have to go and meet the man. That would probably take care of things. He probably had nothing between the ears. And she wasn't interested in all brawn and no brains. In fact, she wasn't interested in a man, at all.

- o -

Leading his string of riders toward the stables, Scott McCord could hardly stop chuckling. After an hour of paying half attention to the idle chatter of his riders, he'd found himself suddenly alert

15

and on guard as they'd approached the condo with the woman in a white terry cloth robe on the patio drinking her coffee and reading a book. He'd seen her long before she noticed him.

He'd kept his eyes focused straight ahead as he rode past her, yet he felt her gaze and steady appraisal. There was no question the long-legged beauty was Traci Steele. Did Ms. Steele realize how much bare leg and thigh were revealed by the parted robe? He'd bet his ranch she didn't.

- o -

On her second morning at Live Oak, Traci floated in the outdoor pool and listened to birds calling to each other. She was pleased to have the pool to herself, though it was surprising how few guests she'd seen since her arrival. Perhaps they were off doing touristy things, or maybe lounging in bed.

Again, she heard the steady clop, clop of horses; McCord was likely leading another trail ride. She'd read about his trail rides in the resort brochure back in her condo. That wasn't her thing, but she did need to walk over to the stable and introduce herself.

She couldn't put the meeting off much longer. Cassie would probably call and ask how things were going. Already Traci's mind was growing stale. She needed a case to work: *any* case. Even as a little girl she'd enjoyed working puzzles of all types: jig-saw, cross-word, anagrams. She'd have to explore the cowboy puzzle that she'd named Mustache. Maybe he'd surprise her; maybe he *did* have a brain. That would be a shock.

Pampered. She'd seldom had that sensation. The Olympic size pool proved to be just what her body longed for. Her father had often described her as the family's steelhead—the fish determined to swim forever to return to its home. She couldn't help it if she felt freer in or on the water than anywhere else. The water was always buoyant and supportive.

Usually when she sailed she was either alone or with good friends. She could let down her guard and be herself. Why had Cassie led her to believe she'd be able to sail any day she wanted during her stay at Live Oak? That was only true if you were a daredevil driver willing to tackle the roads between Buteo and San Diego.

Of course that was an apt description of Cassie—daredevil.

Traci swam lazily across the pool. Daredevil was about the last descriptor anyone would use to describe her. Traci frowned. She'd always played it safe. The biggest risk she'd ever taken was leaving her father's practice to go to the prosecutor's office. That was huge, but it hadn't changed her lifestyle. According to Cassie, she buried herself in cases and other peoples' problems and didn't take enough time to live.

Maybe her friend was right. But she'd gotten a lot of scumbags off the street, and that was worth something. She'd known Cassie since the two of them were roommates in college. Cassie probably knew her better than anyone. But did any person really know another?

Traci closed her eyes. Cassie had always been so envious of her long legs and large breasts. From Traci's point of view, Cassie's smaller frame was much more desirable. But it was her destiny to walk through life with men ogling her breasts and buttocks while trying to maneuver her into bed.

She sighed. Why hadn't she been born ugly?

Chapter Two

Carefully placing one foot directly in front of the other like a fox, Traci entered the stable.

The pungent odors of horse manure and leather greeting her weren't totally unpleasant, but she preferred those of the Arboretum, or Lake Michigan. Traci stepped down the middle of the stable avoiding the outstretched heads of horses seeking attention and treats.

How could she appear casual when every animal in here wanted a piece of her? Where the hell was McCord? He popped up when she didn't want to see him and vanished when she did.

Traci glanced down at her white tennis shoes. They were the best she could do. She didn't own a pair of boots, and tennis shoes had to be better than sandals or heels. She frowned. Her shoes were not going to come out of this adventure untarnished. At least she'd had sense enough to put on a pair of jeans, and the light sweater helped with the chill.

Coming to the end of one barn, Traci saw an imposing sign at the entrance to another declaring that resort guests were not allowed beyond that point. She paused and lifted her chin. Although she was a resort guest, she was here on business. And she might be a city girl, but she knew better than to shout in front of a barn full of horses to get McCord's attention.

Without further deliberation, Traci moved into the second barn. Even to her untrained eye, she recognized quality when she saw it. These horses with angular, dished out heads were classy; some had a look of disdain. They were friendly, but they weren't the lushes who had greeted her in the first barn. They might want to be petted just as badly as the others, but they weren't about to let a stranger know that.

Becoming slightly steadier on her feet, Traci continued her search for McCord. She heard a male voice and slowed her approach. The voice was coming from the end stall.

"You're gonna be okay, girl."

Traci warmed at the man's soothing tone.

"You just took a bad step, that's all. Don't know who was more startled, you or the bobcat. This wrap will help keep the swelling down. I'll check on you later."

Traci knew immediately when Scott McCord saw her standing there staring wide-eyed like some kid on her first visit to a zoo. His eyes narrowed and then grew cold.

Without a word, he closed the stall door quietly, grabbed her by the elbow, and escorted her to the sign between the two barns. She was so shocked by his rudeness she could neither speak nor resist.

Pointing at the sign, Scott McCord demanded, "Can't you read? I thought lawyers had to read to get through law school. Guests are not allowed in this barn. These are some very high priced Arabians."

"You may unhand me, Mr. McCord," Traci replied, attempting to reclaim her calm prosecutorial composure. "I will try not to alarm your sensitive horses. And I am not here as a guest. You and I have some business to discuss."

McCord dropped his hand from her elbow as if she were on fire. His surprise gave her the advantage. He clearly knew who she was, so why didn't he know why she was there?

"I'm Traci Steele, Mr. McCord, but then I assume you already know that or you wouldn't have made the lawyer jab."

"I know who you are." His voice was frosty. Then his eyes softened. "We have a mutual friend, Cassie Travers, who called to say you would be staying at the Oak for a while."

Traci thought his mouth turned up just a little beneath that full mustache.

"So how is the conniving Irish woman?"

Traci couldn't help but smile. "Ah, we do have the same friend, Mr. McCord."

"Call me Scott," he said, pushing his chocolate brown Stetson off his forehead. "We're not big on formality out here."

Traci's eyes narrowed. She didn't like being on a first name basis with the hunk of a man. It felt too familiar; too dangerous. But neither could she offend Cassie's friend. "Then I guess you can call me Traci; I'm sort of on vacation."

"Sort of? I thought that's why you're here."

"Cassie didn't tell you?"

"Tell me what?"

Traci watched the man's muscles tense. Scott McCord was again on guard. He'd been so at ease with the injured horse. She scowled. Why hadn't Cassie told him why she was here? An oversight? Hardly.

"I'm supposed to be doing Clint and Cassie a favor by taking their condo for a couple months. I didn't want to do it, but Cassie really twisted my arm."

"I can believe that." There was no mirth in his words.

Traci hesitated. McCord crossed his arms over his massive chest as if he already knew he wasn't going to like what she had to say. "Seems strange that Cassie or Clint didn't inform you, but the way she convinced me to come was to help solve some kind of problem you're having with horses coming from some track or other. She never did explain the situation much."

"Shit!" McCord exploded. "Now what the hell does that woman think she's doing? I may owe her a lot—"

Without another word, the wrangler started to pace between the two barns. Traci tried not to smile at his slightly bowed walk. His boots were so run down at the heels they looked inadequate for walking. Abruptly, he came to a halt in front of her. He stretched to his full height, no doubt trying to intimidate. If so, he was successful. Traci took a step back from his accusing glare.

"Lookit, lady, I don't know what your gig is, but I don't need any help from a lawyer. Especially a female one. Cassie really screwed up this time. I was pissed when I thought she was trying to find me a wife, which she has threatened to do on countless occasions. But this..." He paused to catch his breath. "This is too much. Thought maybe Clint might get a private investigator working on this stuff. But you?!" He shook his head and turned away.

What the hell did he see when he looked at her? Probably some pampered, ineffective female. Or at least his stereotype of one. How dare he impugn her abilities!

She pressed on in spite of the surroundings. "Listen, you pigheaded macho man." Traci flinched at her loss of cool. A courtroom was a better place for arguing than the alleyway between two barns. "It wasn't my idea to get involved in your business. But I want you to know that I am a top notch investigator for the Cook County State's Attorney's Office. That happens to be my gig. I came out here to help, but it will be just fine with me if I never have to step into this stable again.

"And as far as that other matter is concerned — the little wife — I can assure you it's not me. I am not in the market for a husband or for a man. And if I ever am, I won't be looking for someone who has better manners with horses than with women."

McCord's face turned several bright colors before he spun on his heel and walked rigidly into the first barn she'd entered. In a matter of seconds, she heard a truck start up, its gears grind and its tires spin as its driver tore out of the gravel parking area.

Traci leaned against the stable wall for support and breathed deeply. So much for prosecutorial composure. She must be in more need of a rest than she'd imagined. There was no reason why she should let such a man get under her skin. If he didn't want her help, so much the better.

Traci grimaced, closing her eyes against the scene in her office when Cassie had first offered the Live Oak condo. Cassie had a lot of explaining to do. Traci looked forward to watching the redhead squirm.

She stared at the space Mustache had last filled. A wife! It might take Cassie Travers a lifetime to explain this one.

- o -

Pausing to look across a valley on his ranch, Scott could breathe again. Tightening the barbed wire with a bar that he held with one hand while hammering a staple into a post with the other, he couldn't think of anyone who had ever made him enjoy the onerous task of fence mending as much as Traci Steele. He was hard pressed to understand what had happened that morning. It was a full four hours later, and his gut still churned like a casino slot machine.

But she'd entered his inner sanctum without permission. Who the hell did she think she was?

Pulling snug a second barbed strand, Scott placed the staple. He swung and hit his finger; the wire snapped loose. "Son of a bitch," he howled, dropping the hammer, pulling off his glove and sucking on his finger. "Damn that woman."

He sat on the ground and watched a red-tailed hawk soar high overhead. Was it hunting for prey? Or was it merely enjoying the wind currents it rode round and round?

Scott sighed deeply. He'd been an ass. Made a fool of himself. And why? Cassie Travers, that was why. He didn't have to look any farther for the culprit. Hell, Traci Steele was no more than a pawn in one of Cassie's grand schemes.

He figured he owed the Steele woman an apology, at least. He didn't doubt she was some kind of top-drawer investigator. She seemed top-drawer everything else. And it sounded like she wasn't any more interested in romance than he was. Though she didn't have to try to cut his legs off just because she wasn't interested in a man or a husband.

Scott felt his blood warming again. Why did it matter to him what the woman thought of him? She might look like some damn Celtic goddess, but he wasn't interested. The woman was an expert at sneering.

Maybe they could work together to ferret out who was behind his horse troubles. She was here. And if he cooperated with her, maybe then Cassie Travers would get off his back. The lawyer's intense dislike for him should make her safe enough to be around.

Later that afternoon, parking his truck at the stable, Scott McCord marshaled his defenses and readied himself to go through with his plan to appease the Chicago attorney. Why did he feel like he had his tail between his legs? Because he'd overreacted, that was why. He was still angry with himself about that. She was right: he'd never be so rash with a horse. You could ruin a good horse by overreacting.

He walked slowly toward her condo. Glancing to his left, he stopped and frowned. Why should it surprise him to see her playing tennis at the resort's elaborate tennis complex? He walked to an entrance and watched.

Tennis had never been his game. He swung a tennis racket like he did a baseball bat, with the same result. Only home runs didn't count in tennis.

Traci served two aces in a row, her long arms reaching high for the ball and then rocketing it across the net. Her opponent was handcuffed on one smash and never moved an inch on the second.

The first thing Scott noticed about his future sleuthing partner was that she played to win. The guy she was playing against was overmatched, and she showed no mercy. She wasn't toying with the blond-haired poster boy; she was slaughtering him. With both hands gripping the racket, Traci Steele generated a lot of controlled power.

26

The tennis and racquet club was open to the community as well as to resort guests. Scott knew her opponent was a local who often tried to pick up games and women. At the moment, the man was drooling over his opponent so much he didn't seem at all bothered that she was demolishing his game.

The second thing Scott noticed was Traci's graceful movements. Even with her height, she moved with ease and efficiency. The short tennis skirt showed off her lanky legs. Each muscle flexion seemed pronounced and intentional. Scott chewed his lower lip. Traci's white blouse was loose fitted, giving her room to breathe. He figured she was wearing one of those fancy sport bras, because her breasts bounced hardly at all. Briefly, he imagined how much they would bounce if they were set free.

"Shit," he muttered to himself. "She's class. She wants to win. She's off limits." Scott tipped his dark Stetson low over his eyes and prepared to wait for her to finish off her partner. He'd come this far to apologize; he wasn't going to back down now.

- o -

Traci's body tensed the moment she realized Mustache was watching. She immediately served two aces. Why did she have to show off? Maybe he'd understand she wasn't just some klutz Cassie Travers had pulled out of the gutter. She looked at

27

the strained face of her opponent. There was no remorse in her heart for him. He'd been much more interested in leering at her body and calling out sexual innuendos than matching her level of play.

She loved to play tennis, particularly against men; seldom did she regard her opponents as more than that. Opponents to be beaten fairly, but beaten soundly. On the tennis court as well as in the courtroom, she played to win. Her father's daughter, she'd never been taught any other way.

She volleyed. Why had McCord shown up? Obviously, he'd come seeking her out. She doubted he was an avid tennis fan. Breaking her opponent's serve, Traci moved quickly to end the match.

"I always treat the victor to dinner," the blond man said, approaching the net, not looking at all surprised or hurt by his loss. "You have a killer serve. Bet you got a lot of moves you haven't even shown me."

With practiced patience, Traci replied, glancing over at Scott McCord, "Sorry, I've got other plans. Thanks for the game."

"Oh," he said, following her line of sight. "Assumed you had better taste than that."

"My taste is none of your business." Ignoring the man's protest, Traci turned and walked toward the waiting Scott McCord.

- o -

"Nice guy," Scott said, nodding toward the man still glaring at Traci's back.

"He's a creep. And can't play tennis worth a damn." Traci removed her headband and shook her dark hair loose. "So what are you doing here, McCord? Thought you had a thing against lawyers—especially female lawyers."

"Yeah, well, about that." Scott shifted his weight from foot to foot. "I guess I overdid it some. Imagine Cassie wasn't much straighter with you than with me."

"It's a good thing she's some two thousand miles away." Traci gave McCord a half smile. "So was that an apology of sorts?"

"Of sorts. I'm not generally such a bastard around women."

"You mean I attract your worst qualities?"

"Don't know about that. Look, I just think we got started poorly. Maybe you *could* be of some help. And then we could get Cassie off both our backs."

"You sound like a reluctant partner."

"Didn't say I was ecstatic about working with you. It wasn't my idea, you know." Scott looked up at the early evening sky. "Oh, hell. Why don't I take you out to dinner, and we can decide whether or not we can work together?"

Traci's eyes widened in surprise; streaks of crimson moved up her neck. "I don't know about dinner."

"I'm not after your body, Ms. Steele, if that's your concern. I'm not like that bunny hopper you were playing tennis with." Scott folded his arms and peered closely at Traci. "I'm trying to determine if I can trust you with my horse problem. We can discuss it over dinner. I'm not talking about anything fancy. Just a Mexican hole in the wall down the road a piece. Chalk it up as a business dinner. But I'm buying."

A wisp of a smile crossed Traci's lips. "In that case, I accept your invitation. I'll go up and shower and meet you at the stable in twenty minutes. If that's okay."

"Sounds fine with me. I need to check some leg wraps anyway. Twenty minutes. You sure you can be ready that quick?"

Traci chucked softly. "Let's say thirty minutes."

Taking long strides, Scott headed toward the stable. God, he liked to hear the woman's throaty chuckle. He expected Traci Steele didn't laugh enough. He wondered if she ever played. Just playing for the fun of it. Not playing to win.

Maybe he could loosen her up a little. If nothing else, his pace was a lot slower than the lawyer's. Damn if he was going to rush around as if there would be no tomorrow. At least he'd take time to experience the day, which he expected Cassie's friend seldom did.

- o -

Traci let the shower spray cascade over her body. It felt good. It relaxed her muscles. She'd enjoyed beating the hustler. Humbling such a guy was always satisfying. Discerning what he had really wanted was not difficult. She frowned. McCord provided a more complex puzzle.

She expected the wrangler was right when he said he wasn't interested in her body. So why had she flushed at his brazenness? Traci ran the bar of scented soap over and under her breasts. She was used to being ogled. Some men were bold about it and some tried to be discreet. McCord fell within the discreet category. But he noticed, she was sure of that.

Why didn't that bother her more? It should. She'd given up trying to look dumpy to throw men off. She'd given up eating herself into a blimp. Instead, she'd become very savvy at reading their cues. McCord was not an easy read. Why did she think he could be trusted?

Traci poured shampoo on her hands. Was it that he was Cassie Travers's friend? Maybe. But Cassie had tried to set her up with men before, and some of them had not proved to be very damn trustworthy. Why? For some reason she suddenly remembered Mustache's tone and words to the injured horse: "You're gonna be all right, girl." A wisp of a smile flitted across her face.

Traci sipped her wine and sighed. She loved the long narrow Mexican cafe. There were plenty of people eating at nearby tables. The low lighting fostered an air of intimacy, but not necessarily romance. The candle on their table flickered, a sign of a draft drifting through the old walls.

"This place has been here a long time," McCord informed her. "It was built in 1902 and has always been a restaurant of some sort or another. There are stories that it catered to the merchants of San Diego as well as folks still looking for gold in Alpine and nearby."

Scott McCord looked more comfortable than she'd seen him. He enjoyed telling stories, particularly about the region.

"So your family has been here a long time."

"Yep. Eighteen-sixties. Most of the land Live Oak is on was once owned by McCords. We ran cattle, mostly. Helped irrigate the valleys and attract fruit growers and turkey farmers."

"Turkey farmers?"

"Yep, Ramona area during the thirties was known far and wide as the Turkey Capitol of the world. Used to have Festival Days honoring the damn bird. My family supported the turkey farmers, but we raised cattle and horses. When Thanksgiving comes around, I prefer ham."

"Here's your chicken enchiladas, ma'am," said the waitress, placing a platter in front of Traci. "And your burritos," she added, nodding at Scott, showing plenty of white teeth. "Enjoy."

"Thanks," they responded in unison.

"Where does the name Buteo come from?" Traci asked between bites.

"I guess the settlers who named the place saw a lot of hawks. Buteo means soaring hawks. If you haven't seen any yet, you will." Scott dug into a side order of refried beans. "So tell me how you know Cassie Travers."

"We've known each other since college days. We were roomies. And we've been part of a small women's group for a long time. Cassie's my best friend."

"Or you wouldn't be here."

"Exactly."

"So why don't you like horses?"

"Huh?"

"With Cassie being a horse trainer now, I'd think you'd be more comfortable with them. You looked like you were walking on eggshells this morning when you tiptoed around the stable."

Traci shrugged, swallowing water from her glass. "Just because we're friends doesn't mean we have to share the same interests."

"No, don't suppose so."

"I've been to Arlington Park a few times to watch one of Cassie's horses run, but that's all. I'm a city girl. She grew up in the country."

"You never went through the horse crazy phase that most girls go through?"

"Oh, a little, I guess. I took some riding lessons for a bit. But it got to be too much trouble." She shook her head. "My mother died when I was young. My father had enough to do to raise me without succumbing to the whims of a young girl."

"Oh."

Traci peeked over her shoulder to watch a young couple dancing in front of an old juke box. Actually, they were hardly moving at all. There was no space for dancing. The couple seemed more interested in rubbing up against each other anyway. Traci looked away quickly. She didn't like the way McCord's mustache turned up. Was he mocking her?

"So how do you know Cassie?" she asked, deflecting any potential comment about the dancers.

"Actually, through Clint. He and I went to Utah State together. He majored in criminal justice, and I was in sociology until my dad got sick, and then I came back to run the stable. My older brother took over more of the day-to-day management of the ranch."

"And you and Clint stayed in contact."

"You bet. He was a good bud. And later when he married Cassie, I got to know her too." He winced. "You don't have to know her long before she starts taking a personal interest in your life."

Traci smiled. "She never will stop being a social worker—horses not withstanding."

"She means well." Scott scowled at his own words. "But sometimes that's not good enough. Cassie can overstep; and she's one stubborn woman."

"I suppose you're right. I've known Cassie for much of my life." Brushing back her hair, Traci wondered how Cassie would feel if she heard them discussing her in this way. Flattered, no doubt. Reaching for her wineglass, she said, "Cassie wouldn't do a thing to harm a friend, but she can become overly enthusiastic about what she thinks a friend needs to be happy."

Scott nodded.

"So, tell me about this problem you're having with some race horses. If we can get to the bottom of that quickly, Cassie might let up a little."

Wiping his mustache with a napkin, Scott peered at her as if he didn't believe Cassie would leave them alone that easily. McCord seemed as wary of Cassie as she was. Maybe they were both equally determined to keep Cassie out of their personal lives.

"There's not a lot to tell you," Scott said. "It's as much a gut feeling as anything else."

"That's fine. Unless you have a body, missing property, or a threat, you are often left with gut feelings. I often trust my own." Traci pulled a pen and notepad from her purse. "So tell me about your gut."

Eyeing her notepad, he quipped, "Pretty low tech. No tape recorder? No laptop?"

"I have both at the condo. Don't you think they might be a little out of place here?" She glanced around the café.

"Okay. Over the last six months or so I've fallen onto a string of bad luck with the horses that are being sent to me from the tracks. These horses are placed with me so they can be away from the competition of the track. They rest up, and then I get involved in retraining them before they go back. They might be at the ranch for thirty to ninety days. A few stay longer."

"Kind of like a vacation and retooling," Traci

said, jotting notes on her pad.

"Yeah, that's it. Only the retooling hasn't been going so well lately."

"Oh."

"I send the horse back as fit as can be, and too many of them either arrive not ready to run, suffer an injury within a week or two, or just never race up to their potential." Scott shook his head and folded his arms. "It makes no sense."

"Not just bad luck? Cassie says horseracing involves a lot of luck—good and bad, but mostly bad."

"That's true. But this is happening too often."

"Are the horses associated with particular owners or trainers?"

"If there's a pattern, I can't find it. I work with a half dozen trainers. Most have had problems with horses coming from the ranch."

"Wow." Traci set her pen down. "Maybe *you're* the target rather than the horses."

"Maybe." He arched an eyebrow. "I doubt it, but it certainly feels like it at times. More likely someone is trying to get a betting edge."

"How about jockeys? Any patterns there?"

"Don't know. I haven't really had time to explore all of this." Scott tugged at his mustache. "Maybe it's all in my mind. Thought a private investigator might be able to sniff around and tell me if I had anything to worry about."

Traci tried not to respond to his fingers pulling on his mustache. Why was that simple gesture so suggestive? Quickly closing her eyes, she sought her balance. "Okay," she said, looking at the source of her discomfort. "You haven't given me much to work on. I'll need the names of horses who have had problems along with their owners, trainers, jockeys, and any other handlers. I'll probably need to see how your operation actually works.

"What happens at the ranch? How are the horses transported back to the track? Who receives them there? And particularly, in whose care are these horses for the initial week or two back at the track? I'll have to do criminal history checks on anyone who comes in contact with those horses." She eyeballed McCord closely. "That includes you and your employees." She was pleased to see he didn't flinch.

Drawing in a sharp breath, Scott said, "I can see you're going to be thorough." He smiled. "I wouldn't expect anything less from a top notch investigator."

Traci grabbed her napkin, unhappy with the fact she was blushing like some fresh law school graduate. "Be that as it may, when can I start?"

"I thought you already had...Why don't we begin by showing you the setup at the ranch? My assistants can handle the stable."

"Okay. That sounds fine."

"I'll pick you up around ten o'clock—you are here to get some rest and relaxation. Oh, and when we're done at the ranch I'll give you a riding lesson."

"Uh, uh. No way." Traci shook her head

vigorously. "I don't do horses."

"If you want to help solve this horse problem, you're going to have to get much more comfortable around these animals than you are. I can't be taking you to the backside at Santa Anita the way you were this morning. We have to build up some of your horse confidence, Counselor."

"I don't know," Traci backpedaled. She knew he was right, but she hadn't been on a horse since before...She hadn't been on one since she was fourteen. There had been a brief time when she'd talked her dad into letting her take lessons.

She'd loved the majestic beasts—and then she'd had no time for them. She'd made no time for them. And now she had this uncontrollable fear.

"I'll make sure it's a good experience for you."

Traci lowered her gaze. She couldn't read her own feelings—a tumultuous mix of hope and fear, wanting to trust but desperately trying to keep a door shut somewhere in her inner recesses. Why should this matter so much?

"Do you want to lie around for two months being bored to death?"

How could the man put his finger on her makeup so easily? "No," she replied, meeting his gaze again.

"If you want to work this case, then you'll have to be around horses."

Did he see her fear?

"Come on, Traci Steele. You don't strike me as a woman who is easily frightened. You help me with the case, and I'll help you overcome your fear

38

of horses. I'm an excellent teacher; you couldn't be in better hands."

Biting her lower lip, Traci hesitated. Silence prevailed. Apparently, he was done pushing her. Thank goodness for that. What to do? She could fly back to Chicago and tell Cassie she tried and things just didn't work out. She could just sit by the pool for weeks on end. Or she could accept Mustache's challenge. Most likely, he was a good teacher. McCord began again to smooth out his hairy lip and Traci cast him a half smile.

"All right," she said at last, her eyes softening. "I'll give it a try, but only because it will help me investigate your case."

"Great! The first thing we'll do in the morning is take you to a store where you can buy the proper duds for working with horses."

Traci's smile faded.

Scott chuckled softly. "You'll need boots with heels, a riding helmet, gloves, and boot-leg levis. Oh, and riding a horse doesn't simply mean sitting on a horse's back. It means some hard work. It means grooming and mucking out stalls. Are you going to be up for all of that, Ms. Steele?"

Traci kept her grimace to herself, not appreciating McCord's obvious glee at her expense. She'd made her decision and she'd stick with it. So much for the bikinis and sun-washed beaches. Bring on the blue jeans and horse manure.

Well, she'd dispel this wrangler of any notions that Traci Steele was afraid of hard work. With aplomb, she'd accept his challenge and keep her eyes open to come up with an appropriate daring payback for him. Two could play this game.

Inexplicably, she suddenly looked forward to this contest. Why did she sense Cassie smiling over her shoulder?

Chapter Three

Wincing at her reflection, Traci hoped she didn't look too much like a drugstore cowgirl.

She stood in front of three full length mirrors outside the fitting room of Harrison's Clothing Store. It wasn't Victoria's Secret, but it had everything from filmy lingerie to western boots. Glancing down at her newly acquired boots, she nodded again, approving of Scott McCord's taste. So many of the women's boots seemed so gaudy, but he'd suggested a rather plain design with low cut riding heels.

Functional and durable, he'd said. They might be made for riding, but she was finding it difficult to walk from one section of the store to another.

Looking over her shoulder at Mustache, who appeared most uncomfortable standing in the ladies apparel section, Traci admitted she enjoyed shopping with the man. He'd been helpful and supportive when she was hesitant or undecided.

Surprisingly, he made no attempt to rush her. Weren't all men supposed to do that?

She turned to determine whether the jeans were okay in the back. Peering into the mirror she saw Scott look quickly away. Had he been checking the fit of her jeans? It sure looked like it. Was that a blush she saw creeping up the back of his tanned neck? Traci's lips curled up. Looked like the jeans fit fine.

Traci admired the pale yellow long sleeved shirt with indigo ribbing over each breast pocket. Nothing in her closet at home came close to that.

"You look stunning, ma'am, if I may say so," said the middle-aged store clerk who had been a big help. Batting her long eyelashes, she added, "I think your man thinks so, too."

The clerk looked at Scott for affirmation. He blanched and then stuttered, "I'm not any woman's man."

"Oh, I'm sorry," the clerk demurred, "I just thought…you two seem so well matched. I guess I made a mistake. I—"

"It's okay, Ma'am," Scott said, tugging on his Stetson. "Of course, you're right. She is stunning. How about a hat?"

"Oh, yes," the clerk said, taking Traci by the hand and leading her down another aisle. "With your creamy skin coloring, you'll need to be well protected. The sun can be torturous here even in winter."

She settled on a low crowned dark brown Stetson. It went very well with the rest of her outfit and McCord had described the hat as functional and durable. Those two words seemed to be the best he could say about anything. She peeked at him from under her hat. He looked functional and durable, too.

Scott stood anchored in the middle of the aisle with his arms folded across his chest. He hadn't known what he was getting into when he agreed to help Traci Steele select riding clothes. Hell, it only took a man ten or fifteen minutes to choose and put the leftover change in his pocket.

They'd been in Harrison's for nearly an hour. Between the store clerk and Traci, they'd decided she needed to try on almost everything in the store.

Stunning. The word didn't even come close to describing how Traci Steele filled out a pair of jeans and a shirt. Her lengthy legs seemed to go on forever. And her contoured rear had him swallowing hard. And he was envious of that yellow shirt hugging her breasts.

No way did he want to get involved with the woman Cassie Travers had sent him. But he was in trouble. Traci Steele exuded beauty, seductiveness and vulnerability. He wanted to cuddle her and protect her. Hell, he wanted those damn shapely legs wrapped around him. He stalked toward the exit.

He straightened his shoulders. *McCord, you got to get control of yourself.* The woman reeked of big city sophistication. She probably had lawyers and stockbrokers hanging all over her. Probably had a hard time deciding which man she'd bed on any given evening. *When she looks at you, she just sees a cowboy.* And that was the best way to keep things.

43

"It is beautiful country. And so vast." Traci scanned the horizon, which had to be miles away. It was broken up by foothill after foothill. And then to the northeast there were snow capped mountains. Far below, she could make out the rutted road Scott's truck had followed to this high plateau. She stretched her back and shoulder muscles. She couldn't remember ever having a bumpier, bouncier ride. Relieved to be standing on solid ground, Traci deeply inhaled the cool mountain air. "How high are we?"

"About three thousand feet," Scott answered. "Most of what you see off to the east and south is federal or state land. A third of those houses to the west weren't here two years ago. Hardly any, five years ago. Now houses seem to be creeping up and down every valley like molten lava."

"You find the advance of civilization distasteful."

Scott shrugged his shoulders. "Doesn't matter what I think. How about some lunch?" Scott motioned toward the truck. "I've got coffee, ham and cheese sandwiches, apples, chips, and Danish."

"Sounds fine." Rubbing her hands together, she added, "The coffee sounds great."

"Yeah, that wind makes things a little nippy. It can be hot in the valley and still cool up here. You want to eat in the truck or outside?"

"It's not that cold. Let's eat out here."

Traci was surprised how good a ham and cheese sandwich tasted. Even the chips. When had she last eaten potato chips? McCord hadn't said much at all during lunch. Maybe that was a cowboy thing. Brushing Danish crumbs from her lips with her fingers, she chuckled. There was no need for napkins. "So, all that land to southwest is McCord land?"

"Pretty much. We used to own a lot more, but each generation seems willing to part with some of it."

If she was going to find out what was behind the problems with McCord's horses, Traci had a feeling she needed to know as much as she could about the man and his family. There had to be a motive, a reason for someone to compromise McCord's business. "So your family put roots down here about a century and a half ago."

Scott nodded. "Shortly after the war, in 1866, Ezra and Zachary McCord came west from New York. They bought several thousand acres that had originally been part of a land grant. Over the years the land has been used for grazing cattle and horses and harvesting hay, barley and rye. McCords played a major role in starting the town of Buteo. They needed a place for supplies. It took days to drive a wagon into San Diego."

He gazed across the land. "Yeah, McCords have been in this valley for a long time. That means something to me, though sometimes I feel fenced in by it. Its roots and heritage. I guess someone in the family has tried just about everything imaginable to make a living."

"But no one tried turkeys."

"Nope. No one tried that." He gathered up the remains of their lunch. "Guess we ought to show you the actual operation." He smiled, pulling down the brim of his hat.

Traci ducked her chin. Seemed like every time the man tugged on the brim of his hat, there was trouble ahead.

"If you're going to do a thorough investigation, I guess you'll have to meet people involved in all aspects of the operation? That includes folks at the track and here at the ranch. Probably at the stable too."

She stood and brushed off her Levis. She scowled. "So how are you going to introduce me? I should've thought of that earlier. I wouldn't want your family to get the wrong idea about us."

His shoulders sagged. "There's nothing to hide. You're helping us sort through some problems. I don't know what's eating you, Ms. Steele, but I didn't walk out of a cave yesterday. I don't have designs on your body." He paused. "But if I did, you'd be the first to know. And I'd woo you like you've never been wooed before. And you'd want me just as badly as I'd want you. You see, we McCord's have been in the business of wooing for generations. But you can relax. I am not interested in you, in that way."

Seething, Traci stalked toward the pickup. Of course she'd have to meet his family. Why hadn't she thought of that? She did need a rest. And how

46

could she let him get away with such brazenness?

Yet, she'd brought it on by implying that he might be interested in her as a woman. So he wasn't. He was quite emphatic about that.

And why did that bother her? Wooed. She blew compressed air through her closed lips. Hadn't men stopped wooing women decades ago? Scott McCord might not live in a cave, but what century was he from?

It seemed to Traci that they'd been driving for hours, although she knew it wasn't nearly that long when they finally topped a rise and started to descend into a gorgeous tree-lined valley. On the other side of a meandering stream just below the next hill sat a group of buildings comprising a substantial compound.

Two houses about a hundred yards apart anchored the ends of the half circle. The nearer one was quite large and rambling. The other newer looking one was more compact. Two large barns were set back some from the houses. Other storage sheds and stacks of large round bales of hay filled out the picture. Extending from the buildings up the gentle slopes was one fenced-in pasture after another, each holding two or more horses of various sizes. This was a serious horse ranch.

Hesitantly, Traci glanced over at Scott, who had said not one word since they'd left their lunch site. He might be slow to anger, but he also seemed quite slow to calm down. She, on the other hand, was ready to get to work.

"There's trouble," Scott warned, nodding in the direction of a pasture where a single rider chased a dozen horses. "Stay put," he ordered. "I'll be back as soon as I can."

Traci watched Scott jump out of the truck and dash toward the barn. Shortly, she saw him re-emerge on top of a horse and race off in the direction of the "trouble." When Scott joined the other rider, they worked as a team, riding their horses close to the ground, seemingly gliding first one way and then another, gathering the scattered horses into a bunch and then herding them toward a pasture near the barn. Traci caught her breath. It was like watching a ballet without the accompanying music.

As the riders neared, she could see that the second rider was a woman; long blond hair flowed behind her like wheat before a strong wind. Traci's heart clutched. She couldn't explain the immediate torrent of jealousy sweeping through her body. Why had she assumed McCord was unattached?

Traci stepped out of the truck and stretched her muscles. She'd been sitting and waiting too long. She walked toward the barn she'd seen McCord and the woman enter.

Standing in the shadows of the barn, Traci stood and watched and listened. She felt a twinge of guilt for spying. But it was only a small one. Wasn't she supposed to be investigating? That meant surveillance and finding out all she could, even about her client.

"That was close," Traci heard Scott say.

48

A high pitched feminine voice responded, "Yeah, good you came along when you did. Something scared the hell out of those horses, and I really want to go back and see why that section of fence was down. Could've been a cougar, I suppose."

"Or maybe a two-legged polecat."

"Right. Too many things have gone wrong lately. Accidents may come in threes, but how many threes do we have to go through?"

"Don't know. Let's get the horses put away. I've got someone I want you to meet. She may be able to help us with our problem."

"A woman." Traci shrank back from the incredulity of the blonde's voice. "You're going to accept help from a woman? This woman I've got to meet. It'll take quite a woman to get Scott McCord to willingly accept help."

"I don't know so much about willingly," Scott grunted. "But she's here through a mutual friend. You remember Cassie Travers from Chicago?"

"Of course. The one who agrees you've been a bachelor for far too long."

"Damn. Anyway, Traci Steele is some kind of prosecutor from Chicago vacationing at the Oak. Cassie thought she might be able to help us out."

"And she's not bad to look at either, I bet."

Scott hesitated. Traci held her breath. "No, she's not bad to look at. In fact, she's a long-legged beauty. And it would be a hell of a lot better if she were fat and ugly."

Traci nearly giggled as she backed out of the

49

barn and retreated toward the truck.

"Now just who might you be, sneaking around my property?"

Traci stiffened at the accusation and the gruff, cutting female voice. She turned slowly and looked down at a thin rail of a woman for whom seventy had to be a long ago memory.

The woman removed her Stetson and banged it against her hip. Steel gray hair formed a single braid down her back. Her eyes were coal black and accusing.

She had to be Scott's mother. Who else would claim the property as her own? Instinctively, Traci held out her hand in greeting. "I'm Traci Steele, Mrs. McCord. Your son brought me out here and then left me because there was some kind of problem with some horses. I was trying to find him."

The old woman squinted at Traci. "He's never told me about you. And seems to me you were going the wrong way to try to find him, backing out of the barn the way you were. Unless you're one of those city folks afraid of their shadow."

"Well, I am from Chicago. But..."

"So you two have met," Scott boomed, rapidly closing the distance between the barn and where Traci and Mrs. McCord stood. The blonde jogged to keep up with him.

"Hardly," the older woman grunted. "Saw this woman snooping around and thought I'd better find out what the hell was going on. Says you brought her and sort of dumped her on the spot."

Traci swore she saw a trace of a smile flicker across Mrs. McCord's lips, but she couldn't be certain.

"We had a situation to take care of in paddock four," Scott responded easily. "Now that it's taken care of, let me make the introduction. Ma, Penny, this is Traci Steele. She's from Chicago, and she's going to help look into the problems we're having with the horses going back to the track."

"What the hell! We don't need no help from an outsider." Mrs. McCord narrowed her eyes at her son. "You never take help from a woman; seldom even from one within the family."

McCord appeared flustered, if not embarrassed. Traci tried not to smile. "Well, she's different, Ma. Let me explain."

"Damnation, I'm not going to stand out here and catch my death of a cold while you sputter around trying to tell me why you brought a fancy woman onto this ranch to help us solve our problems." Turning to Traci, she said, "Come on inside. The pot is on."

Traci followed in step along with Scott and the young woman named Penny. It sounded like Penny was family, one way or another. Traci glanced quickly at Scott. His stony features looked straight ahead as he followed the lead of the tiny matriarch. Penny, however, met Traci's glance and gave her what Traci assumed was a supportive smile. Why did it feel like they were bad children being taken to the woodshed?

The main house was impressive. It was stucco

with red tile, like everything else in the area. But it had additional character. It slouched a little with age. It was dusty and seemed to appreciate the shade of the large oak trees nearby. There was nothing new or contemporary about the house. It looked like a reservoir of memories.

As they marched through a porch into a large kitchen, Mrs. McCord shouted orders in Spanish to a woman whom Traci assumed was a housekeeper or cook. Listening to the instructions, Traci glanced toward the floor not giving away her urge to smile or her knowledge of Spanish. Maria had been told to prepare another plate for supper for their guest and that she was to use the best china and silver.

"Now then," Mrs. McCord said, looking at Traci while grabbing the coffeepot and four cups. "I'm Sally McCord, Scott's mother. He hasn't said any more about you to me than he likely has about me to you. So who are you? And why should I be pleased that you're here to help us? And quit gawking at her, son. You'd think you'd never seen an attractive woman."

"She's here because..."

"I can speak for myself, if you don't mind," Traci interrupted, waving off Scott. "Now, Mrs. McCord, as I said earlier I'm Traci Steele."

"Just call me Sal, everyone else does."

Taken aback by the hint of admiration in the woman's voice more than by her desire for informality, Traci continued on. "Okay, Sal. I'm staying at the Live Oak for a couple months of rest and relaxation at the suggestion of a good friend. In Chicago, I'm an Assistant State's Attorney for Cook County."

Traci tried not to react to the woman's sharply raised eyebrows. "As it turns out, my friend is a friend of Scott's. She and her husband own racehorses, including some that Scott works with. Cassie suggested that I might be able to help. That's how she twisted my arm to get me to come out here."

"Cassie. You mean, Cassie Travers?" Traci nodded.

The old woman hacked a deep throaty cough that Traci recognized as a cigarette cough. Turning to her son, she said, "Well, why didn't you tell me that in the first place. If Cassie sent her, she's got to be good. Damn good."

Now it was Traci's turn to blush. She watched the beaming smiles of Mrs. McCord and Penny. It was like old home week, but she still didn't recognize the home.

"Of course we all know Cassie. She's the spunkiest lady I've met in a long time. If you can keep up with her, Traci Steele, then you can keep up with the McCords."

Traci stifled a chuckle. "I've been trying to keep up with Cassie for years; seldom am I successful."

"Somehow I doubt that," Mrs. McCord said. "This is Penny McCord, my oldest son's wife. My youngest," she said, scrutinizing Scott, "doesn't have one. Penny and James have darling ten-year-old twin daughters. They live in the house down the lane."

Penny smiled warmly. "You'll get used to our ways if you hang around here much. I don't suppose we're as tactful as folks back in the city. But we mean well."

"Dammit, girl," Mrs. McCord groused, "don't go apologizing for my behavior in front of me. At least have the decency to wait until I'm not here."

"There's no need for anyone to apologize," Traci interjected. "I'm just relieved to know that maybe we can work together. If you don't want my help, that's okay too."

Mrs. McCord flashed her son a look that Traci could not decipher. This was a tight family and they obviously had their own ways of communicating.

"Nonsense," Mrs. McCord said. "If Cassie says you can help, then maybe you can see something that the rest of us can't. Sometimes it's beneficial to add new blood to the lines."

"Huh," Traci muttered.

"Don't mind, Sal," Penny said, eyes sparkling. "We're happy to have you working with us. Anything I can do for you while you're here, let me know."

"Well, if she's going to work with us, why don't she just stay here?" Mrs. McCord said. "There's plenty of room."

"No," Traci and Scott said in unison.

"I appreciate your offer, Mrs...Sal, but I'm really quite comfortable at the condo, and quite frankly, I need my privacy." She paused. "I've

54

been through a lot lately." She sighed. "My father passed away three months ago. Part of what I need on this trip is alone time."

A flicker of pain crossed the older woman's face before she responded, more slowly. "I understand completely, Traci. But any time you get lonely, or if you think my son isn't treating you right, you just come and talk to Sal. I've been through a lot of grieving in my time. You could say I'm an expert at it."

Traci smiled, holding back tears. "Thank you, Sal. I'll remember that." Shuddering, she turned toward Scott and said, "It's been a long day. I think I'd like to wait a bit before meeting more folks. It would be good to go back now."

Scott looked at her and then at his mother who nodded her assent. There would be another time to share a meal. Traci appreciated the woman's understanding. She stood to give her farewells to the women. Then she and Scott left the house and headed for his pickup.

Traci brushed out her hair preparing for bed. She'd been jumpy ever since they'd left the ranch. Before, actually.

She tightened the white robe and studied herself in the vanity mirror. She wouldn't deny that she was pretty, but she was no super model, either. Across the years, she'd learned how to dress well for her size and build. She'd better look good — she spent enough on clothes. She needed to look good in the courtroom, and that made her feel good.

Still, she generated more attention from men than she wanted. Like Scott McCord.

Traci grimaced at her reflection. She'd always thought her nose was too long and too pointed and her face too angular. She ran a finger along her jaw line. Her glossy black hair was a source of pride. And her eyes were naturally dark and sparkling.

Wetting her lips, she smiled. Yes, she had a mouth that could pout, exhibit toughness, or reflect gentleness on demand. How often had she practiced before a mirror, getting ready for moot court in law school, trying out just the right expressions to emphasize her opening and closing arguments? Visual impressions did make a difference. She knew that. In many respects, she was an actress, only her stage was the courtroom.

Standing, Traci placed one foot on the stool, and her robe fell away displaying her best assets. She had strong, shapely legs and thighs. What had Scott said to his sister-in-law? *She's a long-legged beauty.*

Why did it matter what Mustache thought of her? Traci twisted her lips to one side and then relaxed them. It mattered. It shouldn't, but it did. But he claimed not to be interested in her in that way. Why wasn't he interested? What would she do if he was? What could she do?

Traci's brow furrowed and her eyes darkened. She jerked her robe open and twisted her nipples roughly. She gasped. Her face contorted, conforming to what she knew was the ugliness of her breasts.

She despised them. Her breasts were far too large, and even at the age of thirty-five, they sagged. She looked like a cow. If he ever saw her breasts, he wouldn't be calling her a beauty.

They had pulled and twisted her nipples, heedless of her screams. They'd called her breasts oversized watermelons. Grotesque. Whore's tits. They were like signal flares telling the boys she was easy. But she wasn't. Yet they'd still had their way with her.

She'd been so shamed. All because of her breasts. Even now her muscles quivered, remembering.

Traci raised her chin, disregarding her tearstained cheeks. That was why she couldn't care what Scott McCord thought of her as a woman. It would be enough if he thought of her as a competent lawyer, as an able investigator.

Quickly she switched off the bathroom light before she could see the lie on her face.

- o -

Several miles away, Scott McCord carried square bales of hay from the hayshed to the barn. He should be asleep, but his mind wouldn't stop churning. This was better than lying in bed staring at the dark.

It felt good to work his muscles. They'd been tense all day. That woman had a way of getting him tied up like a rodeo roper tied a calf—the calf thought he could move on his own, but couldn't quite get up.

Traci Steele. What was he going to do about her? Even his mother liked her. She'd tried to be her usual intimidating self, but Traci had stood her ground. Then that talk about grieving. At times Traci seemed quite open and forthcoming, and then suddenly a steel curtain would close behind those lovely dark eyes.

She was big city and he was country. She was probably classical music and he was country western. So why bother?

Scott shook his head and walked toward the pole shed for another bale. He hadn't decided to bother. In fact, he'd decided he wasn't going to bother.

So why the hell did the woman bother him? She was no doubt a competent lawyer, but why did she have to be so damn seductive? The way she walked, the way she turned up her lips in a knowing smile, the way she paused to think through a response, the way her eyes twinkled when she thought something was funny, the way pain made her vulnerable.

He sat on a bale. She was only going to be around for two months, if she lasted that long.

Why was he wasting so much time and energy on the woman? Traci Steele had a life, and that life was in Chicago. He doubted either one of them was interested in a fling.

So he'd work with her to help discover what was happening with the horses, treat her with the respect she deserved, even enjoy being with her, but he wouldn't try taking their relationship to a place where they would only hurt each other.

Clearly, she'd been hurt enough, and he wasn't eager to go through another emotional buzz saw. He'd seen enough already. Traci Steele wasn't as together as she wanted the world to believe.

Chapter Four

As planned, Traci found Scott the next morning at the resort stable corral saddling a couple horses.

"So you look ready to tackle this part of the case," he said, grinning at her.

"As they say, *looks can be deceiving*." Traci ignored Scott and looked at the two horses. They looked domestic enough. "Are you certain this is really necessary?" she asked, hoping she didn't appear quite as petulant as her words implied.

Continuing to smile as if he had nothing else to concern himself with, Scott replied, "Of course. We can't have our hotshot attorney looking like a greenhorn on the backside."

Traci gave the man an icy glare. "I'd like to think you're talking about the track."

Scott frowned, removing his hat. "Ms. Steele, I don't know how to convince you that not everything I say is laced with sexual innuendo. Now, why don't we try to get you sized up with this saddle? Hold your arm out at a right angle touching this part of the saddle."

Traci did as directed and Scott lengthened the stirrup so it tucked under her arm pit. "Okay, that's a beginning. We may change it once you're astride. But before you mount, I want to show you a few things. You have ridden before, right?"

"Yes, a few times, before. I was much younger then."

"Right. Well, it's not that different from riding a bike: once you've done it, some things remain the same."

"I don't remember a thing."

"That's okay. Your muscles will. Now then," Scott said, placing his finger between the cinch and the gelding she would ride. "This guy thinks he knows a thing or two. When I first tightened this cinch, he filled up his lungs hoping I'd be satisfied and forget to come back and check again. This saddle would slip either when you attempted to mount or maybe a few minutes later. Never get on a horse without double checking the tightness of the cinch." He pulled up on the strap and tightened it by two notches.

Traci nodded. "How old is the horse? He is handsome."

"Yeah, he's a deep bay gelding quarter horse. Cory is fifteen years old and knows pretty much how to behave." Scott looked at Traci. "But he is a horse. And horses do startle. All my horses are well trained, so you shouldn't have to worry much. He's used to cars and trucks, kids on scooters, and just about anything else that I can think of that might scare him, but you still need to be prepared for him to startle. Don't panic. That will only serve to scare him more."

"Are you trying to scare me?" Traci laid a hand on Cory's withers. She drank in the smell; she'd forgotten how rich and musky the horse's scent could be.

"Not at all," Scott said. "I simply want you to know that you are on a good horse and in capable hands, but you also have a responsibility, and that is to be as calm and reassuring as you can. Are you ready?"

"I guess." She'd come this far—there was no turning back now. "Okay, Cory, I'm one of the good people." Traci lifted her foot to place it in the stirrup, missed, and stumbled.

"That's all right," Scott said. "I'll give you a hand. Although you probably do a lot of exercising, you'll use some different muscles riding a horse. Put your foot in my hands." He cupped his hands and held them low for her.

Traci did as instructed. "Now grab some of his mane with your left and the front of the saddle with your right. Heave ho, here we go." Scott lifted and Traci pulled herself into the saddle. She appreciated the fact that Cory remained standing like a rock throughout this process.

"Now settle into the seat. Let your legs hang naturally. Good. How do they feel? They look about right."

Wiggling her feet, trying to remember what it was supposed to feel like being atop a horse, Traci felt remarkably fine. She even managed a grin. "Feels okay. Now what?"

"Here are the reins. All my horses are trained to neck rein. You need to keep contact with the bit, but not much. If you want him to go to the right, just lay the left rein against his neck and pull out with your right hand. If you want him to the left you do the reverse. Like this. It also helps if you look in the direction you want him to turn. These are all cues that guide Cory.

"There are many more involving knees, legs, balance and so on, but this is enough to get started. To get him to go, squeeze your knees gently and say *walk on*. If you want him to stop, say *whoa*. Draw out the word, and don't whisper. At the same time shift your weight back in the saddle."

"This is more complicated than preparing for law exams. How am I supposed to remember everything?"

Scott laughed. "You don't have to. Cory knows what to do. And I'll be right here. Okay?"

Traci looked down at him and inhaled. "Okay."

"We're not going to try anything fancy today. We're just trying to help you get your horse legs under you. I'll start by leading him on this long lead rope first. Here we go."

Before they were half way around the corral, Traci could feel her hips naturally rising and falling with the movement of Cory's hind legs. It felt good. It felt comfortable.

"Try to keep your eyes looking out ahead of where you're going. If you keep looking at his ears, you'll throw your weight forward and put both of you off balance."

"Right."

"You're looking good. Now give him the stop command."

"Whoa."

"Very good. He was listening to you, even though I was by his side. I'm going to unsnap the lead rope."

Scott walked toward the center of the corral and crossed his arms. "Okay. Start him off."

Traci tried to hold the reins firmly but not too tight. She shifted her weight slightly forward and said, "Walk on." Immediately, Cory responded and made his way around the ring.

"Get him to stop," Scott instructed.

"Whoa," Traci commanded and Cory came to a slow halt.

"That's fine. Next time try to shift your weight back a little. You were giving him a bit of a mixed message there."

Traci nodded.

"Okay, we'll try that again. Only this time I want you to turn him to the right and left. Don't turn him all the way around. Just kind of move in a serpentine pattern."

"You mean like the canyon road."

Scott grinned. "You've got the idea."

Ten minutes later Scott said, "That's probably enough for one morning. How do you feel?"

"Fine," Traci said, "I'd forgotten how exhilarating this can be. I know we just took baby steps today, but I liked it."

"You'll want to hit the Jacuzzi later. Your leg, thigh, and hip muscles will be begging for attention."

Once they'd unsaddled Cory, Scott waved to an

assistant to take the horse. The young woman gave Traci a toothy smile and led the gelding toward the barn.

"Next time, we'll have you groom him. That's an important part of developing a relationship with a horse, but you have a one day reprieve."

"You're a hard taskmaster," Traci complained, amazed that she could hardly put one foot in front of the other. She grabbed Scott's arm for support. "I think you were right about the Jacuzzi. Maybe I'll go to the pool and spend the rest of the day floating and then sit in the hot tub. I couldn't have been on Cory that long, but wow. My thighs are burning."

"You go on ahead. If you want to come by late this afternoon to talk about the case, I'll be free, or we can wait until tomorrow."

"No, that should work. I ought to have my body together by then. And I want to get a list together of what I need from you in order to begin checking on individuals and so on."

"How about four-thirty? I should be available by then."

"I'll be here." Traci grinned lamely. "If the body's willing."

Two hours later, stiff but refreshed, Traci entered the resort office to pick up the local paper. Like everything else at the resort, the office area was plush. On one side was a counter used by staff. A large gas fireplace glowed softly on the wall across from her and a bar extended from the wall on her right. Plush leather chairs, mahogany end-tables and reading lamps provided the large room with a slightly aloof aura.

"Ah, Ms. Steele," the manager said, sending her a beaming smile. "Have you been enjoying your stay with us? I hope everything is satisfactory."

"Everything is just fine, Mr. Humphries." Did the man sleep with a smile on his face? "The rooms are spacious and tasteful and I love your pool area."

"Well, we do try to do things right here at the Oak. I noticed you playing tennis the other day."

"Yes, you have a first class tennis facility."

"And have you made it over to the stables yet?"

"Yes, and I have the sore muscles to show for that." Traci thought the man looked too pleased. "You can be justifiably proud of the Live Oak. It's first class all the way."

Mr. Humphries nodded, clearly basking in her praise.

"So who owns this place? Who's responsible for all of this luxury?"

An undecipherable flicker crossed the manager's eyes and his smile weakened momentarily. "It's a consortium of folks, a corporation," said Mr. Humphries, finding his voice. "Why are you concerned about who owns the place, Ms. Steele?

"I'm not concerned." Traci folded and unfolded the newspaper she'd pickup from the desk. "I just want to know who to write a thank you to when I've completed my stay."

Why did she have the feeling that the smiling manager would be happier if she had poked him in the eye with a pointed stick? "Well, why don't you just write it to me here at the Oak, and I'll hand deliver it to the next corporate meeting." The man's smile was withering.

"I'll do just that. So tell me about the bus trip to Mexico."

Traci took another ten minutes to listen to the value of going on the resort-sponsored trip to Mexico. The manager visibly relaxed, apparently back in his comfort zone doing something he enjoyed.

At four-thirty, Traci walked into Scott McCord's small stable office. Sparse but neat. Sparse didn't surprise; neat did.

He looked up from his paperwork and nodded. "So you're still alive. How are the muscles? I've got coffee brewing, if you want some."

"No coffee, please. I'm coffeed out already. The muscles are okay. I've found some I didn't know I had." Traci sat down in a straight-backed wooden chair.

Scott grinned knowingly. "We take the pelvis for granted."

Traci flinched.

"I'm sorry," he quickly said. "That just popped in my head. All riders who haven't been on a horse for a long time complain about stretched pelvic muscles." He leaned back in his swivel chair. "So you said you had a list for me?"

Traci reached into her purse and pulled out a small notepad. "I'd like names of your employees here and at the ranch, of trainers you accept horses from, of the owners of those horses, of persons responsible for transporting the horses from the ranch to the track, and of individuals who work the horses at the track."

Whistling softly, Scott stared at Traci. "You don't want much. I'm not sure I can come up with names of everyone who has contact with the horses at the track. What will you do with those names when you get them?"

"Run criminal history checks and begin to see if there are any connections between trainers and owners or between employees here and people at the track."

"And just how do you do that? I'm not sure I want to treat my friends and employees like one of them is a crook."

"One of them *is* a crook."

"Oh." Scott threw his Stetson on the desk. "Maybe I'm wrong about all of this. Maybe all of these occurrences are simply coincidences."

"But you don't think they are."

Scott shook his head in response.

"Then we need to get to work and ferret out the culprit so we're not suspicious of innocent people." Traci crossed her long legs. How many other victims had she talked with over the years like this? When confronted with what was required of them to help identify an offender, they'd back off because they didn't want to hurt a friend or relative. She watched Mustache sort it out. She wouldn't rush him, but if he gave her the go ahead, then they would pursue every avenue available.

- o -

Scott twisted his mouth. She was waiting for his signal. He hadn't expected they'd have to involve everybody he knew in this search for what was going wrong. He closed his eyes. There was a lot riding on his gut instinct. Maybe he was wrong. But this was worse than a string of bad luck.

He sighed. Traci Steele had put on her professional aura. She was tightly wrapped in impenetrable armor. If he let her investigate, she'd be a loose cannon. He remembered her tennis playing and shuddered. He hoped his friends and employees didn't have anything to hide. But some bastard out there was up to no good, and it was starting to imperil his family's reputation. And then there were the owners of the horses, like the Travers — they deserved to be treated fairly.

"Okay," he said. "We'll proceed. I'll get a list of names, but I want to be involved in this every step of the way."

Traci smiled thinly. "Don't trust me? Or afraid of what I'll find?"

Scott threw up his hands and stood a moment with his back to her. Slowly, he turned around to face her. "Let's get one thing straight," he said, his voice lowering an octave. "You work for me as a private investigator."

"Actually, I think I'm working *with* you," Traci replied evenly. "But I want it clearly understood that if we discover a crime has been committed, then I will be turning over that evidence to the appropriate authorities."

"All right. Of course. So why the hell are we arguing?" He sank back down in his chair.

"I didn't know we were. I thought we were establishing the ground rules. You want to be integrally involved in the investigation, and if we find something amiss, I'm obligated to report it no matter who is involved, including you."

"Now that's a joke, right?"

"I assume it is."

"You're one cool lady, aren't you?"

Traci arched her eyebrows.

"Okay, I'll work on it tonight. I should have most of what you want by the morning." Scott threw her a quick half smile. "I'll have a list ready when you come for your riding lesson."

Traci flashed him a warm smile in return. "I think riding lessons is the part of this arrangement that you like the best."

"Maybe. It's what I know the most about."

"So tell me about this set-up. How many employees do you have? Do any of them also work at the ranch? Is this a seven day a week operation?" Traci picked up the notepad and reached for her pen.

"I guess the investigation is about to begin."

"Oh, it began long before now."

Scott frowned, ignoring her remark. "I have three employees working here. In the summer months, we add four part-time workers. There isn't nearly as much interest in riding this time of the year, but we stay busy. We don't operate on Monday."

"Does the resort make money off the stable? Does it pay for itself?"

"Most years no, but it wasn't intended to be a money maker."

"Why not?"

"When Live Oak was originally built, it was set up to serve the needs of the local community as well as folks who would buy into the resort one way or another. So as you probably already know, the stables, tennis and racquet club and golf course are open to anyone living in the area."

"Even if they don't earn their own way?"

Scott smiled at the question. "Well, that actually only applies to the equestrian center. My father sold the land that all of this sits on, in part to make some money, but largely to give back to the area that had supported our family for generations, to preserve a way of life that involved horses. I don't remember the specifics, but the center is part of the resort as long as it's in the public interest."

Traci whistled softly. "That's as good as tenure."

"I suppose. So why all the questions about Live Oak? The problems are happening with horses coming from the track, not with the horses stabled here."

"I know, but this is part of the whole context," said Traci, jotting on her notepad. "We really aren't certain whether you're a target or a bystander. We don't have a motive."

"Motive? This is horseracing, darling." Scott sneered. "Everyone is looking for an edge—better feed, aqua baths, magnetic wraps, shipping in from high altitudes, running horses when they are young, waiting until they mature—if it can be thought of, it's been tried. Some unscrupulous folks, though, take that edge-seeking beyond what's legal. Motive? The motive is to win. I suspect you know something about that."

Traci swallowed hard. "I may want to win, but I compete on a fair playing field."

"Right," Scott said, pulling a horse magazine from a pile. He thumbed its pages idly.

Traci pressed on, "So is it correct to say that the equestrian center is used more by the community than by folks staying at the resort?"

"Oh sure. Lessons and rides. Some board their own horses here and we take care of them. Some board and do their own work. Some use the riding facilities but maintain their horses at home. There are many different ways of using the facility."

"But it still doesn't pay for itself?"

"I already said that."

"How about the golf course and tennis facility?"

"The golf course holds its own. Some years the tennis facility is a regular cash cow. I'm sure I don't know why."

"Your tone would suggest that some folks make

comparisons and the horse part of the business comes up short."

"Some folks are too new, or fail to remember why this center is so important." Scott glanced at his watch. "Shit, I've got to get going. I'm supposed to help the twins with a weanling."

"This is a start," said Traci rising from her chair. "Oh, by the way, who owns the resort?"

Scott halted putting on his jacket and frowned at Traci. "Who owns Live Oak? There are a bunch of folk like the Travers who own some of the condos. Other units are rented out on a timeshare basis."

"But who owns those units and manages the place? Who owns all these fine facilities, including the stable? Who do you work for?"

"You sure as hell ask a lot of questions, Counselor." Scott shrugged into his jacket, preparing to leave. "There's a corporation called Snowden that manages the place and owns the largest percentage of the Oak. I've got to run. See you."

"Sure. Thanks."

- o -

Groaning, Traci struggled to sit up and place first one foot on the floor and then the other. She flung the coverlet to the end of the bed. God, her complaining muscles screamed. There were aches upon aches. Coffee. She needed the nectar of the morning, and fast. But she couldn't move quickly

74

enough.

Traci grabbed a robe and made her way to the kitchen. She couldn't believe the effort it took to put one foot in front of the other. Her pelvic muscles resisted any movement. Just because she sat on a horse for twenty minutes or so? She'd thought she was in pretty good shape.

Gradually, as if her muscles began to remember why they existed, movement became easier and pain diminished. But it was only after that first cup of coffee that she began to believe she still had a future.

With coffee cup in one hand and a banana in the other, Traci moved to the glass-topped dining table. Taking another sip of coffee, she booted up her laptop and began putting together her to do lists.

McCord was turning out to be a bigger mystery than she had expected. Was he hiding something? Why had he dashed off yesterday in the middle of her questions? Did he really have a prior appointment?

Her fingers ran nimbly over the keyboard resulting in a list of questions and things to do.

Questions:
1) McCord hiding?
2) Motive?
3) Players?
4) Interconnections of players?
5) Who wins what?
6) Who loses what?

7) Access to horses?
8) Resort ownership?

To Do:
1) Get Roberta to help with computer checks.
2) Begin interviewing players—ranch, stable, track, resort.
3) Work with horses (groan, groan, groan).

Traci smiled at her list. Now that the aches were retreating before the rising sun, she looked forward more than she'd expected to her next horseback lesson. There must be something visceral she'd been unaware of that those magnificent animals were touching deep inside her soul. And she knew McCord was right: she had to be more relaxed around them in order to do her investigation. And perhaps understanding horses and people who worked with them might better sharpen her insights in the case.

Chewing thoughtfully on the banana, Traci wondered what Roberta Turner would think when she asked for her assistance. There was no one better with a computer and tracing people, especially those who didn't want to be traced. She and Roberta had worked together in the investigation wing ever since Traci joined the State's Attorney's Office. Roberta would be happy to help on her free time, and the more the case became as challenging as Traci was beginning to think it might, the happier her Chicago based friend and colleague would be.

Traci squinted at the screen, nodding her approval. She pushed the save button, saved everything to her back-up thumb drive, and logged off. Within an hour she had to be showered, dressed, and ready to take on both Cory and Scott McCord.

A shower would relieve some of her body aches in preparation for riding Cory, but what, if anything, would prepare her for combat with McCord? She wished he'd turned out to be a toothless, grossly overweight, conceited man.

Stepping into the shower, Traci grinned. McCord might be self-conceited, but he certainly wasn't hard on the eyes. She sobered. If one wanted to look.

Chapter Five

Cory snorted into the unseasonably crisp air, apparently impatient to begin. His rider sat, poised, with a satisfied grin, looking equally eager.

"You remember everything I've told you?" Scott asked, still holding the lead rope.

"Of course," Traci replied, with a trace of smugness.

"Don't grip those reins too tight, or Cory will think you want him to back up. Now, concentrate on your riding, not on that list of names I gave you. There'll be plenty of time for you to look them over later."

Traci loosened her grip; she tried to sit assured, deep in the saddle. The list? What list? She really had forgotten it, stashed away in her gear bag in the stable. He didn't have to remind her that riding a horse required full concentration. Turning her head toward him, she saw the mixture of seriousness and excitement in his eyes. Was Mustache always so excited about teaching a woman how to ride?

McCord detached the lead rope from Cory's halter and then walked along the side as Traci guided the gelding into the corral.

"Take him around the corral like you did yesterday," Scott instructed. "Get used to him at a walk. Then try the neck reining exercises—first one direction and then the other."

With increased precision, Traci followed Scott's directions and Cory moved accordingly. Pleased with herself, Traci tried not to become bored. After all, what she was learning she had learned many years ago.

"Feel with your buttocks. Let your body rise and fall with Cory's hind legs. That's it. Doesn't that feel better? More comfortable?"

Surprised by these renewed sensations, Traci nodded. "Yeah, it's free flowing. Like swimming without feeling the resistance of the water."

"I wouldn't know about that," Scott grunted. "Bring him to a halt. Good."

He came over and put his arm on the saddle's cantle. "How are you feeling? Ready for the next plateau?"

"Sure. What's next?"

"We're going to move to a trot. You've trotted before?"

"Yeah, when I was a kid."

"Did you learn to post?"

"No, my lessons stopped before we got that far."

"Just as well. Posting looks sort of out of place in a western saddle. Cory has a fairly smooth trot. And he has two gears—a slow trot or jog, and a fast trot. We'll just try the first gear today. You squeeze your knees and release, and he should move into a slow trot. You may want to cluck at him a little. When we get ready to move on to the

80

fast trot, you'll squeeze your knees again while at the jog and he'll pick up speed. Sort of like a manual gearshift on a car."

"I wouldn't know about that; I've only driven automatic."

Scott grinned. "Remember, you can always put him in "park" by saying *whoa* and shifting your weight back in the saddle. At a slow trot, your body should be able to absorb the gentle up and down motion. When we get around to a fast trot, you may want to stand in the stirrups enough not to feel the pounding. The canter is a much smoother gait, but we're a ways from trying that. So are you ready?"

"Let's go." Traci patted Cory's neck, hoping that he remembered how to shift gears smoothly.

"Why don't you begin by putting him in a walk? Good. Now when you're ready, just gently squeeze your knees."

Traci squeezed and Cory strode off in a trot. She bobbed about more than she liked. How many times had she been envious of women with small breasts?

Mustache was probably enjoying the show. She gripped the reins tighter. Was this the slow trot, or had Cory skipped a gear?

"Stay focused. Keep your heels down. You're going too high and forward in the saddle. Keep your hands down."

Traci heard Scott's words, but her body refused to respond. Cory picked up speed. The corral fence posts whirled by as if she was on a carnival ride.

Her world was spinning out of control. Her right foot slipped out of the stirrup.

She heard Scott hollering for her to bring Cory to a halt. She tried; she really did. The "whoa" command remained stuck somewhere in her larynx. Reflexively, she squeezed her knees, trying to reestablish her grip on the horse. Cory responded by going even faster.

Traci's torso was flung up and down with increasing force. The saddle pounded relentlessly against her bottom.

Her mind went blank and then clicked into a horror she'd tried hard to repress.

Again they spread her legs wide apart like she was a wishbone. Again she was being pounded. Her hips, her pelvis could hardly withstand the force. Her inner thighs chaffed from the friction. Her womb had been invaded, never, ever to be the same again. Traci shrieked.

"Don't! Please stop! You're hurting me—let me go!" Traci screamed to the past and to the present. She felt herself floating. Maybe there would be escape, this time.

And then there was darkness.

- o -

Scott McCord stood at Traci's emergency room bedside. He must look a mess. A nurse had already asked if he wanted a sedative. *Hell, no.* He wasn't going to soften his guilt with drugs.

God damn, how had it happened? He replayed

the scene over and over again. He still couldn't understand it. One minute Traci and Cory had been working together as a team, and the next she was tossing about like a child's rag doll.

Until she landed in the dirt. He hadn't been able to move fast enough. Her words and the magnitude of her distress had temporarily paralyzed him. Without a doubt, this accident involved more than a woman learning how to ride a horse. But she was his responsibility, and he had let her down.

So there Traci Steele lay, ashen, but breathing steadily. The doctor said nothing was broken. There were no apparent internal injuries. She'd be bruised some. And they'd want to keep her overnight to check for a concussion.

He followed behind the gurney when they moved her from emergency to the second floor. No one seriously challenged his presence. Since he didn't know about her insurance carrier, he'd signed to cover financial responsibility. Looking at the pale woman, who was becoming a bigger mystery every day, he knew she wouldn't be pleased he'd taken over. But they could straighten things out later.

During the night, Traci came to enough to complain to a nurse about the IV, but he could tell she still had little understanding of where she was or what had happened.

Scott dozed off and on until sunshine bounced off his closed eyelids. Sputtering, cussing himself for having fallen asleep, he pushed himself up in his chair and looked at his patient. She stared back at him with a wan smile on her lips.

Leaping to his feet, Scott fumbled for words. She held out her hand to him; he clasped it between his own.

"Hi," Traci said softly. "You don't look so good."

"Maybe." Scott ducked his head so she wouldn't see the moisture forming in his eyes. "You don't look quite ready to walk down a fashion show runway, either."

"I'm sore and maybe a little weak, but otherwise I'm fine," Traci offered. "So where am I?"

"You're in the regional hospital. The doc wanted to keep you overnight for observation. They couldn't find anything wrong other than being knocked out. Do you remember what happened?"

He watched the competent lawyer withdraw behind shuttered eyelids. Her body quivered and then gradually calmed. She stared at him with renewed energy. "Yes, I remember. It wasn't Cory's fault."

"No, I should have—"

"It wasn't your fault, either. It's hard to explain. I lost control of Cory. And then I got into a terrible place, and I lost control of myself." She smiled weakly. "But I'm alive. I've survived worse." Traci squeezed his hand. "Please don't blame yourself. You didn't do anything wrong."

"So are you going to tell me about it? Somebody

hurt you badly." His fingers curled into a fist.

Traci pulled the covers up around her shoulders. She shook her head. "Can't talk about it. Wouldn't do any good anyway." She smiled lamely. "You're a good man, Scott McCord. Maybe someday."

"Okay. I won't push you."

Traci grinned. "And I signed all the liability release forms at the resort. So you don't have to worry about that." She laughed. "Just what a horse trainer needs is for a crazy female lawyer to fall off a horse and sue."

Looking chagrined, Scott stood. "That never occurred to me. But I guess we're done with riding lessons."

The look on Traci's face turned fierce and determined. Not for the first time, Scott was thankful he'd never had to take the woman on in an argument that mattered.

"Isn't there an old adage that says, the best remedy for being bucked off a horse is to get right back on?" She raised her hand to ward off Scott's protest. "Maybe a few days' rest would help. There are some things I have to work on before Cory and I go trotting off into the sunset."

"During the night, I was thinking that maybe we ought to have you do more groundwork anyway. We're just trying to get you comfortable with horses and help you understand what we're all about a little more. I've got a couple of weanlings and three yearlings I've been helping the twins with, but there would be plenty of room

85

for you. And since you'll be staying with us for a while, that might be the natural thing to try next."

Traci shot straight up in bed. "Ouch!" She lay back down and turned her head toward him. "Staying with you? Who says?"

Scott grinned broadly at her. "Don't get your nose out of joint. The doc wants you to be around people for a few days just in case. In case you get wobbly, faint—I don't know all the whys and wherefores. I'm sure he'll tell you when he makes his morning rounds.

"Ma will be thrilled to have you even if for a few days. And you haven't met the twins yet. And that's where the young horses are, anyway." Why the hell couldn't he stop babbling? Maybe he'd hit his own head and hadn't realized it.

She cast him a hard glare and then softened. "Okay. You and your family are the only people I know out here. But it won't be longer than absolutely necessary. I'll be going back to the resort as soon as I can."

"Of course. You'll likely be bored out of your gourd in a few days anyway." Scott stared at Traci again as if to satisfy himself that she was okay. "So, I better go call my mom and let her know what's happening."

- o -

Traci watched the tall man move gingerly out of the room. He looked totally out of place in a hospital. She shuddered, curling her toes. She'd

86

been touched by Scott's genuine concern.

He'd blamed himself for her accident. How could she ever tell him? She shook her head, feeling her professional aura reclaiming its rightful place around her. She didn't have to tell him. He was a client, if not a suspect, in a case she vowed to continue working. A cowboy client, and that was that.

Closing her eyes and letting her head fall deeper into the pillows, she realized she had to be very careful. The look in Scott's eyes had been more intimate than maybe even he was aware. Her accident had moved them to a slightly different plateau. At least for a while, he and his family would be her caregivers. She would try to gracefully accept. But that didn't give him a right to know how soiled and debilitated she really was. Traci clenched the sheets. Why? Why couldn't she just let it go?

"Do you like him?"

Traci glanced down at the source of the high pitched voice. It was Susannah; she knew that to be the case, because she wore her golden hair up in a ponytail. Her twin sister, Rebecca, wore hers loose, falling down her back. Traci had been informed that when the twins came over to work with their Uncle Scott, he required they wear their that way so he could distinguish one from the other.

Susannah was much more outgoing than her thoughtful sister, but otherwise there seemed little to distinguish one from the other. The ten-year-olds showed remarkable patience and skill with the weanlings and yearlings. She had yet to see them ride, but Susannah had told her they both could ride like the wind and had been on horses before they could walk. Traci didn't doubt either statement.

Resting her arms comfortably on the top rail of the corral fence, Traci peered out at Scott rubbing a blanket over a weanling who stood solidly still, as if to move would break a mysterious spell. The young colt's mother stood by paying close attention but showing no inclination to interfere. Traci had been told that this "sacking out" process was very important for helping the weanling develop trust in humans.

"Well, do you?" Susannah insisted. "Do you like him?"

"I think he's adorable," Traci replied. "His deep chestnut color is quite stunning. And I like the way he seems to wink at me when I get close to him. What do you think?"

"I think you're not paying attention. I don't mean little Dasher." Susannah puffed out her cheeks. "I mean my uncle. Do you like my uncle?"

"Oh." Traci gasped and looked down at the well scrubbed face radiating innocence. Backing away from the fence, Traci tried to find the right words to satisfy the young girl's curiosity. It was a simple question. So why couldn't she find a simple answer? This was not a court of law. "Of course I like him. Your uncle seems like a nice man."

"Nice man," Susannah squealed. "Uncle Scott is a stud!"

"A what?" Traci's hand flew to her throat. She frowned at the girl. Where had innocence gone? Quickly, she turned her eyes toward the other twin pulling on her arm. "Yes, what is it, Rebecca?" Traci wanted to kiss the girl for interrupting.

In a very quiet, even voice, Rebecca said, "A stud is slang for a very sexy man, Ms. Steele. That's our Uncle Scott. So, do you like him?"

"I said I liked him," Traci responded too sharply, chafing under the twin inquisition. "I don't know about him being sexy, though."

"See, I told you," Susannah said, grabbing her sister's arm. "Told you lawyers lie, and she's one of them."

The girls scampered toward the barn. Traci thought her skin might burn to a crisp. How could she let two ten-year-olds embarrass and insult her and get away with it?

She could sure understand why Scott said *twin* stood for trouble. Outgoing or reserved, they were both little devils; they knew it and enjoyed it. They meant no real harm; they were playing with her. Traci managed a grin. Sometime in the future she'd pay them back. She was good at biding her time.

Hearing Scott call to her, she redirected her attention back toward the corral where he had set the weanling free to roam. The first thing young Dasher did was sniff his mother for assurance. Then he high-stepped toward Traci. Caution overtook the young colt when he was three feet away from the fence. Holding his ground, leaning and arching his neck as far as he could, he stretched to sniff her extended hand. Moving his forelegs six inches closer, he rubbed his nose against her palm. He closed one eye, bared his teeth, but did not nip. Then he whirled quickly and gamboled away.

Traci laughed at the colt's antics. He was already a master of approach-avoidance. She decided it was a skill of males in all species. Yeah, she liked him a lot.

Her attention shifted to Scott, who studied her with an odd look. He was probably pleased she'd showed no fear when the weanling advanced. But there was more to his look than that. Was it admiration? Was it wistfulness? Was it longing?

Certainly not longing. The twins were right: that solid hunk of a man was a stud. And she didn't need a ten-year-old to tell her what that meant: Danger!

He ambled toward her, his hips swinging in a cocky, confident manner. "I thought the girls were going to stick around and help," he said, looking toward the barn.

"Guess they made other plans," Traci replied, afraid she showed more of her ire at the twins than she wanted. At least when they were around, she wasn't alone with him. His mustache curled up as she studied him. She relaxed a little. She still thought of him as Mustache; that seemed much less threatening.

"Those two can be fickle at times. They're quite a pair. What one doesn't think of the other will. But they wouldn't hurt a flea, and they're both going to be damn good horsewomen. Already are for their age. Susannah's pretty good at barrel racing, as long as she can keep her mind off of boys." Scott removed his hat and scratched his head. "I thought boy stuff came later."

Traci grinned. It was clear they both thought the younger generation should be more innocent that it was. "Guess they're precocious about such things."

Rubbing his hand across the top of the railing, Scott appeared to reflect on her observation. "Well, maybe Susannah. But Rebecca—she's too shy. She won't be thinking about boys until she's eighteen."

"I wouldn't count on that, cowboy." Traci chuckled.

"Do you know something I don't?"

His face, his lips were uncomfortably close. Traci sidestepped. "Well, are you going to let me work with my favorite yearling, or are you just going to stand here until you make a fool of yourself?"

Scott jerked backward as if she'd slapped him. "Lady, you sure know how to cool the juices." He shook his head. "Sure, Ransom's waiting in the next paddock. Let's go get him. I'll give you the halter and lead rope and you can bring him into the corral."

Crawling between the rails, Traci realized she'd just dodged a kiss. Why would he want to kiss her? And in broad daylight, at that? Why did men ever want to kiss a woman? Right. She shuddered and picked up the pace as they headed toward the next pasture.

Her spirits lifted immediately when she saw the half Arabian Saddlebred. He was a beautiful multi colored specimen with a nicely arched neck and a tail that rose when he trotted. He was a mixture of gray, russet, and white.

When he noticed them approaching, he whinnied softly and advanced toward them at a slow trot. Horse people called that gait a trot, but she thought the word "prance" captured much more the mood and presence of this animal. While not yet fully grown, he was certainly fully into himself.

This was the fourth morning they'd worked together. Traci confessed she preferred working with a horse from the ground rather than from its back. Without incident, she attached the halter. With a modest amount of confidence, she led Ransom into the corral and stopped in front of Scott.

"Good job," he praised, rubbing his hand across the colt's muzzle. "Why don't you take him through his paces? Go around clockwise and then counterclockwise. Bring him to a halt with the *whoa* command, tugging gently on the lead rope twice first to get his attention. He wants to please—you can see that in his eye. But he can't if we don't communicate our wishes."

"Sort of like with Cory."

"Yeah, Cory moved into a fast trot because he thought that was what you wanted. He was probably as surprised as you when you hit the ground. Now remember, this guy is still learning all the basic cues, and sometimes he likes to play around. Okay, he's yours."

Traci took a deep breath, calming herself. She knew if she stayed calm the colt would more likely be calm too.

For the next ten minutes she led Ransom around the corral—to the left and then to the right. She had him turn away from her and around her. They would halt and she would praise him. Once he nuzzled her pocket with his nose. "Not yet," she told him, "we're not going to turn you into a lush by giving a treat every time you do something right."

"Okay," Scott said from the center of the corral, "you're doing real fine from the left side, but remember we have to make sure he's comfortable with you on his right side. So change sides and keep working on the *walk-on* and *whoa* commands and getting him to turn on his hind quarters."

Traci did as instructed. She didn't enjoy working from Ransom's right side as much. It was her weaker side, given she was right-handed and now had to lead with her left. But they'd tried it okay yesterday. "Walk on," she commanded and Ransom responded by stepping off crisply. By the time they reached the far corner, he was leaning on her quite severely.

"Remember the bubble," Scott said. "Give him

a sharp elbow. Protect your space, Traci."

Right. Elbow. She jabbed Ransom with her left elbow. He didn't budge. She jabbed him again, harder. The colt moved away, leaving her space to walk comfortably beside him. She had reestablished her "bubble." Scott had told her Ransom had to learn not to lean on her, whether they were working with him in the ring or grooming him. He would only grow bigger.

"Okay," Scott said. "That's enough for today. We don't want to overextend his patience and attention span. As he matures, both will increase."

Later that afternoon, Traci stood at the counter in the large McCord ranch kitchen slicing carrots, potatoes, and onions while Scott's mother slathered a home recipe honey glaze on a large ham and Penny carefully iced a triple layer chocolate chiffon cake. It was going to be a festive evening, and the McCord women were not leaving anything to chance.

It was Scott's thirty-eighth birthday. A fact he'd never mentioned to her, but his mother and sister-in-law had shared that vital information. They'd given Maria the night off to fix one of his favorite meals themselves. The entire McCord family would gather in the seldom-used dining room for the celebration.

During her four-day stay, Traci had grown accustomed to Mrs. McCord's crustiness. The woman unsuccessfully tried to hide a big heart and kind spirit. Penny had proven more elusive. She stayed busy managing her daughters and working beside her husband on the ranch. Both of them worked hard and were welcoming, but quite reserved. She hadn't exchanged more than three sentences with Scott's brother, James. "Welcome to the ranch. Thank you. How are you? I'm fine," was the extent of their interaction.

Scott had a suite of rooms in the upstairs of the main house; his mother's bedroom and sitting room were downstairs. She wanted it that way, Mrs. McCord had said, to afford her son some privacy. She really didn't want him moving out of the house. Living alone in the damn place, she'd said, would be like being in one of those old cold castles with hidden dungeons she'd read about as a little girl.

"There," Mrs. McCord said, standing back to better observe the ham. "I think it's ready. Scott likes my honey and mustard glaze spread on thick; it gives the meat a thick crusted covering." She turned and smiled at Traci. "I think you'll like it. That should be enough vegetables. I'm gonna grab a cup of coffee after putting this thing in the oven. Why don't we sit down and take a load off our feet for a minute? It's still a little early to start the vegetables."

Traci didn't hesitate. If she chopped another vegetable she'd develop a new kind of carpel tunnel. The mounds of carrots and potatoes were huge. And her watery eyes attested to the number of onions she'd sliced.

She sat at the kitchen table across from Sal.

Penny pulled up a chair and joined them. Penny spoke first. "Being single, do you have much chance to cook?"

"Not like this. I've never cooked for this many people." Traci sobered. "We had a housekeeper who would cook when asked too, but my dad preferred to eat out at restaurants with friends. There wasn't a lot of opportunity to cook until I left home. And then it was usually what to cook quickly that was still nutritious. My college roommate and I—that was Cassie—used to do a lot of stir-fry cooking."

Sally McCord wrinkled her nose. "I've seen some of those recipes in magazines. It's a wonder you're not just skin and bones."

"We're pretty much meat and potatoes here at the ranch," Penny said. "James and Scott wouldn't have it any other way." Her chin jutted forward as if she were arguing a point. "But I imagine I should be teaching the girls how to cook a variety of dishes. They'll not likely live out their lives on ranches. Ranchers are a disappearing breed."

"I'm sorry to hear that," Traci responded. "It seems so free and remote out here. The views are breathtaking."

"Few folks want to start out ranching," Mrs. McCord said, lifting her coffee cup to her lips. "There aren't enough of those so called amenities."

Traci blushed. "You mean like the phone line not being able to handle data for my Internet access." She'd apologized before for overreacting to that reality. She wasn't going to again. But lack of that kind of access did contribute to her sense of detachment. There were moments when that was comforting, and then other times she felt so isolated and out of touch with the real world she wanted to scream.

Both McCord women stared at her, apparently expecting more.

"It is a gorgeous place to visit," she added, "but I do wonder how you are able to deal with the isolation."

"This ain't isolation, girl," Mrs. McCord said. "You should've been here when our ancestors were settling this country. It took days to get to San Diego. Now you can be there in an hour or so—if it ain't the rainy season and the road ain't out."

"James thinks we ought to set up a dude ranch."

Sally McCord scowled, but Penny hurried on. "Like you say, Traci, people like to come to this kind of place to visit. They might fantasize about staying, but they won't. We know of thriving dude ranches in Montana, Colorado, Wyoming. Why not here?"

"Because I don't want it, that's why!" Mrs. McCord's neck muscles stood out and perspiration beaded her brow.

Flares flashed behind Traci's eyes. She'd stumbled on to a family squabble. She wasn't about to take the side of either woman. There was little doubt where Scott stood on the question: with his mother.

"So tell me, Mrs. McCord," Traci began and

then halted, catching the import of the older woman's frown. "I'm sorry. Sal. Tell me why you and your husband decided to sell land for the development of Live Oak."

Sal snorted and lowered her eyes. "Wasn't my idea. My husband felt we owed something to the community. I expect he was right, but I hated like hell selling any of the land. Oh, the resort was going to happen one way or another. If we didn't sell the land, someone else would. This way, we retained some control over how it was developed."

Traci sat up straight and wished she had her note pad handy. "So what kind of control did you retain?"

"Don't try to appear disinterested," the older woman groused and then a grin spread across her face. "You're not chopping vegetables; you've got that investigator look on."

"I'm sorry. I guess it's a habit."

"No need to apologize. It's what you do. My husband and I wanted to make sure certain things happened with that land that benefited everyone in the valley." Mrs. McCord paused and cast a meaningful look at Penny, who glanced away.

"Mainly, we wanted any recreational facilities to be open to the community. We didn't want the place to simply cater to the rich. From the beginning, the equestrian center was to be available to anyone living in the area, and in order to maintain the quality of the place, a McCord would be in charge of that operation as long as a

McCord desired the position."

"Really! I didn't know that." Traci tensed. Why hadn't Scott told her that? It might have no bearing on the case, but it would have been nice to know. "Scott did say something about the equestrian center being grandfathered in such a way that it would continue as long as it was in the public interest."

"Yeah, my husband thought that was a well turned phrase. So, whoever owns shares of Live Oak, there is that clause they must buy into."

"So who does own Live Oak? It sounds like it's been sold more than once since it was developed."

"Isn't that the case with most of these places? That's why it was so important to get those understandings in binding legal jargon. Snowden Corporation owns the largest share, but many of us own a piece of it."

Traci tried not to jump out of her chair. "You mean you own part of Live Oak?"

"Of course. We have from the beginning. Didn't my son even tell you that?" Her lips turned up in what Traci described as a wicked smile. "My, my he really is a cagey one. He must get it from me."

"So how much does your family own, Sal?" And why hadn't a certain cowboy with a gigantic mustache only matched by his ego shared that information? He damn well knew she wanted to understand the financial holdings of Live Oak.

"I think we still own about fifteen percent. Originally, six families that had deep roots in this valley owned ten percent each and an outside developer owned the rest. That balance has shifted over the years, but no single individual or group owns a controlling amount. That's why there are so many battles on the board of directors."

"So your family has a seat on the board of directors?" Traci asked, leaning forward.

"Of course. We have from the beginning."

"And who fills that position now?"

"Scott. Naturally."

"Naturally." Traci sat back in her chair. There were more questions, but those she would pose to a different person. What the hell game was Scott McCord playing?

Traci maintained a cheerful presence throughout Scott's birthday meal, but she still reeled from the information shared by his mother.

She glanced at him sitting across from her. How could anyone eat as much food as he and his brother did without looking like plump elephants? Neither brother was in danger of that fate. Scott laughed easily at a joke Susannah told. Traci noticed Rebecca peering at her intently and wished she knew what the girl was cooking up now — girls, she corrected herself.

When everyone chimed in on an exaggerated version of happy birthday, Scott puffed up his cheeks and blew out all the candles with considerable aplomb, if not grace. A grin worked its way across Traci's face as he opened an envelope containing a handmade gift certificate for any of the local clothing stores. She'd wanted to return the favor and take him shopping. Scott nodded his thank you and said he'd show her how men shopped. Penny rolled her eyes and his mother groaned.

The twins could hardly contain their excitement. They insisted their uncle save their gift for last. Finally, he hefted a fairly heavy but loosely wrapped package. Traci had no idea what it might be. As he ripped the tissue, a lariat was exposed along with a large card.

"Thanks," Scott said, smiling at his nieces. "This will come in handy, I'm sure."

He looked at the hand-drawn card and his features clouded over. The girls were tittering behind cupped hands. Traci reached for the card to pass it around as they had the others. It depicted a large man with a huge mustache in a cowboy hat lassoing a tall woman with pitch black hair. And it read: "Happy Birthday, Uncle Scott. You can do it. We know you can! Susannah and Rebecca, your favorite nieces."

"Oh," she gasped. How many shades of red were there?

Glaring at his nieces, Scott said, "I hope you have had your fun. Maybe you're my favorite nieces because you're the only ones I've got."

James grabbed the card from Traci and immediately bellowed, "Out of here, both of you! Go home and go to bed. We'll talk about further punishment tomorrow."

"Oh," Traci intervened. "Don't punish them on my account. I'm sure they didn't mean any real harm."

Ignoring her, James pointed toward the door, his voice lowered. "Now! Go!"

Both girls pushed their chairs back and tiptoed meekly through the dining room doorway and into the kitchen. Once they were outside their hooting could be heard by everyone.

Traci didn't know whether to laugh or cry. How could anyone stay mad at those two for more than a minute? Scott was the first to break out laughing and she joined him. She thought James turned purple.

"I wonder where those girls get their wicked sense of humor," Sal grumbled. No one answered. "Must be from their grandfather, because there ain't enough present here to fill a thimble."

Traci followed Scott to the barn to make the last round of checking on the horses for the night. Although the weather was hardly cold by Chicago standards, this was still winter for southern California, and most of the horses were brought in before the sun went down.

She loved the barn at this time of night. It was so quiet. An occasional snuffle could be heard. The poor lighting only enhanced the dreaminess of the setting. A few horses stuck their heads out over stall doors to inspect visitors. Scott stopped to pet or speak softly to a horse here and there. His eyes were constantly moving, making sure nothing was amiss.

Standing in front of one stall, Traci held out a

carrot in the palm of her hand.

Ransom stepped from out of the shadows, bared his teeth, and took the carrot without nipping her hand. He stepped farther forward, encouraging her to scratch his neck.

"You have the smoothest coat of hair, little one," she said softly. "Maybe they should've called you Silky."

Traci didn't startle when Scott came up behind her. She just glanced over her shoulder and smiled. "I think this is my favorite time of day at the ranch, when everything is slowing down and becoming still."

"It's always been mine," Scott replied. "I'm surprised to hear you say that, though. I figured with the fast pace you're used to, this would be dull."

Traci continued petting Ransom thoughtfully. "I suppose it surprises me too, now that you mention it. I'm not sure there is anything comparable in my typical day. Maybe when I make sure I've saved everything before turning off the computer."

He laughed and she did too.

- o -

Scott watched the woman he'd grown to respect and appreciate savor the aura of the dimly lit barn. The light cast a gilded sheen off her dark hair. She was certainly something to look at. She seemed softer at night, here in the shadows of his work.

He placed a hand on her shoulder and felt her

flinch, but she didn't move away. She turned to face him. He couldn't define the look in her eyes. Curiosity. Hesitation. Wonderment.

"I'm sorry," he said, "if the girls embarrassed you early this evening."

Traci gave him a half smile. "No matter. They're just a couple pranksters." She breathed deeply. "I'm working on something. I owe them for more than that. Their time will come."

"Uh, oh. That sounds serious. Maybe I should warn them about the danger that lurks around them."

"Don't you dare. I just want them to know they can be the object of pranks too."

"They're not half bad artists, really."

"You noticed. I tried not to, but you're right. I thought they had you drawn real well. Big head and all."

"Big head?"

"Uh, huh."

Seeing hesitancy but no red flag, Scott lowered his lips toward hers. He brushed those pink lips with his mustache. Then he traced them with the tip of his tongue. She leaned into him, and he nibbled on her upper lip. She let out a deep breath and relaxed. Only then did he place his lips over hers. Only then did he place his arms around her back, pillowing her breasts against his chest.

– o –

104

Traci tried to breathe. His mustache was so soft it felt like a hundred feathers tickling her upper lip. She wanted more of him, but he maintained a glacial pace. She stood on her toes, but he only nibbled. And then she felt him pull her close. His mouth was on hers. She opened her mouth greedily. His tongue entered without further invitation. She'd never been kissed so thoroughly. Reciprocating, Traci wet his mustache with her tongue. And then she bruised his lips with her own. Since when had she become the aggressor?

And then she felt it—his hardness pressed against her crotch.

Traci yanked herself out of his arms and leaned against the stall, hunched over, clutching her knees, catching her breath. "Oh my," she said, her voice strained. "No more. Please." She held up an open palm to punctuate her words.

Scott stood still. "I didn't mean to scare you."

"It's not you," Traci explained in a rapid fire monotone voice. "I shouldn't let you kiss me. I shouldn't have gotten carried away. I'm sorry. Don't make any more of this than it was—a mistake in judgment."

Standing his ground, Scott folded his arms. "I disagree, Counselor. I know my body pretty well. And the way your body was responding, I'd say there were no mistakes in judgment."

Traci pulled herself upright. "You don't understand. If it helps your male ego any, yes, I enjoyed the kiss. I enjoy kissing. But no more." She paused, brushing hair from her face. "I'll want to go back to my condo in the morning after working with Ransom. You and I have to return to a professional plane. I need to get on the internet so I can really play with some threads surrounding your case. I trust you will take me back."

Scott kicked at the dirt floor. "Of course I'll take you back, but don't count on one kiss being all there is between us, woman. That wasn't just any little kiss. That was a kiss that mattered. And I'm not about to forget it."

"Maybe you should be trying to remember more important things," Traci retorted, "like appraising me of all your involvements and interests in Live Oak. I expect to hear from you, directly, about your family's ownership in the resort and your working relationship with its board of directors. I don't like playing with half a deck, Mr. McCord."

"Well, I don't like playing with half a deck either, Ms. Steele." Scott slammed his fist into a stall door, spun around and stalked out into the night.

Again, Traci watched the man escape her wrath. She blew air out between her lips. He was right. That was a kiss that had curled her toes. If she'd had her watch on it might have stopped from the energy collision. But he was wrong. It didn't matter. She couldn't let it matter.

- o -

Scott stopped walking when he came to the pond across from his brother's house. He listened to the night sounds. He listened to his heart pounding. There was no way he could have anticipated the power of that kiss. He'd simply wanted to kiss the woman. Who knew where it might lead?

She turned him hard and mushy in a moment. And then she'd broken off. There was fear in her eyes. She had to know he would never hurt her. But she seemed only interested in denial — denying herself as well as him.

He shook his head, bent over to pick up a flat pebble, and skipped it across the pond. And now she knew about his family's ownership in the resort. It was bound to come out at some point. He should have just told her.

But from the moment he saw her climb out of her red rental car at the resort he'd felt a pull, an attraction. It hadn't been only her full breasts and curves; it was how she'd thrown herself across the car roof in utter exhaustion. She'd survived something harrowing. Her vulnerability was as apparent and enticing as her beauty.

He hadn't wanted to get involved. Not with Traci Steele. Not with a woman Cassie Travers sent to him. It was better for them both for her to believe he was just a simple cowboy rather than a fairly wealthy rancher, horse trainer, stable manager and whatever else somebody wanted him to do.

Not involved? He was involved up to the tip of

his heart. And it *did* matter. That kiss might have been the single most important event in his life. It was too early to tell, but he would be willing to take some bets on that. "Another plateau," Scott mumbled. "I've got another plateau or two in mind."

"Sounds like you're developing a new skill, talking to the fish."

Scott didn't turn; he didn't have to. "You're out late tonight, James."

"Yeah, well, the household has seen happier nights than this one."

"Don't be too hard on the girls. They didn't mean anything bad to happen."

"They never do, but they've got to learn not everything that seems funny to them is funny to others."

"Traci's taking it fine."

A long silence hung between the brothers as each looked up at the stars blinking against the dark low sky.

"What the hell is that woman doing here?"

"You know. We've talked about it before. She's here to get some rest, and to help us sort out what's going wrong with our horses."

"Seems like she and you are together a lot."

"Yeah, I suppose we are. We have to be. And frankly, she's not bad to hang around with."

"Great. You mean the twins were right?"

Scott said nothing.

"You'd better watch out, little brother. That woman is big city, snooty uppity. She'll eat you up and spit you out for breakfast. She's a witch. She's a—"

Scott grabbed his brother by his jacket collar. "Shut up, James. I'm not asking your advice about women. Never have and never will."

Freeing himself, James stepped backward and nodded. "Okay, little brother. But I've warned you. You mess around with lawyers, and you're going to wind up the one hurt. Our daddy would be the first to tell you that, and you know it."

"That might be true, big brother, but our daddy ain't here, and you sure as hell aren't about to fill his shoes. Why don't you go back in and make peace with your family? I'm going to go to bed."

Chapter Six

Closing the condo door behind her, Traci leaned against it and drew in several deep breaths. The ride from the ranch to the resort had been quieter than any funeral she'd attended. And it had taken every ounce of her reserve not to throw herself into Scott's arms when they got out of his pickup to seek forgiveness and understanding. She still savored the scent and touch of his soft mustache upon her lips. Closing her eyes, Traci alternately congratulated and chastised herself for maintaining self-control.

Reluctantly, she pushed away from the door and dumped her few things on the living room couch. The red light on the phone blinked, reminding her there was another world out there beyond the resort and the ranch.

The hairs on the back of her neck stiffened. Something wasn't right. Cautiously, she moved from room to room. Everything looked the same, but it wasn't.

Someone had been in her condo.

Then Traci laughed, somewhat alarmed at her own slightly hysterical sounds. Of course. The cleaning crew came in twice a week. Still, it was comforting to know she'd had her laptop with her at the ranch, even if she'd been unable to use the internet. She'd always had the habit of backing up her computer work on a flash drive. One could never be too safe.

The phone rang and Traci picked it up. She smiled at the nearly panicked voice on the other end of the line. "Oh, it's you," she said.

"I'm okay...No, I haven't been here for several days. I'm sorry you worried about me, Cassie, but I didn't know I was required to check in. Yes, I love you too. Yes, I've met McCord. His whole family sends you their love. Right. That's where I've been these past several days. I fell off a horse... Stop laughing. Yes, I got on a horse. No, no one took a picture. Actually, I'm working with a yearling—leading him and simple things like that. Ransom is adorable. Scott thinks I need to be comfortable around horses before we travel to a couple race tracks and talk with trainers in their barns and such. Yeah, I guess it matters.

"Yes, he's a nice man. No, not in that way." Traci's chest constricted. "At least, I don't think so. Don't sound so smug. Scott's very pissed at your matchmaking efforts. Don't even try to deny it. By the way, where's the beach? Right, just a short drive away.

"I'm not sure there is a case yet. But now that I'm back here, I can really get started. Can you believe I couldn't get e-mail out at the ranch because of poor phone lines? I'll keep you posted." Traci laughed. "Yeah, those sweet little darlings are right in the middle of things. I don't know which one is worse; while Susannah is leading them into trouble, Rebecca is conjuring up their next foray. Exactly, they're a hoot all right.

"Twenty below? Real temp, not wind chill? This is feeling better by the minute. It must be brutal just getting the chores done. Don't turn into an ice cube. I'll let you know if I learn anything and need any assistance. What do you mean, let yourself go? I enjoy myself. Right. I love you too. Bye."

Carefully, Traci placed the receiver back on its cradle. *Let yourself go.* Why did those three words sound so simple when someone else said them? How could she let herself go with him, when she couldn't be free with herself?

Enough! Enough! There were things to do. A shower. A little grocery shopping. Pulling together her thoughts on the developing case. And then gathering her wits and emotional protection for the three o'clock meeting with Scott McCord to go over the lists.

She'd made it clear she wanted no repetition of the kiss. He wasn't about to leave it be. If he felt any of the sparks and skyrockets she'd felt when they were crushing each other's lips, how could he? How could she? But she had to leave it be, and she would.

Funny, she had always thought the sparks and skyrockets were fantasies that writers made up in their romance starved minds. But something explosive had happened during that kiss, and it wasn't just in her mind. There was no need to deny. She was a cool-headed realist, and he'd shaken her at her fiery core. That kiss had been soothing, enticing, and pure abandonment. They'd played with liquid fire and she'd only been singed by its heat. The results could have been worse. A lot worse.

- o -

Scott McCord sat on his swivel chair staring at the feed mill calendar hanging above his desk without actually focusing on any single date. He twisted first one way on his chair and then the other. He picked up a pen to make some notes about a horse's nutritional intake. He laid the pen down.

Scott stood and paced. He stopped and shoved his hands in his pockets and sighed. Damn that woman! She was making him fidget, and he didn't like fidgeting.

He prided himself on dealing with women on his terms. With Traci Steele, he didn't know if he had any terms anymore. How could she have hooked him so? Had she given him a magic potion when he wasn't looking?

What was it about her? Her feistiness? Her beauty? Her strength? Her vulnerability? He'd always liked a strong woman, and he certainly wasn't immune to beauty, but he'd never been a rescuer.

But her withdrawal had more to do with her than with him. She reminded him of a quarter horse reluctant to race again after being bumped badly in a couple of starts. He'd helped those horses by providing space for them to win back their confidence and trust, in themselves and in their trainer. He'd had to take the pressure off the horses without giving up on their ability to run.

"Yeah," he grumbled. "Take the pressure off. Off her or me? What a kiss! I'm ready to shift gears, and she's sitting there stuck in park."

Be calm. Be honest. Maybe she hadn't had much honesty with men. Scott raised his eyes to the ceiling. It wasn't like he'd really inspired her confidence and trust thus far. How long had he thought she'd be nosing around without finding out about the McCord family and Live Oak?

"Knock, knock," Traci said, rapping lightly on the office door frame. "Is it okay to come in? You look very ponderous. Heavy thoughts or heavy heart?"

Scott smiled at her instant blush and motioned for her to sit down. "Both, I imagine. Can one have heavy thoughts about a heavy heart?"

"I suppose," Traci replied, pulling a notepad from her purse. "So why the cloud of secrecy about your family tie-in with the resort? Surely you knew I'd find out. Or was it a test of my skill?"

Chuckling, Scott said, "That would be a nice way out for me. But since one of the conclusions resulting from my heavy heart thoughts is that I am going to be as honest with you as I can—no games—I won't take that out."

"Okay," she responded evenly.

"I imagine there were two reasons, really, and

115

I've just come to realize the second. When I first saw you by your car that afternoon you arrived after the rain storm, I was struck by your beauty — as much as by your presence. You were unsure, yet relieved and confident. You exuded class and sophistication. And you were the bait that Cassie Travers used to set a trap. I figured at the time that you were aware of that."

Traci shook her head.

"I know it was pure Cassie. But I didn't want to get involved with any woman, particularly a big city lawyer. I certainly didn't want you to see anything in me that you might like." Scott glanced away from Traci's intense stare.

"So that explains why you were so gruff at first."

"Yeah, I overdid that a bit, but I figured you'd expect that behavior from a cowboy."

"Yes, I think I'm understanding some of this now. You didn't want me to know you had wealth and status, certainly enough to match my own." Traci covered her mouth, and still failed to contain a soft laugh. "You were scared of me, and I thought I was afraid of you."

"Be that as it may, I'm not a person to be feared." He paused and gazed at the feed mill calendar. Turning back to Traci, he said, "To be perfectly honest, as I got to know you better, as I started allowing myself to be attracted to you, I didn't want you to think I was only capable of doing a job that had been handed me on a silver platter."

"Oh."

"I'm sure Ma told you the stable is to be managed by a McCord as long as there's one interested in operating it."

"She did."

"Well, James, being the oldest, was groomed to run the cattle ranch, and most of his time is taken up with that huge responsibility. Our father groomed me for this position. And it's been rewarding. I'm much more at ease dealing with the public than James ever will be. But I had to have more than this, and that's why over the years I've developed the connection with trainers at race tracks and have worked with their horses needing rest, recuperation and retraining."

Scott steepled his hands and met Traci's gaze openly. "So, you see, at first I didn't come clean because I didn't want to be attractive to you, and then I didn't say anything because I thought you'd think me some kind of pampered youngest son."

- o -

Traci leaned back in her chair and took in the candor of the man before her. When had anyone tried to be this honest with her? And what had he found so attractive about her that he wanted to so impress? She wasn't going to go there. Not now.

But he certainly seemed less intimidating now. And *she* hadn't been the only vulnerable one.

"It never occurred to me that you were anything but a hard working, generous man.

You're a cowboy, in my eyes." She blushed. "But that's not bad. You make a living working with horses. And that requires a lot of hard work. I'm not at all certain why my perception of you should matter all that much, but I'm glad we've at least cleared the air.

She paused. "So, you sit on the board of directors representing the McCord interests."

Scott hesitated. "Yeah, we don't meet more than twice a year, but I show up for the meetings."

"So, you know all the folks with financial interests in Live Oak."

"Sort of." Scott folded his arms and leaned back in his chair. "The local owners show up and the managing corporation sends a representative or two, but I don't know who is behind the corporation. But don't you think you're pushing the resort ownership a little hard, since my withholding information had to do with us rather than with the problem I'm having with my horses?"

Traci nodded. "You're probably right. I imagine I'm pursuing that lead now because it's the only one available to me. Now that I'm back with e-mail I can work with a friend and colleague in Chicago who's a wizard on a computer and getting behind corporate roadblocks, and we'll start checking your lists of trainers, owners, employees and so on. And I want to start interviewing folks. When can we visit the track?"

"Most anytime," said Scott, looking amused. "You seem to be able to make your way down a barn walkway without looking like you fear for your life."

"What about my work with Ransom? Should that continue?"

"It would be good for you and him. At least twice a week, if you can fit it in."

"Good, I'll miss him when I go back home." Brushing hair away from her cheeks, Traci asked, "And how about Cory?"

"Ah, Cory. I think riding him has taken on a greater personal challenge for you than getting comfortable enough to be around horses."

"I imagine it has." Traci felt her cheeks warm before his steady gaze. "Leaving it go as it is feels too much like losing, and I don't like that feeling."

"Okay, maybe after we come back from LA, we can see how you feel about getting on Cory again. We'll spend a day or two up there and visit Santa Anita, Los Alamitos and Hollywood. Only the first two are running races now, but horses are still training at Hollywood."

"Two days probably makes the most sense, given what you've said. Give me a day or two to go over your lists, and then I should be ready."

"Great—I'll make reservations."

"Two rooms," Traci said, arching her eyebrows.

"Of course," Scott replied. "And what about us, Traci Steele from Chicago? Where do we go?"

"There is no us." Traci didn't like the tremble so apparent in her voice. She clutched her pen tightly.

"I think there is, or at least there could be."

Traci shrugged her shoulders.

"I've been very candid with you. That kiss last night in the barn ignited something I've never felt before. I'd like to find out more about its source and what it means. Can you really sit there and say it didn't do anything for you?"

A long silence ensued. Was it her heart she heard beating, or his? "No," she whispered.

Scott leaned over and placed his hands on top of hers and looked into her eyes. She didn't have the strength to move a muscle even if she'd wanted to. And she didn't want to. If life could stop right there, she could swim in the pools of his gray eyes for eternity.

"Then let's at least remain open to one another. I don't want to push you. I won't hurt you, but I need to be able to talk with you about things that matter, and feel your touch—like now. You are so warm. What do you say, Traci? Can you risk being open with me? Even a little bit."

Traci tried to focus on him through watering eyes. She wanted to shout *no* and run, but her body refused to move. He seemed so large, yet so gentle. She'd seen him coax horses, big and small, and she knew he was doing the same with her.

She'd seen him work miracles with those magnificent animals. Could he work a miracle for her? At last, she nodded and mumbled, "A tiny bit. But I've got to go right now."

Scott squeezed her hands. "I know you do. I'll check in with you tomorrow to finalize our trip to LA."

"Here it is," Scott said, with a catch in his voice. "You can feel the place vibrate." Scott pointed across the panorama of the Santa Anita backstretch. "This place works like a finely tuned Swiss watch. It has to, in order for the trainers, grooms, exercise riders and everyone else to get their work done between five thirty and ten thirty a.m."

They walked past barn after barn. Clutching her coffee mug between her hands for warmth against the early morning chill, Traci marveled at all the activity taking place in a fairly quiet manner. Each barn seemed like a beehive, with men and women leading horses to and from the track, to and from wash racks, or just to and from anywhere to be closely inspected by trainers, grooms and owners and occasionally veterinarians.

Glancing at Scott, Traci thought she could hear the man's heart pounding in his chest; a vital spark emanated from him that she hadn't seen at the stable, with his family or even in the corral working with the weanling. She'd felt that spark only once before — in the midst of their embrace in the shadows of the McCord barn.

She tried to appreciate what he was feeling. Yes, she confessed, she was impressed with the controlled chaos taking place around her, not unlike a courtroom before the judge enters. But good grief, it was six a.m. They'd awakened at five. When she'd ducked her head out of her hotel room, he'd thrust a coffee mug and bagel at her and told her to hurry. She hadn't had an appetite for the bagel at that hour, but the coffee proved to be a lifesaver, and she'd already refilled it from his thermos twice. Five o'clock in the morning! Five o'clock was supposed to register at the end of the day.

"It looks like they have to cram a whole day into a few hours. Is that because of the racing schedule?"

"Yeah. There has to be time to prepare the track for racing and to settle the horses down before the crowds gather.

"Does each horse have to go to the track every day?"

"Not necessarily. Depends on the horse, where that horse is in its conditioning schedule, and how the trainer prefers to work a horse."

"So the trainer is a manager of people and animals. Sounds like a lot of judgment calls."

"Sure is."

"Could mistakes in judgment contribute to the kinds of problems your horses are exhibiting?"

Leaning against a post, Scott shook his head. "Highly unlikely. When a horse leaves the ranch, I've personally assessed that the horse is fit and ready to compete or at least undergo rigorous training. If there is an error in trainer judgment, it would be mine."

"And that might happen occasionally, but not this often."

"Right." Scott pointed at a horse and rider trotting by on the track. "Traci, look at that chestnut. He's favoring his right foreleg ever so slightly. Can you see he doesn't quite put his entire weight on that foot? Hopefully, the rider will report that or the trainer will notice. Most will. Some will ignore it."

Traci stared hard at the horse. She squinted. The damn horse looked like any other she'd seen that morning: a perfectly healthy specimen. "I give up," she said at last when the horse had trotted a considerable distance away. "You must have magnifying glasses for eyes."

"That's all right. It probably takes years of experience to see some of these things."

"So is there such a thing as a typical day at the track?"

"Sure. It usually starts at five a.m..." He grinned at Traci's involuntary shudder. "Each horse will usually be given a little snack to keep them quiet and wait their turn. Like people, some horses are more patient than others. Of course, you don't want to work a horse on a full stomach.

"A groom or the trainer will check the horse out for any injuries or heat that may have been accidentally caused overnight or left over from previous work. The animal is tacked up, and if all goes well the exercise rider arrives just as the horse is ready to go to the track. The rider will receive instructions from the trainer for that day's exercise regimen. Once the animal returns from a workout or routine exercise, the tack comes off and a blanket goes on and the horse is walked through the barn area by a groom or assistant groom for a half hour or so to cool the horse down. Then the horse is returned to the stall where he'll be groomed, and they'll do leg wraps and medications if necessary.

"Usually, by ten or so the horses are having their breakfast. As you'll see, most trainers mix their own feed right here on site. Each horse has its own dietary needs. On the day of the race, they'll typically only have water and hay. Evening feed is usually around four or four-thirty. Again, grooms and trainers will be eyeballing each horse to check for problems."

"How about vets?"

"Vet checks, dental appointments and shoeing generally occur in the mornings."

"Dental appointments?"

Scott laughed. "Yeah, good dental care is important for the well being of a horse. Bad teeth can cause pain and distraction; poorly worn teeth may mean that a horse can't eat its feed adequately."

"Wow. I had no idea there was so much involved in all of this."

"Hah, what I'm telling you and what you see is only the tip of the iceberg."

"What about between ten and four? Are there people around these horses?

"There is track security. You do have to have a pass to be back here in the stable area. During the off hours you may find some grooms hanging around, mainly socializing. Or there might be a horse that needs checking. Sometimes owners will come by and visit. Mostly, it's quiet."

"Would a person up to no good be more likely to be seen during the hours of high activity or during the quiet hours?"

"That's hard to say. If the bastard is well known, he might simply be accepted as part of the woodwork. A stranger would likely stand out at any time. This is a fairly tight community. If you don't belong, you'll be noticed."

"So whoever is getting to the horses is likely an insider."

Scott's neck muscles tightened before he responded. "That's a reasonable conclusion, Counselor. It's one of our own. But enough of that—there's a man we've got to see."

Scott strode off like a boy set free in a toy shop; Traci hurried to stay in step.

"Well, look at what the wildcat drug in from the mountains," a stocky man shouted, sticking his head out of a nearby doorway.

Both men took three strides toward each other and then slapped each other on the back as if they needed resuscitation. Traci grinned. That must stand for a male hug of affection.

Scott turned and said, "Clyde, I want you to meet a friend of mine from Chicago, Traci Steele. Traci, this old varmint is Clyde Laskins; he and I go back to rodeo days. We've competed against each other, I dunno, maybe since age eight or so."

"That's about right," Laskins agreed. "This man's as stubborn as a mule and as wily as a range bull."

Traci laughed. "I've noted both characteristics."

"Okay. Enough." Scott raised his hands. "I know it's a busy time, but do you have a few minutes? It's important. Traci's not only a friend, she's also a private investigator looking into some of the problems we've been having."

Laskin's eyes clouded briefly. "Sure," he said, grinning. "I don't have much opportunity to talk with investigators. Follow me."

They sat in a cramped office next to horse liniments and stacks of Daily Racing Forms. Traci listened to Laskins describe what had been happening on his end.

"I don't know, ma'am, how it happens, but the morning after they arrive back, or maybe the next day, the horses come up lame, or develop a fever, or become colicky. There's no rhyme or reason. It doesn't happen to all the horses." Laskins frowned at Scott. "But trainers are starting to grumble about it. Even had an owner wondering why I still ship his horses to McCord. This thing is going to get worse soon if we don't figure out what's happening."

"So do you check the horses when they arrive back from the ranch?" Traci asked.

"Sure, we look them over."

Traci looked over at Scott. "Maybe those horses will have to be monitored closer. If someone is getting to them, they're either doing it when they get back to the track or before."

"That costs money and time," Laskins groused. "My people don't have either."

"If it can be established that these aren't just

126

random occurrences, we'll pay for the extra monitoring," Scott informed Laskins. "Til now, I haven't been convinced that I wasn't just having a streak of bad luck. But the frequency has increased. And as you've said, people are starting to make noises about it. We'll come up with the extra security if need be."

"All right. That'll help a lot. It's damn creepy to think someone is routinely walking in and out of here and drugging a horse or doing whatever they're doing." Laskins glanced quickly at Traci then at Scott. "I'm no fool. I know shenanigans take place at the track now and then. But this is more than occasional abuse. Much more, I think."

"So who is responsible for the horse when it arrives back in your barn, Mr. Laskins?"

"The hauler will turn the horse over to a groom or an assistant groom. My man has to sign for the horse. If I'm here, I might do it, but the groom is empowered to receive the horse. The care of the horse is then the responsibility of a particular groom.

"I have twenty-three people working for me, Ms. Steele. This place operates smoothly, for the most part. That requires a lot of managing of horses and people. Most of the barns are similar."

Traci groaned. Scott had already told her the problems with the horses involved at least a half dozen trainers. That could be over a hundred people. Plus track personnel. "I can't talk with everyone who might come in contact with a horse."

Laskins chuckled. "You're welcome to try, but most of my people have English as a second language, if they have it at all. Whatever you do, don't tell them you're a prosecutor. Ma'am, we do our best to check green cards, but we don't examine them real close. I'm more concerned about whether a man or woman can handle a horse."

Traci released air slowly through pursed lips. She shook her head at Scott. "Why don't you show me what happens as these horses come and go? Maybe I'll want to interview some of your people later, Mr. Laskins."

Standing, Scott shook hands with Laskins. "Thanks for taking the time to talk with us, Clyde. Is Barrows here today?"

"Sure. He's up in the stands timing some of the workouts. Good to meet you Ms. Steele." Laskins extended his hand. "If I can help more, let me know. We've got to keep this big galoot out of trouble, you know."

As they walked toward the track, where horses were doing sprints and exercise riders were cooling down their mounts, Traci struggled to make sense of what she'd learned. "So, any number of persons could come in touch with a horse within forty-eight hours after its return?"

"Sure. Most anyone in a given barn. There are some track personnel around and about."

"Vets?"

"Yeah, but you wouldn't have to be a vet to

dose a horse."

"No, I imagine not, but I don't want to overlook anyone at this point."

"Well then," Scott drawled, "your suspect list might as well include everyone who works at the track, the stables and the ranch."

Traci smiled lightly. "It does." She chuckled at his scowl. "Somehow I think we have to find the connections between the horses and the trainers and or owners. Even if grooms will talk with us, I doubt they'll share their suspicions. And we have to establish motive."

"I told you motive is clear," Scott replied. "You're involved in horse racing, Ms. Steele. People want to win. Some will do anything possible to do just that."

"I'm sure you're right, Mr. McCord." Traci stopped walking and turned to face her client. "So tell me, how many other ranches doing what yours is doing are reporting these kinds of problems? Have you heard of any? Have you checked?"

McCord frowned and then grinned. "You sure look sexy when you get your dander up. You may have a point. I don't know about other ranches; I haven't talked with any of the others. This is a problem you don't really want to talk about unless you have to. You'd be surprised to see how rampant the rumor mill can be at a track." He paused and glanced thoughtfully out at the horses working on the track. "You may be right, though. I haven't heard of any other problems. But why would I be singled out?"

Chapter Seven

"This is exquisite; very classy." Traci loved the view and ambiance of the clubhouse restaurant high in the stands of the Santa Anita Racetrack.

After leaving shedrow mid-morning, they'd gone back to their hotel rooms to nap and change clothes and now were sharing a mid-afternoon lunch while watching the races. From their table they could see the horses on the track. For an even better view, they could walk down several steps and stand in front of the floor-to-ceiling windows. Or they could watch the changing odds and then the progress of the race on the TV monitor at their table. If they wanted to bet, they could make wagers at counters only a few feet away.

"White table cloths and more silverware than I know what to do with," Scott said, lifting his beer in salute.

Traci clinked her wine glass against it and smiled comfortably. "This is quite the life, Mr. McCord. Expensive horses. Wining and dining in elegance. And people who look like they belong in Hollywood."

Scott chuckled. "Many do. But I'm looking at the classiest, sexiest woman in the entire place." Scott traced the back of her hand with an index finger.

Watching his gaze soften, Traci tensed only a little. She didn't want to mislead him, but the setting and the man were so right. "You've a lot of blarney; must be a lot of Irish mixed up in your Scottish blood." She pulled back her hand and took another bite of her lamb loin chop. "This is absolutely delicious; the Rosemary does wonders for the meal. How is yours?"

"Can hardly go wrong with Black Angus New York Sirloin. Would've preferred baked over scalloped potatoes, though. And you're on the mark about the Irish. It comes from my mother's side."

"Bet you don't like quiche, either." Traci laughed at the face Scott made. No, he wouldn't like quiche. He was a steak and potatoes man. He was a man of the earth; even in these rich surroundings, there was a primal element to Scott McCord—an element that drew her like a magnet and repelled her at the same time. If she crossed that invisible line of nearness, would she ever withdraw unscathed?

"Now, here's a race I want to see," Scott said, pointing at the screen. "Smooth Ivory spent a couple months at the ranch recently. She's number eight. Check out your program."

Picking up her program, Traci was uncertain what she was expected to notice. She knew very little about deciphering all the numbers and small print, though serious handicappers could spend hours attempting to decode those data to speculate on how each race would run. Glancing across the page she saw nothing, and then the obvious leaped out at her. "Oh my, Cassie and Clint own the horse. Wait till Cassie hears I saw her horse run. Do you think it will win?"

"Unlikely. The horse is a natural router and this is a sprint. I expect the trainer is trying to get her to develop a little more early speed. If she's toward the front early on today, even if she fades later, look out next time when she returns to a route."

"So will you bet Smooth Ivory to win today?"

"I might put her in a small exacta or two, but I won't pull out the credit card."

"We've seen four races and you've only bet one. Don't you like to gamble?"

Scott smiled broadly. "Sure I like to gamble. It's like life. Some things are worth more of a gamble than others. Take you, for instance. You're worth staying at the table to see if my luck changes."

Impetuously, Traci darted her tongue out at him. What had prompted her to do that? His laughter didn't suggest he'd been put off at all. Why, she'd just done something one of the twins would have done. For a brief lightheaded moment, she felt good about that. Trembling slightly, she said, "So some races aren't worth betting."

"A sure way to lose at the races is to think you have to bet every race. In some cases, the favorite is nearly certain of winning and is going off at such low odds there's no value in taking the risk. Some other races may be so contentious you can't narrow it down beyond four horses." He leaned back in his chair. "To bet seriously, I would've spent last night handicapping. No, today is just a fun afternoon with you. No serious betting today."

"But you're still gambling," she countered smugly.

"Oh yeah, you can count on that."

Again her heart fluttered. Somehow she knew she could count on that. Was that a sure bet? She'd come to enjoy the repartee with Scott far beyond any banter she'd had with other men. Banter with him tested both skill and will.

But there were predefined limits to their game. She knew that; he didn't. She didn't want either one of them to be hurt, but she couldn't walk away from the game just yet. There was that force of energy between them that seemed to have a life of its own. Acknowledging that force startled her. For the first moment since meeting Mustache, she wondered if she controlled their game and its outcome.

"Will you be wanting dessert?" inquired the waiter.

"I'll have your Individual Fruit Tart," Traci said.

"An excellent choice, ma'am."

"And I'll have the ice cream."

"Sir?" The waiter frowned. "We don't sell ice cream."

"Sure you do. Says so right there—however you pronounce the damn thing." Scott jabbed a finger at the dessert menu.

"Oh. Of course. The Profiterole Trio. Good choice."

134

As the waiter left, Traci tried to hide her giggle behind a menu. "McCord, you're an original. No question about that."

He gave her a lopsided grin, not appearing embarrassed at all. "It's a nice place, but they ought to print their menus in English."

- o -

Coffee was served with dessert and Scott sipped his watching the gleam in Traci Steele's eyes. She was an enigma — so full of passion and yet so hidden. Was that part of her allure? Was it innate or practiced?

Here he was at one the best tracks in the country paying more attention to a woman than to the horses. What the hell was wrong with him?

He'd sure like to know what she was really thinking, not just what she chose to reveal. She fit in this upscale restaurant with these people, many of whom wore their wealth on their wrists, fingers, and necks. Yet there she sat in a black jersey top and pants that hugged her like he so wanted to. The only jewelry she wore was simple silver loop earrings and a gold watch. Her lips had a light pink cast and her dark eyes sparkled as if protecting inner mysteries.

Traci Steele was pure enchantment. And he'd been enchanted even though she hadn't deliberately set out to catch him in her web. If she could, she'd choose to run from him. And perhaps that was the greatest mystery of all. Why didn't she run? She could be on the next plane back to Chicago if she wanted to. Certainly she didn't stay just because of the case they were working on. They both knew Clint Travers had contact with others who could do all of this investigative leg work. So he frightened her, yet she stayed.

Travers. Good God, he'd tried to repress the fact that Cassie had set them up. Scott blinked. Maybe she wasn't far off the mark. But it was still galling to think she'd had a hand in getting him involved with a woman. It was sort of like being sent a mail order bride. And in this instance, he hadn't even read the ad.

Whoa. Back up there, old boy. He'd better scratch that five letter word *bride* from his thoughts. He watched Traci nibble at her dessert. She wasn't ranch material.

She was big city. But she certainly presented an intriguing challenge. And he seldom backed away from a challenge.

He followed her with his eyes as she tucked the menus in her bag. She smiled at his unstated query. "It's legit. Says right on them: *Please take home, with our compliments.*

"The watercolors are beautiful. The artist has really captured the mood and spirit of Santa Anita. The jockeys and horses look almost alive, in a surreal sort of way. She's good, and I'm taking home some souvenirs. I might even frame one of them. Your menus have different scenes than mine. Do you mind if I take those too?"

Scott placed his menus in her outstretched

hand. "Didn't know you were a collector of racetrack menus."

"I appreciate quality art wherever it appears."

"Me too," he said, smoothing back his mustache and appraising the woman's beauty with a well trained eye. "I prefer mine very alive, on four legs or two."

He smiled at her glower before she looked away. He guessed she wasn't about to get into a discussion of the relative merits of various art forms.

- o -

After the races and after the sun had set, Traci and Scott sat at a picnic table in the shadows of the now empty clubhouse waiting for a man Scott wanted to see. He'd been too busy earlier in the morning.

His name was Harry Barrows. Scott claimed that Barrows had done just about everything one could do at the track, from grooming to training. In his youth, he'd even been a jockey. Now he was known as a clocker.

He was one of the people who carefully scrutinized the horses as they worked in the morning and recorded their official finishing times. Barrows knew everyone at the track. He'd agreed to meet with them because he owed Scott more than one favor. He'd chosen this time and this place.

"Ah, there you are," said a gruff voice. A rather

bent man in a dark hooded jacket approached their table. He shook Scott's hand warmly and then directed his gaze at Traci.

He didn't smile, but he nodded and shook her hand as Scott introduced them. He sat down across from them with his back to the track. "So how can I help you, McCord?" Barrows asked, keeping his hands tight around his coffee mug.

"Thanks for meeting with us, Harry. I'll let Ma know you're still kicking."

"Guess she must be, too, or I would've heard different."

"She's fine, more ornery than ever."

"I can believe that. So what do you need?"

"Information."

"Thought so."

"We're having trouble with some of our horses when they come back to the track — not performing the way they should."

"Heard a rumor about that just the other day."

"What did you hear?"

"Only that a couple trainers are wondering what the hell is going on and how long your string of bad luck is going to last."

"Ms. Steele is helping us investigate the situation. We're beginning to think this string of bad luck is man made."

Barrows looked sharply at Traci and then spat on the concrete. "Don't know that a woman's gonna help much with this, but you're better looking than most of 'em he brings by."

"Mr. Barrows, my looks don't have anything to

do with anything," Traci sputtered. Out of the corner of her eye she caught a glance of Scott trying to hide a smile with his hand.

"It's okay, Traci. He was just complimenting you." Grinning at Barrows, he went on to say, "She's also a damn good investigator, Harry. I'd appreciate it if you'd let us know if you hear something of interest."

"I'll do what I can." Barrows fumbled with his jacket zipper. "Didn't mean to offend you, ma'am. If you have any questions, McCord knows how to get a hold of me. Now, if you don't mind, I'd like to get some shuteye. Mornings come early around here."

"I'm becoming very aware of that. And you didn't offend me. Sometimes, when I'm over stressed, I get a little touchy. Sorry about that. If I have questions, I'll take you up on that offer. Maybe we could have lunch someday. It appears that you know Scott McCord quite well — maybe even some of his secrets."

The old man chortled. "That I do. That I do. You call, and I'll find a private place for us to talk."

Traci watched the man disappear into the deeper shadows of the building.

Without further comment, Scott stood and said, "Okay, let's get out of here. It's too damn cold to think clearly about horses or anything else."

"You wimpy southern Californian," she chided. "This is hardly a chill from where I come from."

"Right."

But Traci didn't complain about being hustled toward their car. She was eager to try out the rental car heater.

With Scott behind the wheel, Traci watched Santa Anita fade into the night. There had been a lot of mystery there. Much of the conversation with Barrows seemed to take place in code, leaving her uninformed. "So who is Harry Barrows? You don't seem like the best of friends, yet he knows you very well. Do you think he told us everything he knows? Can he be trusted? And how does he know your mother?"

Scott looked away from the road long enough to give her a grim smile. "We're not buddies, but we're more than mere acquaintances. Can he be trusted? With my life. How does he know my mother? He's her brother."

"Oh my goodness!" Traci's hand flew to her mouth. "That—"

"That old crusty guy who appears nearly down and out is my uncle."

"There's got to be a story behind this."

"Oh yeah. My dad hated his guts. End of story."

"But your mother—"

"My mother loved my dad and she loves her brother, even though they've been estranged most of their adult lives."

"But your dad is dead now. Surely, the brother and sister can get together now."

"I think Ma would like to, but she doesn't know

how to go about it. She doesn't think Harry will forgive her. And she may be right. Apparently, she wounded him very badly when she married my father, and of course he poured salt into that wound anytime he had an opportunity to do so."

"But you've maintained contact with your uncle."

"Yes, that was important to my mother. He was the only family she had left, and she wanted me and James to know we did have another living relative. We never mentioned Harry to Dad. I'm not sure if he knew we'd meet the guy a couple times a year or not."

Traci watched the lights of the city go by as they traveled back to their hotel. McCord was turning out to have as many secrets as she did. How could his father be so mean and distrusting? She thought of a question she'd meant to ask before. "Did your father support your involvement in racehorses?"

"Not hardly." Scott flipped the turn signal on before entering their hotel driveway. "He did everything he could to talk me out of it. Initially, I got into it as a way to help Clint Travers with some of his thoroughbreds. Then Harry got wind of what I was doing and a couple quarter horse trainers wanted to know if I'd handle their stock, too. I imagine my dad was suspicious of some of my contacts, but I think he knew he'd pushed me as far as he could. If I couldn't work with racehorses, I might have left the ranch."

"You told him that?"

"Uh, huh."

"Wow, that's huge.

"That feels great," Traci cooed. "You have a magic touch."

"Comes from practice—with horses. They're like people and develop muscles knots and tension that can be eased if you learn how to do it." Scott dug his thumb under Traci's scapula; she emitted a low groan.

Her muscles had loosened considerably during the last five minutes or so. They'd come back to the hotel and she'd complained about a stiff neck and a shoulder muscle that wouldn't stop spinning. He'd offered to help. At first she'd said no, but then she relented. She sat bent over in a cushioned chair while he applied pressure to the nagging aches.

"That should do it for now," he announced, lightly running his fingers across her nape.

She sat up and sighed heavily. "That was heavenly," she said. She felt him lift her hair off the back of her neck and felt his breath hovering over his fingers. She didn't move, afraid of ruining the moment.

His lips settled on her neck. His tongue snaked out, tracing the length of her neck muscles. She went still. Heat threatened to suffocate her, yet her skin turned cool whenever he moved on to lick another area. Where he had been, she felt bereft; where he landed, she felt exalted.

He ran his finger along her jaw line and then across her lips. Playfully, she nipped at it and he yelped obligingly.

"You are such a lovely woman. Your skin is more delicious than any dessert at any fancy restaurant." His words of praise were but a whisper.

She knew he wasn't mocking her, yet she still could not believe. He wouldn't think that if he could see the real her. She knew the limits.

He turned her head slightly and then his tongue followed her jaw line to the tip of her chin. She couldn't withhold a chuckle. And then his lips were on hers again. The birthday kiss in the barn was not an anomaly. Again, her body sizzled. He knelt beside her chair in a posture of adoration and kissed her lips, her cheeks, her eyelids. She lost track of where he was and what he was doing.

His tongue parted her lips and she welcomed him. She closed her eyes and responded with her tongue entering his mouth, pushing against him with all her strength. She laced her fingers behind his neck, pulling him farther into her warmth. His tongue began a slow withdrawal and reentry rhythm. She tried to hold him still but couldn't. And then she joined the dance of tongue. He pushed in and withdrew partially and she invaded his mouth, stretching her tongue as far as she could. He quickened the pace; she matched him thrust for thrust.

Although lost in the mutual stroking, Traci remained vaguely aware of her nipples tightening. Then an unfamiliar coiling began deep in the recesses of her loins. It cramped. It burned. Was she going to melt or explode? She didn't lose touch with his mouth. She arched her back, pushing her breasts against his massive chest, seeking relief.

She heard him groan, but paid him no mind. She was having an other-world experience and couldn't pause to listen to him. That inner coil threatened to recede. *No! No!*

A trigger snapped somewhere in her most sensitive tissues. She responded like a sprinter at the sound of the starter's pistol; she drove her tongue faster. She sought better leverage and more contact.

Scott's hands settled on her buttocks, pulling her closer still. And then she exploded. She laughed softly as she soared to heights she hadn't known existed— it was as simple as that. She floated pleasantly for what seemed like an interminable length of time before she realized one of his hands had crept up the inside of her jersey and was cupping a breast while his thumb brushed a nipple through the soft fabric of her bra. Even in the hazy aftermath of orgasm, she knew her limits.

"No!" she said firmly, removing his hand. He sat back on his heels and stared. The shock on his face said it all. But she couldn't have more. She couldn't give more.

He would be repulsed at the sight of her.

"I'm sorry," Scott said, breathing shallowly. "I thought you were enjoying yourself."

Traci blushed. "I was. Thank you for that. But I'm not ready for more." She looked away and

144

then back at him. "I need more time, more space."

Scott frowned and stood. "That's okay. I've got plenty of time."

"I hope," Traci squeaked, "you know I'm not teasing you when I can't go forward."

"I know. That never crossed my mind. But I do wish you'd trust me. Together, we could conquer whatever demons are eating at you."

Traci smiled wanly. "I do trust you, or we would never have gotten this far. This was — was very surprising. I've got to think some. I guess I've got a protective bubble around me, sort of like with Ransom."

"It's been a long day. Knowing you are protected by that bubble, I think I'd better be getting back to my room. A cold shower is what I need right now."

"I'm sorry," she said, standing, brushing her lips across his cheek.

"It's okay. We're making progress."

Again, Traci felt her face redden. "That we are," she whispered. "That we are."

Hugging a pillow between her legs and another to her chest, Traci found comfort but little sleep. She'd only dated a few men. None had had a fraction of the patience of Scott McCord. What was happening to her?

She'd lost control earlier in the evening. She'd become the aggressor. Other women had talked about such experiences while she had remained outwardly reserved and private. Even by her own hand, she'd only been able to approach that cliff with the sheer drop off.

Never had she risked playing the fool by actually stepping off the cliff—not until tonight. That floating sensation stayed with her even now. It was like a sailboat gliding forward steadily in a gentle breeze and then swifter when a stiffer wind filled its spinnaker and then thrown about by the whim of a gale threatening to shatter the mast and then a return to that more steady movement as the force of the wind retreated. What a fool she'd been to let them rob her of that experience all these years.

But she'd lost control of the game she and Scott were playing. Fortunately, she'd regained her senses before he had moved much farther. She squeezed the pillows tight; her eyes closed and then sprang wide. Traci wasn't certain what game she was playing anymore. She loved the repartee and the innuendo—that had always been a challenge—and she was skilled at thwarting unwanted advances. It was a way of life.

This felt different. Dramatically different. Was it her body? Was it him? Was it the two of them together? She wouldn't go there. She couldn't.

She tensed. Minutes passed until she realized she was shaking the bed. Traci sat up and held her head between her hands. What to do? She had options. She was not out of control.

She could hop on a plane to Chicago, but that would be like admitting defeat to Scott, to Cassie, especially to herself. She could continue fencing with the man, but she wasn't certain she could trust her body to maintain the necessary limits.

He would drop her in a minute if he ever saw her hideous breasts. Maybe she should just bare them and be done with it. She didn't want his sympathy. Maybe she should share her whole story. She'd never shared it with anyone.

But why would she? What did she really want from all of this? *More floating and soaring,* her inner voice tempted. *That's what you really want. But you're too afraid to risk.*

She'd once wondered if Scott McCord could work a miracle with her like he did with his horses. He already had. Could she trust him with more? With her body?

With her story? With her heart?

- o -

Scott lay fully clothed on his bed, staring at the ceiling of his hotel room. He was in danger. He'd come to enjoy the tough and able Traci Steele. He'd been surprised by her hidden passion, but it was her seldom shared vulnerability that hooked him like some gullible trout. He'd always fancied himself as wary around women, like a brown trout was around artificial flies. But that combination of toughness, passion, and vulnerability was proving much, much too alluring.

No longer was he convinced he wanted them to solve the case if that meant Traci Steele would be free to return to Chicago. He enjoyed being with her—but he didn't have a clue what he wanted to do with her.

Other than the obvious. Was it simply the challenge of getting her in his bed? It had never been, before. If a woman wanted to go to bed with him, fine. If not, that was fine too. So why couldn't he just walk away from the intimate part of their relationship? Why did he want to go back and get the door slammed in his face again?

Maybe because she was opening it up bit by bit, and he wanted to learn how far she would widen that opening the next time. Maybe because he wanted to taste more of her passion. Maybe because he wanted to help her discover herself.

Scott chuckled aloud. Maybe because he wanted her to help him discover *him*self. He pulled on his mustache. He'd hardly ever worked with a horse that didn't teach him something about himself.

But what was the end game in all of this? He couldn't see any happy resolution. Maybe simply playing the game made it worthwhile. What did he have to lose? His heart. Scott sighed into the darkness. No way. She was still sophisticated big city. And he—he was simply who he was. He'd never eaten quiche, and he wasn't about to start now.

- o -

After breakfast, Scott drove Traci's rental car down the coast heading back to Buteo. They'd been on the road for more than an hour when he turned into a rest area, commenting that he must have had too much coffee for breakfast.

Traci chuckled. "Fine with me. I've been drinking coffee since six. Oh my, look at that. I've caught glimpses of the ocean, but we'll be able to really see it from here."

Without waiting for him to turn off the engine, Traci bolted from the car and ran to the top of the hill overlooking the Pacific. When she got there, she just stood, held out her arms and breathed deeply. Although the beach was a couple hundred yards beyond a fence, she could see waves swell and unfold, sending her a private message of invitation. Two large sail boats were visible straight out from where she stood. And on the horizon miles away she could make out the dim outline of three tankers probably heading for Los Angeles.

Gulls flew overhead squawking their familiar calls. Traci glanced down at a sign on the fence that she hadn't noticed in her rush to see the ocean. She took a step back. The sign read *Rattlesnake Warning*.

She heard Scott chuckle from behind her. How long had he been standing there?

"Shouldn't have to worry about the rattlers yet," he said. "They should still be holed up. But as we get warmer days like this morning, there always could be an early one out and about."

Traci nodded and focused on the sailboats; she could make out individual people on each. How she longed for that kind of freedom, to glide along the surface with a stiff wind at her back. She hugged herself.

That was the place. *That* was where she could share her story. Would Mustache go sailing with her? Without looking at him, she smiled; he wouldn't like the idea one bit. That might even the score some for her having to ride horses. But more importantly, that was where she felt safest.

"Looks like you've discovered an old friend," Scott said.

"Oh, I have," she replied, glancing quickly at him and then back at the ocean. "The water nourishes my soul. I'd hoped to be able to sail often during these two months. That was another carrot Cassie used to get me to agree to come out here. Cassie didn't mention the winding roads between Live Oak and the beach."

"You're only an hour or two away."

"Yeah, if you don't mind being a daredevil driver. Why do you think I'm letting you do all the driving? I'm a flatlander, I'm afraid."

"So what's so fascinating about the water?"

"This isn't just water. This is the Pacific Ocean. People come from all over to walk its beaches, to dip a toe in, to surf, or to sail. I'd love to be out there on one of those sailboats." She turned to face Scott and asked, "Do you sail?"

"You got to be kidding!" Scott crossed his arms and raised both eyebrows. "I drink water. I sit in it in a Jacuzzi. I'll even wade in it to fly fish, but I don't get on it. I can't float and can hardly swim."

"That's hardly a reason not to sail. You don't

know what you're missing. They make excellent life preservers today."

"Right."

"I'd love to take you sailing, Scott. You're an excellent riding instructor, and I'm an excellent sailor. I've been sailing ever since I was a little kid. You'd be safe with me."

- o -

Scott's heart beat rapidly. How could he explain to her his fear of the water? Not of water, as much as being more than six feet from shore. That was how he'd convinced himself to fly fish; he figured he could stretch the six feet back to shore if necessary. And it had been, on more than one occasion.

There was a dreaminess in her eyes when she looked at the ocean that reminded him of a caress. The ocean breeze blew her hair off her face and billowed her skirt. He recalled her seductive words: "You'd be safe with me." His gut clenched. She'd become the temptress. Was she simply goading him into doing something he dreaded even thinking about? Was this just a game that he had no intention of playing?

"No way are you going to get me on a damn boat." He could not explain his own reaction to the disappointment and tears that marred Traci's features. It was like he'd just devastated her. Why was going sailing so important? If this was a game, she should be happy. She won. She'd called him

151

out and he refused.

Slowly, it dawned on him that much more was at stake here. He wasn't quite certain what. But there was much more to it than testing his courage. "It's pretty important to you, isn't it? That you take me sailing."

She nodded and glanced away at the ocean. He stepped to her side and wrapped an arm around her waist. She laid her head on his shoulder. Warm tears wet his shirt.

Scott breathed deeply trying not to cry himself. "So how far would we have to be from shore? And it would have to be a large boat. I'm not going out there in some little thing that will tip over if I blow on it."

He couldn't fathom why her body was now shaking worse than before and why she still sobbed. What had he said wrong now? Patience, he told himself as she curled one arm around his back and the other around his chest. They stood that way for long minutes. He didn't disturb her by talking, yet he took great pleasure in her hips and breasts crushed against him. For the moment, they were at peace.

That filled him with thankfulness and it scared the hell out of him.

"Can I borrow your handkerchief," Traci whimpered, at last stepping out of their embrace.

She dabbed her eyes and smiled uneasily. "As to your questions, I'll make sure we keep the shore in sight. And I'll rent the largest sailboat I can manage alone. It will have a cabin so we can go below to eat. It will have bunks, but I don't suppose you'll want to stay on board overnight." She laughed at Scott's sharp agreeing nod. "I realize I'm being a basket case, and I don't want you conceding to do something you really don't want to do. But I do appreciate you considering it." She pecked him on the cheek and headed for the bathroom.

Scott stared at the woman's swaying backside and tried to breathe normally. He glanced back at the ocean and shivered. What the hell was he getting himself into? He walked back to the car kicking himself for being such a soft touch.

Scott glanced at Traci, who had turned quite pensive after leaving the rest stop. She turned to face him. He tried not to let her skirt riding high on her thighs distract him.

"I wonder," she said, "Do the trucks hauling your horses stop at any rest areas?"

Scott frowned. "I don't know. I imagine it depends. They certainly could."

"It's something to check out. Stopping here or stopping for gas somewhere. I hadn't considered those possibilities. Someone could get to the horses in transit."

"If they knew when the horses were shipping out."

"Exactly.

"This has been an extremely helpful trip, Scott. I hope we didn't use up too much of your time."

"I got a lot of business done, too. Besides, we're

supposed to be doing this investigation together. But I'll need a few days at the ranch before tying me onto a boat."

Traci chuckled and trembled slightly. "That's fine. I need to follow up on some of these leads and check in with Roberta. There'll be time for sailing, if you still want to."

"I said I'd do it," Scott grunted through clenched teeth. He pushed the gas pedal down and the Grand Am leaped forward sharply. "I don't go back on my word."

Chapter Eight

"Why does that not surprise me more?" Traci held the condo phone between ear and shoulder while typing the information Roberta relayed.

"So we can't get behind Snowden Corp. Yet. I hear you. If anyone can, I know you will. The president, vice-president, and secretary are clean so far. And the treasurer shows up on our organized crime files as treasurer of at least a half dozen other small corporations. Okay. Let's keep digging.

"I agree. There has to be more. I'll send you lists of names we've generated here of horse owners, trainers, employees and so on. I'm curious to see if there are ties with any of those folks and Snowden.

"You're right, of course. The Oak could be clean, which I seriously doubt. Or more likely, we've stumbled onto something bogus but entirely separate from McCord's problems.

"Appreciate your help.

"I'm not as bored as I thought I might be.

"No, I don't have visions of riding off into the sunset with some cowboy. Love yah. Bye."

Traci hung up the phone and rubbed the bridge of her nose. So far nothing had come from her crosschecks of names. Criminal history background information was still being run.

So, was Mr. Humphries aware that at least one of his bosses lurked around with the bad guys? She'd bet he was. What about others at the resort? She'd have to be doubly careful not to appear suspicious.

From what Roberta had indicated, they were dealing with small fry, maybe individuals on the fringes of organized crime. In some ways they could be as dangerous as the big boys.

How much would Snowden risk? It seemed fairly obvious they were using the place to launder money or do something illegal behind what appeared to be a very legitimate front. Once they found out she was onto them, would they stay and fight, or would they run?

Often if the payoff was low, such groups would simply disappear to avoid blowing their cover. There were so many holes elsewhere for them to burrow into. From an economic standpoint, remaining involved with Live Oak might not be worth the unwanted attention.

They'd know soon enough, if she could blow enough smoke. Not yet. She didn't have nearly enough evidence that anything was wrong. Traci doodled on a pad of paper drawing lines between the words Oak, racehorses, and McCord. The connections had to be there. Why couldn't she see them?

They'd been back from LA for two days. She'd caught up on her laundry and grocery shopping and begun to gather information through various computer banks. Shaking her head, she wondered how many persons realized how much of their personal information just sat out there in cyberspace to be tapped into by anyone with half a brain.

She hadn't seen McCord since dropping him at the ranch. They'd agreed she should visit tomorrow to work with Ransom and interview some ranch employees.

She checked her calendar. It was difficult to keep track of the days. That would be Wednesday. Then on Thursday she'd talk with employees at the stables. She was still uncertain at this point about talking with other resort staff. That could tip her hand sooner than she wanted.

Ask McCord for board meeting minutes, she wrote on her pad. Certainly, some kind of minutes had to be kept if for no other reason than to look legit to the local owners.

Cash. Which operations handled lots of cash? Golf course. Tennis facility. She squinted at the words tennis facility. Rubbing her temples she tried to recall. Yes, McCord had said something about not understanding how that facility was able to generate so much income. She'd initially just written his response off as sour grapes. But it was something to check out. Somehow this place was being used by the mob. She didn't think it was just a place for them to vacation.

Traci repeatedly circled the name "McCord". Where did he fit into all of this? Did he know something he wasn't telling her? Did he know something he wasn't even aware of?

And what was she going to do about him? Obviously, she'd neutralized Mustache by getting him to reluctantly agree to go sailing. It was unlikely he would bring that up on his own. So she could just forget the whole thing.

But she couldn't shake the memory of her response to their kisses. She was making progress. Could she take it to the next level? It seemed clear he wouldn't initiate a next step—it was up to her.

So if they didn't go sailing and she didn't share her story, he'd never know the difference. But *she* would. Why was she still vacillating? She hated being indecisive. "But I am," she whimpered. "Dammit." She scratched broad strokes through McCord's name.

"I want you to take Ransom out of the corral today. Young horses can turn sour if there's no change in their routines."

Traci glanced quickly at McCord leaning with his back against the corral gate. Why did she always look for double meanings in his words? His face gave away nothing.

Scott opened the gate wide and Traci walked Ransom through without hesitation. They made their way about a hundred yards before Ransom stopped suddenly where shadows from trees bordering the ranch driveway sliced across in front of them. "Walk on," Traci ordered. Ransom stood braced on all four feet. Traci pulled on the lead rope. Ransom pulled back. Flustered, she turned to Scott for help.

"He isn't quite ready to fully trust you." Scott chuckled lightly. "You're walking away from the barn and the pasture area, so you're walking away from what he knows is safe into the wide unknown. You'll be surprised what horses can convince themselves is spooky. It may be a shadow, a stick they've walked by many times before, the wind, a bird. If you can imagine it, they can imagine it spooky."

"Okay, horse psychologist, so how do I get him to budge?"

"You're trying to get him to trust you—that is, that you won't lead him into danger. Then he'll move." Scott stepped closer. "But sometimes it does take a little convincing. First, you don't tug on him steadily. If you play tug of war with him, he'll win. He's stronger than you. Second, talk to him in a soothing manner. What you say is likely less important than how you say it. Give him the walk-up command along with a couple jerks on the rope, but release as soon as he twitches. If that doesn't work, you can use the end of the lead rope to tap his rear end to get his attention. That's why I use ten foot lead ropes instead of the shorties you often see."

Traci nodded. Ransom had remained like a statue. "Okay, young man," she said, firmly but she hoped soothingly. "Were you listening to all of that? There's nothing here to be afraid of—just the warm sun casting shadows in front of us. No big deal." She looked at Ransom, who eyed her with interest.

159

"Walk up," she ordered and tugged twice on the lead rope. Ransom took two steps forward and stopped again, turning his head to look back toward the barn. "No. No," Traci said. "This way." She repeated her command, but Ransom leaned back instead of forward. Turning slightly she let some of the lead rope through her right hand and swung it, tapping Ransom on the butt. He stepped forward quickly and began to turn around her in order to go back to the barn.

"You've got to talk to him. Tell him *whoa*. Use your elbow. Use your shoulder. He's all over you. Do it now. If you wait much longer, you're gonna be sitting on your rear watching *his* rear dashing for the barn."

Hearing his words of warning, Traci took heed. She lowered her elbow and shoulder behind Ransom's shoulder and shoved with all her might and was amazed that the animal moved over and continued walking forward.

She sensed him getting ready to balk at another shadow and gave him the *whoa* command. He did so and relaxed. Shortly, she asked him to walk on and he did. Over the next twenty minutes this test of wills occurred repeatedly, but Traci was now aware of what to expect and was able to coax Ransom into trusting her enough at least not to bolt and dash for the safety of the barn.

When they got to the end of the lane, Traci had had enough. She turned Ransom, prepared for the distinct possibility that now they would have to work on the *whoa* command. Odd, she thought, half amused—shadows didn't seem to bother young Ransom nearly as much when they were walking back to a place he knew.

And now where the hell had McCord gone? He had been right behind them, but now he was nowhere in sight. She was out there all alone with this horse who had his own inclinations about what they ought to be doing, and her coach had left.

When she and Ransom crossed in front of the main house, the screen porch slammed loudly. Ransom flinched, but she held him in check and reminded him that he was okay. Then she saw McCord approaching with a steaming coffee mug in each hand.

The coffee looked heavenly, but she'd bet anything McCord had slammed that door on purpose. Ransom had to get accustomed to unexpected noises, he'd said earlier. Right now Ransom would have to adjust to her screaming at a certain cowboy for running off and leaving her alone and then nearly scaring the hell out of her and her horse. As if on cue, Ransom raised his tail and made a deposit where he stood. It was his fourth since they'd left the corral. He had no constipation problems.

"You're looking good, Ransom," Scott said, coming to a stop by their side. "Your mistress is looking pretty good too." Scott smiled at Traci. "You're doing fine, Traci. Really. You'll have some tired arms tonight. But you and Ransom are working things out. I think he's learning to trust you — at least a little bit."

Traci flushed with satisfaction. Why did his simple words of praise mean so very much? Well, they did. She hadn't flunked her first solo flight with the yearling.

Not that Scott had informed her she was going to go solo. Wasn't that also how she'd learn to ride a bike? One minute her dad was holding the rear fender, and when she peeked over her shoulder he was standing a long ways behind.

Traci led Ransom back to the corral without further incident. After she removed his halter, he remained by her side wrinkling his nose with expectation. "Okay, you deserve three treats this morning. We might make a team yet." Traci scratched between Ransom's ears as he gulped his treats.

When she stepped through the rails of the corral to join Scott, he said, "I meant it. You're developing him into a real nice horse. And I think he's appreciating all the attention."

"Sometimes he doesn't show it very well," Traci scoffed. "But I do like him a lot. You're right, it's feeling better. Any pithy thoughts while this lesson is fresh in your mind?"

Scott shifted his weight from foot to foot. "I don't know about pithy. You were doing much better anticipating his moves toward the latter half of your time with him."

"You were watching all along, you big faker." Traci arched her eyebrows. "I should have known."

"No matter. You did fine. But you have to continue being decisive. If you aren't, he will be. And sometimes you won't like his choices."

Traci coughed, wondering again about Scott's real meaning.

"I've got to go move some horses from one pasture to another so we don't overgraze any one area. Want to come along?"

"Sure. I've got a ton of questions for you."

"And I bet they aren't about working with Ransom."

"You got that right."

Traci sat in the pickup as Scott drove toward one of the outlying paddocks. She'd already learned cowboys didn't walk any farther than they had to.

"Well, fire away, Counselor. You have my attention."

"Before I begin, I want to thank you again for the fantastic weekend in LA."

"That was pretty good, wasn't it?" Scott smiled without looking at her.

"So tell me how many folks know when you're getting ready to ship horses back to the track?"

With one hand on the steering wheel and the other arm across the back of the seat, Scott glanced quickly at his passenger. "Anybody and everybody here at the ranch. Plus of course the folks who will receive the horses, and a guy or two who transport them."

"You sometimes use two drivers?"

"When we have them available. Just in case something goes wrong, one person can stay with the horses."

"But not necessarily when they go to the bathroom."

"Hadn't thought of that as something going wrong before."

Scott shifted to a halt at the corners of two adjacent pastures. Traci saw the board gate separating the two fields. She followed him when he got out and climbed through the fence to open the gate.

"Stand back," he ordered, when four resident mares came on the fly to inspect what was happening and perhaps to get a treat. Without any difficulty, Scott led them into the next pasture and closed the gate behind them. "There now, young ladies, you have plenty of water and shelter in this area too, and the grass is even better on this side of the fence."

Traci chuckled. "You sure have a lot of lines for the ladies, McCord."

He looked over at her, furrowing his brow. "I've got a few you haven't heard yet, Traci."

Traci took a step back from the heat that suddenly filled the space between them. Nothing had changed in the two day absence. He still wanted her.

She turned and walked back to the truck. Once they were settled inside, she asked, "How about other folks aware of these horses being transported back to the track? People at the stable? At the resort?"

Scott gave her a crooked smiled and turned the ignition key. The engine roared and he leaned back in the seat. "It's no secret. I guess I sometimes say something about it, maybe if I have to be gone ,or if one of them has to sub for a driver."

"Resort employees sub as drivers?" Traci squeaked.

"Yeah, sometimes. It's no big deal. The people who work for me at the stable are very good with horses."

"Okay. Anybody else at the resort? Who else knows?"

Wincing, Scott said, "You have more questions than the twins, and they drive me batty." He blew out a breath of air. "Sometimes guys will just come by the stable or even here and ask."

"They do? Why in the world would they do that?"

"Because they're handicappers looking for an edge. Remember, we talked about that at Santa Anita."

Traci nodded.

Scott put the pickup in gear and they started back toward the ranch buildings. "Red Evans and Bruce Harris stop by often enough to know which horses are going back. They want to know what I think of them, or they may want to look them over."

"You might as well put up neon lights announcing when you're shipping," Traci grumbled. "Isn't there any way to narrow this damn case down?"

"We never considered this end of things to be a problem until you came along." Scott chuckled. He parked the truck in front of the barn nearest the house.

"You can wipe that smug smile off your face, McCord. What do you think about the treasurer of Snowden having ties to organized crime?"

Scott had opened his door to get out but quickly slammed it shut and stared hard at her. "You're not kidding, are you?"

Shaking her head, Traci replied, "He's the treasurer of at least four other smallish corporations in out of the way places. And we know he's on the mob's payroll."

"Holy shit. Wilkins. That scrawny little guy."

"Did you expect him to carry a tommy gun?" Traci snickered. "I think that was the Roaring Twenties. Today these folks are more likely to carry cell phones, laptops, and calculators. Don't get me wrong. They can still be lethal."

"But what does that mean?" McCord turned white. "What does it mean for the resort? For our community?"

"I don't know. They've owned their position for five years. We're checking on money flowing in and out of the place. By the way, do you have minutes of board meetings?"

"Of course I do. I'll give you all the resort files I can get my hands on."

"Good. Scott?"

"Huh."

"Don't tell anyone else about this. Not yet. We don't know what we're into."

"And there may be no tie-in with the horse problems?"

"Maybe not, but I'd lay even odds there is."

Scott nodded. "This could get dangerous."

"Let's not jump to any conclusions. Not yet."

"Do you miss Chicago?" Rebecca asked, her eyes rounding. "It's a long ways from here."

Traci folded the cards she was holding. She and the twins sat on the porch of the main house playing more kinds of poker than she knew existed. "It is a long way to travel."

Funny, she hadn't really thought about her home much at all until the question was put to her. "I imagine I do miss it. I'd miss it more if it were summer time. Then I'd be out on my sailboat as often as I could. Now it's still quite cold. And the piles of snow are turning black from all the dirt and car exhaust."

"Yuck." Both twins wrinkled their noses.

Laughing, Traci said, "It's not pretty, but it does go away when spring comes."

"Spring is already here," Susannah said.

"I'm afraid it comes later in Chicago than it does here. Now tell me, have you girls traveled much?"

They both shook their heads. "We've been to San Diego a lot," Rebecca said.

"And we've been to Disneyland," Susannah added. "But I hated the smog."

"Is Chicago smoggy too?" Rebecca asked.

167

"Yes, it can get pretty bad, but I don't notice it like I did in LA. And there are days, particularly after a summer thunderstorm, when the sky is as blue as it is here and the city just seems so fresh and alive. Then when you're out on the lake and the sun sets slowly over the city...it can be breathtaking."

"I doubt it would take my breath away," Susannah grumbled. "I don't like cities. Too damn many people."

"Susannah," Rebecca scolded. "I think I'd like Chicago. I know I like San Diego. There's so much more to do there than here. But it doesn't have skyscrapers like the kind I see in your town. I'd like to see what's east of these mountains. You know some of my friends have never been out of this valley."

"Yes, we have tall buildings. My dad's office used to be on the twenty-third floor of the Sears Tower."

"Wow!" Rebecca's eyes went wide. Susannah groaned at her sister's enthusiasm.

"I live on the twelfth floor of a high rise and have a spectacular view of Lake Michigan."

"Do you really sail?" Rebecca asked.

"Of course I do.

"I can swim. We learned at camp. But I've never been on a sailboat."

"If you hang around me long enough, sooner or later, you'll have that opportunity."

"So," Susannah said, "do you think you're going to be around a lot?"

Traci opened her mouth and shut it, frowning. Trapped again. It would be difficult enough staying ahead of one ten-year-old, but with two it was nearly impossible.

"I just meant that I like to sail. And if we knew each other very long you'd be invited to come along." She knew that didn't sound much better, but mercifully the girls let it go.

"Now what about this game you two wanted to play so badly? Never thought baseball could be played with cards; this is fun."

"If this is fun, you must like to lose," Susannah chided.

"What do you mean?"

"Our stacks of pennies are three times bigger than yours."

"Well, I'm still learning. You just wait. You'll wish you hadn't taught me these games of chance. I feel like I'm corrupting you—playing poker and enjoying it."

"Don't worry. Uncle Scott and Grandma are way ahead of you."

"Yeah," Rebecca chimed in. "They let us keep the money we win rather than agreeing in advance to divide the pennies equally when we're done. I don't understand why we're playing if we can't keep what we win."

"Can't we just enjoy playing the game?" Those words seemed insulting even to Traci's own ears. Why did you play any game if not to win?

"So have you invited Uncle Scott to go sailing?" Rebecca asked innocently.

169

Traci stared at the young girl. "Now, why would you ask that?"

"Well, you know him better than you do us. And you just said if we got to know each other better, you'd invite us to go sailing with you."

Tracie tried not to smile. Rebecca might already have the skills to be a master at moot court. Her logic was sharp, if not flawless. "I don't think that's any of your business."

"She's asked him," Susannah declared. "She's blushing. I'll bet he said no. Uncle Scott doesn't step off of land for nobody. He doesn't swim. He doesn't even like to fly."

"He gets into rivers to fly fish," Rebecca protested.

"That doesn't count," Susannah retorted, drawing herself up straight. "He still has his feet on the ground."

"Girls, it's time to come home for supper," their mother said, approaching the porch. "Hi, Traci. I hope the girls haven't been a bother."

"No. They've been teaching me more card games than I knew existed. Now, let's divide these pennies up."

Both girls grumbled as they counted. "I wonder if she'll want to divide the pot equally after she learns how to play better," Susannah muttered.

"Bye girls," Traci said as the two of them skipped down the steps.

Rebecca turned, smiled and waved. "I think I'd like to go sailing, Traci. And I know I'd like to see Chicago someday."

Traci smiled back. Why did the girl's hopes flush her with such warm feelings? Traci had never considered herself to really be the mothering type. But then neither had Cassie, and look at her—mother to Clint's two kids and now two of her own, and even Daisy Underwood, Cassie's former foster child, had a baby.

- o -

"You look quite pensive, Counselor," Scott observed, entering the porch from the kitchen. "Did the girls manage to tweak you again?"

"Not really. They always seem to be so full of news and information."

"Probably telling all the family secrets. By the way, supper is going to be a little late. Hope that's not a problem for you."

"No, but I really should head back. I feel like I'm mooching off your mom."

"She doesn't. You intrigue her."

"How so?"

"Got me. You'll have to ask her. I know she thinks you've got a lot of gumption, as she puts it. She's usually not so welcoming to strangers."

Traci flashed an eyebrow. "Maybe she doesn't think I'm a stranger anymore."

"Maybe."

Scott picked up the deck of cards and began to shuffle them, then laid out a game of Solitaire.

"So why do you stay here, Scott?"

"Huh? This is my home. This is my job."

"Yes, but why? You can't fool me. I saw you at Santa Anita. You sparkle when you're around the backstretch or when you're handicapping the races. What you have here is good—but your soul is somewhere else."

Scott scowled and turned up the queen of hearts. No one had ever challenged him in this way. What did she know? This was his home and he liked his jobs. But she was right.

He stared at the cards spread out on the table. "You know why I'm here. It takes two people to manage the ranch and the stables. Dad trained James to take care of the ranch and me to do the stables."

"And if a McCord doesn't run the stables, your family loses control of it. And that's more important than doing what you'd really like to do."

"I don't look at it that way."

"And I'm supposed to believe that the moon is made of cheese."

"You seem to think you know a hell of a lot about my situation. You haven't walked in my shoes." Scott knew he sounded defensive, but the damn woman was prying too much.

"Not exactly, but close."

Scott glanced over at her. Their eyes met and he saw a different kind of pain in hers than he'd seen before. "Go on."

"My father was a very big corporate lawyer in Chicago." Traci looked down at her hands. "He groomed me to work with him in what he liked to call the family business. There wasn't anything family about it. For years I did what he wanted, knowing that my heart was in criminal law.

"I wanted to be a prosecutor to help keep criminals off the streets. He thought that kind of work was dirty and beneath a Steele. By the time I was thirty, I was pulling out my hair. Two years later I finally made the break. The last three years I've been flying professionally. It was the right move for me. So you see," she said, looking at Scott, "I do know something about domineering fathers."

"How did your father take your rebellion?"

Traci chuckled. "Not well, at first. In fact, he didn't talk to me for the first six months after I left the firm. Eventually, he was okay with it. Even he could see I was much happier."

"You're lucky. You made your move before he died. It's harder fighting a dead man."

"I imagine it is." Traci nodded. "So I assume he didn't like horse racing much."

"Despised it. My mother's family with its Irish roots had raced horses as long as anyone can remember. Uncle Harry carried on that tradition. It's one of the reasons my dad didn't like him. And I suppose Uncle Harry helped me catch the bug, although I imagine it was there genetically." He grinned easily. "It was a major battle with Dad for me to carve out enough space at the ranch to do what I do with the racehorses. He thought it was a waste of time and money."

"Why did he go along with it?"

Scott's features clouded. "He didn't have a choice. We had a major blow-out I imagine we never quite got over. I threatened to leave if I couldn't get involved with those horses. He knew better than to call my bluff. So here I am."

"And there's a part of you that wishes he had called you. And then the decision would have been made. You might have a string of contenders at Santa Anita. Now you just wonder about what might have happened."

"Something like that, I guess. I try not to think about it much, though. It's over. It's done."

"Why?"

Scott shrugged. "People need me here — Ma, James, the community. And I have a taste of the racing business. And I made a deal with my dad."

"And you don't go back on your word."

"Right."

"So your father controls from the grave."

Scott lurched out of his chair and glared at Traci. After taking a couple deep breaths, he growled, "I think it might be best if you do go back to the condo before supper. We'll see what tomorrow brings."

"I'm sorry if I hurt you," Traci said to his back as he marched down the porch steps and off toward the barn.

- o -

"I'm sorry you won't be staying for supper," Sal said, standing beside the kitchen table. "Maybe it's

174

best. Scott is quite out of sorts this evening."

"Before he talked to me?" Traci frowned. Maybe he hadn't just been angry with her when he stormed off.

"Didn't he tell you?"

"Tell me what? Sal, your son is very skillful letting out news in bits and drabs."

"Well, he received a call from a trainer friend late this afternoon." Mrs. McCord paused.

"Yes?"

Shaking her head, Sal continued, "I don't see any reason to keep it from you. His friend is sending out a truck to pick up the horses he has recuperating here at the ranch."

"Oh my goodness." After he'd gotten that news, she'd prodded him for why he stayed on the ranch.

"Seems like a couple owners complained and threatened to pull their horses away from the trainer. The man is sorry, but he doesn't have much choice. I know that. Scott knows that."

"So the stakes are getting higher."

"You could say so. Scott's reputation is on the line."

"So why are you smiling? Sal, don't try to wipe that smile off your face. Now what aren't you telling me?"

"I'm smiling because I expect you're very good at what you do and will get to the bottom of all of this. And because the pained look on your face goes well beyond professional concern for the case you're working on."

Mrs. McCord squinted and shrugged her shoulders. "You care about my boy. And I rather like that, Traci Steele from Chicago. You're good for him, and I bet he's good for you."

"Well, I never—" Traci sputtered, grabbing on to the back of a kitchen chair.

"You asked." Sal smiled brightly. "If you don't want to know what I'm thinking, don't ask."

Not able to remain aloof, Traci chuckled. "Between you and the twins, I never know what to expect."

"Good. Life's pretty damn boring if there's no surprise."

Chapter Nine

The door buzzer droned far too loudly for so early in the morning. Traci squinted at the clock. The buzzer was incessant. After depressing the offending button, she scrambled out of bed and grabbed her terrycloth robe. She flipped the coffeepot on as she hurried by the kitchen. Thank goodness she'd put all the ingredients in the night before.

She flipped the lock on the door and opened it. The buzzer stopped immediately. Mustache stood there with a sheepish grin holding a bouquet of freshly cut pink and white flowers.

He glanced down at her bare feet sticking out beneath her robe. "I hope I'm not too early. Didn't mean to wake you."

"The flowers are lovely," Traci said, reaching for them. "You're not too early; I'm making coffee. Come on in."

Traci pulled a tall glass from the shelf and put the flowers in it, then poured coffee and handed him a cup. It was fresh and thick—just the way she knew he liked it. Traci pulled the robe sash tighter, walked into the living area and settled on the couch. Scott sat across from her in an easy chair.

"So what do I owe this early visit to, Mr. McCord? Last I checked there are no cows here that need to be milked."

"Yeah, I imagine it's a bit early, but I got the horses at the stable fed. Then I found these flowers and couldn't wait any longer."

"You mean these are flowers from the resort."

"Sure. I own them. At least part of them."

Traci held a hand to her mouth and giggled. "What will the maid think? Management will probably accuse me of cutting their precious flowers." Traci sobered. "So why are you here, McCord?"

"Needed to apologize for kicking you out yesterday. That wasn't very neighborly of me."

"Your mom tell you to say that?"

Scott frowned. "No, this was my own idea. Figured she must've gotten wind that something happened, though. There wasn't any supper when I got back to the house."

Traci's lips turned upward. "That sounds like her, all right. Do you suppose she and Cassie confer about us?"

"I've begun to wonder."

"Well, I need to apologize too. I pushed you pretty hard. Too hard. What you do with your life is your business. We've both done things we might like to do over. And I imagine we've both made do with some things that seem unchangeable."

Scott smoothed out his mustache. "I admire your guts, Traci. That had to be real big to go against the wishes of your father."

"It was that or suffocate. I waited too long as it was. But I didn't have other family members depending on me like you do. You've done what was right for you."

"Maybe." Scott shrugged.

Traci glanced down at her bare feet and blushed. She looked back at him. He had that crooked smile again. This was far too intimate. She finished her coffee and started for the kitchen. "Would you like more coffee?"

"Sure. I thought there was more to that line than that."

Traci looked blank. When she remembered the words *tea or me,* her skin turned pink.

Scott stood. She raised her hand. "Sit back down," she commanded. "I'll get the pot."

"Yes, ma'am."

Traci felt a lot safer knowing he wasn't coming up behind her. She had to get a grip on herself. Was he preparing to force the issue between them? She couldn't let that happen. Not yet. Not now. Not here. Traci willed her hand not to tremble as she carried the pot and filled his cup.

When she returned to the couch, Traci relaxed. She had to find a way to tell him her story. The sailboat felt so right for her, but she knew Scott would never bring that idea up. Did she have the courage to raise it?

Scott cleared his throat. "So what is this bet the twins have going?"

"I don't know anything about a bet. We just played poker for pennies, but I made them give those back after the game."

"I don't mean that. Rebecca is betting that you'll

179

get me to go sailing, and Susannah is saying it will never happen. Don't know what they've wagered, but certainly something that's important to them."

"They did what?" Traci covered her mouth. "Those two imps; sometimes I want to throttle them."

"You might have to get in line for that."

"I never told them that I wanted you to go sailing. We just talked about sailing and stuff."

"They're pretty good at reading between the lines when it comes to stuff. So when are we going to do it?"

"Sailing?"

"Sailing. What else are we talking about?"

"I didn't think you wanted to go."

"I said I would."

"Thought maybe you'd forget."

"Did you want me to forget?"

Traci sighed. "Honestly? Yes and no. But what do we do without letting one twin win over the other?"

"I'm not about to worry about that. If one of them is right and one wrong, that's the way it is. They made their bet without consulting me."

"Maybe they'll learn something from this yet."

"I wouldn't count on it."

"I'm not."

"So when? It's been nearly eighty degrees now for a couple days, so I imagine you're itching to go."

"It'll be cooler on the water," Traci warned. Why wasn't she more relieved? She hadn't even had to bring up the topic on her own. Why was she so nervous? He didn't know the reason for going out on the ocean.

She didn't have to tell him anything, really. They could just sail and come back. Or she could take one of the biggest risks of her life. "How about Monday? There'll be fewer people on the water than during the weekend. And the weather is supposed to continue heating up. That'll give me time to make some calls and get a boat set up along with provisions."

"Doubt I'll be all that hungry."

"I always take along enough for a couple days just in case there's any trouble." She smiled at Scott's arched eyebrows. "I'm not expecting trouble, but it's no different than you planning a trail ride into the mountains. You take along enough supplies just to handle an emergency."

He nodded. "I guess that makes sense, though I don't like to think about emergencies on the water."

"We'll be fine." Traci squeezed the bridge of her nose. She knew they would *do* fine on the water, but she wasn't at all convinced they'd *be* fine.

An hour and a half later, after Scott left for the stable, Traci sat with a foot tucked under her in a cushioned chair with the file open to board minutes of July fifteenth the previous year. She whistled softly and wondered why Scott hadn't mentioned the discussion of closing the equestrian center and replacing it with more condos.

Someone had gone to quite a lot of work to come up with estimated costs, savings and profits.

She glanced at the list of attendees. McCord hadn't been present. A couple other local owners opposed the idea because of the benefit of the equestrian center to the community and cited the original agreement when the McCords sold the land for building the resort. No motion had been made. And the topic did not reappear in subsequent meetings.

Had it been a trial balloon to see what kind of response it would receive? Interesting that the notion was trotted out when McCord wasn't present.

Still, why hadn't Scott mentioned this? She laughed and banged a hand against her forehead. She'd bet almost anything that Scott McCord seldom if ever read board minutes.

Motive was beginning to emerge. Money. Profit. With the equestrian center gone, the resort could expand to almost twice its existing size. And the directors would not have to deal with a McCord on the board.

She needed to get her hands on the original agreement between the McCords and the Live Oak Board of Directors. Was there any way the board could get out of its agreement without discrediting Scott McCord?

If he were discredited, pressure would be placed on him to resign from the board. And would a scandal lead a hotshot lawyer and a judge to determine that closing the center would be in the community's best interest?

She hated to think what money placed in the right hands might produce if it got that far. An interest group would be formed to improve the image of the community, move it into the new century. It could no longer benefit the few who wanted to play at being nineteenth century cowboys. Make room for progress. Bring in more people who would spend more money and boost the economy to attract still more dollars.

The argument might boil down to—could the community afford to waste such high quality land and tax base on the desires of a few horse people?

Traci tensed as these possibilities came to her. Surely there were those who detested the smell and presence of horses. The key in such a battle for the public will would be the McCords. If they couldn't marshal support within the broader community, the odds might very well tip in favor of those who desired *progress* and an enriched tax base.

"Whew." Traci leaned back. She was onto something. She'd have to try it out on Scott. Would he be surprised? Would he even take her hypothesis seriously?

Traci leaned back and rested her chin on her chest. It was also time to have a serious talk with Scott's mother.

As Traci drove down the McCord ranch lane she saw Sally McCord kneeling in her garden. The older woman stood and waved. Traci climbed out of her car and headed toward her.

"Good morning." Sal brushed the back of a hand against her brow. "He's not here. Sorry you wasted your time driving out."

"That's okay. I didn't come to see him. I came to see you."

"Oh." Wariness clouded the woman's eyes. "Well, I don't have time to gab." Sal surveyed her and turned her back to Traci. "You can talk to me while I work if you like. If I don't get this ground prepared soon, it'll be too late. Nobody else around here seems to care whether we have a garden or not."

"What can I do to help?" Traci asked.

Sal turned and ran her eyes over Traci's long fingers and manicured nails. "There's a spare set of gloves in that pail over there. You could use this small trowel and dig out the weeds threatening to take over my hibiscus plants. Just make sure you only take out weeds."

"Okay. I can do that if you show me what not to dig up."

With surprising patience, Sal gave Traci the necessary time until both women were comfortable that she wasn't about to destroy a treasured plant.

They worked side by side, each kneeling in the soil still moist from an overnight dew. "Guess you haven't spent much time in a garden," Sal said, after a bit.

"There's a first time for everything."

"That's what they say. So what brought you out

184

here to see me? I don't think you came to just help me with my garden."

"No." Traci took careful aim with her trowel to get deep below the weed's taproot without cutting it off. Sal had warned her that merely slicing the root would only mean the "little bastard" would rise again to plague her. Sal took her garden very personally. "I was wondering if you have copies of the original agreement between you and your husband and the Live Oak Board of Directors."

Sal glanced sharply at Traci. "Of course I've got it. You don't throw that stuff away. So why do you want it?"

"I want to make sure I have the exact wording regarding the equestrian center and its place in the life of the resort and the community."

"So you've found something, have you?"

Traci stopped digging and shook her head. "Not really. Just a couple things raise questions."

"And you're not going to tell me what they are?"

"I'd really prefer not to. Everything is so speculative at this point."

"Harrumph. If I really wanted to know, Scott would tell me. He never has been good at keeping secrets from me."

Traci groaned. "I'm never sure he's telling me all he knows."

"You're not family." Sal gave Traci a curious smile. "Although if you hang around here long enough, I may have to adopt you or something. At least you can pull weeds."

"So will you show me the agreements?"

"Certainly. There's nothing to hide. Though I doubt it has much to do with what's happening here either. This sun is getting down right hot. I need a drink." Sal stood. "Why don't you come with me?"

Traci followed her lead. They walked to the east end of the garden and stopped under a giant oak tree. Resting between two of its exposed roots was a large thermos and a stack of cups. "Made this lemonade myself," Sal said. "Have some."

Lifting a cup to her lips Traci tasted the liquid. Its tartness initially startled her and then the flavors of the drink caressed her taste buds. "This is delicious, Sal. My goodness, I've never tasted lemonade like this before."

Sal grinned. "Fresh lemons help. And a fresh lime doesn't hurt either. Of course, I won't tell what all is in it. But it does pack a little wallop, doesn't it?"

Traci's eyes widened. Now she really was curious about the ingredients, but wasn't about to ask. Some of Sal's secrets would remain secret.

"You have a spectacular garden, Sal," Traci said, her eyes scanning the nearly quarter acre lot. "It must be something when it's all in bloom."

"It's quite robust and splendid—a rainbow of colors really. But I like it now," there was an audible catch in the woman's voice, "when there's just a dash of color, a little red, a little yellow over there, and of course the purple. This time of year the garden gives me hope; it contains a promise of more to come."

Traci noticed a faraway look in her eyes. Sal continued, "There's a fragility about a late winter early spring garden that begs for attention. It's not a feeling I often get from the summer garden in full bloom."

Sal shook her head and set her cup down. "That's a lot of prattle from an old woman. Don't imagine it makes a damn bit of difference to the plants whether I'm here or not."

"You know it does," Traci responded, realizing Scott's mother was embarrassed for sharing her feelings. And Traci wasn't at all certain she knew what had really been shared. "The plants and weeds would choke each other off if it weren't for you caring about them."

"Perhaps. So tell me about your father. You said he died only a few months ago. How did he die?"

Traci looked down at her glass and sighed deeply. Sal had turned the tables adeptly. Traci had tried not to remember. It was only moments earlier when she'd been digging in the ground that the image of that large hole in the cemetery had reappeared in her mind.

She'd gone on with her life, certainly more than she could have if she'd remained in Chicago. But the hole still awaited her. It had been filled with a casket and with dirt. But it was not covered over.

"It was a massive heart attack. There was no chance, really. The doctors did what they could, but it wasn't enough. They'd warned him for years. He'd had several minor attacks."

"But he pushed himself twice as hard."

Traci looked at Sal leaning against the tree. There were tears in the woman's eyes. Traci nodded.

"It was the same with my Bruce. Stubborn. Proud. Thought he was invincible. When the doctors warned him to slow down, he pressed even harder to show them they were wrong."

Again Traci nodded.

"I was mad as hell at that man. Still am, I suppose."

Horrified, Traci looked away from the woman's intensity. Was *she* angry with her father for dying? There had been all that other grief—but anger about his dying?

No anger that he hadn't taken care of himself and had robbed them of years of sharing their lives together? Tears ebbed down her cheeks. Her stomach clenched. She tried to keep the sobs from starting. She was unsuccessful.

Mrs. McCord slid across the grass between them and put an arm around Tracy.

"I don't want to be angry with him," Traci moaned. "But why didn't he listen? Why did he have to die and leave me alone?"

"I don't know," Sal said. "I doubt that we ever will. The questions are important at first. Then I'm not sure they are anymore. Maybe they get in the way of us getting on with our lives. There's so much to grieve—the dead are only part of that."

Traci tensed, bringing her sobbing under control. Sal might not ever give her such an opening again. Would the woman even talk about it? Her son had kicked Traci off the ranch the day before; maybe it would be his mom's turn today. "You're talking about your brother, Harry Barrows, aren't you," she said gently.

Sal's nostrils and eyes flared. She stiffened. Traci was certain the woman was going to explode. And then she softened. She smiled weakly. "So you've met Harry, have you? I wondered if he'd show up when you were in LA." She paused to study her garden. Traci wished she were a mind reader.

"Most families have an underbelly, I guess. I loved my husband, Traci, but I also hated the bastard."

The bitterness in the woman's voice shocked Traci, but she was careful not to register any of that on her face.

"I didn't realize what was happening at the time. Oh, maybe I did, but I was too caught up in being courted by a dashing young man from one of the old pioneer families of the valley. My family was Irish—recently immigrated—and my husband never let me forget it. He hated everything Irish.

"My family leased a bar and raised racehorses in the back forty. None of them amounted to much, but my family had raised racehorses in the old country for as long as anyone could remember.

"When my parents were killed we lost the lease on the bar, and Harry did everything he could to hold on to those horses. That was about the same time Bruce showed up and swept me off my feet.

189

Why he loved me I've never quite been able to figure out. Maybe I was the forbidden fruit that he had to have. I really can't complain about him. He cherished me. Gave me fine children and security.

"But all of that came with a price. I sold my brother and my history. I'm no better than those brothers in the Bible who sold their brother into slavery or left him for dead or something." Sal shook her head. "I was all the family Harry had. I ran away from him and never looked back. I don't know whether I'm more angry with my husband or with myself." Her shoulders slumped against the tree trunk. "Myself, I guess."

"So why don't you go see Harry now?" Traci asked, laying a hand atop Sal's. "There's no one to stop you now." Traci felt Sal tremble, and she was having a hard time not doing so herself.

"Too much has happened. Too many years have gone by. He won't forgive me now. Why should he?"

Grinning, Traci said, "Don't you read the endings of stories? I think those brothers who left their brother for dead were later forgiven by that brother."

Sal met Traci's look and then darted her eyes away. "Those brothers were probably a lot younger than me and Harry." Sal squeezed Traci's hand. "So, Traci Steele from Chicago, you've learned some of what you came to learn. Maybe even a bit more. I'm going to give you a bit of advice, and I think you realize it's well founded. Grieve the death of your father. Honor him, but don't idealize him; and live your own life, not the one he might have wanted for you."

"Do you think Scott's living his own life?"

"Of course he is," was the sharp retort. "What else would he want? Other than maybe a wife and kids. He's very happy here." Sal scowled at Traci. "Has he said anything different?"

"No." Traci smiled. "I just saw another side of him when we were on the backstretch at Santa Anita. That's all."

Sal nodded knowingly. "Unlike James, Scott has that horseracing bug that nips many of the Irish. But he works hard with those horses right here on the ranch. He doesn't have to go anywhere else to find what he already has."

Abruptly, Sal lurched to her feet. "Enough of this girl talk stuff. That should be enough to last me five years. I'd best get back to my garden or it'll rot from lack of attention. And you, young lady, I'm sure have many things you'd rather be doing than tending my garden."

"How about the papers, Sal?" Traci got to her feet.

"Oh, right. I'll go get them and meet you at your car. I won't be but a minute."

Traci walked back toward her car. Once again she was being ushered off the McCord ranch. Sally McCord surprisingly had more grace about it than her son, but nonetheless their discussion was finished. Girl talk, indeed!

Traci rushed into her condo and dumped her

bags on the dining room table, then quickly began to leaf through the papers Sal had lent her. With her index finger going down one page after another, she scanned the materials. It was a very complex document making sure the McCords would get appropriate tax benefits for the portion of the land that was a gift as well as the conditions regarding the purchased land.

Traci's finger moved back up the page. Gift. Nobody had said any of the land had been a gift. She read more of the details. "Aha," she muttered as she read. *Ten acres or about are given in trust to the Live Oak Board of Directors for the purpose of establishing and operating an equestrian center for the benefit of resort owners and guests and for the community at large. It is envisioned that the center will be a multipurpose facility offering opportunities for trail rides, boarding of horses, riding lessons, training and other services to the community as deemed appropriate by the Board. The center is to be under the direct supervision of a McCord family member as long as one is available and interested. That individual will also sit on the Board of Directors.*

Traci skimmed over more legal jargon until her eyes fixed on the sentence she'd been looking for. *The equestrian center is not intended to be a profit making venture; it will continue in operation as long as it remains in the public interest.*

Slippery. Not a word about who decided that it remain in the public interest. Likely no one imagined that such a question would ever realistically be raised. On the surface, the agreement appeared quite ironclad. Still, she worried about the public interest clause, and about what would happen if a McCord did not have a seat on the Board.

She scribbled a few more notes on a legal pad. Her hypothesis about motive still held. If anything, it was strengthened. When would someone in the community begin a campaign against the stable?

Traci scowled at the agreement; she wished that the *public interest* clause didn't exist. Why hadn't they used language like "in perpetuity"? That would've been stronger. No doubt Bruce McCord liked the sound of public interest better. Traci smiled thinly. She wouldn't be at all surprised if the man hadn't gone against the advice of his lawyer, thinking he knew what sounded better in the local newspaper.

Later that evening Traci sat in front of her fireplace watching flames leap from a burning log. She remained nervous but satisfied. Only two hours earlier she'd completed making arrangements to rent a sailboat for Monday. She'd debated between a sloop like the one she owned or a tri-maran like one a friend of hers sailed. She'd been leaning toward the tri because of Scott's fear of the water. Three hulls would look a lot safer to him.

Her decision was clinched when she talked with the man at the harbor who told her a Corsair F-28 was available. That was perfect. It was the exact model her friend owned. It was noted for its stability, and was easy for one person to manage. It was doubtful if Mustache would be much help with the actual sailing.

How would he take to the water? While she was looking forward to handling the tri-maran, she wouldn't actually take it through its paces with McCord on board. But it would still be good for her soul to feel the waves beneath her, to know again the wind stinging her cheeks, and to experience that sensation of being at one with the sea.

Frowning, Traci hoped that would be enough support to enable her to go through with telling Scott her story. If she didn't take that opportunity while on the boat, it would be a story untold.

Chapter Ten

Barbecued chicken sizzled on the oversized grill hanging on a tripod over a wood fire. Traci's mouth watered. On her drive to the McCord ranch that Sunday morning, she hadn't known if she'd have an appetite, because she wasn't really sure she would be welcomed by everyone. Yet Penny had called the night before to invite her to the family barbecue. She wondered if Sal had put her up to it; there was no question the family matriarch would have had to approve. Maybe the woman had gotten over being miffed with the outsider's questions.

Everyone seemed warm and welcoming and her appetite had clearly been stimulated by the grilling chicken. James was doing the cooking. She'd been told he was famous for his barbecue skills. He did seem to have a flair for it, with his chef's hat and an apron that no doubt had been a gift from the twins. "Favorite Dad. Favorite Chef. We want more!" it read.

Penny came out of the back door of their house carrying drinks: a beer for her husband and Scott, and a glass of lemonade for Sal and Traci. Traci hoped that accepting more of Sal's lemonade might go a ways toward smoothing out ruffled feathers. "Penny, are you sure there isn't anything

I can help with?"

"How close are we on the chicken?" Penny hollered over at James.

Her husband turned over a chicken breast. "Five minutes ought to do it."

"Yeah," Penny said to Traci, "another set of hands could help. I don't know where those girls disappeared to. They're seldom around when you need them." Penny scanned the area around the barns. "If they're late, so be it. We're not holding up the meal."

Traci followed Scott's sister-in-law to the kitchen. It was a very modern kitchen. Traci had expected something more like her image of a traditional farm kitchen, but every modern convenience that one could think of decorated the kitchen: microwaves, food processor, cook-top stove, double ovens, side by side refrigerator with ice dispenser. The cattle business must be doing fairly well.

"Why don't you dump that bag of chips into a bowl? We'll use these plates," Penny said, reaching into the cupboard. "Sal doesn't like to use paper plates—they're not strong enough."

Traci nodded and opened the bag of chips. "This is a very nice place, Penny."

"It's more than we need, really, but James's dad built this house when he knew we were getting married, and he didn't leave anything out. Sometimes I think it's too much. So it sounds like you're taking Scott sailing tomorrow."

Traci grinned. "News really travels around this

place."

"That's big news."

"Going sailing?"

"*Scott* going sailing is big. He's afraid of water, and he's always thought yacht clubs were for those snobbish folk down in San Diego or up in LA."

"People who sail are supposed to be snobs?" Traci asked with her voice rising.

Penny blushed. "I don't mean you. Scott doesn't mean you." She averted her eyes and scooped potato salad into a bowl. "It's just that you seem to be able to get Scott to do things that no one else has."

"You make me sound like some spider playing with a fly. Scott's a big boy. I think he chooses what he wants to do; I couldn't make him do something if he didn't want to."

"Oh, I didn't mean to offend you," Penny said, turning to face Traci. "I like you. You're a breath of fresh air around here. Even Sal likes you. I'm just amazed at Scott. That he's actually choosing to go sailing. These McCords can be quite stuck in their ways."

Traci chuckled at Penny's attempted diplomacy. "I kind of guessed that." She heard James shouting from the backyard. "Sounds like the chicken's ready," she said, picking up a tray of food.

"Yeah, we'd best get this food out there." Penny reached for another food tray. "Just don't let Scott swamp the boat tomorrow. He doesn't know the

197

first thing about sailing."

"We'll be careful," Traci replied, walking out onto the patio.

In a matter of minutes, Traci sank her teeth into a chicken thigh that was neither too well done nor too uncooked, which was her typical experience with grills. "Compliments to the chef," she said, looking over at James. "This is excellent, and I'm not usually a big fan of barbecues, but this is fantastic."

"Thanks." James beamed. "Thought I might like to be a cook someday, but I'm satisfied with grilling."

"You should taste his salmon," Penny said.

"He does a pretty mean steak too," Scott added. "Don't know why it's so good when he does it, but it is."

"It's all in the sauce," Sal said, lifting up a half eaten chicken breast. "You put the right sauce on a piece of meat and you've created something worth remembering. James does that with steak and chicken. I do it with ham. But I'm glad I never had to make my living cooking."

James winked at Traci. "I've often said if we ever get the dude ranch going, I'll trade in my spurs and be the cook. I'm fascinated with big cook stoves and griddles. And that's what we'd have."

Sal frowned and chased potato salad around on her plate. Scott shook his head. It was Penny who broke the uncomfortable silence. "What do you do for relaxation besides sailing, Traci?"

Recognizing her responsibility to divert a family

clash, Traci responded quickly. "Sailing is what I like best, but winter does come early and stays late in Chicago...Well, let's see."

She saw Scott grin at her. He clearly knew she was filling air time. "I like to read novels. And in the winter time, I'll go up to southern Wisconsin and cross-country ski. But I guess I don't do a whole lot. Sounds pretty boring, I imagine."

"Sounds like you work too hard chasing criminals," Sal groused. "You need to play more."

Scott laughed. "You're one who should talk, Ma."

With her eyes snapping, Sally McCord responded, "Maybe I play more than you know."

"Speaking of playing, where are those girls?" Penny brushed strands of blond hair off her cheek. "I told them we would be eating at noon. They can tell the time by the sun."

"I'm done eating," Traci said, rising from her lawn chair. "I'll go see if they're down around the barn."

"You eat like some damn bird," Sal observed, shaking her head. "How will you ever be able to cook for a man, when the time comes?"

"I'll tag along with you, Traci," Scott said, scowling at his mother. "There'll be plenty of food left if we want some later."

Traci matched her stride with Scott's as they hurried toward the barns. "Things were getting a little squirrelly back there."

"You got that right. I don't know why James bothers to bring that hair-brained idea up. It just sets Ma off. He knows it will."

"Sounded like he might prefer to do something other than what he's doing."

Scott stopped and rounded on Traci. "Do you see yourself in everybody? No, strike that, Counselor." He nodded. "I'm sorry. You may be right. I've just never thought about it that way. It's hard to believe James would be doing something he didn't want to. He and Dad often fought like cats and dogs, but James wound up managing the ranch. I know he's had his ups and downs, but for the most part I always thought he liked what he was doing."

"Your dad seemed quite adept at dictating what would happen after his death, whether people liked it or not."

"You're talking about me again," Scott growled.

"No." Traci shook her head. "I won't go there. Your mother loaned me the agreement papers between your parents and the Live Oak board at the time of sale. They really do have that equestrian center locked in pretty good. Wouldn't you say that's trying to make sure people do what you want even after you're dead?"

"Suppose so." Scott turned and walked to the barn. "Is there anything wrong with trying to help the community?"

"Not at all." Clearly, Scott didn't want to deal with the obvious—with his father's efforts to control events after his death. This wasn't the moment to try out her hypothesis about a motive. He seemed prepared to discount whatever she said that had anything to do with his father.

"There they are," Scott said pointing toward the fence-line on the far side of the paddock. "I thought it would be something like that."

Traci held a hand over her eyes shading them from the sun and looked where Scott was pointing. "What is it? They seem to be just waiting out there by that scraggly oak tree."

"Hop in the truck and I'll show you."

Tracie held on to the door handle as the pickup bounced across the pasture land. Why was this mode of transportation desired above walking? She saw the girls gesturing excitedly toward the tree. When Scott stopped the truck in front of it, Traci couldn't imagine why so much fuss was being made about a cat stuck up in a tree. She looked again. That was no ordinary cat. She looked at Scott.

"It's a bobcat," he said. "The girls likely treed him and are trying to wait the cat out. That won't happen. The cat knows he's safe as long he doesn't come down. He looks quite relaxed, if you ask me."

Narrowing her eyes at the scene, Traci found it hard to tell if the cat was relaxed or not. She knew the girls weren't; they ran toward the pickup—Susannah to Scott's side and Rebecca to hers—both chattering as fast as words could tumble from their mouths.

"We were just walking along minding our own business when we saw him in our path," Rebecca said.

"And we chased him into the tree," Susannah chimed in. "And he won't come down. I wanted to climb up after him."

"But I thought we should just wait." Rebecca looked back at the cat licking his paws as if he had no worry at all. "I don't think he's coming down."

"Not anytime soon, I expect," Scott said. "And certainly not while you're here posing a threat. Climb on in the back. You're mother's worried because you didn't show up for the barbecue."

"We missed it? Oh, no." Susannah kicked at a tire. "Barbecue chicken is my favorite."

"There's still plenty left," Traci said.

"Yeah, but now we'll have to do the dishes, because we were late," Rebecca complained. "I don't know why Grandma can't get used to paper plates."

Traci smiled at the puzzled ten-year-old. "I guess your grandma has a lot of things to get used to."

"Ain't that the truth."

The short drive back to the house was uneventful. Traci peeked at the girls riding in the back. They seemed quite mellow, apparently preparing themselves for a lecture from their mother and for doing the dishes. Scott was also lost in his thoughts. She expected the bobcat had already escaped to a safer place.

As they got out of the truck, the girls dashed ahead, eager to deal with their mother and dig into the chicken. Traci caught Scott by the arm. "Six-thirty, tomorrow morning."

He nodded. "I'll be ready."

"I think you'll like the sailboat I've rented. But I won't tell you about it. I'll let you see it for yourself. By the way, what are you planning to wear?"

Scott looked down at his jeans and boots and then back at Traci. She shook her head. "No cowboy boots on sailboats. Don't you have any tennis shoes?"

Pulling on his mustache, Scott said, "I may have a pair buried in my closet. May take most of the night to find them, but they should surface at some point."

"How about shorts?"

"Shorts? Me?"

"It's gonna be hot out there tomorrow. You'll roast in jeans. Shorts, a tee-shirt, and a windbreaker would be what I'd suggest. And sunblock."

"I used to play basketball in a community league. Had to wear shorts for that. They're probably wherever the sneakers are. Didn't know I had to get naked to go sailing."

"It's okay, cowboy. I'll be there to protect you."

"Yeah, but will you keep me warm?"

Traci blushed and Scott grabbed her by the elbow. "Come on," he said, "we'd better get back out there on the patio. Never know what those twins are saying about us by now."

Glancing up at the cloudless turquoise sky, Traci sucked in more of the ocean air. The westerly breezes provided adequate wind for sailing, but not enough to cause choppy waves. She couldn't have asked for a better day for sailing with a greenhorn.

She glanced across at Scott, who sat stiffly with his back imprinted against the rear of the boat as she moved nimbly about maintaining the sails and directing their voyage. There was a cove she was headed toward. She'd checked it out with folks at the harbor; it sounded like a quiet place to have lunch. Traci chided herself for the slight tremble in her hands. All she had to do was tell him, and then they would probably be able to put this romantic nonsense behind them. They were both mature adults.

McCord didn't look very mature at the moment, sitting there in his life jacket hunkered down as if expecting a wave to throw him overboard. At least he had owned a pair of sneakers, but his bare legs looked extremely white, as if they'd never seen daylight. Traci guessed that cowboys seldom rode in shorts. He'd resisted wearing them until she goaded him into it. The air temperature was in the eighties, and there was going to be plenty of sunshine.

The tri-maran proved an excellent choice. It handled very well, and although Scott wouldn't admit it, she knew he liked the idea of three hulls. "Isn't this great?" she said for probably the tenth time.

"Yeah," Scott replied, looking toward shore. "So do we have a place we're going? Or is this it?"

She frowned. She wanted him to enjoy his day. "There's a cove about twenty more minutes from here. I thought we'd take down our sails and stay in there for awhile. We can check out the food I stowed in the galley. We can eat outside or inside."

"It is a bigger boat than I expected," he admitted, flexing the fingers of one hand while still holding on with the other. "The three hulls sort of lure you into thinking you're safe."

"I hadn't noticed."

Giving her a lopsided grin, he said, "Don't make fun of me. I didn't make fun of you when you were uneasy about getting astride a horse."

"I know, and I am sorry. If you've never been on a sailboat before, this has to be a little bit creepy. I've been raising and lowering sails since I was kid. It would be at a terrible loss if I couldn't ever ride the waves again."

"Oh, thanks for taking it easy with this monster. I have a feeling you could make it go a lot faster than you are."

"Oh, yeah. She's sleek and she's fast." Traci chuckled as Scott's eyebrows shot upward. "Maybe another day we can show you what it can really do. But I can't tell you how much this does for my soul, Scott." She breathed deeply again. "This is pure peace. I wish things could stay like this. Do you ever wish a moment could last forever?"

"Guess so, now that you mention it. But then maybe that moment wouldn't be so special."

Traci nodded. They'd reached the cove. Shortly,

she took up some sail and began maneuvering them toward the middle of the cove. With the sails down, she released their anchor. Soon they were bobbing gently with the ebb and flow of the waves. It was a precious soothing motion for her.

Scott rose to stand beside her and wobbled on unsteady feet. She reached out and grabbed hold of him to guide him into the main cabin.

"Think my legs went to sleep," he grumbled.

"You need to get up and move around more—stretch your legs."

"Right. I feel like I'm the rubber duck bouncing in the bathtub at the whim of a four-year-old. Is this thing ever going to steady down?"

Traci shook her head. "Not unless the wind dies down completely. Then we'd have to use our engine to get back."

Pulling food out of the small refrigerator, Traci said, "This probably wasn't a very good idea bringing you out here. I'm sorry if you're not having a good time."

"I'm doing okay," Scott said. "It's all new to me: the motions, the movements, seeing the shoreline getting farther away. This is better. The cove, I mean. Really, it is. I don't want to make this a downer for you; I know you've looked forward to it a lot. And you look very at home out here."

Scott paused. "I didn't know you could look prettier than you do standing there in your white robe when somebody gets you out of bed too early in the morning. There were times when you were

206

doing your thing with the boat when the sun shone off you..." Scott searched for words.

Traci's chest tightened and her ears felt like they would implode.

"I haven't spent much time imagining mermaids, but I expect you would have filled that image quite fine."

Finding her tongue, Traci quipped, "I didn't know you saw anything but the shoreline. Would you like something to eat?"

"Not hardly," Scott said. "You go ahead. I'm fine. By the way, what do you do here if nature calls?"

"There's a head right over there. You'll find it a little cramped, but it works."

"I'll be damned. You could stay on this thing for days."

Traci smiled. "People do all the time. You want a drink?"

He hesitated.

"You don't want to dehydrate, and if your stomach is off a little, a soda might help."

"All right," he said, taking the can from her.

For several minutes, Scott seemed content to watch her nibble on crackers and cheese, carrots, and sliced apples. His voice suddenly broke the silence. "How can you exist just eating that stuff?"

"I brought sausage for you if you want some."

"No thanks." He paused. "Well, I guess Susannah loses."

"What?"

"The bet. Here I am. You got me to go sailing

with you."

"Oh, I forgot. I wonder what they bet," Traci said, putting away uneaten food. She opened a can of soda for herself and sat back down across from Scott. Her heart was beating faster than after a four mile run. How was she going to begin? She'd gotten this far, but there was no script from here on out. She ducked away from his curious gaze. What was he expecting would happen?

- o -

Scott tried not to scowl. Now what? He knew Traci Steele well enough to know that there was more to this than a quick sail to a cove and an attempt to have lunch. Maybe this whole elaborate set up was simply to prove that she could get him off the land, or that she was better at some things than he was. God, he already knew that. She didn't have to take him out on the water to make that point.

If she had simply wanted to sail, she could have done that at any time during her stay. He would've driven her into the city if need be.

Another woman might have brought him out here to seduce him, but not Traci. It wasn't a bad idea, but he wasn't sure how he would function. This constant bobbing and weaving made him feel like he had a monstrous hangover.

Though he was feeling better than when they started out. Then, he hadn't been at all convinced he'd make it without making a deposit or two in

208

the great Pacific.

Thankfully the stomach had subsided some, but he sure wasn't going to risk putting any solids into it. Maybe the soda helped some.

She sure was a looker. Traci brushed her hair back off her cheeks only to have it fall back again. He knew she was having one of her indecisive moments. There wasn't much he could do about that. He waited. Her eyes drooped, giving her that pained vulnerable look again. He was afraid she might erupt if she didn't speak soon. She'd better stay together — there was no way he was going to get them back to shore. He hadn't even seen a single oar on board.

Traci folded her arms tightly across her chest; she moved her lips to speak, but words failed to come out. At last she said in a plaintive child's voice, "I don't know how to begin; how to do this."

He watched her shoulders tremble. He wanted to reach across the scant space separating them and hold her, but instinct told him not to. "I'm no fool, Traci. I knew we were out here for a reason. Just take your time and tell me what you have to or do what you must."

"Okay," she said, drawing deep breaths. "It's about us. You seem to think there is an *us*. There can't be. No, please don't interrupt. I've gotten this far, let me go on."

Scott nodded, slumping back on the bench seat.

"You keep saying I'm beautiful. But I'm not. If you could really see me, you'd know I speak the truth.

"I've told you I'm ugly, but you still pursue me, leaving me no choice." Her hands shook and her cheeks turned red, but Traci managed to pull the windbreaker over her head. Her tank-top followed that. She reached for the front clasp on her bra, not acknowledging his protests.

Her breasts sprang out.

He found it impossible to breathe normally.

Quickly she covered her standing nipples with her palms. Tears eased down her cheeks and she dropped her hands to her waist. "See. See how ugly they are? They're like oversize melons. They're whores' tits."

"They're lovely; they're precious," Scott said, hardly able to remain sitting. He was afraid to move, very unsure what was happening or about to happen, but aware that the situation was fragile and he had to let her go on. But those round full breasts caused an immediate erection that he tried to hide by crossing his legs.

"They said they were ugly," she went on as if Scott hadn't spoken. "They said they were slut knockers." Traci's voice had turned shrill. Her fingers pulled and twisted her nipples — not in an arousing way, but apparently to punish.

"So you see," she shouted, turning her attention back to Scott, "I am ugly. You don't want to be associated with this kind of ugliness. Now we can go back. You see, there is no us. There can never be."

"Traci," Scott said, softly. "Traci, listen to me.

You are not ugly. You have beautiful breasts. Many women have breasts that size—many very nice women. They appear quite normal to me. Very loveable and kissable, in fact."

Traci flinched backwards and turned her head away.

"I'm not going to touch you, Traci. You know that. I wouldn't do that without your permission." He waited until her gaze met his again. "Who told you that you were ugly—that you had whores' tits? Who told you those things?"

"My cousin and his friend," she whimpered. Her eyes had that vacant looked he'd seen when horses were paralyzed with fear.

"They were wrong, Traci. Terribly wrong. You have beautiful breasts. You are a beautiful person. The most beautiful person I've known. What makes you feel ugly, Traci? You can tell me. I'm not going away. What makes you feel ugly?"

"It's not a feeling. They made me ugly. They made me dirty. They raped me. My own cousin and his friend. I still can't believe I let them do it. But one sat on my breasts while the other pounded in and out of me." Traci looked at the floor, not focusing. "And then they changed places. All the time they were screaming about how ugly I was. They were doing me a favor; they were breaking me in. The only kind of guys I'd ever attract were those looking for sluts. They said I'd have plenty because my breasts screamed easy lay.

"I am so ashamed. So ashamed. Of my body. Of my breasts." She sobbed harder. "Of letting them do that to me."

Scott couldn't wait any longer. "Traci, I'm going to come around and sit by you. Is that okay?"

She nodded, sobbing harder still.

"I'm going to hold your hand, okay?" Again, she nodded.

"Good. I just need to touch you a little," he said, rubbing his fingers lightly across the back of her hand.

She sobbed and nodded again.

She still looked beyond thinking, so he just sat there content with stroking her hand. After long moments, Traci took halting breaths matched by halting sobs. He didn't alter his finger movement. Her leg collapsed against his and he tried to send her positive energy where they touched.

- o -

Gradually, Traci came back to awareness behind closed eyes. She was totally exhausted. He was still there. She basked in the warmth of his touch. But now what? She hadn't mapped out this scenario. He was supposed to be mad at her and eager to get back to shore. She was supposed to be talking with him about being mature and that they could still be friends, but just friends. Now what?

She tried not to let her heart soar. Was this his sympathy she was receiving? She'd gone ahead and shown him her breasts before sharing her story because she didn't want him to respond out of sympathy. Anything would be better than

212

sympathy.

Traci opened her eyes and looked at him. There he was, meeting her gaze steadily. His smile was comforting. His eyes were filled with powerful emotions. She didn't think sympathy was one of them.

"Okay, cowboy, talk to me," she said shakily. "I'm sorry if I embarrassed you."

Scott narrowed his eyes. "Embarrassed me? I'm...I'm honored that you'd take the risk of sharing with me. I truly am. And if I had those bastards here, I'd break their necks."

"I know." She shuddered. "But they're not. Thank goodness."

"This will sound prejudiced, but they sound like a couple of street kids gone wild."

Traci sniffed. "Both are products of private schools. Upper class kids can be just as violent and nasty as other kids."

"Apparently. But they were wrong. Not only in what they did, but in the tapes they left in your head. You, Traci Steele, are the most gorgeous woman I've ever known. And I wouldn't trade those breasts in for any others."

Traci wiggled her upper body and gave him a half smile. "I've detested these breasts for so long, but I've never figured out how to trade them in on smaller versions."

"Good."

"So now what?"

"I'm curious—did you bring me out here in the middle of the cove so I would run from your so-

213

called ugliness?"

Traci shook her head. Her voice trembled slightly as she answered, "No. To make sure that *I* didn't run from my ugliness. I had to tell you. I had to show you."

"Because there might be the possibility of an *us*."

She nodded. "I've only dated a few men since I was fifteen. They gave up long before I was ready to accept their advances. But they weren't much of a loss."

"But I might be a loss?"

"Don't let it go to your head, cowboy."

"Now that's my girl. I have some thoughts. About us."

She nodded and waited.

"Now that I know what happened to you, I can understand better why you can be so passionate one minute and then it just turns off the next."

"Yeah, so?"

"I'll be honest with you, Traci. I don't know where all of this goes. But I do know that I find you to be an incredibly attractive woman. You can be a pain in the ass at times, but for the most part a delightful pain in the ass." He paused and studied her thoughtfully. "My suggestion is this. Why don't we just move forward in baby steps? Telling me your story isn't going to make all the damage those two did to you go away overnight. But I do want to touch." He rubbed her hand again. "If I can't touch, I think I'm going to explode. And I want you to know how beautiful you really are."

"But—"

"You are, Traci. You really are."

"I can't believe I'm sitting here beside you with my breasts exposed like this."

"May I touch them?"

"I don't know," her eyes widening. "Do you really want to? You're not repulsed by them?"

"I'll say it a thousand times if necessary. I find them very appealing. They are so round and perky. They look just right."

"You can try touching them, if you want to."

Scott turned slightly toward her and ran a finger along the underside of a breast. She tensed and then watched his finger move over and around its crown. He brushed the nipple, which now stood erect seeking its own attention, whether she wanted it or not. Sharp currents shot from her breasts to her loins.

He put an arm around her and she turned to place her lips on his. It seemed like the natural thing to do. He rolled her nipple between finger and thumb. The tingling sensations were exquisite. She didn't want them to end. His tongue probed the warmth of her mouth and she reciprocated.

Wildly, her mind leaped from thought to thought. He hadn't withdrawn from her. He wanted more. She hadn't withdrawn from him. *She* wanted more.

Suddenly, he broke off the kiss and moved back to the seat across from her. She felt bereft and cold. He must have come to his senses. Her lower lip

215

quivered.

"Traci, I had to move over here. We can't go that fast. You're not ready. And I only have so much self-control."

Traci's spirits soared. She wasn't accustomed to having such power over men. She knew what he was talking about, though. And he was right. They needed to slow down, or everything could blow up in their faces.

"I think maybe I'd better get dressed."

"That would help a lot. Your breasts are a real turn on to me. I wonder how those bastards got the idea that they're ugly."

Flustered, Traci had difficulty clasping her bra. Tossing it aside she said, "To hell with it," and doffed her tank top and windbreaker.

Traci stood and laughed at his lusty look. "Maybe we'd better get you back to land before you become as loony as one of those Irish leprechauns."

Chapter Eleven

Darkness had settled in long before Traci drove herself back to the resort. She was exhausted. She was relieved. She was ecstatic. Scott hadn't fled. He had simply listened and held her.

There would be more hurdles. But the wall she'd climbed earlier that day had always before appeared unscalable and with no way around. Now she could look back at the wall; it still cast a long shadow, but she could see that it was a shadow because of light filtering around its edges.

As she walked from the parking lot up the stairs to her condo, she noticed some muscles aching that she hadn't felt for a long time. Then she grinned broadly remembering how McCord had nearly fallen on his face when he'd stepped off the tri-maran onto the dock. He complained about being woozy and that his legs couldn't support him. He'd said he knew she was intoxicating but hadn't realized to what extreme. She'd pointed out to him if he'd gotten up and moved around more on the boat, use of his land legs would have returned quicker. Recalling how her pelvic muscles felt the first day after sitting astride Cory, she thought turnabout was fair play.

Traci put her key in the door and twisted the knob. It didn't turn. She twisted the key again and the door opened. Frowning, she stepped into the condo. She was certain she'd locked the door on her way out early that morning, though it had been quite early, and maybe she'd forgotten.

The hairs on the back of her neck rose. Something wasn't right. Grabbing an empty wine bottle, Traci held it as a weapon and moved cautiously from one room to another. Each time she flipped on a light switch, her heart pounded in her throat.

She was alone. But someone had been there; she knew it. And the maids came in to clean on Wednesdays, not Mondays. Walking back through the rooms, Traci examined her surroundings more closely.

Yes, the yellow pad she'd been working on at the dining room table had been moved. She had a habit of leaving the pen or pencil she'd been using on top of the legal pad, so it would be there when she needed it next. The ballpoint pen sat on the table beside the pad.

Traci bent over to look at the pad. The top sheet bore no imprints at all. Someone had ripped off a couple sheets trying to figure out what she'd been writing.

Thankfully, she'd thrown the original in the fireplace the night before.

She checked the wastebasket. Yes, someone had sifted through it. She'd opened a carton of mocha cappuccinos early in the week; that carton was now near the top of the wastebasket. Someone either was not very competent at searching a place, or was leaving subtle hints that she was being watched. Traci expected the latter to be the case. Subtle hints could not be mistaken for vandals.

"Shit," she muttered, "the computer." Traci rushed to the bedroom dresser where she'd stored it, brought it out to the dining room table and booted it up. It purred. Traci sighed relief. Windows popped up okay. She clicked on "open files." The screen remained blank. Her heart sank. She tried again, but knew the effort was fruitless. Her C drive had been cleaned of all document files. They probably had been copied first.

With her fingers trembling slightly, Traci reached for her purse and took out her backup thumb drive. She put it in the USB port and clicked on "open files" again. And the list of available files appeared. She opened one to be certain. The computer, itself, was functioning fine.

She leaned back and studied the screen without focusing on it. Somebody definitely wanted her to know they knew what she was doing. If they'd simply wanted to know what she knew, they would have copied her files. But they wanted her to know they knew. It was an explicit effort to scare her.

Although she didn't like being threatened, it certainly wasn't the first time. Threats and intimidation came with her chosen work. Nor was it surprising. She'd interviewed enough people by now that word had to be getting out. Clearly, someone was not happy with her rummaging about. Who? Why?

Traci glanced at the clock. It was after midnight. Tomorrow — no, later in the day — she'd go back over her notes. She had to be missing a link. And now somebody knew how close or how far away she was from solving this puzzle.

If she was close, then the heat would be turned up. If not, whoever was behind all of this could simply afford to wait her out, let her grow tired of the case. They also would know that she wouldn't be hanging around forever.

Turning off the lights, Traci went back to the bedroom, determined not to let the bad guys spoil what had been a momentous day.

Shyly, she examined her nude body in the bathroom mirror. She lifted a breast and choked on her tears. He liked them. No, she corrected herself — he *loved* them. She shook her head. How could he? But he did. She'd seen the adoration in his eyes — that hadn't been sympathy. It was more than compassion; it was passion. Scott said they were delectable.

What would it feel like to have him lick them? To suckle them? She closed her eyes, imagining. Her nipples pebbled and elongated. She brushed them lightly, remembering his touch. She shuddered, opened her eyes and smiled at herself in the mirror. No, she wasn't going to take herself there. She wanted to wait for Mustache. "My God," she gasped. What would those hairs feel like on her skin?

After turning off the bathroom and bedroom

lights, Traci crawled into bed, held a breast in the palm of each hand and drifted off to sleep replaying the sensations of his fingers that had given her a new self-image and renewed hope.

The phone rang early the next morning, although Traci had at least had time to eat a toasted bagel and was on her second cup of coffee pondering her next steps.

"Hello," she said into the mouthpiece.

There was a brief silence and then, "Oh, I'm sorry Traci, I was just making notes. Oh, before I forget it, Alex wants to hear from you."

Traci stilled but managed a cool response, "Okay Roberta, I'll call him later this morning."

"I've run into a dead end. Oh damn, there's a knock on my door. Talk with you later, Trace."

"Take care. Bye.

Quickly, Traci pulled on shorts and a polo shirt, grabbed her purse, and filled a tote bag with her laptop and note pads. She paused at the door to collect herself.

Deliberately, nonchalantly, Traci walked to her car and drove off toward Buteo.

Without speeding, she headed to a payphone she'd seen outside the post office. A chill swept through her body as she tried to take in this new information that her phone was tapped. Roberta had used the code words, "Alex wants to hear from you." She didn't have to say anything else other than provide an excuse for the brevity of their conversation.

There was a pay phone at the resort, but she didn't want to be seen using it even if it was clean. And her cell phone was useless; she might as well be shouting into a CB. Pulling out her phone card, Traci punched in the appropriate numbers.

"Hello."

"It's Traci."

"Thought that might be you. No ears?"

"Shouldn't be. I'm at a pay phone in Buteo. So what do we know?"

"We know someone is watching us and trying to cover trail faster than we're tracking."

"Can you determine the source of the tap?"

"We're working on it. Right now all we know is you've got an extra set of ears."

Traci sighed. "Why do you have to be so melodramatic?"

"It's boring looking at computer screens all day. Aren't you at least a little concerned?"

"It's not the first time. The important thing is that our equipment worked." Traci glanced at a man walking toward the phone booth. He kept walking and climbed into a brown car.

"You still there? I'm about to fall asleep."

"Sorry, Roberta. I'm a little jumpy this morning. Someone has been playing around with my computer files."

"Oh my God. In your apartment?"

"Uh, huh. That's probably when they bugged the phone. No need to be overly alarmed. I figure they're trying to find out what I know and scare me off at the same time."

"Like that will work. The more they push you, the more you'll dig in."

"Anything else on your end? Have you found any more links? Possible leads?"

Roberta cleared her throat. "You're beginning to sound like the Traci Steele I know so well. Impatient. Eager for the kill. I thought you were on vacation and this was something to keep your mind occupied a little."

"Right."

"Okay, let me see, what was I calling you about initially?" Traci shifted in the booth so her notepad was accessible.

"We have some new criminal history information on a few people that might prove interesting. Let me see. Yes, Susan Larson, who works for Laskins, one of the trainers. She's been working for him for three years. She was charged with theft and also for breaking and entering before going to work for him. There were no convictions. Charges were dropped."

"Do we know why?"

"We're working on that."

"I want to know who went to bat for her." Traci's pulse quickened. Who would help a young woman out of a jam? And who might later want to call in a debt?"

"Also, Ellen Zastrow."

"I know her. She works for Scott at the stable. Quiet. Unassuming. Good with horses."

"She spent some time in a juvenile facility in Massachusetts on a prostitution conviction."

"Holy shit. I'll bet no one knows about that."

"Hope the wrong person doesn't know. She might be quite vulnerable to pressure."

"You're right about that." Traci shook her head. "I've been in this business a long time, and I still get surprised over and over. I'd bet most anything that Ellen is trying to keep her life clean."

"Speaking of surprises, listen to this one. James McCord."

Traci's heart sank. She'd dreaded that Scott's brother's name would come up in her net of suspects. It had only been a feeling, but she knew better than to ignore such feelings.

"What about him?"

"The man has a penchant for casinos." Traci groaned and closed her eyes.

"At least he did about three years ago. Not in California, though. He'd go to Laughlin or Vegas and run up some pretty big debts. Everything was comped for him except his losses. We're still working on it, but the pattern is that of a sucker rather than a professional gambler. At one point he owed three casinos a combined hundred and fifty thousand dollars."

"Damn."

"I'd say he's having a hard time even paying the accumulating interest. Although over the last year he's managed to cut that debt by more than half. Down to fifty thousand."

"Wow."

"Right. Where did he come up with that kind of dough?"

"Can't imagine anyone else here knows about any of that."

"That's all I have at the moment."

"That's a lot, Roberta. Thanks. Though I wish I didn't have to know some of this. This will be devastating to the McCords." Images of Susannah and Rebecca flashed through Traci's mind. Then Penny. Then Sal. And at last, Scott. She couldn't tell them. She wouldn't tell them. Not yet.

After trading niceties with Roberta, Traci hung up the phone and staggered to her car. She gripped the steering wheel tightly, wishing she was on her sailboat.

Why did innocent people always get in the way? She knew James well enough to know that he was blustery, yet unsure of himself. He wasn't an evil man; he might be weak, but not evil. She knew the same was true of Ellen Zastrow. And although she hadn't met Susan Larson, she was most likely a hardworking woman trying to put her past behind her.

And now Traci had to dredge up the past not only for Susan, but also for Ellen and James. Each person was vulnerable. Each was susceptible to pressure applied by an individual threatening to expose them, or possibly to their own greed. Still, there was no direct link between any of them and the string of bad luck occurring to the horses. And she wasn't about to share their dirty laundry even with Scott until she could reasonably draw such a link.

225

When she drove into the resort parking lot, she saw Scott brushing down a horse across the entrance in front of the stable. Smiling, he waved for her to come over. Traci put on what she hoped was a happy face and made her way across the parking lot.

"So are you able to walk this morning, McCord?" she teased, approaching him. "Your legs didn't look like they were doing too well last night when I dropped you off. We've got to get you out on the water more often."

Standing on the other side of the gray filly, Scott continued brushing the animal's back. "Walking is better than it was last night," he admitted. "But most importantly, I can still ride."

His grin was infectious. "I'm happy for that, Scott. I didn't think a day of sailing would permanently disable you."

"It was good," he said, holding his hands still. "I don't think I've ever had a more profound experience." Putting the brush down, Scott began massaging the gray's shoulders and then worked his fingers gently but firmly down the filly's spine.

Traci watched, mesmerized by the movement of his fingers. She swore she could feel those powerful fingers kneading their magic on her.

"So how are you feeling, Counselor?" he asked with a wry smile. "The day after. You must be wiped."

Stepping over to the horse, Traci ran her hands over the horse's neck and shoulders. "Yes, but not just because of yesterday in the boat. That was very special, Scott." Her fingers touched his briefly. "But so much has happened since then."

"Oh." Scott continued digging his fingers along the gray's spine and the animal responded by stretching its back seeking even more attention.

Traci laughed. "You sure do have an effect on the ladies, McCord. Well, to begin with, somebody was in my condo while we were sailing."

Scott's hands stopped moving. He scowled. "Are you sure?"

"Oh, yeah. There were little telltale signs. The garbage was rearranged. And all my C drive documents on my laptop were erased."

Scott tensed and the filly did also. "I'd better put Hazel, here, in her stall," he grunted. "Why don't you join me in my office? I've got coffee brewing."

Shaking her head, Traci stepped back. "I think it's better if we talk out by the corral. Fewer ears."

"Okay." Scott frowned. "I'll bring out a couple coffee mugs."

In only a few minutes he rejoined her. "Why do I have a feeling that we're into more of a cloak and dagger mode this morning?"

"Because someone was in my condo and my phone is tapped."

Scott rubbed the back of his hand against his mustache and stared out across the corral. "This is getting serious."

"Yes, it is."

"This means you're onto something."

"It means someone is afraid I might stumble across something." She leaned against the corral fence. "But I don't know if what that someone fears is at all connected to the problems with the horses. Access to the condo and a phone tap points to resort personnel and professional criminals. We know the resort has a foul nest; maybe that's all their interest is about."

"But you don't think so."

She squinted at Scott. "How's your mood, McCord? I've got a further hunch about motive, but you're not going to like it."

Scott's shoulders slumped. "Don't imagine my feelings matter much at this point. This is a bigger, more complicated matter than I ever expected. So what do you think?"

"It's a hypothesis only. As I told you, I've gone over the agreement between your parents and the original resort board."

"Yeah, I remember." His eyes hardened. "You thought Dad did a good job of controlling the future from his grave."

"Are you ready to listen? I don't want to revisit that issue. I'm sorry I ever mentioned it."

"Okay, spit it out. Tell me your hypothesis."

"Did you know that at a board meeting you missed, management presented a proposal to tear down the stable and replace it by expanding the resort twofold?"

Scott glowered at the stable and then back at Traci.

She watched his fingers curl into fists. "I guess

not," she said. "McCord, don't you even read the board minutes?"

"Who has time for that crap? So tell me what happened."

"No motion was made. A couple of local owners reminded the board about the original agreement and about what the McCords have always done for the community."

"Good." Scott's nostrils flared. "So that's done."

"Maybe. I've been going over the agreement very carefully."

He nodded.

"On the surface, it appears ironclad. I'm sure it made for a nice splash in the local papers, if not the San Diego papers."

"It did both." Scott smiled. "Dad was very pleased with it and Ma was ticked that the details leaked out."

"I wonder how they leaked?" Traci ignored the warning glare she received from him. "Anyway, the language *public interest* is slippery. That's the kind of language that keeps civil lawyers in business. I don't understand why they didn't say *in perpetuity* – that would've been a lock."

"Probably was too much legalese for dad."

Traci pursed her lips. "In any case, that language looms as a loophole. If..."

"If what?"

"If you can be discredited. If a group of folks could be organized to oppose the place of a horse stable for cowboys in the midst of an upscale progressive forward looking community. That would be a lot more easily accomplished if you and your work could be seen as shoddy, perhaps bringing unwanted negative attention to a community that covets privacy. And maybe, just maybe there might be a few folks here, even old families, that wouldn't mind seeing a McCord get his comeuppance."

Scowling, McCord folded his arms across his chest. "That's a lot of thinking you've been doing."

"Does any of it seem at all plausible?"

"Maybe. Occasionally we see a letter in the newspaper questioning the existence of the stable in what you so aptly called an upscale neighborhood." He spat on the ground. "Funny, some of these folks will spend a hell of a lot of money to get their kid a competitive horse, all the clothes and trimmings that go along with competition, but they would rather drive miles out into the country to a facility than walk down the street to one."

Traci nodded. "I've heard that one before. I want a group home for juvenile delinquents, but not in my backyard."

Scott nodded. He drew a line in the dirt with the toe of a boot. "To be honest, I imagine there is a family or two who has harbored resentments against the McCords over the years. I expect my father and grandfather and those before them did a lot of good for the area. But sometimes they didn't mind running roughshod over their neighbors to do it."

"We'll help you whether you want our help or

not."

"Yeah, something like that."

"So what else do you know?"

"That's about it," she lied.

"That's all you're going to tell me."

Traci bent down and picked up loose dirt and sifted it through her fingers. When she looked back at him, there were tears in her eyes. "Scott, I would trust you with my life. But there are pieces of information I can't share with you. We have a few possible leads based on criminal history checks. I have access to that information because I am an officer of a court. I'm sorry I can't share that with you."

Scott grabbed her hands and rubbed the grime off them. She trembled at the intimacy of his touch.

"It's okay," he said. "I understand your professional responsibilities." He glanced away. "I guess I'm a little worried about what we might find if we go on."

"I know," Traci whispered. Of course he must be wondering if the culprits would include friends or even family. "But you have obligations to your trainers and your owners."

"I know I do. Keep digging, Traci. I don't think we have a choice."

Traci felt his eyes probing the depth of her own.

"But what of the danger? You don't carry a gun, do you?"

Traci bubbled with laughter. "No, I don't. Those things can be harmful to your health. So far, the danger level really hasn't risen, though. I'm being warned that someone knows what I'm doing and that I perhaps would be wiser to leave things alone." She saw his eyebrows arch. "But I don't have any more choice about proceeding than you do. It's not in my makeup to walk aware from a case because of threats."

"So be it. When can I see you next?"

Her breath quickened. She didn't need him to use more words to know what he was talking about. She wet her lower lip. "You want to come by tonight? I can cook some. I make pretty good spaghetti."

"Sure. Maybe your place is bugged."

"I'll make a sweep. I doubt they'd bother, given that they wanted me to know they'd been there. But if the condo has been compromised, I'll find it."

"You're an amazing woman, Traci Steele."

Traci smiled. Her pulse returned to near normal. "Don't you forget it, cowboy. See you tonight. Seven o'clock. Don't be late," she said over her shoulder as she sauntered back toward the resort complex.

- o -

"You can count on that," Scott shouted, admiring the swing of her buttocks and the taut thigh and leg muscles that scrambled his brain.

He wasn't at all certain where his relationship with the Chicago lawyer was going, but he was eager to get there. No, he counseled himself, patience. He had to remember she needed time. They both needed time. And patience. And cold showers.

So what wasn't she telling him? That bothered him some, but he did understand and appreciated her professional integrity. He just hoped she wasn't going to dig up something on a good friend. That could be rough.

- o -

"That was an excellent meal, Traci," Scott said. "You shouldn't put down your cooking skills."

That was at least the third time he'd said those exact words. And Traci thought *she* was the nervous one. They sat side by side on the couch. A log burned in the fireplace countering the evening chill which seemed more pronounced in the southern California foothills on days that reached eighty degrees than was her experience in the mid-west. She was pleased her spaghetti had been a hit.

But now what? They both knew what was expected, but neither seemed comfortable taking that initial step.

Scott drained his beer. Traci watched him turn to her with that crooked grin of his.

"Guess the script is missing," he volunteered. "I haven't felt this inept since high school."

Traci nodded. She'd always felt inept.

"Do you have any CDs for that CD player over there?" Scott asked.

"Some."

"Anything slow we could dance to?"

Traci went into the bedroom and rummaged through her CD case. Her fingers felt like five thumbs. Finding what she wanted, she put it in the player and soft music filled the room.

"Much better," Scott said, rising from the couch and extending his hands to her.

She kicked off her flats and stepped into his arms. Was she in a trance? He held her close; her breasts nestled against his chest. It felt good. It felt right. Their feet hardly moved. They swayed to the music. There was no hurry.

She wanted to taste and savor the moment. The press of her body against his, his aftershave enticing her senses, his hand resting on her lower backside. Intimate and right. She didn't want him to let go. Ever.

- o -

Scott filled his lungs with Traci's fresh scent. He wanted to be gentle with her, but her body filled his empty spaces so well that he lost track of his intent. He pressed her body to his as if afraid they wouldn't have another time like this. Scott closed his eyes and swayed with the music, rubbing his nose and jaw through her ebony hair. It was like touching silk. He breathed deeply and her scent caressed his soul. She wasn't supposed to have such a powerful impact on him; he was here to help her overcome her past, not to succumb to her innate charm. He was cowboy and she was big city. *Don't forget that. Enjoy. Please her. But don't forget.*

Through how many songs had they clung to each other? He couldn't remember. They moved hardly at all. There was a waiting and a longing that palpated between them. Scott couldn't wait any longer.

He lightly kissed Traci's forehead. She didn't retreat. Instead, he heard the softest of moans come from her lips. It was the best music he'd heard all evening. He kissed her closed eyelids and nibbled on her brows. She giggled softly and noticeably relaxed in his arms. His tongue followed the lines of a high cheekbone and ducked under her hair to explore an ear. Again, he was emboldened by her corresponding moan. He ran his tongue along the entire length of her nose. It was his turn to groan. "I love your nose," he whispered.

Scott caught her laugh between his lips; she placed her hands around his neck and drew him tighter. Her lips tasted faintly of strawberry. It was *her* tongue that initiated, that probed his mouth. Not to be left behind, he darted his tongue into her warm interior. Was she sapping his strength? He could no longer stand. Scott went to his knees and Traci followed suit. There they remained trading pecks, soft kisses, and bruising kisses. Hands moving as if of their own accord traced shoulder and back muscles.

Breathless, Scott broke off and leaned back. He

saw smoky passion in Traci's eyes. Questioning, but no fear. "May I," he asked, extending his hands toward her breasts.

She chewed on her lower lip and nodded. He cupped a breast in each palm and studied Traci's wide open eyes. She smiled a little. He reached for the top button of her blouse. Her eyes narrowed and then she relaxed again. He maintained direct eye contact as he unbuttoned the remaining buttons. She didn't waver when he lifted her arms and removed the blouse.

Softly, he ran a finger along the top edge of the bra, outlining each breast in turn. His fingers met at the front clasp. Traci flinched just a little as he undid the clasp. For several moments he held the open clasp in his fingers before lifting his hands and exposing her gorgeous mounds.

Scott leaned back and sighed, admiring her beauty, seeking permission. She smiled demurely. Gliding a finger under each breast, he said, "These are absolutely perfect. I love the way they turn up, like they have minds of their own." He winked at her. "Now why should that surprise me?"

- o -

Traci chuckled. "I'm pleased you like them. They seem to have lives of their own when you caress them like that." She hardly recognized her own voice, thick with passion. She believed him. He wouldn't lie to her about her breasts.

What would he do next? Her lips dried. She wet

them with the tip of her tongue. What did she want? She wanted to feel his mustache against her skin. But she couldn't tell him that. She wanted to feel her nipples against his skin. She couldn't tell him that either. But she could do something about it.

With slightly trembling fingers, Traci reached across the space that separated them and started to unbutton his shirt. His nostrils and eyes flared, and that pleased her immensely. Having this kind of power over a man intoxicated and frightened her.

Thankfully, he understood what she wanted. Scott didn't even remove his shirt—he just hugged her to his bare chest. She closed her eyes and reveled in the sensations of skin rubbing skin. Hers rubbing his. His rubbing hers. If someone froze them into a statue at this moment, she'd not complain at all. Her nipples grew painfully hard. She brushed them against his, seeking relief.

He leaned back and she was grief stricken with the loss of contact. And then he bent forward and trailed his tongue along the underside of one breast; his mustache hairs brushed her extended nipple. "Oh my," she mumbled, staying very still.

The soft hairs tickled and coaxed. His tongue warmed her flesh. She waited. On the edge of nowhere, she waited. She felt his breath encompass her nipple. His tongue nearly touched it but slid on by to lave the upper side of the areola. She felt her body involuntarily try to redirect his attention. She wanted his tongue. She wanted his mouth covering that nipple. How could he not know that? Her body squirmed. Almost as an observer, Traci was embarrassed by the need of her body, yet she wanted his mouth on her now more than anything she could imagine. She knew it was just a matter of time, but could she wait that long?

She moaned satisfaction and relief when at last the tip of his tongue grazed her overly alert nipple. He pulled on it gently between pursed lips. Traci closed her eyes and went inward; she had no choice. Her body demanded her complete attention. Scott took the nipple in his mouth and then the areola. Traci tensed. He began to suckle. She squirmed. He stayed with her. She relaxed and let the sensations wash over her.

He suckled as if she were the gift of life. It was his adoration as well as the physical touch that sent her soaring. But he wasn't done. Amazed, Traci shot her eyes open briefly as he took as much of her breast as he could. She felt his tongue twirling as his head bobbed up and down. If she had had any milk to give, Scott would be drowning.

"Oh, my God," she screamed, hugging his head tighter against her body. Then she floated in space. It seemed like hours. She simply floated and soared, rejoicing in the freedom of release, in the responsiveness of her body, in having a lover.

Traci was jarred back to the present when she felt coolness where his mouth had been. She opened her eyes and saw him staring at her. She gave him a half smile and fell into his outstretched arms. And then she sobbed. Why the tears? Why now? She couldn't explain them, but thankfully she knew she didn't have to.

"You'd better put this back on before you get chilled," Scott said, pulling her blouse around her shoulders.

She put her arms through it, but didn't bother to button it. "Are you okay?" she asked.

"I'm fine," he said. "That looked pretty good for you."

"Pretty good?" Traci leaned back against the couch. "That was phenomenal."

"I think we're making progress, Counselor."

"The evidence is quite convincing," Traci quipped, stretching her arms above her head and yawning. "I think I'll sleep soundly tonight."

Well after midnight, Traci rolled over and tucked a pillow between her legs. Sleep refused to come. Her body was exhausted, but her mind raced. What was happening to her? Why worry? It was fantastic.

But it shouldn't be this good. Why not? The voice inside was relentless: *You don't deserve it. No matter what he says, you're damaged goods.* Her eyes popped wide open. No, he'd made her feel again. He made her feel whole. Like he would with any of his horses. But she was more to him than a horse. Wasn't she?

She didn't know; they hadn't really talked about their feelings. She hadn't thought beyond the fact that what he was doing with her was fabulous. Was he on a mission of mercy? Did she care? What did he get out of all of this? Where did it all lead? What next? What, indeed? There was no doubt they would be together again. She wanted that very much. But where would he want to take them then, and could she follow his lead?

Chapter Twelve

The next morning Traci stood across the counter from Mr. Humphries, who wore his fixed smile as if it were body armor.

"So are you still enjoying yourself, Ms. Steele? I thought we'd see you poolside or on the tennis courts more than we do."

"I'm quite able to fill my time. And it has been particularly nice since the weather turned so mild."

"The weather is always an unpredictable matter here in the hill country. So is there something I can do for you?" The manager opened his calendar notebook expectantly.

"Matter of fact, there is. I'm curious. I'm certain that in a resort this fine you must keep a record of whenever staff enter a unit."

"Of course we do."

"Could you check who was in my condo last Monday?"

Unruffled, Humphries thumbed through another calendar. Maybe she was going down a blind alley.

"Yes, here it is," Humphries said, giving her a satisfied smile. "At eleven fifteen, house repair went in to check on air-conditioner filters. It's that

241

time of year to get ready."

"Do you have a name?"

Humphries frowned. "That is unusual. There's no name, just that the task was completed."

"That's unfortunate."

"How so?"

"Someone needs a reprimand for leaving my unit unlocked."

"Oh, my." Humphries jotted a note on his calendar. "I'll look into this. Leaving a unit unlocked is inexcusable. Someone could have been there in the dark waiting for you when you returned."

"No harm done this time. Maybe you could issue a memo reminding staff to be more security conscious."

"Good idea," Humphries said, nodding and writing another note to himself. "You may be assured that it will be done. And Ms. Steele..."

"Yes?"

"On behalf of Live Oak, I do apologize for any inconvenience or alarm that this incident may have caused you."

"It's okay. As I said, no big deal. But we wouldn't want it to happen again. Have a good day, Mr. Humphries."

Halfway back to her condo Traci suddenly stopped. The only moment she'd not seen the fixed smile on Humphries lips was when he talked about the possibility that someone could have been waiting in the dark for her return.

How had he known she hadn't come back until

well after dark? A good guess. Maybe.

"Ms. Steele, I've been waiting for you to come see me." The meek voice belonged to Ellen Zastrow, who was sitting across from Traci in Scott's stable office. Ellen fidgeted with the work gloves she held in her hands.

"I just want to ask you a few questions."

"I know who you are, Ms. Steele. Scott told us you're investigating all the bad things happening to his horses. I don't know anything about it."

Traci watched the woman duck her eyes downward. Of course, Scott would tell his staff to cooperate with her. There wouldn't be any sneaking up on folks around here. Ellen raised her eyes and Traci saw fear and fierce determination.

"You know about me. I can tell. I liked this job. A lot. I've been here nearly two years, but you can't walk away from your past. That's what one of the juvenile detention workers told me. I didn't want to believe her."

"She was wrong," Traci said. "And I'm not here to dredge up those things you're trying to put behind you."

"You're not? I sold myself in order to escape things that were worse. Only I was caught instead. But maybe that wasn't so bad, because here I'm making a good living and hanging with decent folk. Not bad for a girl from the wrong side of Chelsea."

"You've come a long way, Ellen, and I don't want to destroy any of that. I haven't told Scott

243

about your history."

"You haven't? I wouldn't do anything to hurt Mr. McCord."

Traci flinched at the adoration so evident on the young woman's face. No, she wouldn't hurt Scott. At least not on purpose. "Has anyone else approached you about your past, Ellen?"

"No," Ellen replied, her eyebrows arched high. "I'm always so afraid it will come out. People won't understand. Why should they?"

"So no one is using you to get information about Scott and his racehorse operation?"

Ellen shook her head. "If anyone knew—besides you, that is—I would just move on. It wouldn't be worth the risk to stay."

Traci nodded. The determination on the young woman's face said it all. Ellen Zastrow was no longer on Traci's suspect list.

"I do believe you, Ellen. And I hope you know you have no reason to leave this job on my account."

"I know."

Both women stood and Traci gave Ellen a brief hug. Smiling, Ellen pulled on her gloves and headed for the Arabian barn.

Traci leaned against the office wall. When had she become so soft? She'd been around abused and self-abusing women for years. She'd helped them in a variety of ways, but never before had she stepped over that professional line with a hug.

Was it California? Was it McCord? She was changing in lots of ways. She wasn't entirely sure she liked that.

Traci glanced around the laundry facilities. It looked like she was the only one doing laundry on Wednesday afternoon. That was good. She hated having to make small talk while folding her lingerie. She'd been surprised but pleased to have had the area to herself each week on her wash day.

Sitting in a plastic straight-back chair, Traci scanned the pages of a novel while waiting for the wash cycle to complete. There hadn't been enough time for reading. But she wasn't complaining. The washing machine stopped. She put her book down and transferred those clothes to a dryer. Her second load would take a little longer.

As Traci slammed the dryer door shut, she heard a couple women from the housekeeping staff enter the other end of the small building. Only a thin wall separated the guest laundry room from the resort laundry. The women seemed upset about something. Traci listened more closely. Thank goodness for her three months in Guadalajara and all the Spanish training she'd had.

Listening, Traci chuckled and grinned broadly. She understood why the women were so upset.

"He shouldn't be allowed to snoop on us," one woman said.

"We already have a supervisor," complained the other. "That's one too many." That comment was followed by laughter.

"Humphries is a mean man. He threatened to recheck my green card if I didn't do what he wanted."

"The bastard."

"Fortunately, the gringo has no staying power. I can go down on my knees for two minutes if that means he won't stir up trouble with immigration. That's a small price. And I do mean small."

Both women howled loudly.

Traci resisted slamming her book on the counter. What did these women have to endure to keep a paying job? Humphries probably thought sexual favors were his fringe benefits for the taking. Apparently, he didn't always hide behind a smile.

She'd be pleased if the man became a casualty of her investigation. The two women she'd overheard would likely agree.

She hoped her meeting the next morning with Mrs. Herb Bergstrom, a small percentage owner of Live Oak, would give her more ammunition to nail Humphries and his bosses.

When Traci entered O'Neils, Mrs. Bergstrom was already at a table and waved at Traci to join her. A contemporary of Sally McCord, the woman wore her gray hair in a serviceable bun. She had an easy smile and seemed quite comfortable with herself.

It was only after exchanging pleasantries and ordering that Traci was able to check out her surroundings. Signed photographs of Hollywood stars hung on the walls. Framed playbills and thank you notes were also displayed. Most of the memorabilia came from the forties, fifties and sixties. She recognized John Wayne, Roy and Dale Rogers, Bing Crosby, Clark Gable, Jane Russell, Paul Newman, Robert Redford, Marilyn Monroe, and Jimmy Stewart. Most pictures had been taken right there in the diner.

"I see you appreciate our little hole in the wall diner," Mrs. Bergstrom said.

"Have all of those folks been here?"

"Certainly. This entire region was a draw for Hollywood. Still is today, to a lesser extent. People wanted to get away from the heat and the smog and the fans. They might come up here before or after the horses ran at Del Mar. The place had a charm they were looking for back then.

"And the woman who built this place, Margaret Mary O'Neil, was a character like no other. She drank her whiskey straight, smoked cigars, out-cussed most men, and had a heart as large as a gold mine. She said she could shoot the rattles off a snake at a hundred yards. That included two-legged snakes. Yeah, she was a draw all right. She should have been in the movies."

Traci chuckled. "She sounds like quite the woman."

"She was that. But she died at least a dozen years ago. Nowadays, we're either too crowded or too quiet. Depends on who you talk to. But you didn't ask me to breakfast just to hear about local color."

"No, but I could listen for hours." Traci leaned back to let the waitress set their meals on the table.

She picked up a fork and cut into her scrambled eggs. "So you've been a part owner of the Oak since its inception?"

"Me and my husband, but he died two years back."

"I'm sorry."

"Yeah, well it happens. You pick up and go on."

"Has Live Oak been a good investment for you?"

"Surely has. It turns a nice profit. Can't complain about that part of it at all."

"But you do have some complaints."

The gray-haired woman scowled and wiped the corners of her mouth with a napkin. "The board meetings are boring as hell. And those out-of-towners can become quite heavy handed."

"You're referring to the attempt to close the equestrian center and build more condos."

Mrs. Bergstrom smiled. "Scott said you'd done a lot of homework already. Yeah, that was probably the boldest effort on their part. Although there have been others. Each year they send a man around to buy us out. They don't have a price big enough to get me to sell. Don't know about some of the others."

Traci leaned forward. "Let me get this straight. Snowden tries to buy out the smaller owners each year?"

"Of course. That's what I just said. So far only one family sold, and that's because the original owners died and their children who live, I think in Georgia, didn't want to hold on to their shares.

Wish they had told me. I would have paid more just to spite Snowden."

Pursing her lips, Traci jotted notes on her pad. "So it may simply be a matter of time before Snowden owns controlling interest in Live Oak."

"Probably. People die. Corporations don't." Mrs. Bergstrom smirked. "At least not the ones I'd like to see die."

"So, if you don't mind my asking, what did Snowden do to you that has made you so bitter toward them?"

Mrs. Bergstrom glanced at her plate and then back at Traci. "They're heartless bastards. There was a man on my doorstep the day after I put my Herb in the ground. Never a word of condolence. Implied that a woman wouldn't be welcomed on the board of directors."

"But you are."

"Damn right. The only one so far. And I'm not a milktoast about it, either."

Traci beamed. "I'm sure you're not, Mrs. Bergstrom."

Beckoning the waiter for more coffee, Traci went over her notes. "Tell me, Mrs. Bergstrom, do you think the equestrian center is valued by the local community?"

"I know what you're thinking. Public interest. My husband told Bruce McCord that that language was goofy, but the man wouldn't listen. I don't really know the answer to your question. In the beginning, local folks thought it was a grand idea. A lot of locals still rely on the center for boarding and training their horses.

"But this community is changing. New people are coming in. They just want to have a home in the hills. They might spend two to four hours commuting. That doesn't leave much time for horses. I don't know what would happen if the issue ever came to a referendum."

Traci nodded and closed her pad. It was a matter of time. Everything seemed to be a matter of time. How much time would it take before the entire equestrian project unraveled one way or another around the McCords' ears?

"Oh," Traci said, "one more thing. Is there anything else you want to tell me? Something I haven't asked."

"I am a little curious," Mrs. Bergstrom said. "What about Scott McCord's other business?"

"What do you mean?"

"People are whispering about troubles out at the ranch with the racehorses. Used to be folks around here thought Scott McCord walked on water when it came to working with horses. Now there's some serious head scratching going on. I hope he can straighten things out quickly. But I guess that's where you come in."

"We're working on it, Mrs. Bergstrom." Traci felt her pulse quicken. "I can pretty much assure you those troubles have nothing to do with a lack of skill on Scott's part."

"You think those ranch problems are tied into the resort?"

"I didn't say that, Mrs. Bergstrom. That would

250

only be speculation at this point."

"You may not be free to speculate, Ms. Steele, but I have no constraints. If someone is out to cause trouble for the McCords, I wouldn't look farther than Snowden."

"Why?"

"They have a lot to gain if the equestrian center no longer existed. No McCord on the board. A free rein for expansion. Profits would skyrocket. And we're doing pretty good already."

"You'd gain along with Snowden."

"Yes, economically. But if Snowden gets majority control of the Oak then the board meetings will be that much harder to stomach. And I don't like the bastards they send in here to tell us what we ought to want and not want. No, profits aside, I'm in McCord's corner. You can count on that. You might tell him that. And when you see Sal, tell her for me not to remain such a stranger. I'd like nothing better than to talk flowers with that woman. She has a green thumb I've always envied."

"I'll do that, Mrs. Bergstrom."

Traci left the diner chock full of nostalgia and headed for her car. Was the equestrian center ultimately doomed to being just another picture on the wall?

Traci stopped at the stable parking lot in order to double check a few more facts with Scott. When she stepped out of the vehicle, she was assaulted by shouts and screams entirely uncharacteristic of the stables.

Scott emerged from the barn on a dead run. "There's been an accident," he shouted. "Get back in the car. I'm driving."

Traci tried to swallow; her skin went clammy. Who? His mother? The twins? What was happening? She wanted answers, but the terror on Scott's face left no room for questions. She dashed around to the passenger side of the car. Scott was already backing up before she closed her door.

In a matter of minutes, they were headed down the narrow road toward Escondido. She couldn't focus on the roadside fence posts flying by like runaway kites before a gale force wind. Checking on her driver, she saw a man familiar with high speed chases down winding, hilly country roads. Oddly, she didn't feel in danger. But Scott looked like he'd come face to face with one of his worst nightmares.

"Scott, I need to know what's happening. Is it one of the family? I have to know." Traci twisted her seatbelt in her hands.

He glanced quickly at her as if he'd been unaware of her presence and then turned his attention back to the road. "No. Sorry, I should've told you immediately. But we've got to get out there fast." He shook his head. "There's been an accident involving the van hauling two horses back to Santa Anita."

"Oh, no." Traci's hand flew to her mouth. "Is everyone... Is anybody hurt?"

"Apparently, the driver has some bruises." Scott

bit his lower lip. Traci watched him fight back tears. "They had to put down the mare; she snapped both front legs in the collision. The gelding fared better."

Traci put a hand on his thigh. "I'm sorry, Scott. That's terrible."

"Yeah. They say things like this happen, but that doesn't make it right."

"How did it happen?"

"Blew the right front tire." He glanced at Traci; his eyes widened with pain. "I checked those tires myself a week ago. They had plenty of tread. They must have hit a sharp object."

"Maybe."

Long minutes passed. The landscape remained a blur to Traci. She couldn't shake the feeling that this wasn't the kind of accident Scott thought it was.

"We should be just about there," Scott said. "It's amazing Dennis could keep the truck from going over the side." He shuddered.

"This must be it," he said as they came up on a long string of backed up traffic. At least half a dozen buzzards circled above the hill. Horns blared at them as he drove up the wrong lane making their way over the rise. The police officer blocking traffic was upset even after Scott identified himself as the owner of the truck, but did direct him to park the car on the side and to proceed to his driver and the investigating officers.

Traci tried to breathe regularly as they

approached the van. A man in a Hawaiian shirt and shorts walked a bay horse up and down the side of the road. She guessed he was a passerby who knew something about horses. Scott stopped briefly to examine the horse and grunt thanks to the man, who nodded in return.

Then they moved closer to the trailer. She could see the large rear end of the mare protruding from the open backdoor. Rigor mortis was already setting in. The stench of death nearly overwhelmed. What had been a lively, proud animal and someone's dream of the big race horse was now simply a carcass growing colder with each passing moment. Traci trembled at the loss and at the precariousness of life and dreams.

She watched Scott approach the animal and go down on his knees. He placed both hands on the mare's rump. He whispered some words, but Traci couldn't make them out. Scott stood with shoulders slumped, shook his head and walked toward the front of the vehicle, where a state trooper was filling out forms and where Dennis Anderson stood. Traci had interviewed Dennis earlier. He'd been laid back and rather comical. Now he appeared shell-shocked.

Looking over the scene, Traci decided Dennis had to be both lucky and very skillful to have jackknifed the truck and trailer across the road rather than plummeting down the steep ravine. It was probably the sudden change in direction that had snapped the mare's legs, but if truck and trailer had gone over the side, they would still be searching for bodies.

As she made her way around to the front of the truck an officer stopped her. "Lady, do you belong here?"

Traci flashed a smile and her ID at Officer Brown. "I know this is not my jurisdiction, Officer Brown, but I've been working with Mr. McCord investigating some difficulties that he's been experiencing of late."

"So." The man folded his arms across his chest.

"So, I'm wondering what you typically do with an accident like this."

"What do you mean?"

"That tire, Officer Brown," she said, pointing to the shredded right front tire. "Do you usually try to determine how the blowout happened?"

The officer shrugged. "Usually, ma'am, it's pretty obvious. The tire wore out. Or it hit a sharp object. I looked at this one already." He bent down and lifted some of the remaining tire. "The tread looks fine. They'll be no fine on the truck owner for driving an unsafe vehicle. That's often the case.

"My guess is the driver hit something sharp. Might have been a pointed stone. Could have been a piece of glass or a nail that worked its way into the core of the tire—although that should have caused a slow leak instead of a blowout."

Traci stared at the shredded remains of the tire wondering if there was enough left to ever tell them what had caused the accident. "A bullet would cause a blowout."

The officer frowned. "No doubt about that,

ma'am."

"Do you check for that?"

"Frankly ma'am, assuming a bullet caused a blowout is not high on my list of possibilities. But you seem to think that might have happened here."

"It's certainly possible, Officer Brown. The shooter could have easily been positioned in that line of trees across the ravine."

The officer looked in the direction she was pointing. He scowled. Traci couldn't determine whether he was suspicious of her or of the possibility that this accident was no accident.

"Do you think there's enough left of this tire for forensics to make a determination?"

"Perhaps. If there's any reason to suspect foul play, we'll definitely send the remains of the tire up for the lab boys to play with it."

"What's the chances of finding the bullet?"

"If there was a bullet, ma'am, I'd say the chances are slim to none. We haven't been treating this as a crime scene. It was an accident scene. Police cars have been in and out, as well as an ambulance, which we didn't need. The wrecker's already begun its work," he said, pointing to the large tow truck that had come up the hill from Escondido. "On top of that, drivers were edging their cars around this scene to get by before we arrived. If there was a bullet, it's likely miles down the road embedded in the treads of someone else's tire."

"But you'll look."

"Of course we'll look, now that there's a reason for suspicion."

"Thanks, Officer, that's all we can ask."

Traci glanced back down the road and recognized a second pickup and horse trailer from the ranch approaching. Once the gelding was loaded and headed back toward the ranch, Traci caught up with Scott.

- o -

Scott leaned against Traci's car staring at the troopers examining the ground. And he waited. But he wasn't waiting for them. He was waiting for the rendering company to come and pick up the mare. He'd dreaded making the call to Edwards, the trainer at Los Al, but he had. His instructions were to dispose of the body and to send him the bill. Edwards had been upset but understanding. And he'd send his own trailer out to the ranch to pick up the gelding.

No more business from Tom Edwards and his owners. But Scott knew that wasn't what was turning his guts inside out. He peered at the mare lying there in the trailer. Bad things happened to horses. That always seemed to be the case. They could step in a gopher hole and break a leg. Get the colic and founder. Cast themselves in a stall and break a leg trying to get up. Eat a poisonous weed and drop dead on the open range. He'd seen it all, but he would never get used to it.

He spent most of his waking hours trying to

keep horses alive. And now more rumors would spread about Scott McCord's negligence. *Doesn't the man even know enough to keep good rubber on his trucks and trailers?*

Scott slid to the ground and leaned against the Grand Am. He put his head between his knees. He knew the tread was good on those tires. But that wasn't what would hit the local papers.

Groggily he became aware of Traci's long fingers massaging his stiff neck and shoulders. He welcomed her presence. He welcomed her touch. But what was she making of all of this? He'd heard bits and piece of her conversation with the trooper. Did she really believe someone wanted to discredit him bad enough to risk killing a horse or even a person?

It made no sense. He felt so numb. He'd sent Dennis back to the ranch with the other pickup. The wrecker would haul this rig into Escondido. He'd worry about that later. Now he wanted to be anywhere but here. Yet he felt obligated to wait on the rendering truck.

Scott tried not to think. Her fingers rubbing his back helped some, and he appreciated her silence.

At last the rendering truck had come and gone and they'd started the drive back up the canyon. Scott had asked Traci to wait in the car while he helped take care of the mare. He noticed she hadn't complained about being excluded.

As they entered Buteo, Traci asked, "Are you hungry?" He shook his head. Food had no appeal to him at all.

"Why don't you come up to my place? Let me get you a drink. You don't look like you're ready to go back to the ranch."

"Okay." How could the woman read his mind so easily? The ranch was the last place he wanted to be. Not true. That would be better than standing there beside the road watching flies fighting for space on a dead horse. He wasn't ready to face his family. He was letting them down.

- o -

They sat on the floor, each of them holding a beer, each lost in thought. Traci warmed remembering the last time they'd been on this floor. Those memories were delicious, but not tonight. Scott needed her tonight, but not in that way.

He looked haggard and drained. She wasn't sure what to do. Running a finger over the hand resting on his knee, she asked, "Do you want to talk about it? It might help."

He shrugged.

"That horse was very important to you."

"She was a living being," he mumbled. "Majestic. Proud. Vibrant. And then I got my hands on her, and look at her now."

"So you're responsible for the mare's death?"

"I can't duck the responsibility."

"But it was either an accident, or someone deliberately shot that tire."

259

"In any case, I failed to protect her."

"That's bullshit!" Traci pulled back, surprised at her own anger. "I'm sorry, Scott, but I'm not going to let you wallow around in self-imposed guilt."

He glared at her. "What do you know about guilt?" he demanded. "I was *born* guilty."

Traci frowned, but didn't say a word, afraid she would stop the man from grieving.

"My brother was the first born and therefore inherited the right to manage the ranch. My birthright was the stable, but it wasn't enough, in my judgment. Dad knew how I felt about it. But the McCord philanthropic legacy was my responsibility. Not to accept that mantle was to reject my father and everything he stood for."

Scott brought the beer to his lips and swallowed. His eyes were fixed on the blank television screen. She knew he tried his best to ignore looking at her. But he was wrong; she knew about shame.

"I ran away when I was twelve." He stopped speaking.

"Where did you go?" she prompted.

"To Uncle Harry. When Dad got me back he nearly skinned me alive. Ma tried to get me to tell them why I ran, but I wouldn't talk. So life went on. I almost didn't come home from college. I'd planned on getting my degree and moving on. And then Dad got sick during my senior year. So I came back to the ranch. He wasn't overly thrilled that I completed my degree by taking some

260

additional courses at San Diego State. But it was something I started and something I had to finish."

"So what did your mother or your father say when you said you wanted a different kind of life?"

"I never told them."

"You have trouble asking for things for yourself, McCord." She ignored his glare. "Why don't you ask?"

"Shouldn't have to ask," he mumbled.

"Not everyone is good at mind reading."

"The horses meet my needs just fine. They don't ask you to do the impossible. And they reward you for being there."

"And they cause you a huge amount of grief when something goes wrong with them. Or when they die."

Scotts eyes clouded over with tears. "Yeah," he managed to say before sobbing. She moved to him and he rested his head on her shoulder. Traci could feel his body shaking against hers. She rubbed his back and brushed her lips against his neck. In the recent past, those lips had carried a message of erotic passion. Now they were sending unspoken words of compassion. Her cowboy was in pain, and she wanted to help it go away.

Her eyelids flung wide. When had he become her cowboy? A wisp of a smile formed on her lips. At least for the moment, he was her cowboy. She'd deal with the ramifications of that thought later.

They clung to each other for several minutes. His sobbing ceased and he still held her. When had he last cried in front of another human being? He couldn't remember a time. He'd always done his crying in a horse stall or astride a horse racing the wind.

This was a very special woman holding him. He'd begun to figure that out, but he knew that now without a doubt. With her, he didn't always have to be the strong one. With her, the possibilities seemed limitless. And yet so limited. Sometimes it was too easy to forget that she was a big city lawyer. Sometimes he just wanted to forget. But he wouldn't stay in that place. Not tonight.

He backed out of her arms and smiled weakly. "Thanks," he whispered. "You're something else. I didn't cry like that at my dad's funeral."

"Maybe I have a talent for making grown men cry."

"I don't know if it's a talent, but it does feel like an anvil has been lifted off my back." He looked sharply at her. "You really think someone shot that tire and caused the accident."

"That's the most logical explanation, given what has been happening, and given that the truck had perfectly fine tread."

Scott shook his head. "It's hard to believe anyone could do that. They could have killed Dennis."

"Yes, they could have," she replied. "Obviously, it wasn't the intent, or they would have shot him instead of the tire, but then it would be clear to everyone this was no accident."

"The bastards," he shouted. "What do they want? Why me? Why now?"

Traci placed her hands on his fists. "I don't know the answer to those questions. Not yet. But I expect we're getting closer, and that's why the stakes are rising."

- o -

Traci wrapped him in her arms. She held him tight, willing him relief. A half hour later, her eyelids popped open. Scott was snoring softly with his head pillowed on her breasts. She smiled. Her newly discovered breasts had become quite nurturing.

Carefully, she moved him so he was prone. She collected a blanket and a pillow from the bedroom and covered him where he lay. He was exhausted — probably both by the events of the day and by the events of the past.

Traci curled up next to her cowboy and held him. She wouldn't press herself to analyze her sense of satisfaction.

Chapter Thirteen

Familiar scents, exotic scents assaulted his nostrils. Without opening his eyes, Scott stretched stiff muscles and then settled back to savor those early morning smells: coffee, bacon, eggs, toast, lavender soap, and a female scent that filled the void. His taste buds ached for the coffee whose aroma carried a pungent nutmeg scent peculiar to the kind Traci made. His stomach growled its impatience responding to the bacon, eggs and toast. The lavender soap told him she'd already showered and was ready for her day.

Slowly Scott cranked an eye open. His lips turned up in a smile. That female scent sat directly across from where he lay. She was reading a novel and her robe had fallen away, displaying plenty of thigh, with a leg bouncing to an unheard beat.

His entire body warmed when she raised her eyes, saw him watching her, and matched his smile with one of her own. "Good morning, sleepyhead," she said. "I was about to wake you. Breakfast is made. Can I bring you some coffee?"

Scott sat up and ran his fingers through his thick dark hair. "You're a fantastic picture to wake up to." He appreciated her immediate blush. "Why don't you pour me a cup and I'll go wash up?"

He glanced at the clock and scowled. "I haven't

slept this late in a long time. No need to rush now. Ellen has the horses fed and is probably preparing for the morning trail ride. Never thought you were a sedative, Traci."

She smiled brightly. "I just lull men into my web and put them to sleep. It's not surprising you slept so long. Yesterday was a terribly exhausting experience."

Scott stiffened at the images of the dead mare flashing before his eyes. He headed toward the bathroom.

Five minutes later he pulled out a chair at the table and sat down to share the breakfast Traci had prepared. She stared at him with an unreadable look before reaching for her fork. Scott was struck by the intimacy that hung between them. He'd had his share of women, but he couldn't remember one who had made breakfast for him. Or maybe he'd just forgotten. He didn't expect he had enough time left in his life to forget this breakfast or the woman who had cooked it.

There existed an unmistakable warmth between the two of them. It seemed almost sacred, like being swallowed up by the stars hanging low over the mountains on a crisp night, or when a newborn foal was able after much effort to stand on wobbly legs, or when he'd held Traci in his arms on the sailboat after she'd shared her story.

Did she feel it? He watched her sip her coffee. He thought she did. Confusion danced in her eyes. Longing and fear fused to form a mood he hadn't witnessed before. She looked at him steadily, chewed on her lower lip and then looked away as if she couldn't quite describe what was happening either. Maybe that explained the silence.

- o -

Traci wiped her fingers on a napkin in an attempt to calm her nerves. She should've dressed before he awakened. Why hadn't she? This was far too intimate. It was like she'd made breakfast for her man and they now sat there eating it, neither one quite sure what to say, afraid to say anything that would burst the bubble surrounding them. Why was sharing breakfast with Mustache so romantic?

Maybe because this act foreshadowed a possible future even more than his suckling her breasts. Traci felt her cheeks warm, but she couldn't shake the thought and didn't really want to yet. Was it her domestic instincts taking over? She'd always felt those were rather underdeveloped.

The future. She repressed a tremble. The future had an end date. Four weeks from today she would be flying back to Chicago, leaving this luxurious resort and all its warmth behind. She eyed McCord trying to fathom what he was thinking. It was impossible. Neither one of them had intimated any kind of future beyond the end date. That was the end game and the end of the game.

Unwanted and inexplicable tears threatened; she contained them by yawning and pretending to rub sleep from her eyes. Traci sighed. She was a woman of reality, not fantasy.

"So," she said, smiling at Scott's sudden flinch. Had he been experiencing anything similar, or was he just trying to sort out who might have taken a shot at the pickup hauling his horses?

"So. Where do we go from here?"

His seductive smile warned her to be more specific.

"When will you ship some more horses to a track?"

"Oh, that," he replied, continuing to smile as if he enjoyed her distress. "Three will go out tomorrow morning for Santa Anita."

"Really." Traci sat up straight. "I want to follow that trailer. I wanted to do that anyway. Now it's a must."

Scott furrowed his brow, casting a skeptical look. "That could be dangerous."

"I doubt anyone will be foolish enough to shoot at your truck or trailer again. Unless they can actually find evidence that the tire was shot out, yesterday will still be written up as an accident. Two in three days would raise law enforcement suspicions to mount a full investigation." She shook her head and rose to refill their coffee cups. "I don't think the mob or anybody else will want to attract that much attention."

"You're probably right." Scott stood and followed Traci into the kitchen. "But you won't go without me."

Traci stared at the man. His face was contorted

with concern and demand. She decided not to challenge his command. Besides, she liked having him drive those damn twisting roads. "All right. What time do we leave?"

"Horses will be loaded and ready about six o'clock."

"Doesn't anything happen late on a horse ranch?"

"Not much. Unless a guy gets hung over and beds down at his woman's condo."

Feeling her cheeks burning, Traci said, "Do you believe your family thinks we were..."

Scott chuckled. "It doesn't matter what my family thinks. You and I aren't kids, Traci. We're both a heck of a lot closer to forty than twenty. If we want to sleep together, they aren't going to complain. Hell, Ma is probably pulling weeds in her garden hoping that I'll finally produce some grandchildren."

Traci pressed her backside against the counter. With her mouth wide open, she was unable to locate her voice.

Scott held up his hand. "Now, don't get me wrong. That's not what I'm after. Just don't worry about Ma. She'll be much more disappointed when you go back to Chicago than over the fact that we're spending time together."

Still speechless, Traci nodded.

"Thanks for breakfast." He paused and placed a hand on each of her shoulders. "Thank you for being there yesterday and last night. What you said, what you did, means a lot to me."

Scott leaned into Traci and pressed his lips lightly against hers. She responded without hesitation. He backed away and said, "Later."

Traci nodded again with her throat constricted and watched him open the door and close it softly behind him. She didn't move from the kitchen counter. She let trapped air escape through her lips. This network of relationships was getting more jumbled than she'd ever imagined. Grandchildren?

Later. Her heart warmed at the way his lips had formed that single word. It had been a word of promise. Expectation made her skin hum and nipples swell. While a reservoir of fear still resided deep within her body, hope was beginning to work its will. The power of fear was eroding in the face of hope.

Dead ends. Traci hated dead ends. The only good thing about them was setting them aside and moving on. But they inevitably managed to waste a lot of time and energy.

She and Scott stood by her Grand Am in the Santa Anita parking lot. Following the horse trailer from the ranch had proven to be uneventful. There were no shots. No one approached the horses when the driver stopped at the rest area. And the horses arrived seemingly as healthy as when they left the ranch. It had been a slow trip. She'd shuddered when they passed the site of the accident and wondered again how the driver had managed to keep from going over into the ravine. Scott had tensed then, too, and said very little throughout the remainder of the drive.

Her interview that afternoon with Susan Larson had generated no new information. Susan had been on vacation when two of the incidents occurred. And she appeared too much in love with horses to purposely cause them harm. Like Ellen Zastrow, the woman was getting on with her life and eager to keep her past relegated to the past. Traci hoped she'd allayed the woman's fears. Her secrets were safe with Traci.

Now they waited. Scott slumped against the hood of the car and she stood beside him staring at the parking lot entrance. "Are you sure he'll show?"

"He'll come." Scott shrugged. "Harry's never been known for his promptness. He said three o'clock. I'd say three fifteen or three thirty."

"Is tardiness a family trait?"

Scott frowned at Traci. "I hadn't noticed. Am I often late?"

Traci shook her head. "No, I suppose not. You just don't show up at board meetings, and you neglect to tell me things you think I should find out on my own."

"Oh that." Nonplused, Scott chided, "You sure do have a long memory, Counselor." He nodded toward a faded green pickup turning into the entrance. "Barrows is here."

A smile crossed Traci's lips as she took in the sight and sounds of Sal's brother's arrival. Calling the vehicle a rust bucket would have been kind. It

271

sloped to the right. When had anyone checked its shocks? The noisy tail pipe was attached to the frame with a coat hanger. And the pickup belched twice when Harry Barrows turned the engine off.

"Good afternoon," Harry said, not getting out of the truck. He nodded at Traci. There was a twinkle in the man's eyes that she hadn't noticed the first time they'd met.

"See you still have your friend, son. You're going to damage your image if you keep showing up with the same woman all the time."

Ah, now Traci understood the twinkle. Sort of. What kind of image did Scott have at the track?

Scott ignored the old man's comments. "How you doing, Harry? Sounded like you might have some news."

Harry spat a stream of tobacco juice three feet from where Traci stood. She tried not to jump. He nodded at her and grinned. This was one man she would never figure out. One moment he talked as if she wasn't there, and the next he seemed to flirt with her in the way of old men.

"Heard you had a bad time of it a couple days ago."

All of Traci's senses went on alert.

"You could say that," Scott said, with an edge creeping into his voice.

"Sorry about the horse. Someone is being very stupid. Killing a racehorse is not a way to win friends at a track."

"Is there talk?"

Barrows grimaced. "There's always talk at a

track. You know that. What's interesting is that no one can point to an owner or a trainer gaining from what's been happening." Barrows coughed. "I've talked very confidentially with a steward here. We even went over betting records on races where horses ran poorly or were scratched prior to the race. Nothing seems out of the ordinary. Longshots weren't all of a sudden winning.

"There's a growing feeling that you're the target, Scott. Somebody is trying to bring you down. I've had more than a couple trainers come and tell me they weren't sending you anymore horses until this all settles down. They want you to know it's nothing personal."

"So you're the messenger."

"It's easier for them this way. They don't want to get caught up in your troubles."

Scott sighed deeply. "No, I can understand that. So, is that all you've got?"

Barrows glanced at Traci and narrowed his eyes before responding. "Just that finding something on this end may be more difficult than on your end. Whoever is behind all of this has to have sources of information that tell them when you're shipping horses."

Scott's shoulders sagged. "Yeah, I know. Traci's been interviewing everyone. So far nothing's turned up."

"I must admit I'm curious," Barrows said, addressing Traci. "I've heard tell you've talked to a lot of folks here and at Los Al and it sounds like you've done the same back in Buteo. So why is someone after dunderhead?"

Traci shifted her weight from foot to foot. "It's only a hunch," she said, hoping she could trust the man. She remembered Sal and decided to take the risk.

Barrows leaned out the pickup window and grinned a toothy smile. "You're talking to one of the best hunch bettors around, ma'am. So what do you think?"

"That someone is trying to damage Scott's reputation in order to get control of the Live Oak stable and close it down so they can build more condos."

Barrows whistled lowly. "So you don't think the reason behind all of this is the track, either."

"No, I don't."

Looking at Scott, Barrows waited.

Scott scowled and threw up his hands. "I don't know. I thought she was way off base at first. Now, I don't know. Maybe. But why attack me by hurting my racehorses, if the stable is the objective?"

Barrows squinted. "You got to admit it served as a useful diversion. And I bet eyebrows are being raised in Buteo about how well you're managing your horses. People don't like to be associated with fallen heroes."

Traci wanted to ask what the man meant, but Barrows started up the noisy engine and in the midst of backfiring exhaust eased down the parking lot toward the exit before she had the chance.

"What was all that about?" she asked of McCord as he ducked into the driver's seat of the Grand Am to drive to their hotel.

Looking thoroughly disgusted, Scott growled, "Who knows what that old man means?"

"He certainly seems to think the community of Buteo sees you as some kind of hero."

"Okay, you got your teeth into something so you won't let go until someone tells."

Traci wasn't put off by his sarcasm. "You're absolutely right. So what are you trying not to tell me now?"

Scott sighed and slowed down to the speed limit, nearly causing a wreck. "It wasn't much, and it happened years ago. Not many remember anymore, I'm sure. Hardly matters."

"So try me. Bore me with the facts, cowboy."

"I pulled a girl out of a burning car when we were in high school."

"Wow."

"It was prom night. Several of us drove in a caravan from the high school gym to the restaurant where the post prom party was to be held. It had been raining, so the road was still wet. The guy in front of me took a sharp turn too fast.

"He was thrown from the vehicle on impact and died instantly. His date had sense enough to wear a seat belt. All of it happened right in front of me. I scrambled to the passenger side of the car, then broke the window to help pull Nancy Freeholt from the car.

"The back seat was burning. We didn't get fifty feet from the car before it blew. We were both singed and pretty shaken, but that was about all. Nancy had some cuts and bruises from the crash, but not even a broken bone. Everyone thought it was miraculous she survived."

"You *were* a hero."

"I didn't do anything anybody else wouldn't have done. Hard to think of yourself as a hero when you see one of your best buddies, mangled and dead on the ground."

"But the town treated you like a hero."

"Yeah, it was pretty embarrassing for a while. My dad didn't let them forget, either. Thank goodness I left for college about five months later. Uncle Harry shouldn't have brought it up. Nobody remembers that stuff anymore."

"Does Nancy still live in the area?"

"Yeah."

"Somebody remembers."

Scott glanced at Traci. "But it has no bearing on the situation we're looking at."

Resting her chin on a hand, Traci said, "Probably not. But there are people who get excited about a hero or heroine, place them on a pedestal and then harbor a nagging hope that the person will fall, making it clear the hero is no better than anyone else."

"I'm not any better. Wasn't then. Nor now."

"Of course you weren't, but some likely thought you were."

Scott shrugged his shoulders. "Maybe. So what

are you getting at?"

"I'm not sure," Traci admitted. "I know from interviewing your employees and people in the community that you are a highly respected horseman. You come from a prominent area family. You are or have been regarded by some as a community hero.

"There must be some envy out there, Scott. I expect Snowden is planting seeds to fuel that envy and make people wonder about whether the local hero has clay feet. And maybe some might clap their hands with glee to discover that he does."

Turning into the hotel parking lot, Scott shook his head, "You sure do come up with some farfetched scenarios. Is that what they teach you in law school?"

Traci paused with her hand on the car door before responding. "You look at a horse from all angles before buying it, right?"

"Of course."

She gave him a satisfied smile. "I'm trained to look at a case from all angles before considering it closed."

Looking defeated, Scott nodded, "Okay, you win. I'm not up for trying to match wits with you tonight. My stomach is off and my head is splitting. I'm going to go take a nap."

"Should I wake you for dinner?" asked Traci, trying to mask her disappointment.

"No, you go ahead. I may catch up with you later. If not, I'll see you at breakfast."

Traci ordered dinner through room service and spent most of the evening curled up with a novel. Finally, she got ready for bed. She'd stayed up later than usual thinking, expecting, hoping that Scott would come by. He never showed.

Had she offended him by pressing about that hero business? Or maybe he was finally coming to his senses about her. Had he lied about loving her breasts? No, Scott wouldn't lie to her. He might not volunteer all the truth, but he wouldn't lie.

So much had happened in the past several days. Was it still less than a week since they'd gone sailing? He hadn't held her in that way since Tuesday night. She'd given him many comforting hugs around the accident, but that was different. Her skin warmed and chilled. She wanted to feel his lips and mustache on her skin. She wanted to feel his tongue swirling around her nipple. God, she wanted him to suckle her like he had before. And he'd never even knocked on her door.

Traci was so angry she could scream. It was a good thing Mustache wasn't there right then. She'd probably say something she'd regret later. She'd carve him up like those turkeys he so detested. Traci punched up her pillows before climbing into bed. By morning, she'd be in control of herself again. She dreaded the hours in between and hoped sleep wouldn't take forever to overtake her wakefulness.

Feeling lower than a coward, Scott tried to rest. He'd ordered up room service and drunk more liquor than he intended, but at least he stayed put, as if he were in jail.

For the umpteenth time he pondered why his uncle felt it necessary to mention that hero stuff. It only served to dredge up horrifying memories, and it made Traci Steele think more of him than she should. A hero would have stopped his buddy from driving drunk. He hadn't told Traci that they'd all stopped for drinks at Nancy's house before leaving for the restaurant on that fateful prom night. He never could forgive himself for not demanding that Adam and Nancy ride with him and his date. He had at least been wise enough to nurse a beer or two. Adam had chased his beers with whiskey.

So what if he had clay feet? Everyone did.

Was he trying to be a hero again by avoiding Traci? He couldn't trust himself with her. She wasn't ready for what he needed. And at least tonight, he was too near the edge to touch her lips or feel her passion when nibbling her breasts without wanting more; much more.

Maybe it was the accident with the mare getting killed. Maybe it was his uncle bringing up things best forgotten. Maybe it was her body displayed in a hugging tank top and short skirt. Maybe it was his own fears of where they were headed. He wanted her. That was true even when he first saw her step out of that red Grand Am. But now he wanted much more of her, and that was scaring the hell out of him.

He rolled over on his stomach imagining her beneath him. Quickly he rolled back. His life was complicated enough without getting hung up over a woman.

Particularly a woman who lived two thousand miles away. Particularly a woman named Traci Steele.

- o -

The following morning neither Traci nor Scott broached the kinds of thoughts they'd had the evening before. There was little conversation, and most of it was chatter about the weather, the Cubs' chances in the coming baseball season, and the qualities of a good wine versus a good beer.

Traci studied the changing landscape as they retraced their way up the foothills. Spring in Chicago was usually a drawn out drab affair. Here, spring was exploding. Flowers of all shapes and sizes bloomed in broad variety of reds, yellows, purples, and oranges. The cornucopia of hues boggled her mind.

Glancing upward, Traci smiled. Sunlight reflected off a red-tailed hawk soaring on the wind as if it were free to explore the entire universe. While she'd never been very mystical, she wondered about the import of seeing the hawk. At that moment the bird banked and swooped low across the road in front of the car. Traci gasped.

"How beautiful," she whispered. "It's like magic, the way that hawk glides and maneuvers."

Scott glanced at Traci and grinned. "The red-tailed hawk is fairly common around here, but it's unusual to have one swoop down and greet us like that. Many cultures regard the hawk as a messenger from the holy."

Traci frowned. "Do you believe that?"

Shrugging his shoulders, Scott turned on to the ranch road. "I don't believe or doubt. If an animal like a horse, whose instinct it is to flee from humans, allows a human to get on his back and ride away, then anything is possible."

"We really do ask a lot of a horse, don't we?"

"Oh, yeah. It's said by some that appearance of the red-tailed hawk is a call to be open to new ways. It may look beautiful, Traci, but that hawk that just passed in front of us is a fierce bird and kills in a matter of seconds."

"And yet it's so graceful."

"Yes, it may be reminding us that balance is important. Some say the red-tail awakens one's kundalini associated with the base chakra, which is red and is the seat of passion."

"I didn't know that," Traci whispered. "I have a friend in Chicago who's into the chakras, kundalini and all that energy stuff. But she never said anything about the red-tailed hawk."

Scott chuckled. "There probably aren't a lot of them flying around Chicago."

"No, I imagine not. We're more famous for

pigeons. So McCord, how do you know all of this stuff? That sounds pretty far out for a cowboy."

"Really? Maybe. I guess it probably is. But I read a fair amount about native mythologies. First Nation. Celtic. African. Russian. Myan. They interest me. My degree is in sociology, but I particularly liked cultural anthropology."

"But why? It's so...fanciful."

"Maybe because I spend most of my time with animals and out in nature. It's a real world out there. Birthing. Living. Dying. Can we learn from that world? Is there intention from that world? I don't know. But I am willing to remain open — or at least I try."

"The message of the hawk?"

"Right." Scott turned the Grand Am down the ranch driveway. "I don't know if they have feelings, but did you know that red-tailed hawks mate for life?"

A sudden chill swept over Traci. All the conversation about kundalini and hawks and intention scrambled her brain, but mating for life was a concrete experience that she couldn't misunderstand. Because she couldn't think of anything clever to say, she remained silent.

And she knew one more thing: Scott McCord was much more complex than she'd ever imagined. Her pulse quickened as she played back the image of that red-tailed hawk swooping across and tipping its wings in front of them.

A messenger? She doubted that. But could she remain open to new possibilities?

Later that afternoon, Traci stooped over Ransom's left hoof picking out dirt and stones. What would her girlfriends think if they could see her now?

"You're gonna tip him over if you keep raising his leg like that," Susannah said.

"Oh my goodness," Traci said, lowering Ransom's foot. "I must have wandered. I didn't even hear you guys come up."

"Grandma says if you let your mind wander when you're working with horses, you'll wind up sitting on your ass faster than you can spit."

"Susannah," Rebecca scolded.

"Well, it's what she says."

"In any case," said Traci, untying Ransom, "it's good advice. And it is something I have to continue to work on. Sometimes my mind wants to go in twenty directions at once."

"That's how it is with me at school," Susannah said. "But the teacher doesn't understand when I try to explain."

"No, I suppose not. Let's put this guy in his pasture." Traci opened the gate. "So do you like school?"

"I don't."

"I do."

Traci smiled as she removed the halter from Ransom. She didn't have to guess which twin said what. "So what do you want to be when you grow up?"

Without any hesitation, Susannah piped, "I

want to be an NFR barrel racer."

James, who had just walked up behind his daughters, beamed with pride. "And there's no doubt that she'll be one of the best. She's already the best barrel racer in her age group in this part of California."

"Yes, I've seen you practice before. You do ride like the wind." Traci brushed a hand across the girl's blonde hair. "It would be great to see you compete before I leave. And what about you Rebecca—what do you want to be when you grow up?"

"A lawyer."

"Oh my, really?" Traci responded, noting the dark scowl on James's face.

"Yes, I want to help put the bad people in jail."

Traci smiled. "Well, sometimes we can be more helpful than simply putting them in jail, but I understand what you mean."

"So when did this come about, young lady?" James challenged. "Have you been hanging around Ms. Steele too long? I've never heard you talking about wanting to be a lawyer."

Rebecca turned and faced her father. "No one ever asked me." She shrugged and rubbed the toe of one foot over the other. "I've always wanted to be a lawyer since second grade, when the principal kept me after school because I wouldn't come down from my favorite tree when the teacher said to. Recess wasn't over. It wasn't fair. Lawyers help keep things fair."

"Well, I never." James looked at Traci, and she

284

saw rage and fear.

Without taking his eyes off Traci, James said, "Girls, you run along now and wash up for dinner. I have to talk with Ms. Steele for a minute, and then we'll be right along."

"Okay," both girls said before darting toward the house.

Traci sighed. Was he only upset because his daughter wanted to be a lawyer? He was on her interview list, but she dreaded bringing that up.

"This isn't the time or place," James began, "but we need to talk."

"Of course," she said evenly. "Where and when? Do you want to come to the condo?"

"No." James shook his head. "That won't do. There's a park about two miles north of Live Oak."

"Yeah, I've walked there and back."

"Good. I've got to go down to the city tomorrow. I'll be back mid-day on Tuesday. Why don't we meet about four thirty that afternoon? If you walk, that might be better."

"Sure," Traci said without hesitation. "I can do that."

"See you then." James spun on his heel and stalked away.

The man was on the brink. He clearly had so many emotions bottled up inside it was a wonder he didn't have a heart attack. Her stomach curled. Her worst fears were about to come true. She'd found the source of information about shipping horses from the ranch to the tracks. There'd been plenty of circumstantial evidence, but she'd have a confession by Tuesday evening. Why didn't that elate her? She only felt dread.

And now she had to eat dinner with a family that didn't know how close their world was to blowing up around them.

Chapter Fourteen

Traci checked her watch again, picking her way along the path behind the resort.

Time had dragged these past two days. She'd talked with two more Live Oak investors; they'd given her essentially the same story Mrs. Bergstrom had. Neither of them was fond of Snowden management and each praised Scott McCord, but each also took the opportunity to attempt to get information from her about what was happening at the ranch. Rumors were flying.

She'd spent as much time as possible doing laps in the pool, and had finished her laundry early that morning. But no matter how much busy stuff she managed to do a part of her mind stayed focused on the upcoming meeting with James McCord.

While she didn't like the strain in her relationship with Scott, it had at least been easy to avoid him. He was the last person she wanted to see before talking with his brother.

Traci entered the park and walked along a wide path used by walkers as well as horseback riders. Oak trees and eucalyptus lined both sides. A small creek trickled on her right.

As she rounded a bend in the trail, she saw James McCord sitting on a picnic table. She'd never doubted he would be there. It was ironic, given his distaste for lawyers, that she might be one of his last hopes.

He was dressed for ranch work with his broad western hat, blue work shirt, Levis, and scuffed up boots. She guessed he'd parked in the lot at the second entrance a quarter mile farther up the path. That was a fair distance for a cowboy to walk. But then, he clearly desired privacy.

"Good afternoon, James," she said, coming to a stop in front of him.

He nodded, making no move to get up. He just sat on the picnic table with his long legs draped over the side, staring at the ground. At last, he rubbed a hand over his thigh and looked up. "Ah hell, guess you probably know why I asked you to meet me here."

The pain in his eyes ripped at her. "I can guess."

"I'm the one you've been looking for." He sighed deeply and looked for a long time at one of the gigantic live oaks before continuing. "I'm the one informing them when horses are leaving the ranch for the track."

"Them?"

James's eyes glazed over. "Don't really know. I leave a message on an answering machine. I never talk to anyone."

"But somebody had to ask you to do this." Traci ran her fingers through her hair. "This is tied into your gambling debt, isn't it?"

James's eyebrows arched. "Figured you'd know about that too, but hoped you didn't." He swiveled about on the picnic table, checking his surroundings before proceeding. "Yeah. I got a call from a guy with no name telling me if I would call the answering machine number the day before Scott was to ship horses to a track, I would be doing someone an important favor."

Traci nodded. "They didn't say why they wanted the information?"

"Nope. And it wasn't until I looked at my loan account with the casino that I realized how significant the information was."

"How much were you paid?"

"It varied some between five and fifteen thousand a call."

Traci whistled softly. "That was enough to get your attention, and to keep you quiet."

"I only owe thirty thousand now. And I haven't been in a casino or played a round of blackjack for over two years."

"It's hard for me to say congratulations, given your betrayal of your brother."

James jumped to his feet and glared at Traci. She recoiled. They were alone. She'd be safe with James if she didn't send him over the edge. She softened her tone. "I know you had to be in a bind to do that. Why don't you tell me about it?"

"A bind. That's a nice way to put it. A hundred and fifty-thousand dollars worth of bind. I could hardly find enough extra money in the ranch accounts to keep up with the interest. That money doesn't come cheap."

"I'm sure it doesn't. How did you get in their

clutches in the first place?"

"Stupidity." He slammed a fist into the table. "I couldn't quit. Too proud to admit I lost. I knew the next hand would put me in the black. My luck would change if I just hung in there long enough. Stupidity."

"Your family doesn't know?"

"Of course not. My dad told me before I married to always have a private checking account tucked away for emergencies."

Traci blinked and gasped. "You mean your father had such an account."

"Sure. Don't look at me that way. I have no idea how he used it. After he died, I went to the bank and nosed around, and sure enough, there it was. It was held jointly in my name. There was more than fifty thousand in it."

"That was your initial gambling stake."

"Yeah, thought I could triple it or quadruple it and have the start up money for the dude ranch and maybe set up something for the girls' college. Ma wasn't about to fork over any money to help with the dude ranch idea."

"No, I suppose not. So then you started borrowing from the casinos?"

"Yeah, I'd get them paid off and then borrow some more. Until I couldn't pay them off anymore."

"So providing information about the horses turned out to be a way of paying off your debt."

"Yeah."

"Did it ever occur to you that someone was

290

trying to destroy your brother's reputation in order to gain control of the Live Oak equestrian center?"

"Only in the last month or so—probably about the time you started snooping around. I hadn't given it a lot of thought before then. Scott never said much about the horses having problems on the other end."

"And when you did figure it out, what did you think?"

James sneered. "At first, I thought this might work out better than I thought. The debt would be paid off, and Scott wouldn't have to baby sit at the stable anymore but could come back home and help set up the dude ranch. He's much better working with the public than I am."

"So what changed your mind? Why are you telling me all of this now?"

"Sooner or later you would've gotten around to me. But the clincher was..." James bent over and grabbed his knees. After taking several deep breaths, he continued. "The clincher was when the mare was killed in the accident last week. I can't have anything to do with that. I help bring these animals into the world. I don't kill them."

He paused and closed his hands into fists. "Good God, Dennis could have been killed."

"So you didn't leave a message about the horses being transported to Santa Anita on Saturday?"

"No, I didn't. Don't know how long it will be before they learn I'm no longer cooperating." James's hands trembled slightly before he stuffed them into his pockets.

Traci looked up at the robin's egg blue sky and saw a bird soaring high above. She knew it was a hawk. Was it a red-tailed? She placed her hands on her lower back and stretched.

What to do with James? And it wasn't just James. It was also his girls, Penny, his mother, and his brother. Traci shuddered. How would they react to James's treachery?

"So what happens now, Ms. Prosecutor? Do they hang me from the highest tree?"

"I'm sure that won't happen. I'm more concerned about your family."

James's eyes clouded with tears before he looked away.

Traci folded her arms across her mid-section. She was about to break every boundary she'd ever placed between herself and a client—but this wasn't really her case. She'd come out originally to help a friend resolve a problem. Resolution wasn't clear, but at least this part was in focus. James was at serious risk, and time was short. Traci pulled out her checkbook.

"What are you doing?" James asked, backing away from her and into the table.

"I'm writing you a personal check for forty thousand dollars, Mr. McCord." She watched his mouth fall open and his jaw muscles working.

"I can't take your money!" He pulled himself up to his full height.

"No you can't, but you will." Her words were softly spoken, but contained a hard edge. "Why?

Three words: Penny, Susannah and Rebecca."

Sobs racked James body. Traci let him cry it out. She didn't want to touch him. She wasn't entirely convinced she wanted to help him, but there was no question she wanted to help his girls. And they didn't need to know what their daddy had done out of greed and fear.

Traci picked up a small stone and laid it on top of the check she'd placed on the picnic table. "Don't try depositing this until tomorrow afternoon. I'll have to move some money around tonight." She snorted. "Don't think this is a gift."

"I didn't," James managed to say in a strained voice. "I'll pay you back."

"Damn right you will, with ten percent interest." Traci paused and gave James a half smile. "I think you're worth the investment. I know your kids are."

"But why? How can I thank you enough?"

"Those girls deserve more than having to write letters to their father in prison. I expect you to pay a lot of attention—loving attention—to them. You support them and their dreams, whatever they might be." Traci watched him flinch and nod in agreement.

"And let's just say that I've got the money and you need it. You'll pay it back. Either because you want to. Or because you'll be too embarrassed if you don't. Or because you know what I know about you and your private account. One more thing. After I'm paid off, I expect you to close that damn account."

James nodded. "You really don't need a rich husband, do you?"

Traci looked at him and laughed. Her eyebrows arched in comprehension. "You mean you thought I was after Scott for his money."

James shrugged, looking sheepish.

"No, I don't need a man for his money. I don't need a man at all, really. I may want one someday, but I sure as hell don't need one."

Breathing deeply, Traci tried to calm herself. It wouldn't do any good taking her anger out on James when much of it needed to be directed at his brother.

Certainly, he didn't believe she was after his money! "Scott will have to be told about this."

James looked sharply at her.

"Not about the loan, but about what you did."

"I'll tell him."

"See that you do it today. I'll try to avoid him until tomorrow, but I won't keep this from him."

"That's it?"

"For now, it is. As I learn more, I may be back to you with further questions, and I expect full cooperation."

"You'll get it. You can trust me."

"I hope so. For both our sakes." Traci turned her back on Scott's older brother and retraced her steps back down the path. After a few minutes, she broke into a jog. She wanted to sweat. She needed to sweat. Maybe then she could get the distaste of what James had done out of her system.

Nearing the resort, Traci broke into a smile

294

remembering her conversation with the twins the day before. Rebecca wanted to be a lawyer because she wanted to help people make things fair. Maybe that was what she hoped for now—a fair resolution.

But from whose perspective?

- o -

Scott McCord sat on an embedded boulder on a hillside absently tossing pebbles. Cattle grazed the valley below along a stream that meandered, slowly shaping its surroundings as it went. The air was still, even where he sat. He heard the deep chatter of a pair of ravens, but he didn't attempt to locate them. The reddish sun was already lowering toward the horizon. It had felt more like a summer day than the first of March. He smiled grimly. March had certainly come in roaring like a lion.

He stared at his brother, who stood with his back to Scott facing the valley and the ranch buildings far off in the distance. Scott shook his head and threw a pebble as far as he could. Nothing he did could get rid of the bile threatening to suffocate him. He'd hoped his Judas wasn't a friend. He choked. No, it wasn't a friend; it was just his brother.

How could he? Scott repeatedly scuffed his heel on the boulder, scraping off a protective thin layer of rock. What to do? What next? His skin chilled. What would Traci want to do to his brother?

James was still his brother. And then there were the girls, Penny, his ma. "Goddammit," he muttered.

Feeling more numb than anything else, Scott said, "I'm sorry, James, but I don't really have a plan. I need some time to sort all of this out."

Reluctantly, James turned and faced his brother. "I understand. I appreciate you not telling Ma or Penny. They don't need this shit."

"Wish you had thought of that a few years ago."

"Right."

"Did Traci say anything about you being charged or prosecuted?"

Scott watched his brother blanch before answering. "I don't think so. Looks like she's more interested in protecting the girls than anything—and getting to the bottom of all this."

"Really? That's not the way she plays the game." Scott's heart fractured as he thought of the price Traci must be paying in all of this if she wasn't going to push anyone to press charges against his brother.

"She made it clear she wasn't letting me off the hook because of me." James folded his arms across his chest. "That doesn't mean she won't come after me yet."

"I imagine we've got to get the remainder of your debt paid off right away, or you'll really be in trouble." His brother's flushed cheeks raised his curiosity. "I assume there's still more to be paid."

Glancing away, James mumbled, "It's being taken care of."

"Like the rest of it was taken care of." Scott's voice rose.

"No. Nothing illegal." James pursed his lips. "I got a legitimate loan."

"From who?"

"You don't need to know that."

"Like hell, I don't. You've made a number of terrible decisions because of money. If we're going to have any chance of continuing to work together, I need to know who is helping you pay off your casino debt."

James turned his back on Scott.

Scott scowled. "Who have you been talking to?" he asked. A sharp pain shot through his brain as the truth struck him. "Holy shit. How much did she give you?"

"She didn't give me anything," James shot back, whirling on his brother. "It's a loan with interest."

"How much?"

"Forty thousand."

"So she just wrote you a check for forty thousand dollars. And you took it. Why didn't you come to me?" Scott paused. "No, I imagine if you could've come to me, you would've done so a lot earlier."

"Coming to you would have been an admission of failure. It would've been like going to Dad and saying I didn't live up to his expectations. Besides, she had me over a barrel. It seemed the best way out." James removed his Stetson and banged it against his thigh. "She's not going to be happy about this. She didn't want you to know about the check."

"I'll bet she didn't."

"Anyway, she knows it'll be paid back. I got too much to lose if it isn't."

"Sounds like she's got you by the short hairs."

"You could say that."

"One thing I can guarantee you is that woman can be tenacious. If you try and scam her, you'll wish you were just dealing with the mob."

A wisp of a smile crossed, James's lips. "You may be right about that. At least we know she's not after your money."

Scott tensed and then relaxed; he didn't want to knock his brother on his sorry ass, although for that remark he probably should. Instead he said, "Not everyone is driven by money and greed. There's still one more thing I want to know."

"What's that?"

Scott ignored his brother's defensiveness. "Did you really think I'd be happy running a dude ranch?"

"Sure. If you're happy babysitting resort guests, why not do a dude ranch?"

Nodding, Scott sighed heavily and replied, "I think you'd better leave now. There's a lot to sort out. You need to know this, James—I won't tell Ma, but if she ever asks I won't lie for you."

James nodded and walked over to his waiting horse.

With his thoughts in a jumble, Scott watched his brother make his way down the hillside to the valley floor. Why wasn't he angrier? He was

298

overwhelmed by sadness. But he wanted to be angry. How could he continue working with his brother? And why had Traci stepped in to bail out James? Didn't she know he'd find out?

Scott shook his head. He wanted to be angry at Traci Steele for interfering, but he couldn't even do that. He was amazed she seemed uninterested in pressing charges against James—and then the loan!

He tossed another pebble at a nearby tree. What was he going to do with her? He thought of her voluptuous breasts. Oh, he knew what he wanted to do with her.

But there was more to it than that. Much more.

"Shit," he grumbled. She'd be leaving in three weeks. His stomach knotted. Why did that terrify him even more than his brother's betrayal?

He stood and stretched. "Well Counselor, by foolishly making my brother a loan, you have tied yourself to the McCord family for a number of years. What will you do if I want to make that a stronger bond? Will you try to run?"

Scott laughed, suddenly remembering the girls' birthday card. He wondered if that lariat was strong enough to hold Traci Steele.

"Patience," he cautioned himself. "Go slowly."

Walking to his horse, Scott grinned. Maybe there was something to that old belief that something good came out of the darkest moments. His head was clear. And his sights were focused on Traci Steele.

Not just on her body, and not just as a

temporary conquest in a game. No. The game had definitely changed. It had changed before this evening, but he didn't know quite when. Maybe at the accident scene. Maybe at the breakfast table the morning after the mare was killed.

He placed a foot in the stirrup and mounted his horse. As he guided the gelding down the hillside, he grinned again. It was a brand new game he and Traci would play, and there would be no losers, only winners.

- o -

Traci stepped out of the shower and heard her door buzzer ringing. Annoyed, she grabbed a robe off the bed. There wasn't time to dry her hair. Whoever was at the door must be leaning on the damn buzzer.

Peeking through the peephole, Traci frowned, yet wasn't surprised to see Mustache standing on the other side of the door. Didn't the man own a watch?

She opened the door.

"Is it too late to come by?" Scott asked, stepping into the foyer.

"No," Traci said, unsure of what he wanted. Had he come seeking the expertise of a private investigator, or the comfort of a woman? She smiled wanly, not certain what she wanted him to seek. "I guess it's never too late for you, cowboy. I thought ranchers got up early and went to bed early."

Removing his hat, Scott replied, "Most days that'd be true, but this isn't most days."

"So James talked to you."

"Earlier this evening. I've been doing a lot of thinking since."

Traci watched the tall man fumble with his words.

"I needed to talk with you, Traci. Is that okay? I know things got a little out of whack this past weekend, but I need..." He looked at her as if seeing her disheveled state at last. "You must have been getting ready for bed." He put his hat back on. "I can come back in the morning."

"Nonsense," Traci said, reaching for his arm. "Would you like a drink? A beer?"

"No, but I'll have a glass of wine with you." He grinned broadly.

Traci's eyebrows arched. "McCord, I didn't think you liked wine."

"Never said that. You never asked. I actually consider myself to be fairly knowledgeable about California wines. Don't know anything about the foreign stuff, though."

With hands on hips in mock distress, Traci chastised, "Why do you keep doing this to me, McCord? Every time I think I know something about you, you keep changing."

"Thought you tall leggy sophisticated types were only interested in mysterious men."

"Right. Why don't you pour the wine while I go blow dry my hair? You'll find an open bottle of Gossamer Bay Sauvignon Blanc that I just uncorked last night."

"Ah, good choice, Traci. The butterfly wine; one of my favorites," Scott said to Traci's back as she headed for the bedroom.

She turned with a pensive look. "Yes, they have a colorful logo to match the quality of their wines. You do know your wines."

"California wines," he corrected, searching for glasses.

"Upper right hand cupboard," she said, disappearing into the bedroom.

She lifted her hair with a brush and let the blow dryer do the rest. Why was Scott McCord so hidden? There were so many little things about him that just kept popping up. Traci scowled at her image. Had she been any more forthcoming with him?

"Damn," she complained when her neck started to burn from the hairdryer. Annoyed at herself, she switched sides. And why did he decide to share his little secrets when he did? Did it really matter that he knew something about wine? It made him less cowboy and more like her. And that was a problem?

"You're going to set your hair on fire if you take much longer."

She flicked the dryer off and ran a brush through her hair. It should bother her — a lot — that a man leaned nonchalantly against her bathroom doorway as if he was a fixture. But it didn't. She wondered if he knew she was naked under her robe.

302

She wrapped her fingers around the stem of the wineglass he offered. "Do you always make yourself at home?"

"Only when the hostess runs away and hides."

"I wasn't hiding." She tried to give him her best pout. "I was just thinking."

Scott stepped back to let her enter the bedroom. "This is pure luxury," he said, his gaze sweeping from the king sized bed to the wall of mirrored closet doors, to the two large easy chairs and a second fireplace. "I never had a tour of these units before," he added, sitting down on one of the chairs.

Why did it thrill her to know that he hadn't been with another woman in one of these bedrooms? She sat in the other cushioned chair, pulling her robe tight around her body.

"So tell me about James," she said, wanting, needing something to divert her mind and body from the large mustache that sat too comfortably close to her.

"Can't say I was shocked, but I was certainly disappointed." He sipped his wine. "So why aren't you after me to press charges?"

Traci closed her eyes briefly. "He's only the messenger man. We're after a lot more than that. You and he, himself, will probably punish him more than the system ever would."

He gave her a quizzical smile. She let out a small sigh before continuing. "Ah hell, the girls don't deserve to have their father dragged through the courts and the local paper."

"Figured it was something like that. They have the ability to kind of wrap your heart up in strings."

Traci shrugged. "They're pretty good at that, I suppose."

"Does that explain the loan too?"

"That bastard!" She shook her head. "He wasn't supposed to tell you."

"I'm a pretty good interrogator when I need to be."

"That you are, cowboy."

"So what did you hope to achieve by loaning James the money?"

"Something had to be done quickly to clear his debt with the casino. He'd already stopped making the calls. He wasn't going to turn to you. He would've had to go to another loan shark. That would've been a mistake."

"Another one. He says you've got him fairly hemmed in regarding payback."

Traci chuckled. "I hope he thinks that. I want my money back."

Scott leaned closer and narrowed his eyes. "Sounded like there was more to it than that."

Angry she couldn't keep the tears from welling in her eyes, Traci blurted out, "I told him to spend quality time with his daughters and to support their dreams, whatever they might be."

"Ah, that sounds more like my girl." Scott moved to kneel beside her chair and ran his hand gently up and down her arm. "We all had fathers who were quite practiced at ignoring us."

Tears flowed down Traci's cheeks. She nodded in agreement and tucked her feet under her body. "They deserve more. Both of them. They shouldn't have to wait until their thirties to follow their hearts. Ah, hell." She stared at Scott. She hated blubbering. Traci leaned over and reached for the box of tissues sitting on the dresser and her robe fell away, exposing a breast.

"Damn." She grabbed the box and sat back down. His hand rested on top of hers before she had a chance to cover up.

"Don't," he said. "Remember, I love your breasts. I think we both could use a little loving tonight. I know that breast could."

Traci giggled at his blurred image. She wiped away tears and blew her nose. Her words were muffled from emotion. "So now my breasts speak to you. You really are a mystic." She made no effort to stop his hand from cupping her breast.

She watched him stare deep into her eyes seeking permission. If he looked much longer he'd touch her soul. She nodded. "Expect you're right, cowboy. I need to be held and kissed. And I can't think of anyone I'd rather have hold me and kiss me than you."

"I certainly hope you can't." He reached for her empty glass and set it aside, then took her hands and pulled her up. She went willingly into his embrace. Her lips found his and nibbled on his mustache.

"Ouch," he said. "You're one dangerous lady."

She grinned and darted her tongue into his

open mouth. He turned her gently. Traci felt the bed against the back of her legs. She caught her breath. Her eyes flared wide.

"Don't be alarmed," he whispered. "I need to see all of you. I want to kiss all of you. We won't do anything you don't agree to."

Traci laid her head on his shoulder. She knew her heart was pounding so loud the room should be vibrating. It pleased her to notice his heart pounding against her breast. She wanted to do this for him. For them. She knew she could trust Scott. But could she trust herself?

She pulled away from their embrace. "Okay," she murmured. With shaking hands, she untied the robe and it fell away from her shoulders into a heap at her feet.

The catch in his breathing, his beaming smile and his admiring eyes made her toes curl. He was pleased. Scott McCord didn't have to say a word. He found her pleasing. He wanted her.

"You're...gorgeous," he stuttered. "My God, you're even better than my fantasies."

Even standing there stark naked, Traci couldn't pass that up. "You've been dreaming about me, McCord?"

"More than I would like to admit. You're something else, Traci." He stood as if glued in place.

Traci couldn't figure out what to do with her hands. There were no pockets, so she reached them out to Scott. "I thought you said something about more kissing. Or are you just going to stand there and gawk?"

"Not at all," he said. Holding one of her hands tightly, Scott pulled back the bedcovers. "My lady," he said, giving her a bow. "Your bed is ready."

Fear tried to creep out of the recesses of her mind, but it was hushed away when she stared into Scott's eyes. He would not hurt her. She willed herself to relax.

When his lips circumscribed much of a breast she did just that. Closing her eyes, Traci reveled again in the warmth of his mouth. Would she ever get enough of his suckling?

He brushed the other nipple between thumb and finger and she mounted those stairs that would lead her to ecstasy. His lips and tongue ceased moving. "No," she cried out. "Don't stop. Not now." She felt his smile on her breast and then those suckling motions resumed. Pulling his head tight, Traci stepped off into the universe. This one was sweet, not as earth shaking as the one she remembered before, but soft, and lovely.

When she returned, she realized Scott was no longer on her breast, but lay resting his head on her abdomen. She ran her fingers through his hair. Boldly, she whispered, "I want to feel you skin against mine."

His questioning look elicited no more response. Scott stood and removed his shirt, pants and socks. He left on his under-shorts, apparently trying not to alarm her with his nakedness. Though she was more than a little curious, she was grateful for his concern.

He lay beside her and cuddled her to his body. They played, but it wasn't child's play: it was erotic play. He held one of her breasts and rubbed its nipple against his. She raised her other breast and did the same to his other nipple.

"I didn't know men's nipples grew erect like women's do," she whispered.

Amusement flickered across his face. As he rose to his knees, she could see the clear outline of his arousal. She tensed. Then she watched his fingers trace her body as if he was finger painting: from her breasts, along her midsection, thighs, legs, and ankles. She closed her eyes; her muscles turned to mush. When he paused, she moaned softly both thanking him and encouraging more exploration.

When he finished, she opened her eyes and stared into his. They were soft and filled with passion. She could not articulate a syllable, yet she was aware her eyes must mirror his passion.

Without speaking, he brushed his lips across hers. His tongue felt electric as it moved lower. Not fully understanding what he was doing, she realized that it was her center that drew him like a powerful magnet. She felt it pulse, seeking, reaching for something inexplicable.

He laved her belly button.

"That tickles," she moaned, arching her back.

He moved lower and then kissed his way down a thigh; his mustache teased. She shuddered. He stopped. She couldn't understand her own disappointment.

Somehow, even with her eyes closed tight, she could sense him grinning that lazy cowboy smile of his. His lips grazed her inner thigh and he moved upward. Had she spread her legs wide purposefully? Or had they done so on their own volition? No matter, she wanted more.

Traci nearly screamed. Was the man trying to torture her? Good God, she couldn't believe she wanted him there. But she did.

His tongue neared that magnetic force she could no longer control. He paused. She knew he was monitoring her response as if she were a volcano ready to blow. Maybe she was. Again, she didn't know what to do with her hands. She cupped a breast with one hand and snaked another behind his head and tugged gently.

Was that enough of a signal for him? Oh my God, she felt his breath on her pubic hairs. Involuntarily, she tensed. And there it was. His mouth was on her most private place. For a long moment he just rested there. It was an eternity.

And then, his tongue flicked her straining bud. Traci gasped, raising her buttocks off the bed. He stopped. "Don't go away," she managed to say.

"I'm not going anywhere," he murmured.

His tongue separated her folds and Traci bucked against his mouth until without any more warning, she exploded. Parts of her were scattered to the four directions. She lost track of Scott. She lost track of time. She lost track of herself.

In some far off corner of reality or fantasy, she was aware that Scott sipped her juices. And then his head rested on her abdomen awaiting her return.

Later, much later, Traci's eyelids sprang wide open. She glanced down and smiled. There he was. Mustache was snoring gently. She could feel his breath on her belly.

She didn't want to spoil the moment, but she had to go to the bathroom, and soon. *So this is what it's about,* she said to herself. Could anything be more delicious?

She stretched and then frowned. But that wasn't what it was about. She shuddered. There was more. Much more. He'd want more. He'd need more. Was there a chance that she could handle all of it?

You'll never know until you try, she heard an inner voice cry. But she didn't want to risk losing what they had — no, she corrected herself: what *she* had.

Traci shook Scott gently. "Come on, sleepyhead. It's well past midnight. Why don't you just roll over and sleep here tonight?"

"Okay," he mumbled.

When Traci returned from the bathroom, she crawled under her covers and didn't quite know what to do with a man sleeping in her bed. It was king-sized. There was more than enough room. But that wasn't good enough. Without further thought, she lay on her side and backed into his arms, which closed tightly around her.

She smiled, basking in the warmth of the embrace, and began replaying those earlier sensations. Then she jumped. He was erect. And it wasn't a nipple pressing against her buttocks. She tried to move out of his embrace. But every time she moved, he gripped tighter. At last, she gave up, determined to get some sleep. He couldn't stay erect all night. Could he?

- o -

When he heard her snoring regularly, Scott smiled into her hair. Yes, they were making progress. A lot of progress.

- o -

Early the next morning Traci blinked three times before smiling at the man in her bed, who wore one of those wicked McCord grins. "Hi," she said. "Fancy meeting you here."

"I love watching you when you sleep. So are you ready for the rest of my promise?"

Traci cocked an eyebrow. "What do you mean?"

"I'd said I'd kiss you all over. I missed a few spots last night."

"You are a tease, Scott McCord," Traci said, smiling broadly. And then she stopped talking when he turned her over and started kissing her back. She stretched. "Amazing," she whispered as he ran his lips up and down both sides of her spine. "I never would have thought."

"Sometimes you spend too much time thinking," Scott said, gently pinching her buttocks.

311

That was the last she heard from him for awhile. But she always knew where he was. His lips never left her body. She rolled over easily for him after he'd thoroughly explored her backside. She was pleased and sorry when he again reached his final destination. She wrapped her legs around him, eager to re-experience that exquisite journey, but she knew it would be over too quickly.

Over coffee, orange juice, and toasted bagels, Scott said, "You know, this could be addictive."

"What?"

"Having breakfast with you each morning."

Traci chuckled and felt herself blush. "I don't know about that, but what you did to me last night and this morning might."

"I'm counting on that."

Traci's eyes clouded and she frowned. "So what are you going to do about James?"

Scowling, Scott pointed his fork at her. "You think you ducked one. Maybe for the moment. To answer your question, I don't know. When I think of him, I become numb." Scott placed his hands around his coffee cup. "Things will never be the same again. I'll never trust him like I did before. Maybe I should have listened more to his dreams about a dude ranch."

"Maybe, but I hope you're not blaming yourself. You didn't do anything wrong."

For several seconds, Traci felt his steady burning stare. She couldn't fathom his thoughts.

"Traci, do you listen to your own words? Don't

blame yourself. You didn't do anything wrong."

Traci gasped, looked down at her lap, and fumbled with her napkin. He was right, of course. She hated him for that. She loved him for that. A flash of pain shot from her lower back to her brain. Closing her eyes, Traci tried to maintain her balance, physically and emotionally. What did she know about love? Next to nothing. Would she have the courage to recognize it if it ever happened to her? She hoped so.

She brightened and glanced over at Scott who continued to gaze at her steadily. "I'd like to ride Cory again."

Scott nodded and gave her a half smile. "I think you just ducked another one. It's about time you got up on him again. I'm very booked today. How about tomorrow?"

"That would be fine."

"How about four o'clock or so? I should be getting back from the afternoon trail ride by then."

"I'll be there."

Chapter Fifteen

Later that morning, Traci brought her Grand Am to a stop by the phone booth near the post office. Earlier she'd received another of those cryptic, breezy calls from Roberta. Whoever was listening in on her phone conversations must have thought her friend was the classic airhead.

As she walked to the booth, Traci grinned. Roberta was anything but an airhead, and she owed the woman a huge favor for doing all of this extra work.

Roberta picked up on the second ring. "Hi," Traci said. "Whatcha got?"

"Hi, Trace. Sorry I haven't been quicker, but I've had to put in very long days at the office. They even had us work last Saturday because of some report deadline for the mayor. Whoopee. Anyway, I've got something good this time."

Traci held her breath and then urged, "Tell me."

"The Snowden treasurer uses his own name, probably because he has to, but the president, vice-president and secretary use aliases. In fact, each has a half dozen or so names, so it's taken time to cross-check and verify what I'm about to tell you."

"So tell me, for God's sakes."

"Now, don't get your back up. I'm into high

drama."

Traci sighed exasperation. "How could I forget?"

"Good. Anyhow, the horses that have done poorly for whatever reason are horses owned by those Snowden corporate officers."

"No shit!"

"Yeah, we ran a check on the owners of horses that have gone through McCord's operation who experience no apparent negative side effects. Those were different folks entirely."

"So it was a set up."

"I'm sure of that."

"But why?"

"I've had the information longer than you." Roberta paused. "Try this on. If these guys were to do something screwy to somebody else's horses, they run the risk eventually of someone calling in the track cops, the horse cops, or whatever they call them at racetracks. This way they kept their troubles in the family, so to speak, and they really weren't troubles anyway except for McCord."

"And for the horses."

"Exactly."

"Thanks, Roberta. This is great." Traci scribbled on her note pad. "We're closing in on them. But we still don't have much to take to any local authorities other than cruelty to animals, and we can't even prove that yet."

"That may be extremely difficult," Roberta replied. "We'd have to catch someone in the act."

"That doesn't seem very likely. Keep combing

our leads on the resort. Something much bigger than the horses is going on here. Pay close attention to the tennis complex cash flow."

"Will do."

"These guys are into something more than harming the careers of some low to mid range claimers."

"Appears like you'd better get back here pretty soon, woman. You're starting to sound like them."

Traci frowned. "Like who?"

"Like those cowboys who like their horses fast, their whiskey straight, and their women a little on the wild side," Roberta drawled.

Traci didn't respond.

"So how is your love life? Is that cowboy proving to be a good ride?"

"Roberta!"

"I know. I know. You don't like being teased about men. Someday you gotta slow down enough to make time for a man, Steele. It happens to the best of us. Look at me! I'll stay in touch. Bye."

Traci hung up the phone and leaned her forehead against the phone booth. Would Roberta ever slow down to the speed of a normal fast paced person? Yes, the woman seemed happily married, although sometimes, like now, Traci pitied the man who had to wake up to that chatter every morning. And yes, Roberta was a dear friend and colleague, but one of the woman's most annoying pastimes was fantasizing about her friends' sex life. If a man so much as looked at

Traci or bought her a drink, Roberta had them in bed doing more things that she'd ever imagined possible.

Lifting her head and glancing around, Traci blushed. Not until lately, that was. Recently her imagination had slipped into overdrive. She shivered. God, she loved the feel of his mustache as it roamed over her skin...everywhere...

Traci saw Scott standing outside the corral with Cory saddled beside him as she walked across the stable parking lot toward them. His broad smile showed he appreciated the view.

She met his smile with one of her own. "Hi," she said.

"Looks like you're ready."

"I'm ready. Are you?"

Traci hesitated, trying to bluff her way through his meaningful stare. "I'm ready to ride this guy. I think I remember about mounting him." She was blushing wildly by the time she pulled the cinch strap tight. Why did the English language have so many alternative meanings?

"Go ahead," Scott instructed. "It's been awhile. I'll steady you."

She appreciated the support, but Traci wondered if he helped all the women mount by splaying his fingers across their butts.

"Let's concentrate on what we're doing here," she mumbled, leaning over to pat Cory's neck.

"Good idea." Scott took the halter rope and led Cory into the corral. "Remember, a soft seat and soft hands can work wonders."

Traci burst out laughing and glanced down at McCord. He wasn't smiling. "I'm sorry," she said. "It's just that it's hard to stay focused when the words you use can...can apply to more than one thing."

"Are we getting you a little hot, Counselor?" He smiled. "That's good, but not what I meant this time. Use that advice now, and maybe we can tuck it away and revisit it later in a more private context."

Traci nodded, closed her eyes and tried to imagine walking and trotting Cory correctly. *Soft hands. Soft seat. Don't cling to him or grab on to him like I tried doing before I fell off. Don't go there,* she warned herself. *Soft hands. Soft seat.*

"Okay," she murmured, opening her eyes. "I'm ready."

"Good. Begin with the walk."

She walked Cory clockwise and then counterclockwise.

"You're doing real fine, Traci. Nice hands. Nice seat. Are you ready to try the slow trot?"

She glanced quickly at him and nodded, surprised by her own confidence.

"When you're ready, shift your seat a little forward, give him a little more rein, and tell him what you want. And don't forget to breathe."

Traci smiled. Breathing was often the most difficult part. She did as Scott instructed and Cory moved out in a rhythmic gait. It was a slow trot. It felt natural. The sitting trot, at this slow pace, was easy.

After several minutes of taking Cory back and forth between the slow trot and the walk, she brought the horse to a halt before Scott. His smile warmed her heart, but not as much as knowing that she'd conquered a long standing fear. But there was one more thing she wanted to prove to herself before she dismounted.

"You're doing great, Cory. Do you think you're ready to do a fast trot for me?"

Scott scowled. She flashed him a pleading look of determination. "Are you sure?" he asked.

"Yes, I'm sure. It's terribly important. You've helped me a lot, Scott, but I have to do this. You can't sit in the saddle for me."

"I wish I could."

"I know. So what's your advice?"

"Start with the slow trot, and when you are relaxed, squeeze him with your knees and maybe cluck at him. He'll get the message. But Traci, as soon as he responds, you have to relax your seat and your hands. Trust Cory's movements to prompt your body's movement. Remember to stay fairly straight but not rigid. Relax."

"A hell of a lot to remember."

"Yeah, I know. Once you start moving with him, don't even think about what I've said, just move with the horse."

"Right." Traci knew if she listened to any more advice her muscles were certain to lock up. "Here we go."

Did her outer smile match her inner smile? She'd transitioned from the slow trot to the fast trot. Cory didn't hesitate. Briefly her thoughts jumbled, and then she succeeded in turning off her mind and she rode by feel.

She shifted her seat back slightly and asked Cory to walk. Traci was thrilled at the gelding's response. He never missed a cue, and apparently neither did she.

Stopping in front of Scott, Traci dismounted and her legs nearly gave out. Scott grabbed her and laughed. "That was fantastic, Traci. But you'd better give your legs a minute or two." He reached for her and drew her into his arms. He removed his hat and kissed her.

Gleefully, she returned his kiss, then stepped back and glanced around to see if anyone was watching. Cory snorted.

"It's okay," Scott said, "but you should know I don't kiss just any student who rides well."

"I should hope not," Traci retorted.

Traci watched Scott unsaddle Cory. "Roberta told me an important piece of the puzzle this morning."

Scott threw a stirrup over the saddle and turned to face Traci. "Really. And you're just now telling me?"

Shrugging, Traci said, "I wanted to stay focused on riding."

"All right. So what's up?"

"Each of the horses with a problem at the track is listed as owned by one of the many aliases used by the Snowden president, vice-president, or secretary."

Traci watched Scott for any sign of reaction, but he simply pulled the saddle off Cory and started carrying it toward the tack room. He was mulling this new information over. There was no question that Snowden was directly involved. He hadn't wanted to accept her hypothesis — now there was no choice.

Scott re-emerged from the barn to retrieve Cory. He looked at Traci, but said nothing. She followed him into the barn. It wasn't until after he'd taken the bridle off and turned Cory loose in his stall that he spoke. "I guess that just about nails it. You were right all along. It's Snowden behind all of this." He waved his arm to include the entire equestrian center.

"Looks like."

After hanging up the bridle, Scott offered, "Come on into the office, the coffee is on.

"So what now?" he asked, a few minutes later, leaning back in his desk chair.

"Roberta and I are still digging. We don't have enough to go to anyone in authority yet. We know what's happening, and we think we know why. But that doesn't mean we can prove it."

"A tire shot out. Horses coming up lame. Horses not able to compete." Scott shook his head and reached for his coffee.

"Facts, Scott. Those are facts, and the links are circumstantial at best." Traci stood and stretched

322

aching muscles. She'd have to ride more often. Her Jacuzzi would be a welcome respite. But she had to deal with McCord first.

"I expect we'll find something yet about the resort itself that's goofy. These guys don't want to expand just because they're into meeting middle and upper middle class America's need to experience California sunshine. Something else is going on here, and we're going to find out what it is."

Scott grinned. "You've really got your teeth in this one, don't you, Counselor?"

Turning her head sideways, stretching a neck muscle, Traci responded, "I play to win, remember. I put the bad guys behind bars; that's what I do for a living."

"And you seem to enjoy doing that." Scott steepled his fingers and peered at her through narrow eyes. "But not James."

Traci winced. It was maddening that Scott McCord was so good at finding her soft spots. "No, not James."

"Though that bothers you. That you got close enough to the family that it matters."

"Family should matter more to him," she blurted out.

"No doubt." Scott turned silent.

"And what about you, McCord? How are you doing with all of this? Seems like nearly everyone you trusted for a good number of years is turning against you." Traci folded her arms tight across her chest. She didn't like her own accusatory tone.

Why did she need to hit him over the head with those betrayals?

"It hurts, if you want to know the truth." Scott set up straight. "Of course, you probably don't understand, because you don't let yourself trust enough to risk being hurt."

Traci felt herself wither under his cutting words. Was he right? He was so adept at finding the chinks in her armor. She tried to breathe, tried to find words as hurtful.

And then he was up gathering her in his arms. "I'm sorry," he whispered into her hair. "I was angry at what you said and retaliated without thinking. I know you're working hard on trust. With Ransom. With Cory. With me."

Traci felt his hands gently massaging her lower back.

"Maybe we should recognize that both of us are hurting and doing the best we can to move on." He leaned back, looked at her and pecked her nose. "Can we go back to about five minutes ago and start over?"

Sniffling, Traci nodded. "You left one thing out. I'm working hard to trust *myself*."

Again, Scott hugged her close. Her fingernails dug into his shoulders, but he didn't complain.

"You were great with Cory earlier," he whispered. "We're chasing those demons, yours and mine. We'll get there."

"I hope so."

"I know so."

Traci nodded, wishing she could believe. She

didn't even recognize who she was any more. One minute she could be her old self—the competent, no-holds-barred lawyer—and the next minute she was an unraveling emotional ball of yarn. And she didn't like being a yoyo. She wanted her old self back. Her eyes popped wide open. Did she really?

Saturday morning had been mellow, thank goodness. Traci sat on the top rail of the corral watching Susannah take her mare around the barrels. The past week had made for raw nerves—pleasurable and painful. It was good to do nothing but be present for the girls. Rebecca sat at her side offering a running commentary on what Susannah was doing right and when she didn't adequately prepare her horse for making a tight turn. Mostly, Rebecca had words of praise, but as she pointed out, there was always room for improvement.

Traci glanced at the ten-year-old sitting beside her and wondered if she'd been as serious herself at ten. She supposed she was. Looking back on it, she wished there had been more room for play. At least Rebecca had a keen sense of playfulness to go along with her sometimes overdeveloped seriousness.

Traci heard Scott hollering her name and turned to see him running toward the corral. So much for a mellow morning. Scott McCord didn't run anywhere unless there was big trouble.

"We've got to get to the Oak stable quick," he shouted.

"What is it? What's wrong?" she asked when

they met and walked with lengthening strides toward his pickup.

"Ellen called. She thinks someone tried to poison the Arabians."

"Oh my God," Traci responded. "That would be a disaster."

"That's a fact. Thirty dead expensive Arabians, and the resulting headlines would be enough to close the place down for sure."

Ellen Zastrow waited for them at the barn entrance. She looked as white as a clown's face and she was trembling so hard that Scott took her in his arms and held her for a few moments before speaking.

"If it wasn't for the old mare, I would have fed that hay to all the horses," she mumbled. She stepped out of Scott's arms and looked at Traci, her eyes filled with apology.

Traci shook her head slightly. She doubted Scott had even noticed that exchange. Traci hadn't experienced any jealousy when he moved to comfort Ellen. Yet the young woman was aware of that possibility. Traci wondered how many people knew about her and Scott.

"So tell me what happened," Scott said, leading the way to the Arabian barn.

"Sheba sniffed the hay and turned her back on it. At first, I thought something was wrong with the mare. So I went in the stall to see. When I laid my hands on her nose, she started throwing her head around and backed into a corner. Twice I approached her and she did the same thing."

They had come to Sheba's stall and Traci peered in at an old horse who looked so docile she doubted the animal could get excited about much of anything.

"So how did you suspect the feed?" Scott asked, examining the hay across the alleyway.

"I'd been around spoiled feed several years ago and had a horse react sort of like Sheba. Refusing to eat. And not responding to me. So I went and washed my hands. When I re-entered the stall, Sheba came over and accepted a carrot like nothing was wrong."

"I'll be damned. Thank God you were here and knew what you were doing. I don't know if I would have suspected anything more than a colicky horse."

Traci watched in alarm as Scott brought some hay to his mouth. He chewed and spit.

"Something's wrong with the hay, all right. It's not the same. We'll have it tested to find out for sure. In the meantime, I'll bring out a load of new hay from the ranch and take this stuff out and burn it. Security will be in place before the day is over." Scott removed his hat and brushed his hand against his beading forehead. He looked at Ellen and then at Traci. "This shit has got to stop."

Both women nodded. She must be getting closer than she thought. The direct attack on the stable indicated that somebody was getting desperate. Why?

"So why don't you call in the cops, Scott? Someone is trying to destroy us."

Traci saw Sally McCord's neck muscles tighten. This was a woman used to getting her own way. Traci couldn't tell if she was more angry or frightened. She'd guess the former.

Hesitating, Scott glanced at Traci before answering his mother. They stood on the edge of the flower garden where they'd found his mother puttering. Scott had felt a need to inform her of the assault on the stable. Traci wasn't so sure she would have said anything yet.

"If we did that, the effect might be just as bad as if they had succeeded in poisoning the horses."

"What do you mean?"

"Their investigation wouldn't remain confidential. Word of the attempt would be in the paper. How many people do you think would want to stable their horses with us then?"

Sal nodded, laying her shovel down. "You're probably right. I hadn't thought about that. I'm going to get some of my lemonade. Either of you want any?"

Scott declined, but Traci accepted. Whatever was in the lemonade might steady her nerves.

"So, Traci Steele from Chicago," Mrs. McCord said, handing Traci a full glass, "when are you going to nail those bastards to the wall? This has gone about as far as it better go."

Traci took a sip of lemonade and smiled. "Soon, I think. Whoever is behind all of this wouldn't be so bold if they didn't think we were closing in on them."

"Harrumph, you better be right." Sally McCord's eyelids narrowed. "And you'd better be careful, young woman. You're gonna be as welcome around that resort as a skunk at a lawn party."

"I've got to take that load of hay out and burn it and then take another load into the stable," Scott said, looking at Traci. "You want to come along?"

"She'll stay and help me in the garden. She's had enough of sleuthing for one day," Sal said, handing Traci a trowel.

Without comment, Traci took the trowel. She wished she could wipe that smile off of Scott's face. She'd have to deal with him later.

She and Sally McCord worked side by side for nearly an hour without many words being spoken other than the older woman telling where to dig and where not to.

Traci had to admit it did feel good digging in the soil. Maybe it was the sandbox she'd never had as a kid. But no matter how much she might be enjoying herself, Sally McCord had more on her mind than weeds.

"Sometimes we don't like to see things that are obvious."

Startled, Traci paused and looked at Scott's mother. "I'm sorry, what did you say?"

"I said, we don't like to see some things that are right before our eyes."

Traci hesitated. "Yes, I suppose you're right."

"No need to look so dumbfounded. I'm not a

stupid old woman to be protected from the truth."

"I never—"

"I know." Sal's shoulders slumped. She remained on her knees with her eyes closed. She looked like a woman in a confessional.

Tears crept down Sal's cheeks. She turned to face Traci directly. "I knew there had to be someone here at the ranch providing information."

"Oh." The back of Traci's gloved hand rose to her mouth.

Sally McCord sighed loudly. "I don't know why he did it. If it was money problems, he could've come to me. But he didn't." She paused. "Was he jealous of his brother?"

Traci froze in place; where was Scott when she needed him?

"We tried to raise both boys to be strong young men with good values. Oh, I know Bruce could be hard on them. He had James's life planned before he was even born. I guess I just tagged along thinking that was okay.

"It's not easy being a wife to a strong willed man. But then I was no wallflower myself. So what made him do it?"

Traci shook her head. "It's not my place to say, Sal. But I am sorry. For you. The girls. Penny. Scott. For everyone, including James."

"Oh, I know you can't tell me. Or won't. That's okay. Maybe James will confide in me yet. But maybe it's too late for that. When you have your own children, Traci, don't ever hesitate to listen to them or love them."

Traci's heart ached. She opened her mouth to speak.

"It's okay," Sally McCord said, placing a hand on Traci's shoulder to pull herself up. "I think I need to go lie down a bit. The doctor's been after me to do that, and I've refused. Guess I should learn to listen a little better."

Tears welled in Traci's eyes as she watched Scott's mother shuffle out the garden gate toward the house. The woman appeared much older.

It was happening. The family was strained to the breaking point.

Chapter Sixteen

"My home phone tapped? They wouldn't dare!"

Traci chuckled. Why did the woman always believe she was invincible?

Leaning against a glass wall of her favorite phone booth, Traci said, "I called you back at home when you gave me the news about linking Snowden officers with ownership of the racehorses. The very next day there is a direct attack on the horses stabled at the resort. Only you, I, and Scott knew about the connections. Somehow they know we're closing in, and the stakes are getting higher by the minute."

"I'll run a check on the phone," Roberta said, her voice turning sober. "It's a hell of a way to start a Monday."

"Maybe it helped. We're forcing their hand."

"Yeah, well just be careful, girl. These folks are serious."

Roberta laughed. "I'm going to have some fun with whoever is listening on my phone. I'll get Isabella from Records to call me. We'll gross their "ears" out with phone sex."

Traci gasped. "What about your husband?"

"He can listen in or join in—but we're going to burn the earphones on that snoop who's listening. He'll never know we're playacting just for him."

"I think I don't want to hear any more about your plans for revenge," Traci said. "Just let me know when you've confirmed the tap. Do you have anything else for me?"

"Not much. Part of the problem is finding time to work on this, but there is skimming going on at the tennis complex. That we can confirm."

"Great!" Traci paused. "So why aren't you jumping up and down?"

"Because it's very small potatoes. Maybe it's a training ground for skimming. I don't know. But there's not enough money to draw much attention from anyone. Sort of like somebody cheating a little bit on taxes. It's wrong, but it would probably result in a slap on the wrist or a modest fine."

Traci shook her head. "There's got to be more. That wouldn't justify this charade with the horses. Keep digging on your end and I'll do the same on this end."

"All right. Wish I could meet that cowboy of yours."

"Scott McCord is not my cowboy."

"No, maybe not. But you never mentioned the possibility that he might be the leak giving information to Snowden."

Traci rolled her eyes and watched traffic go by on Main Street.

Bubbling laughter assaulted her ear. "Bye," Roberta said. "Talk to you later."

Some days it was hard to remember that all the aggravation Roberta delighted in heaping on her was worth it. The woman was an expert at sleuthing records and finding things that others tried to hide.

Driving down the highway toward Live Oak, Traci counted her worries. There was Snowden. She had to be closing in on the answers to that puzzle because of the brazenness of the recent attacks on the horses. There was James McCord. Would he pull himself together enough to stand by his family? His intentions were good; she was less certain about his judgment. There was Sally McCord. Had the woman ever been that forthcoming with her emotions? Sally was agonizing over past decisions. She'd have to learn what she could do and move on.

And then there was Mustache. Traci gripped the steering wheel tighter. He would want more from her; he would need more from her. She blinked and perspiration beaded her forehead. Was she ready? Would she ever be ready?

She pulled off on the side of the road and slammed the gear shift into park. She laid her head on the steering wheel and gulped in more air.

And then what? No matter what happened between the two of them, she would be going back to Chicago soon. There must be a dozen good cases waiting for her. Her muscles sagged. Why didn't that prospect excite her?

Pulling herself together, Traci eased the Grand Am back onto the road. She had to get back to Chicago fairly soon or her sanity would be in danger. It would be best to conclude this Snowden case quickly, maybe spend a few days in the pool and then go home.

Eager to get back into her own space after spending the weekend at the ranch, Traci took the steps to her second floor condo two at a time, aware that none of her worrying and sorting had come up with a solution for Mustache. He was causing more aches in her body and in her heart than she'd known possible.

The moment Traci stepped into the foyer, the hairs on the back of her neck rose. *They've been here again.* Easing her way into the living room area, slowly, but steadily, she scrutinized everything. Nothing appeared out of place. Her ears strained to pick up any noise; only the refrigerator hummed.

The bedroom looked the same as she'd left it. She flipped the bathroom light switch on and screamed. Her hand flew to her mouth. Her eyes rounded. The message on the mirror was printed in larger block red letters:

GET OUT BITCH!
WHILE YOU STILL CAN
NO MORE WARNING

And if that wasn't clear enough, on the countertop lay a cheap child's female doll, naked with its dark-haired head sitting between its legs.

Traci collapsed to her knees. She had to get help. She had to get out of there. Where had she set her purse? On the sofa.

She crawled from the bathroom to the living room trying not to think. Grabbing her cell phone she punched in the stable number.

"Hello."

Tears rolled down Traci's cheeks; even his voice was comforting.

"Hello, who's there?"

"It's me." Traci managed to whisper. "I need you."

"You at the condo?" It was a shouted question.

"Yeah."

"Hold on. I'm on my way."

Traci sank back down on the floor when she heard the click on the phone line. He'd be there soon. She smiled through tears imagining her cowboy running as fast as possible coming to her rescue. She grimaced. It might make a nice movie, but it hurt like hell. Only once before had she felt so helpless.

She shook her head. No, this wasn't the same. It was a gross violation, but it wasn't the same. So why couldn't her mind convince her convulsing body? She might have managed the words on the mirror, but the ravaged, naked doll had unhinged her.

- o -

The door buzzer started ringing and never stopped until she yanked the door open. Scott McCord burst into the doorway and clutched her to his chest and she collapsed against him. He

336

kicked the door shut with his foot.

To him, it felt like long minutes before there was enough space between her sobs that he might consider asking a question. He was much relieved, though. He'd conjured up plenty of bad possibilities as he raced across the parking lots.

At least she wasn't bleeding. The place apparently hadn't been ransacked. But something had clearly terrorized her. And Traci Steele wasn't a woman easily frightened.

"Can you tell me what happened?" he said softly into her hair.

She nodded. She backed away. His gut wrenched at the pain in her wide open eyes. She looked like a child awakening from a terrible nightmare.

"I'll show you," she said.

Her hand felt so small in his. He squeezed hers and followed as she led him to the bedroom. There she stopped and crumpled up on a cushioned chair.

"In the bathroom," she croaked, pointing with a trembling hand.

Two strides and he was in the bathroom. "Son of a bitch." His fists clenched. Who would go to such extreme measures to frighten the woman? He leaned his head against the doorjamb. Of course, they couldn't know what they'd actually done.

The intruder wouldn't know that the abused naked doll would have taken his victim back to a rape scene when she was fifteen years old. Just two minutes alone with the bastard. That was all he wanted. That was all he'd need.

He backed out of the bathroom and knelt by a still ashen Traci. Rubbing his hand lightly over hers, he stared into her vacant eyes. "Traci. Traci." He had her attention. "You're going to be okay."

She nodded, but it wasn't clear she believed him.

"We've got to get you out of here."

Again, she nodded.

"I'm going to throw some things in a bag. We can get the rest later. I'm taking you back to the ranch."

Traci's eyes whipped back and forth. "Can you do one more thing for me first?"

"Sure."

"Clean up the bathroom. I can't come back to that."

"Of course."

After he scrubbed the bathroom mirror and disposed of the doll, Traci seemed to improve considerably. There was life in her eyes again. He couldn't discern if it was rage or pain, but at least it was something. Anything was better than that vacant stare.

"Maybe I should've taken pictures for the police before destroying the evidence. I didn't think," Scott muttered to himself giving the bathroom a final look over.

"No. There won't be any police. I'm not going to risk the local cops coming in and mucking things up. We've just about got them. I can feel it in my gut."

"But this," Scott gestured toward the bathroom, "is personal and goddamn scary. You'll at least consent to stay at the ranch until this is over."

"We'll see," Traci said, giving him a quick smile. "I have to get some distance from this and find my equilibrium. Then we'll see."

"If you come back here, you'll just be baiting a trap," Scott argued. "I won't have it. This is my problem, not yours."

"We'll see." Traci's eyes bored into his. "But you're wrong about one thing. If not before, then certainly now, they've made it my personal problem, too."

Scott grabbed her overnight bag. "I can't reason with you when you get in your detached warrior state." He chuckled grimly and glared at her. "I hadn't thought of you like that before. But it's true. You're as much a warrior as any of those Amazon warriors of ancient cultures and myths."

"Such insight, McCord," Traci admonished, arching an eyebrow. "You really should have been an anthropologist. If you don't mind, I'd like you to continue rescuing me, by getting me the hell out of here."

Scott grinned and brushed his lips across her cheek. "Welcome back, Counselor. I've still got my money on you. Those bad guys don't have a chance."

- o -

"So you don't know where Sal went?" Traci sat at Penny McCord's kitchen table with her hands around a cup of green tea. She'd been surprised there was any tea on the McCord ranch. Penny had said she kept some on hand for medicinal purposes. It had to be more effective than Sal's lemonade.

"No," Penny said, her blond ponytail moving side to side. "She told me she might be gone for the day or for several days. She had things to do."

Traci frowned. "Nothing more, huh? I hope I didn't upset her too much on Saturday. Yesterday, she hardly said a word."

"I don't think there's too much to be concerned about. That woman is as hard as leather."

Sipping her tea, Traci hoped that was the case. The old woman had looked pretty down.

"Is it common for her to go away like this?"

"Nope. I can't remember her going anywhere overnight since Bruce died." Penny rose and poured more coffee into her cup. Sitting back down, she scowled. "You know, she did say something that seemed awfully strange."

"What's that?"

"She asked me what I thought about the dude ranch idea."

"Really? What did you tell her?"

"I said I thought it could work. It would be a working dude ranch. We could build cabins for guests. We could even remodel one of the barns into a mess hall and rec center. Scott could still use one for the horses." Penny hesitated. "What do

340

you think about the dude ranch?"

Traci leaned back and chuckled. "Don't think I know much about it. I remember some movie years back with Billy Crystal about that kind of experience.

"I know which one you mean."

"So if James would be the cook, who would be in charge of the guests seeing that they had a good experience with the cattle?"

"Me. I'd be the head wrangler, unless Scott wanted to do that. The other men work for me as well if not better than they do for James. And he would still be involved on the ranch end of things, just not as much."

"You really think it would fly?"

"Sure. Why not?"

"I am surprised Sal asked about it. She's seemed quite adamant when it came to that subject."

"Most subjects." Penny grinned. "But I think she's mellowing some." Penny glanced down at her hands and then continued. "I think you've been a good influence on Sal."

"Me? Hardly. No one influences that woman."

"Maybe, but you've made her realize that Scott may not be here forever."

Traci felt her cheeks warm. "What do you mean? What has she told you?"

Just then the screen door banged loudly as the twins rushed in from the school bus.

"Hi," they both shouted dashing into the kitchen.

After giving her mother a hug, Susannah looked

at Traci. "Thought you went home this morning. If you stay much longer, you might as well move in."

"Susannah," her mother warned.

"We'd love it if you did move out here," Rebecca said. "That would be great for all of us—especially for Uncle Scott."

Traci slid her tea cup away from her. She knew her nose had to be on fire. She glanced quickly at Penny and realized no help was coming from that corner.

Sometimes in the face of high winds it was best to sail back to a safe harbor.

"It's good to see you two, but I really have to be getting back up to the main house. I have to make several phone calls before people close up shop in the east."

Traci rose and left the room as gracefully as she possibly could before the winsome smiles of three curious females.

Traci stopped pacing back and forth and sat down on the couch. She frowned at Scott, who sat in a wing chair staring at the blaze in the fireplace in his ranch living room. "I may be a little more jumpy than usual," she said at last, "but aren't you a little worried about your mother being gone?"

Glancing over at Traci, Scott shook his head. "She's doing whatever she has to do. If she hadn't said anything to anyone about leaving, I might be concerned." He clasped his hands behind his head and crossed his legs at the ankles. "Count on it.

Sally McCord is the last person you want to go tracking down if she doesn't want to be found. I'm curious about what she's up to, but I have no fear for her safety."

Sinking deeper in the soft couch, becoming lost in the flames of the fire, Traci relaxed some. Scott was probably right. Besides, Sally McCord was only on the periphery of the problems at the resort.

"You, on the other hand, are a different matter."

Traci jerked her attention back to Scott, but said nothing.

"I'd like us to get away from this valley for a day or two," he said, leaning toward her. "Clear our heads. Forget about all this crap, if possible. Maybe even play a little."

Traci peered back into the flames. It would be good to get away. She could remain in contact with Roberta if need be. But did she want to be alone with Scott again? Her body warmed at the thought. Yes, she did. "What do you have in mind?" she asked, without looking at him.

"There's an old mining town farther up in the foothills. Julian should be fairly quiet this time of year at mid-week. It's a quaint place known for its apple pies, lattes, history and friendly people."

"That sounds lovely." Traci remained transfixed by the fire. "Where would we stay?"

Scott cleared his throat. "There's a nice bed and breakfast that offers spacious rooms, tranquility, a better variety of breakfast than most restaurants and a friendly hostess."

343

No separate bedrooms. Traci didn't have to ask. Hell, the man had already slept in her bed.

"I don't want anything or anyone to hurt you."

She heard his husky words and knew he was including himself. "I know," she muttered. "But you may be too late." Traci drew her eyes away from the fire to look at Scott. He had settled uncomfortably back in his chair and tried to shield his emotions. She knew her words must have been like dumping a bucket of ice cold water on him.

She managed a furtive smile. "It sounds like a lovely time, Scott. I agree it would be good to get away for awhile." She rose and crossed over to where he was sitting and bent and kissed him on the cheek. "And I know you don't want to hurt me. It's been a rough day. I think I need to go to bed now."

Scott stood and held her. "I know it has. You need your rest. I'll be right down the hall if you need me."

Relief swept through Traci's body; he was giving her plenty of space. "Thanks," she whispered, tilting her head upwards so his lips would find hers. It was a soft gentle kiss demanding nothing, yet filled with promise.

Was she floating? The covers were tucked under her chin and she waited for sleep to overcome her swirling emotions. The near full moon cast soft shadows through the bedroom window. The stillness of the night intruded. The silence pierced her awareness.

She'd only had one glass of wine. Was it the fire in the fireplace? Was it the moon casting its glow? Was it this place? Was it his presence? She was floating; she knew it. And she didn't believe in things mystical.

Her body hummed nearly as much as it did after he'd kissed her all over. Her nipples ached. Her nostrils flared.

Tomorrow night. Tomorrow night. She knew what was expected tomorrow night. By agreeing to go to Julian, she'd joined in an implicit pact. Was that why she was floating?

Pursuing ecstasy or pursuing escape?

Dipping her fingers down to that nest of dark curls between her legs, she was surprised by her own wetness. She smiled into the shadows, resting her hand on her mound. Maybe she was ready.

And then what?

No longer floating, Traci hugged a pillow to her breasts. She did not want to answer. She could not let herself think beyond tomorrow night, beyond California. They had no future together. There was only the moment. She wanted to float, but the realist within had taken over. There was no room to fantasize about Mustache being a lasting part of her life.

- o -

Restlessness threatened to dismantle Scott McCord three doors down the hall from Traci. He couldn't get the vision of her lying nude in his

345

arms out of his mind. She'd looked, smelled and tasted...he couldn't find a single word...delicious, certainly, but more than that. Traci had become a living breathing aphrodisiac.

How much more he could take? The last thing he wanted to do was hurt her, but she was ripping him into shreds. Not knowingly, but just as thoroughly.

Yet, he wanted more than her body. And he was running out of time. He knew the case against Snowden could be wrapped up any day now. Traci Steele would return to Chicago. To her faster paced life. To her job. To her friends. Away from him.

Had she even thought of them together — for a lifetime? He doubted she'd let herself do that.

Scott rolled over on his stomach, ignoring his stiff arousal. Certainly, she would listen to reason. They could make it work.

Groaning, he twisted on to his back. There were so many responsibilities. Even if Traci were to return his love. What about James? His mother? The stables? What of Traci and her life in Chicago?

Scott's mind flew into an endless loop of sorting and yielding. No answers. Exhausted at last, he drifted toward sleep weighted with worry. Would they allow responsibilities to deprive them of each other? Time was running out. The last image to penetrate his blurred awareness was that of a young boy dashing wildly toward a burning car.

"You were right," Traci exclaimed, "this pie is scrumptious."

"Told you Julian is world famous for its apple pie." Scott smiled easily. They sat in a corner of a small store front specialty shop in Julian. Oversized mugs steamed with lattes.

"So, tour guide," she said, "we're at forty-five hundred feet and still only fifty miles from the ocean. That boggles the mind. And we're sharing a heavenly pie. What else should I know about this quiet place?"

"Appreciate it while you can. It won't be that way on the weekend. Julian can become wall to wall cars and people."

"Too bad." Traci looked out the window. "This is so charming. What you just described doesn't fit."

"Many of the locals would agree with you, but it's the tourist trade that allows this place to survive. Bed and breakfasts. Art galleries. History of gold mining. Upscale souvenir shops. Hole in the wall coffee shops like this one. None of these would be here if it weren't for the crowds coming up from the cities seeking fresh air and solitude."

"It doesn't sound like they find much solitude."

Scott sipped from his coffee mug and peered at Traci. "That's an interesting statement coming from a big city woman. I thought solitude for you folk was gathering shoulder to shoulder in some small town and being satisfied that you'd

347

ventured outside the big city."

Traci kicked him under the table. "What do you know about big cities? I find solitude out on the lake. Sometimes even in a park."

"You really are a sailor at heart aren't you?"

"Yes, I am." She laughed. "Unlike you."

"I can learn—if I have the right teacher."

"So, are you coming to Chicago to take lessons?" Traci quipped. When she saw his eyes light up, she realized her mistake. She kicked herself for getting caught up in banter.

"I don't know. Would you like that?"

She must look like an idiot staring wide-eyed at him, but she couldn't find any words.

"If I were to come to Chicago?"

Breathing at last, she countered, "I'm not worried. You wouldn't leave your horses for more than a couple days." She glanced at her watch. "There are a couple more art galleries that I want to browse before they close. We should be going."

Scott shrugged.

She was forewarned by that wicked, slow smile of his.

"But," he said, "you might want to write on your napkin *to be continued*. This conversation is not finished."

"This has been a splendid day, Scott. Thanks for bringing me up here." Traci didn't like the nervous twitter in her voice. Assessing Scott, she wasn't certain he was any less nervous. They had checked into a very spacious room with a bath. A

348

canopied queen-sized bed sat in its center. Three wing chairs were arrayed in a semi-circle in front of a fireplace. The logs were snapping as the fire ate away at them. At the end of the bed was a small mahogany desk and chair. Understated class.

She trembled slightly. Tawdry wouldn't be Scott McCord's style if he was wooing a woman. And there was little doubt left in her mind that was what he was doing.

He'd likely been bothered by her not wanting to pursue the conversation at the coffee shop. There was a part of her that delighted in the fact that the usually so confident man was troubled. Another part of her was totally scared by what he might ask.

She wasn't convinced she could give him her body; she wasn't ready to even consider her soul.

"Yeah, it was a grand day," Scott replied. He turned away from the fire and looked at where she sat. "I really enjoy spending time with you, Traci."

Traci nodded. This was the *to be continued* conversation. "Have you thought about us, Traci?" His voice was so somber it tore at her heart. "After all of this is done? After you go back to Chicago?"

"To be honest, I've tried not to think. I don't want to think." She saw his brow furrow and his shoulders slump. "I don't want to hurt you either, Scott. But we come from such different worlds. I don't see how anything is realistically possible in the long run." She turned her attention to the fire and spit out the words that haunted her. "I don't even know if I can be with a man."

She tried not to cringe before the tension filling every pore of her body.

He let out a deep sigh. "Ah, Counselor, I don't question your capacity to be with this man. Not one bit." He rose and stood before her chair. Taking her hands between his, he said, "Maybe it's time to prove that point."

Her lungs lurched for breath. This was it. She had to know. Maybe she owed it to both of them. Traci turned her teary eyes to Scott and nodded.

He pulled her to her feet and hugged her close. His lips pressed against hers seeking permission. She opened to him and met his demands with her own. She'd never get enough of his kissing.

Scott worked on her blouse buttons and she moved her fingers to his shirt. He was more skilled than she. By the time his shirt was off, her blouse and bra had floated to the floor. Rubbing her nipples against his, she leaned back exposing her neck to his eager tongue. Then he was at her breasts—first one and then the other. When had they become beacons of love? There were no words exchanged. Words were superfluous.

He knelt before her, his hands working the buttons of her skirt. It pooled at her feet. His fingers skimmed her panties down and she stepped out of them. She stood there totally exposed and surprisingly at ease. She wanted his tongue and he didn't disappoint.

His tongue teased and explored her inner sanctuary. She swayed back and forth. There was no warning. She simply shattered before him. Her legs buckled. She heard him chuckle and lift her and carry her to the bed.

Minutes later, she regained focus; she lay in his arms with her back to him. He'd finished undressing; this time he'd removed his undershorts. His arousal pressed against her buttocks. Traci tried not to tense; she wasn't successful. She felt him draw back a little. But he couldn't hold her without touching her, and she did want to be held.

"Are you okay?" he whispered.

She nodded, not trusting herself to speak.

Scott nibbled between her shoulders and she smiled. She rolled over to look at him. Traci tried to stay focused on his eyes; she wasn't ready to look lower. They contained a plea. Again, he was seeking permission. She nodded and closed her eyes.

His fingers revisited her nipples and she lifted her back to welcome them. A hand grazed her abdomen. A finger dipped in and out of her belly button. It tickled. She flinched. Refusing to open her eyes, Traci held her breath as his hand worked lower still.

His palm rested on her mound; she shriveled seeking a corner in which to be alone. She wanted this, she screamed at herself through clenched teeth. She had to find out.

A finger slid along the folds of her most private place. She tried not to squirm. Traci listened to Scott's ragged breathing. She wanted some reassuring words. Right now. But she couldn't ask for them. Were they each lost in their own worlds?

His finger entered, seeking, not demanding. Traci willed herself to relax, but she couldn't.

"So tight," she heard him whisper.

A second finger entered, straining her opening. Traci's eyes popped wide open. She jerked upward and back trying vainly to get away from this invasion. But his fingers went with her and probed deeper.

"No! No!" she screamed. She couldn't comprehend the shock on Scott's face as he jerked his hand away from her. She twisted onto her side. Tears wouldn't stop flowing. Her body convulsed. And then the ugly repressed images flooded her again.

Her cousin's friend pulled at her nipples and sneered his venom while her cousin pounded in and out of her body. She could smell his semen spread across her belly.

"No! No!"

She hugged her knees to her chest. She waited. The images would go away. They always did.

Was it minutes or hours later when she opened her eyes? The room was dark with the exception of the light cast by the fireplace.

She saw him hunched over in an easy chair, his eyes fixed on her, his expression stony. Remembering what had transpired between her and Scott, Traci clamped her teeth trying not to vomit. He had to understand now that it wouldn't work. She couldn't be with a man. Not even a patient man, like Scott. Tears warmed her cheeks.

There was only one thing left to do. She had to get out of there. She had to go home.

She dragged herself to a sitting position and pulled a sheet around her body. "I'm sorry about this, Scott. I want you to take me back to the condo, please."

He jerked his head sharply. "It wasn't you, Traci. It was me. I hurried. I went too fast. I couldn't control myself. Even another few minutes might have made the difference."

"No." She heard the guilt and sadness in his voice, but she wasn't buying that at all. "You could have tried until hell froze over, I would never have been ready. I want to go home now, Scott. Please don't be an ass about it."

He nodded, pulling on his pants. "Okay, get dressed. I'll be waiting downstairs. She knew he had to be as angry as she was hurt, but he had walled in his feelings. And that was okay with her; she was trying to do the same thing.

Right now she just wanted to be alone. She needed to start getting used to it again.

Chapter Seventeen

"All these years, and you never told me."

Sitting on the living room floor of her friend's farmhouse, Traci peered up at Cassie Travers pacing back and forth across the floor. She'd been back in Chicago for two days before driving out to talk with her old college roommate and closest friend.

Numbed by her own story, Traci could only imagine what Cassie must be feeling. She'd left nothing out, ever — not about when she was raped, not about her reluctance to be around men socially, not about the fiasco with Scott McCord. Once she'd started talking there was no way to keep her guts from spilling out. It must have been an assault on her friend.

"It's not that I didn't trust you," Traci whispered. "I didn't want to relive any of it in the retelling."

Cassie stopped pacing and gave Traci a weak smile. "I know that, Traci. It's just...I never recognized what was happening. And then I threw you and Scott together."

"Ah, at last you admit it." Traci shook her head. "I don't blame you. Not for any of it. Even all the stuff with Scott. It was terrible. It was embarrassing. But I had to know what I could do

355

and what I couldn't. Now I know. Now I can get on with my life. End of story."

"Bullshit." Cassie scowled and placed her hands on her hips. "Damn, Traci, I don't want to blubber and I don't want to make you feel worse. Although from the looks of you that may be impossible."

"I'm fine."

"Right." Cassie rolled her eyes toward the ceiling. "As you describe your interactions with Scott, I hear a lot of warm fuzzy stuff, I hear camaraderie, I hear groping on the part of both of you to discover who you each are and what you might become together. Does that sound right?"

Traci nodded her head. "Yes, but that's not all of it. I couldn't shake the past."

"Right." Cassie plopped down on the floor beside Traci. "You were content with remaining the victim."

Jerking away from her friend, Traci said, "That's cruel, Cassie. Even from you."

"I know it is."

Traci saw the tears welling in Cassie's eyes. Her troubles were taking a toll on the small redhead and she vowed to hear the woman out. Sitting rigidly on her hands, Traci said, "Okay, spit it out. You'll bust if you don't."

"It's just that you don't have to continue being the victim of a rape that happened over a half a lifetime ago."

"You weren't there. How do you know?"

Cassie took a deep breath. "I didn't go through

what you did. But you survived, Traci. You're a successful young woman. You're bright and attractive. You're witty and can be lots of fun. In all those ways, you survived. You chose to survive." Cassie chewed on her lower lip. "Only in one area do you choose to remain a victim."

"I don't choose to be a victim," Traci said, her voice weak from sobbing.

"Don't you? Hear me out. Please. You've let those two boys control a most exquisite part of your body and soul for all these years."

"They soiled it, Traci whimpered. "They made me dirty."

Cassie leaned over and rubbed her fingers across Traci's as tears streamed down her cheeks. "They raped you, Traci. They raped an innocent fifteen-year-old girl. And that was a dirty, horrible act, but it didn't make *you* dirty."

"But they laughed at my body. Told me I had slut knockers. Said I was an ugly bitch. Their words still ring in my ears."

"And what about *his* words Traci? What about the man who loves you? The man who you yourself said scares you because he seems to worship those same breasts and adores you as a complete woman?"

"He never said he loved me."

"Because you wouldn't let him."

Traci pursed her lips and nodded.

"How do you feel about him, Traci?"

"It doesn't matter."

"Traci, you're always the one telling me to be

honest with myself. I'm just asking you to do the same."

Traci let her eyes wander across the room. She became aware of the grandfather clock ticking loudly. Funny, she hadn't heard it at all before. Cassie's large gray cat, Bastion, chose that moment to stroll from the kitchen to the living room. He walked directly to Traci and rubbed the back of his head against her leg. In response, Traci scratched the feline's neck.

"Before I can be honest with you, I have to be honest with me," she finally began. "I miss him. I miss the banter we share, the way he smiles, the way he teases his nieces, the way he listens to horses." Traci smiled softly. "I miss his touch, especially his kisses." Traci's muscles tensed. She sobered. "But that's not enough. I can't be a woman with him, Cass."

"I doubt that very much." Cassie's brow furrowed. "I expect there are both emotional and physical hurdles to overcome, but I don't have any doubt that you'll overcome them if you choose to be a survivor."

"That's easy for you to say."

"Yes, it is. I know it's huge for you. All I'm asking is don't sell yourself short. And don't sell Scott short either." Cassie hesitated.

"Yes," Traci chuckled lightly. "As Sally McCord would say, this girl talk is about to end, so you might as well say what you have to say."

"Now there's a gritty woman."

"Her softness might surprise you."

Cassie eyebrows arched. "What I was going to say is in all that you've told me that Scott tried to do for you in being intimate, I wondered what you did for him?"

Traci scowled. "Now what are you saying? Don't talk in circles. Don't be my social worker. Just tell me what you're thinking."

"Okay." Cassie sighed. "The rape was a one-way street. They took. You didn't give anything. Intimacy between consenting adults requires reciprocity. Have you ever asked what might satisfy him? He had to be more than a little frustrated, or he isn't human."

Traci grinned shyly. "He did talk about taking a lot of cold showers. So you think I didn't do enough for him?"

"I'm not trying to heap more guilt on you. You've more of that than you need already. I'm just saying that maybe a little more attention to his needs might take some pressure off of always thinking about what your body is going to do."

"You sound like there's going to be another time with him."

Cassie beamed. "You hear what you choose to hear. Come on, friend." She stood and pulled Traci up. "Clint will be back with the kids soon. Whatever happens between you and Scott is your business. But for what it's worth, I wouldn't give up on him yet. And mostly, I hope you look into a mirror and see not a victim, but a survivor."

Monday morning, Traci sat in Roberta's office.

She glanced around the small glass-enclosed cubicle cluttered with stacks of papers and books. Two computer terminals with two different screen savers flashed a broad array of colors and hypnotizing images. How did anyone get any work done in such a work space?

Roberta claimed she knew what was in each stack, and she'd proven that fact on more than one occasion.

"So the boss isn't going to let you come back yet," Roberta said, chewing on a doughnut.

Traci nodded. She couldn't shake her glum mood. "He thinks I look worse than I did when I left. I didn't need to be reminded that I have three more weeks of vacation left. He wants me to take more than that if I need it."

"You do look pretty bedraggled—you need rest."

"What I need is to get back to work and get focused again. It's all that rest that's driving me up the wall."

Roberta flashed her eyebrows and slurped coffee from a mug that read *Don't worry if I bite your head off—I'll spit it back out.* "So it's too much rest that gave you dark bags under your eyes and a droopy appearance that would rival a rain-soaked cat."

Grimacing, Traci pulled her notepad from her purse. "So let's review what you have on the Snowden case."

Roberta scowled darkly at Traci before replying. "Okay, you don't want to talk about what's bothering you. I can respect that. I'm at a dead end, actually. We've been able to tie their corporate officers to the mob. You've checked out those individuals working at the ranch, stable, and tracks with criminal histories. I've gone over and over again Snowden's financial records.

"I dream about them in my sleep. Something screwy is going on at the tennis complex, but not much. It's sort of like someone can't keep their hand out of the till. It may be an employee rather than Snowden itself." Roberta crunched her fingers. "I wouldn't want to be that person when management finds out. I don't think those guys are big on forgiveness. So what did I leave out?"

"I also interviewed some of the other owners and employees," Traci said. "That didn't turn up much. Nobody likes Snowden, but that's not enough to take to the local prosecutor. Let's see...the crime lab couldn't prove that a bullet caused the blow-out on the pickup, but they believe it was highly likely that it was caused by such a sudden impact. We do know the hay was laced with poison."

"And we know that our phones were tapped and someone wanted you out of there real bad." Roberta squinted at Traci. "That had to be a terrifying experience."

Traci nodded without speaking.

"That probably explains why you're so drawn." Roberta shifted her weight in her chair. "Traci, you look like hell."

"You're reaching again," Traci snapped.

"I'm sorry. I just care about what happens to you. We've been colleagues and I hope friends for a number of years."

"I know." Traci rubbed her forehead. "I'm just not ready to talk about it now."

"Okay." Roberta mockingly slapped her hand. "I'll try not to pry, but you know I'm a snoop. That's why you like me."

Traci chuckled. "And a good snoop you are."

"So tell me, Trace…tell me about Live Oak. You don't have to tell me about the cowboy, if you don't want to. What else did you like about the place?"

Feeling her cheeks turn suddenly warm, Traci fumbled for words. "It's very upscale. The units are lovely and sufficiently large. It was great to be able to cook in rather than go out all the time. Eating out should be special rather than a daily routine."

"Eating out every night might get boring, but I might like to give it a try," Roberta quipped.

"I grew up like that; the novelty of it wears off fast. Let me see. The tennis complex lacks nothing—first class all the way, including every kind of exercise machine imaginable. I spent a fair amount of time in the Olympic-size pool. And at one end was a hot tub; that was pure heaven after riding Cory."

"The horse?"

Traci groaned. "Of course, the horse."

Smiling broadly, Roberta said, "Just making sure. I know you like the water, but I am

362

surprised you spent so much time at the pool. It must've been crowded."

Traci cocked her head sidewise, thinking back. "No, not really. Of course, the first week the weather was quite cool, but after that it was very warm. But I don't think there were ever more than a half dozen people in the pool. And only twice did I have to make small talk with anyone in the hot tub."

"You sure?" Roberta leaned forward in her chair.

"Of course, I'm sure. I don't like to be around a lot of people, particularly when I'm on vacation. You know, Roberta, I was at Live Oak during their off season. The most activity around the place had to do with several condos being refurbished. Why are you looking so strange?"

"That's it. The scam!" Roberta shouted. "It's so damn simple."

"Don't sit there looking smug. What is it? What did I say?"

"Would it surprise you that Snowden Corp. reports year-round near capacity utilization?"

Traci's eyebrows arched. "But they're not."

Roberta waited.

"Oh! I'll be! You're right, it's so simple. It's a money laundering facility. The lower the actual number of guests, the more money they can pump through the resort by inflating their occupancy numbers. You're sure about those numbers?"

"I can print them out for you, but when have I ever forgotten a number?"

Traci jumped to her feet. "That explains the intense pressure to close the stable. Snowden wanted to double the number of condo units and double the amount of illegal dollars they could run through a legitimate operation."

"They had a pretty good thing going until they got greedy and until you came along."

Traci leaned over and hugged her friend. "You're a magician, Roberta. I can hardly believe it was so simple, and it was always there before my eyes. I never had a problem with parking. I never had to wait for a washing machine. Off season is like that."

"Off season for Snowden was a time to get busy and really make some money. So now what?"

Traci sat back down. Her body hummed. This was the moment one lived for in this kind of work. When the puzzle pieces all fit. She wished Scott was there to share in the victory. Traci closed her eyes. She'd have to call him and let him know what was happening and what to expect.

She dreaded making that call. Yet she wanted to hear his voice. And she wanted to know that he was all right. No, she wanted to know that he was hurting as much as she was.

"Traci?"

"Oh, I'm sorry. What did you ask?"

Roberta shook her head. "You're not ready to be back; I'm not even sure you *are* back. I asked what do we do next?"

"We summarize what we have and turn it over to my counterpart in the San Diego County

District Attorney's Office. It's their jurisdiction. We'll let them handle it from here on out. How soon do you think you can get your data together?"

"I'll have it for you by tomorrow morning at the latest. I can drop it by your apartment, since you won't be in here."

"Damn. Okay. I'll type up an overview and a cover letter and contact them in the afternoon."

"So are you going to let your cowboy know about this?"

Traci hesitated and chose to ignore the "your cowboy" comment. "Not until I've talked with the county prosecutor."

The following evening Traci sat at the desk in her apartment and stared at her phone. She had to make one more call. She owed it to him. There was so much to say. And there was so much not to say.

Traci rolled her shoulders up along her neck trying to reduce some tension. It hadn't been a great day, and she still had to call Scott McCord.

Roberta had dropped by the materials she'd promised and Traci had been able to package them into a fairly straightforward document delineating the case against Snowden. She'd made clear those aspects of the case that were well grounded in evidence and pointed out that which remained speculative, such as shooting at the pickup and trailer.

Before dropping the document in the Express mailbox, she'd called the San Diego District

Attorney's Office and talked with Beverly Grayson, Assistant DA. She hadn't been totally surprised by the response she received. The woman's initial coolness had turned irate before settling into a professional calm.

Why hadn't Traci contacted the local office before now? Where was her sense of professional courtesy? Had she violated any laws getting the information she had? And finally, a reluctant thank you for giving them a well developed case, along with a warning to let them handle the case from here on out.

Traci still burned, but she did understand. And she had absolutely no interest in any further involvement in the Snowden case. But there was one more loose end to tie up.

Reluctantly, she picked up the phone and punched the buttons from memory.

"Hello," said the gravelly female voice. "This better not be a sales call. I've had it up to here with you people."

"Sal, don't hang up. It's me, Traci." There was a long pause.

"Traci Steele from Chicago who never said goodbye?"

"I'm sorry, Sal. I had to go. I couldn't help it."

"It's okay. You know you can come back any time."

Traci closed her eyes. God, why had Sal had to pick up? It was bad enough thinking about talking to Scott. "I know. How's your garden coming?"

"It's doing fine. You were a big help. More than

you can imagine." The old woman chuckled. "Suppose you didn't call to talk with me."

"I do have some information for Scott, if he's available."

"He's here. He hasn't done much but mope around since you left. Even the twins are angry with him for not paying them enough attention."

Traci snickered. "That's not hard to picture."

"Okay, girl."

Traci listened to Sally McCord's ragged breathing.

"I just want to tell you one thing. You *can* go back and undo mistakes. You don't have to wait a lifetime to do it."

Before Traci could respond, she heard Sal shouting to Scott, "It's for you!"

"Hello."

His voice sounded deeper and more tired than usual. "It's me, Traci."

"Oh." His defensiveness was obvious.

"There's been a break in the case."

"Tell me about it."

She proceeded to spell out the case as she and Roberta had developed it. There were no interruptions from his end. He simply listened.

"So that's it," Traci said at last. "It was a simple scam that worked for quite a while until they wanted to take over your stable."

"Until they had a hotshot investigator riding their ass."

Traci said nothing.

"So what now?"

"There will probably be a couple investigators wanting to get depositions from you. They'll comb the records and substantiate what we've established."

"What about James?"

"I doubt they'll spend much time looking at the horses. The real focus here is on Snowden's money laundering operation."

"Okay. We all owe you a lot of thanks—including the community of Buteo."

She heard his voice strengthen.

"So what next?"

She closed her eyes and sighed. The silence rubbed her raw. "I don't know."

"Are you okay?"

"No," she whispered.

"Good," he drawled. "I appreciate your honesty. I feel like shit, too."

"But you shouldn't—"

"I screwed up, Traci. That night in Julian. What I understood for passion coming from you was terror. I would have stopped sooner if I'd known."

"It's okay." Traci stood and started to pace absently, winding the phone cord around her body. "Maybe those two emotions have more in common than we like to think."

"Maybe. I'm sorry. I've replayed that scene over so many times, but it doesn't change."

"No, it doesn't." She paused, fighting back tears. "You have to move on, Scott. I can't be the woman I want to be with you. And I won't give you half a woman."

"You still believe that shit."

His words were spoken in anger. She heard him smack his lips together trying to stay calm.

"Lookit," he said, "this doesn't seem to be getting us anywhere, Traci. But you need to know. I guess I need you to know that I love you. I don't really know how it happened. I didn't want it to happen, but it did."

"Don't say any more, please. It's already bad enough."

"We both have a lot of work to do, Counselor. You should know I'm not ready to give up on us. And I can only hope you aren't."

Traci didn't trust herself to respond.

"You're always welcome here, Traci. I love you."

The soft click in her ear was as powerful as a dynamite blast. Traci hung up the phone, walked into her bedroom, flopped on the bed and cried.

It shouldn't be this way. She wanted to be whole again. She wanted to be loved and to love in return.

A week later, Traci's apartment buzzer rang incessantly.

"Shit," Traci muttered, dragging herself up out of bed. She punched the intercom button. "Who is it?" she demanded.

"It's me. Is your answering machine off?"

"No, Cassie, it's not off." She pressed the button to let her friend in the downstairs lobby and then waited for the knock.

It was a bang, actually. Traci opened the door and Cassie Travers stormed in. Traci knew she'd made a tactical error by not returning the redhead's calls.

"What are you doing holed up here like some recluse? You can't move on by shutting out your friends." Cassie pulled herself to her full height and pointed at Traci. "Look at you. You look worse than you did when you first got back from California. So what do you have to say for yourself?"

Traci pulled her robe tighter around her body. She didn't want to argue with Cassie. She didn't have the energy. "Do you want some tea?"

Cassie slapped her own head with her palm. "What do I have to do to get through to you?" She sighed and pulled off her jacket. "Okay, I'll have some tea with you. Along with some toast and jam. And orange juice, if you have any. At least maybe I can make sure you eat something."

Cassie pulled up a chair in the breakfast nook. "So what's happening?"

"They won't let me go back to work."

"And that surprises you?"

Traci looked down at her trembling hands. "No, I suppose not. But it would help. I know it would. Work has always been at the center of my life."

"Maybe that's part of the problem," said Cassie, reaching for a second piece of toast.

Traci made no response.

"So, I understand the case you were working on for Scott has been resolved."

370

"How did you find that out?" Traci's eyes shot wide. There was only one possible source.

"Scott called. Apparently, you haven't been answering his calls, either."

Traci shook her head.

"He's very worried about you."

Traci watched her friend set her mug of tea back down.

"He's very much in love with you, Traci.

Traci closed her eyes and gripped the edge of the table.

"So what are you going to do about him?"

Again, Traci shook her head. She opened her eyes. "Did you just come up to hassle me?"

Cassie reached over and rubbed a hand across Traci's knuckles that were turning white. "No, I don't want to hassle you. But I do want my friend back."

Traci chuckled derisively. "I think you said something like that when you twisted my arm and sent me off to the sunny beaches of southern California."

Scrunching her mouth, Cassie replied, "Yeah well, I guess those beaches were a little farther away than I remembered."

"I wish I'd never seen Live Oak. It's such a horrible nightmare."

Cassie remained silent.

"I never thought I'd find a man who would love me. I had too many scars, emotional and physical. And then I find him..." Tears dripped from her cheeks onto her robe. Traci swiped at them with

371

little effect. "And then I find him and I can't love him. Not the way a whole woman could."

"So you love him."

Traci gasped. "I didn't think it was possible. But I miss him so."

"So why don't you go to him?"

"I can't. I can't love him."

A long silence ensued. Traci didn't know what else to say. There wasn't anything else to add. But she didn't like the scowl on Cassie's face. The woman bit her lower lip.

"Okay," said Cassie, "I may be overstepping, but someone has to tell you this. Love doesn't come along that often in a person's lifetime to simply flush it down the toilet. You know now that you're capable of loving emotionally. Maybe this self-imposed isolation has at least yielded that much."

Traci stared blankly, wishing Cassie Travers would go home. "It hurts more to know I love him than it did before," she mumbled.

"So you have a physical problem that can be worked through."

Traci's loins shriveled.

"You're not the first woman who's ever had difficulty relaxing enough for a man, for whatever reason. There are sex therapists out there that help women and men with these kinds of difficulties every day."

Crossing her arms over her breasts, Traci couldn't respond.

"Dammit, Traci. You can do it. If you don't

want to see a counselor, just about every health store in Chicago sells vibrators, and you always have your fingers. You can do it. If you love him enough. If you love yourself enough. I can't do it for you. Apparently, Scott can't either. Only you can turn yourself into a survivor."

"I think you'd better leave now, Cassie." Traci heard her shrill voice as if it came from someone else's mouth.

"I'm gone." Cassie rose from the kitchen chair and sighed deeply. "I believe in you, Traci. You're made of very tough fiber. You can reclaim who you are."

Traci remained sitting long after she heard the apartment door close. What did Cassie Travers know about this kind of pain? Traci laid her head on the table and sobbed. She knew Cassie had been through a lot of her own pain. Nobody alive was immune from pain of one sort or another. But this was too big.

She was smart enough to know that while her trauma had an external source in the beginning, it now resided within her. And Cassie was right— only she would be able to root it out. But she wasn't at all certain she could. And what if she tried and failed again? She didn't know if she could handle that.

Two days later Traci stood at the Fullerton Avenue beach looking out at Lake Michigan. Thankfully it was an early spring. Her windbreaker protected her from the nip of the day. She longed for the kind of weather that would permit her to get her sailboat out of dry dock. But even standing there feeling the wind bite her face helped. It helped a lot. Why hadn't she pulled herself together enough to walk along the beach before this?

Cassie's visit had been maddening. She still churned over her friend's words, well intended, but so harsh. Surprisingly, she felt better. She'd seen more color in her face this morning, and she was eating better. It had been good to at least share her love for Mustache with Cassie. There wasn't anyone else she could tell.

Traci sighed and watched three gulls perform aerial stunts, seeking food and calling forlornly to any who would listen. She congratulated herself for going by the cemetery earlier in the day. That had been a huge step. Odd — although she still felt sadness standing before her father's plot, she no longer felt so totally alone.

What would Sally McCord have to say about that? What had the woman said? Traci closed her eyes trying to remember. It was something like, "You have to grieve the dead and then move on, never forgetting, but letting them go. There's enough among the living to grieve."

Nodding, Traci hugged herself tightly. "Isn't that the truth."

Above the call of the gulls came a vaguely familiar shriek. Traci glanced upward and searched the sky. It was a cloudless day. The piercing sound came again and she saw its source soaring high above. Traci swallowed hard. She'd never seen a hawk in the city. Of course, they were there. Other people had mentioned seeing them from time to time.

She gasped as the sun bouncing off the hawk's tail sent out rays of red and orange. "Do you have a message for me?" Traci quickly covered her mouth.

She must really be losing it. Scott was the mystical one, not her. Nonetheless, she spent the next ten minutes watching the hawk soar in ever widening circles. She marveled at its sense of freedom and easily imagined the joy of riding the wind without a care in the world.

At last, the hawk faded from sight. Confused by her own remorse over losing contact with the bird, Traci stuffed her hands in her pockets and trudged back toward her apartment.

It had become more of a cell than an apartment. *"But this has been a good day, Counselor. Give yourself some credit,"* she whispered. *"You got out and did some things that needed doing. And then there was the hawk."* Traci came to a halt and frowned. Only Scott McCord called her "Counselor" like that.

She shrugged and walked on.

Traci rolled over and squinted at the clock. The red numerals said four fifteen a.m. She groaned a plea for sleep. For the hundredth time she went over what had happened to her the past few days. The confrontation with Cassie. Cleaning her apartment. Going to the cemetery. Walking the beach. Hearing and then seeing the hawk.

In her semi-awake state, she once again envisioned the hawk. *It soared above her, but much closer than at the beach. She could see its penetrating eyes. They did contain a message. She knew they did, if only she could make it out. The great bird flapped its wings and Traci felt her hair blow before the breeze.*

The breeze was freeing. Her fingers brushed her nipples and then danced across her belly like his had done. She was floating like she had before. She yearned for more. Her buttocks lifted off the bed seeking. And she soared.

The hawk became a dot in the sky. Traci cried out, thinking it had deserted her. The hawk banked into the wind and circled and came back. Repeatedly, the raptor dove down and then back up again in graceful arcs composing its own erotic dance. Without fear, Traci soared and dove with it. She laughed at her new found freedom. She experienced a bliss she'd never known.

Later, Traci was awakened by a strain in her wrist. She felt it before she fully realized the implication. She peered through narrowed eyes as, if not to frighten away the obvious. Three fingers remained lodged in that place between her thighs. Slowly, she pulled her fingers out. She sniffed. She cried. "My God, my God, I did it!"

And then she remembered. "Thank you, hawk. Or whoever or whatever. My God." She pulled her knees to her chest and laughed and cried. These were hot tears, but how much better tears of joy felt than all the tears of pain.

But was that enough? Her heart thudded against her chest wall. She had to know. She had to be able to accept him—all of him, not just his fingers.

Quivering, she rolled over and pulled open the nightstand drawer. There it was. She'd purchased it at a downtown drugstore. It was much longer than her finger, and much fatter.

Short of breath, Traci reached for the vibrator and cussed Cassie for planting the idea in her head that she could do this. She twisted one end and the vibrator purred.

Traci bit her lower lip and moved the love object across her belly. "Goodness," she whispered. "Patience, girl. Go slow. Remember Ransom. Don't let yourself get paralyzed."

She moved her toy lightly across her belly and down and up her thighs. She let out a trapped breath. She eased it closer to her private place until it rested against her outer folds. "Oh my." Slowly, she guided the object upwards until it rested atop her clitoris. Traci arched her back. It tickled. Like a mustache. Her eyes sprang wide. She was doing this for him, for her, for them. It was time.

Her fingers shook. But she managed to lower the vibrator so that its tip was at her entrance. *Slow. Be gentle. Don't rush.* Were those her thoughts? Scott's? The hawk's?

She eased the object in. She spread her thighs, adjusting the angle. She swore she felt herself opening like a flower. The vibrator slipped farther in. Traci gasped. There was little resistance. She pushed a little more and stopped. She shouted, "Yes," and then lay back and enjoyed the moment.

Playfully, she toyed with herself. She moved the vibrator in and out. She turned it up a notch. She crashed around it once, twice and yet again.

Traci turned off the vibrator and lifted it in awe. She blew a kiss at it. "We did it," she murmured. "Thank you, Cassie. Thank you, Scott. Thank you, hawk. Thank you, vibrator. Thank you, me! I'm whole. I'm me again."

Chapter Eighteen

Getting out of the red Grand Am, Traci stretched and looked about the familiar surroundings. McCord's beat up pickup was not in its usual parking spot by the stable. She doubted he'd bought a new one in less than three weeks.

Taking long rapid strides, Traci approached the Live Oak office. Stepping into the lobby, she startled at seeing a friendly face behind the counter.

"Mrs. Bergstrom, what are you doing here?" said Traci, shaking the woman's hand.

"I could ask you the same. Word was you left in a huff. Not that that's any of my business." The older woman paused for a response, but received only a smile.

"Haven't you talked to anyone out here this past week?" Mrs. Bergstrom asked. The woman looked like she was ready to burst with news.

"No, it's been nearly two weeks since I spoke to anyone."

"My, my, a lot has happened. I received a call from Scott a week ago Friday that Humphries had moved out, and would I be willing to fill in until a replacement could be found.

"Over the weekend, the office was broken into and all the records were stolen. And we received

379

word that Snowden Corp. experienced a fire that same weekend destroying the backup financial records." Mrs. Bergstrom smiled sweetly, smoothing out her blouse. "Now wasn't that a coincidence."

Traci's mind was whirling with the news. "They were tipped off about the upcoming investigation."

"Absolutely. But there's more." Mrs. Bergstrom glanced around the welcoming area to make sure no one was listening.

Traci smiled. She doubted there was an eavesdropper given that no one else had come in behind her.

"Last Friday, each of the owners of Live Oak was notified by Snowden that the corporation was seeking a buyer, and by contract we have the first option to buy."

"My goodness," Traci stammered. "I turn my back and the entire world changes. So what are you going to do?"

"The phone lines have been hot." Traci had no difficulty believing that. "It hasn't been formalized yet, but I think a local consortium will emerge to buy out Snowden. We can hire our own management team. And we'll be more likely to keep the community's interest at heart than an out-of-state group."

Traci wasn't particularly convinced. She wondered how much blood would be let when consortium members failed to agree on what was in the community's best interest, but there was no reason to prick Mrs. Bergstrom's obvious euphoria. "Doesn't look like you'll have to worry about being bored for awhile."

"That's for sure." Mrs. Bergstrom picked up a pencil and asked, "Now, what can I do you for? You didn't travel all the way from Chicago to get updated on the local gossip."

"I know the condos are often available by the night. I wondered if I could rent one. I won't be staying tonight, but I need a place to store my stuff. Although I'm not certain how long I'll be staying." Traci frowned. Why was she rattling on so. "Can I pay you by the night or by the week?"

"Sounds like you don't know if you'll be staying a spell or catching the next stage out of Buteo."

Traci bit her lower lip. "Something like that."

"You can have, let's see, room one sixty nine." Mrs. Bergstrom jotted a noted in her logbook. "And you won't be paying us anything. Without you, none of this would be possible."

Flustered, Traci said, "That's not necessary, but thanks."

Mrs. Bergstrom smiled broadly. "Now, why don't you let me get back to work? You dump what you have to in the condo and get out to the ranch. You got a cowboy waiting for you out there. Don't know if I've ever met a more patient man than Scott McCord, but I think he's just about at the end of his rope. Good luck."

"*Thanks,*" Traci whispered.

Walking toward the old woman standing on the

381

edge of her flower garden, Traci tried to maintain her confidence. She resolved not to cry.

A gentle, welcoming smile spread across Sally McCord's lips as she held out her hands to grasp Traci's. "It's good to see you, Traci Steele from Chicago."

"It's good to see you too, Sal. I've missed you."

"As it should be. I imagine you've come to take my boy away."

Traci nearly stumbled.

"It's okay." The older woman wiped her brow with the back of her hand. "I've reconciled myself. Scott would leave anyway."

"He would?"

"With what James did and all, I can understand why Scott needs to be away from here for awhile. And maybe I've held on to him more than I should've. No matter now; he's moving to Chicago anyhow."

"Chicago!"

"Yep, he's worked out some kind of arrangement with Clint and Cassie Travers to work for them to see if he wants to get into training racehorses full time."

Traci's mouth opened wide, but no sounds came out. She watched wide-eyed as Sally McCord bent over to retrieve her hoe.

"So he hasn't told you yet?"

Traci shook her head from side to side, still trying to comprehend the import of what Scott's mother had said. And she thought *she* was the only one who had been working on their relationship these past weeks. What else was he considering, and why hadn't he told her? Traci pursed her lips. Of course she hadn't been returning his calls. And she had a few surprises of her own waiting for him.

"What about the stable?" Traci asked.

"You're buying time, Traci," Mrs. McCord said, chuckling. "That's okay. Now that you're here, you take all the time you need. I've got my lemonade sitting over here in the shade. You want some?"

Nodding, Traci replied, "I think maybe I could use some."

After filling two paper cups, Sally McCord said, "The stables will be in good hands."

The older woman's lips quivered and then her eyes sparkled more brightly. "My brother will be taking over the stables."

"Harry?" Traci placed a hand on Sally's knee. *"That's* where you were when I left."

"Yep. I've got a hard head, but you kinda got my attention. Thought I'd best go see what he was up to. It was my place to take the first step."

"And he welcomed you?"

"Nearly frightened him to death. But once he got over the initial shock we sorted out a lot of stuff and decided we'd best be family for each other."

"I'm really pleased for you, Sal. That'll take a load off your shoulders." Sally McCord shrugged and glanced at her flower garden.

"So Harry's moving here to manage the

stables?"

"Technically, he's not a McCord, which pleases him immensely, but he's close enough to step in on our behalf. And you might as well know James and Penny are seriously looking at what we have to do to turn this place into some kind of working dude ranch."

"Really!"

Mrs. McCord snorted. "Can't say I like it much, but what can I do? They've got to live their own lives. I just told them I won't have any strangers stomping through my gardens or my house. The rest of the place they can do with what they want. Bruce will probably spin in his grave, but so be it."

Traci leaned against the trunk of the giant oak tree, closed her eyes and breathed deeply. "My, you've come a very long way, Sal."

"Kicking and screaming most of the way, but it'll work out. It will be good to have Harry here; he'll help me find my way. So what about you, Traci Steele from Chicago? You look like maybe you've come a long way, too."

"I think so. At least I'm ready to find out what the future holds."

"I'm glad you're back, even for a short while." Sally McCord hesitated. "You're good for him, Traci. I wouldn't let him go if I didn't believe that. And I think he's pretty good for you too."

Setting her cup down, Traci said, "I know he is."

"She's back," the twins screamed together, dashing through the garden gate.

Traci rose and hugged both girls. She smelled

their fresh hair and fresh spirits. Yes, it was very good to be back, even for a short while.

"You're just the two I needed to see. Do you remember that lariat you gave your uncle for his birthday?"

"Sure," they said in unison.

"Can you bring it here without Scott seeing you?"

"Sure we can," Susannah said. "I often take it for practice roping. Do you want to know where he is?"

Traci smiled from ear to ear. "You read my mind. Yes, where is that cowboy of ours?"

"He's working with Ransom in the corral," Rebecca shouted, running after her sister who was barreling toward the barn.

"Whatever you got planned, you're going to have an audience, you know," Mrs. McCord said, getting to her feet. "The twins will tag along."

"And you'll be right behind them."

Traci thrilled at Sal's gravelly laugh. "You're damned right. I wouldn't miss this for anything."

Surprised by her own fearlessness, Traci strode toward the corral with the lariat draped over her shoulder like she'd seen cowboys do. She didn't pay attention to the whispering that followed her.

She knew immediately when he spied her. Scott squinted and took his hat off as if not quite sure of what he was seeing, and then a wide smile broke across his face. As she neared, he tied Ransom and stepped through the rails of the corral.

Without hesitation, he held out his arms and she flung herself against him, nearly knocking both of them over. His lips brushed her hair and forehead. They grazed the tip of her nose and then settled on her lips. It was a gentle, lengthy moment. Traci felt no jitters—only relief at being home.

"Well, Counselor, you seem to have attracted a crowd."

She turned in time to see the twins and their grandmother exchanging high fives.

"And what the hell is the rope for?" Scott scowled. "What have you got on your mind?"

Traci stood back, widened her stance and squared her shoulders. "I'm going to take you for a ride, cowboy, and I didn't know if you would come along willingly."

He tilted his head to the side and gave her one of his lazy smiles. "Whatever you say. I don't think you'll need to hogtie me." He looked at Susannah. "Take Ransom and put him back in his paddock." Directing his attention back at Traci, he said, "I'll need to take a shower. Give me twenty minutes."

As he started for the house, Traci said, "You'll need an overnight bag with stuff for the beach."

Scott stopped and turned back to her with a quizzical look. "So where are you taking me?"

"I'm not telling. It'll be a surprise. I'll bring you back safe and sound. Trust me."

"Right. How come I don't believe that?" He stared at her for several moments. She couldn't read what he was thinking. At last he said, "But I'll play along. You've got class, Traci, and a lot of guts."

"So are you taking me to the Del?" Scott asked, peering over at his driver. He was pleased to see her cheeks crinkle in a smile.

"Maybe. Maybe not," she said. "It's a surprise. Don't you like surprises?"

"Some. Particularly those I spring on others." She drove expertly down the winding foothills. Was this the same woman who swore she'd never manage the switchbacks and dips?

They were headed toward San Diego; that was about all he knew for sure. They'd chattered about a number of things since they left the ranch, some important and some not. But not a word had been mentioned about them. She'd told him how she and her friend had cracked the case and he'd told her about Snowden withdrawing from the fight.

"Sorry you couldn't nail Snowden the way you wanted to."

She didn't take her eyes from the road nor did her smile fade. "Doesn't matter much. Somebody will get them one of these days. Important thing is they left the Oak and aren't bothering James."

"So it doesn't bother you that the bad guys escaped?"

Traci shrugged and grinned at him. "In the course of my life's events, it probably doesn't rank in the top ten."

"I'll be damned," he muttered under his breath. She snickered. She must have heard him after all. He pulled his Stetson down over his eyes and slouched in the seat. Was this the same damn high strung woman who'd left him in such a storm?

"Do you think you're going to be able to hide under that big hat? You know you do look a little odd sitting there with sneakers, shorts, a tee shirt and a Stetson."

Scott sat up straight. Her teasing grated the way she must've intended.

"So..."

Uh oh, Scott's inner voice warned. Her smile had evaporated.

"So, when were you planning to tell me about your move to Chicago?"

Scott jerked forward and glared at Traci. "Damn Ma, anyway. Can't she keep anything to herself?"

"She likes me," Traci said, smugly. "Actually, she assumed you'd already told me. So when would you have? Were you going to just drop by? Or maybe bump into me at the zoo some sunny afternoon? Cassie couldn't have kept it a secret for long. I'm surprised she has this far."

Scott chuckled. "I'm not sure Clint told her. We agreed to work this out behind the scenes in the short run."

"You mean behind my back, don't you?"

"Ah, but it is a gorgeous back, Counselor." He smiled at her neck as it turned three shades of pink.

"Don't try to divert my attention," Traci

complained. "I want to know what you thought you were doing."

"If I tell, will you tell me what you think you're doing driving us to San Diego?"

She shook her head and grinned. "You'll know soon enough." She glanced quickly at him. "Come on Scott, tell me what you were up to."

"I hope it doesn't burst your ego, but you were only part of it."

Her smile disappeared.

"You were only about ninety-nine percent of the decision."

Her smile reappeared and Scott laughed. "Actually, I do need to get away from the ranch, from the Oak, from Buteo for a while. Everybody needs some space. Harry will do fine with the stables. James and Penny need to try their wings without me either propping them up or getting in the way.

"Working with horses is all I've ever really wanted to do. It was pretty natural to turn to my old college bud for some advice. I liked what he had to say." He looked over at Traci. "And it didn't hurt that you'd be a neighbor."

Traci burst out laughing. "Neighbor? Wait until you see how far it is from the Travers farm to the Near North Side."

As they entered the outskirts of San Diego, Scott again tried to figure out where she was headed. He knew it had to be a hotel on the beach.

When she turned left into the wharf area, he groaned. "Not again," he said. "I thought I already passed the test of surviving at sea."

"I think you'll love the trip I have set up this time even better." She stepped out of the car and breathed deeply. Countless gulls filled the air. Their shrill cries touched her soul. "God, I love the ocean."

Scott tried to smile.

"Buck up, cowboy, you'll do fine," she said, grabbing his hand and leading him toward the water. "If you expect to hang with me, you'd better adapt to riding the waves."

He gave her a lopsided grin. "I'll manage. Haven't met a horse I couldn't ride. I guess I'll have to learn to say the same about boats."

- o -

"Just sit aft," Traci said, pointing toward the back of the boat. "Don't go in the cabin until I tell you it's okay."

Furrowing his brow, Scott replied, "Can't I even peek?"

"Absolutely not. No peeking. Now, sit still and look relaxed, I'll get us out of the harbor and then set sail."

"Is this the same boat we had before?" he shouted over the purr of the engine.

"Yep. The Dragonfly."

"That's good. At least it has some good memories."

Traci smiled, cut the engine, double checked her navigation equipment, and began setting the sails.

390

The brisk breeze was sufficient to get her where she was headed. The marine weather station had indicated the wind would calm over night. She turned and watched the setting red ball seemingly expand its rays to color the entire western horizon. They'd be tucked safely in the cove before nightfall. She wasn't sure Scott was ready for nighttime sailing.

They sailed in silence. She'd already turned on the running lights as darkness approached. Not much longer. *A sailor has to be prepared,* she'd always been told. Well, she was prepared. She drew deep breaths, taking courage from the sea. She had no nagging second thoughts. This was what she wanted to do. This was what she must do.

She glanced across at Scott. He appeared uneasy. Was it just the water? He wasn't dumb. He had to know at least part of what she had in mind. Was he worried about what she might expect of him? That he could still blow it again?

She spied the cove and prepared to reef the sails. "Stay put," she instructed Scott. "I'll have us anchored soon."

- o -

Scott marveled at Traci's skill and concentration. He'd stay put, all right; he had no idea what else to do. Patience, he counseled himself. How many times had he thought that since he'd seen her approaching him with that rope draped over her

391

shoulder? He had to admit that was the most beautiful sight he'd seen in a while. Since seeing her naked in Julian, anyway.

His throat tightened. How the hell did one make love on a boat? There was no question that was where all of this was headed. The Del Coronado would have been a lot better.

Control. He had to maintain control with her. He'd gotten them in trouble the last time by pushing too fast. And here he was on a damn boat battling his own fears about staying alive. He looked around the tri-maran. Certainly the boat wouldn't swamp or sink in the course of lovemaking?

"You look a little peaked, cowboy," said Traci, approaching him nimbly from the front of the boat.

Apparently they were as stable as they were going to be. Still, the boat bobbed with the waves. The wind had subsided a little, but to him any wind was a gale if he was on the water. He looked up at Traci beaming down at him. He tried to smile. He thought he actually did a fairly good job.

"Why don't I get us some wine? I'll be right back."

"When do I get to see the cabin? It might feel a little better in there."

"Soon. I'm waiting for the first stars to come out, and then we'll go inside." She returned with two glasses.

"This is good," Scott said, sipping the Riesling. "A good California wine."

Traci smiled. "I didn't want to disappoint you. Look," she said, pointing at the darkening sky, "there's the first star. They say if you make a wish, it'll come true."

"I thought you weren't a mystic."

Shrugging, Traci said, "Tonight, out here, I'm anything you want me to be. I'm anything *I* want to be." She pointed to a spot just above the horizon. "And there's Venus."

"You're wrong on that count, Counselor," Scott said, without looking at where she pointed. "I'm already looking at Venus. She's standing two feet in front of me. I don't even need a telescope to get a better view of her. Although a more complete view would be nice."

Traci's lips turned up. "My romantic guy. Let me escort you to my lair, cowboy." Reaching for his hand, Traci steadied him and led them into the cabin.

- o -

"Holy shit," he muttered. "You've created a love nest."

"You bet." Pleased with herself, Traci couldn't hold back a smile. "Figured the bunks weren't going to work. Too narrow and cramped headroom for what I have in mind. But if you buy enough blankets and sleeping bags, you can fill the footwell and cover the floor and have a lovely space. As you can see, the seats make for nice tables. You may choose from a variety of sausages, cheese, apples, and nuts. And of course there's more wine. Don't worry about the scented candles. They're in protected coverings." Traci pressed a finger to her lips. "And I'll just let you wonder about the oils."

"Wow! You have been busy. How did you come up with this idea?"

"Let's just say," Traci said, pulling Scott's shirt over his head, "I have a lot of experience doing legal research. Recently, I've turned some of those skills to a different kind of research—one that will likely delight you much more."

She bent and kissed his nipples and then stood back. "Seriously, Scott, I've made some big decisions for me and I hope for us. Cassie was helpful in her brutal way, but I am grateful for her."

She ran her index finger down his chest, to his navel, and to the waist of his shorts. "I've done some reading and some experimenting. I believe I've made things possible emotionally and physically, Scott." She was pleased that her voice was steady and strong. "You're not looking at a victim of rape. You're looking at a survivor. At some other point, I'll explain the difference. Now I'm going to show you."

Traci kissed the tears from his eyes. "No tears. Just love me, and let me love you."

"You're the captain of the ship, Traci. I'll follow your lead."

"Thanks," Traci giggled. "You can be my first mate."

394

She chuckled at the low growl emanating from his throat. "Why don't we just dispense with the clothes," she said, pulling on his shorts with one hand and undoing the buttons of her blouse with the other. Soon his hands joined hers and their clothes were cast aside.

"Lie down on your back, please."

Scott did as he was asked. Traci marveled again at his muscle tone. She tried to ignore his stiff arousal swaying slightly before her like a boat in a harbor. It didn't frighten her, but there were others things to tend to first.

She reached for a bottle of oil, spread an ample amount on her fingers and began to rub it into Scott's chest. Leaning over she rubbed one of her nipples against one of his oiled nipples. She filled his belly button with oil until it overflowed. With a forefinger she played in the resulting pool. She was having a tactile picnic.

His fingers grazed her neck and shoulders, maintaining contact, but carrying no command. "I love the mixture of lavender and sage," she mumbled into his abdomen. "How can your skin be so smooth with all the rough work you do?"

Scott moaned.

Traci snaked a hand across his thigh and studied his cock. It was large, but it would fit. She knew it would. This was her man, and he was going to be her first mate.

Tentatively, she reached for him. She grasped him as she might hold a young kitten in her hand. He bucked and then settled. Becoming bolder, she ran her hand up and down his shaft watching it change shape and color.

"Whoa," he rasped, placing his hand over hers. "In your research, did anyone tell you how much a guy can take before he's history?"

"Oh." Traci blinked at him. "Maybe we'd better move on. I might like to do that later. I want to get to know you all over. But first things first." She could feel her own moisture between her thighs; she was as ready as she ever would be.

"I want to be on top," she whispered, moving her body to straddle him.

Grinning, Scott nodded. "Kind of thought that might be the case. Take your time. I'm okay. Now."

Traci took a deep breath, took him in her hand, and guided him to her portal. Her eyes widened as she took a little of him inside. She wet her lips. "Don't close your eyes, Scott. I need to see you. I want you to see me. It's important that we share this as completely as possible."

Was it the waiting, or the hawk, or the vibrator? Whatever. She easily lowered herself, accommodating him completely. He filled her in a way nothing else could. "Oh my," she whispered, settling on his thighs. "Do I have to move?"

Scott chuckled. "You may discover that you like it."

"How could anything be better than this?"

"I thought you said no tears."

"I know. But this is so big. I thought I couldn't manage. The swaying of the boat only makes it more exquisite."

"And there are those beautiful upturned breasts I love so much," Scott said, grazing each nipple between a thumb and finger.

Sensations rippled from her nipples to her abdomen. Involuntarily, her inner muscles gripped his cock tighter. It leapt within her, causing a firestorm to rage through her body. Instantly, she raised and lowered herself over and over again, riding the storm, riding him. Afraid of being consumed — wanting desperately to be consumed.

He joined the race; his thighs drove like pistons against her buttocks. She was riding him; he was riding her. Traci raised her hands high above her head and laughed and cried as the firestorm gathered and centered on that single point of their joining. "Oh, my God, my God," she screamed. Her entire body melted into that tiny space of junction.

From a distance, she heard him calling out her name, "Traci, I love you." She felt him explode deep within her and she crashed around him. "I love you, Scott," she said, pitching forward and crushing her breasts against his chest. "And I'll never let you forget it."

Minutes later, Scott mumbled, "Superb first voyage, Captain."

Traci propped herself up on an elbow, delighted to feel him still inside. "How would you like to sign on as First Mate for a lifetime? I'd even let you be captain from time to time."

"I accept, happily." Scott sighed, giving her his lazy, lopsided grin. "As long as I can bring along my riding gear and tack."

"That can be arranged, cowboy. First, how about another ride without tack? And whatever you do, don't ever shave off that mustache."

- o -

The End

About the Author

Adriana Kraft ~ When it's Time to Heat Things Up

Award-winning author Adriana Kraft is really two people, a husband-wife team writing sizzling romantic suspense and erotic romance. With backgrounds in criminology and counseling, they combine their expertise in the criminal mind, trauma, healing and human nature with a passion for robust sexuality and life-long vitality. Together they have published over thirty romance novels and novellas to outstanding reviews. Long and Short Reviews: *"scorching hot… refreshing… something to read when you want straight up hotness."* Romance Junkies: *"filled with warmth, blazing hot sex, well-developed characters…not for the faint of heart."* Romantic pairings include straight m/f, lesbian, bisexual, ménage and polyamory, in both contemporary and paranormal settings.

We love hearing from readers! If you enjoyed *Detour Ahead,* please consider posting a review.

You can find us and all our links at http://adrianakraft.com.